PRAISE FOR *THE MARRIAGE GAP YEAR*

"I read *The Marriage Gap Year* in one night with a glass
of wine and it was wonderful. The novel is about what
happens in long-term marriages when one partner decides
to take a break. It also serves as a critique of interactions
between Gen X and Gen Z."

Astrid Edwards, host of *The Garrett*, a podcast for lovers of
books and storytelling www.thegarretpodcast.com

"*The Marriage Gap Year* is a daring narrative that challenges
conventional notions of love amidst an existential blundering
into the frontier of midlife. Self-discovery smacks hard
for Emma and Rob as their time apart sets the stage for a
series of transformative events. What makes this novel truly
compelling is its beautifully nuanced portrayal of a shifting
emotional landscape and clash of desires. But its real power
is the poetic skill of Thoraval, a true craftsman of language
and one of my favorite writers. Do not miss this book.
You will laugh, cry and think forever about the characters.
A story of our times."

Rachel Matthews, author of *Never Look Desperate*, *Siren* and
Vinyl Inside (Transit Lounge)

"What a beautiful ending to an amazing book.
I LOVED IT!"

Katerina Gauntlett

"Yannick Thoraval shows us the truth about marriage –
the suffocating weight of over-familiarity, the erosion of
mutual respect, the yearning for disruption and change –
then reminds us of the incalculable value of love, loyalty and
deep human connection. In the age of fakery, the authenticity
of this story is a precious gift."

Sian Prior, author of *Shy: a memoir* and
Childless: a story of longing and freedom

"*The Marriage Gap Year* does not begin or end where you
expect. A wonderful, warm and riveting read about two
prickly people, this is more than a romantic comedy.
It is about what happens when wisdom of experience solidifies
but is not recognized at workplaces. It is about taking the time
to craft something of significance as Rob the builder does.
It is ultimately about how it is never too late to examine
life philosophically to find meaning and joy."

Alice Pung, OAM author of the memoirs *Unpolished Gem* and
Her Father's Daughter, and the novels *Laurinda* and *One Hundred Days*

THE
MARRIAGE
GAP YEAR

YANNICK THORAVAL

First published 2024 in Melbourne, Australia, by Further Publishing
PO Box 12200
Middle Camberwell, VIC 3124
Australia
www.furtherpublishing.com

Further acknowledges the Traditional Custodians of Country throughout Australia and pays respect to elders, past, present and emerging. We recognise and respect the more than sixty thousand years of storytelling, art and culture of Aboriginal and Torres Strait Islander people across Australia.

This is a work of fiction. Characters, institutions and organisations mentioned in this novel are either the product of the author's imagination or, if real, used fictitiously without any intent to describe actual conduct.

A catalogue record for this book is available from the National Library of Australia

Thoraval, Yannick
The Marriage Gap Year
ISBN: 978-1-7635314-0-6 (Australia, UK)
ISBN: 978-1-7635314-1-3 (US, International)
ISBN: 978-1-7635314-3-7 (eBook)
ISBN: 978-1-7635314-2-0 (Audiobook)

Cover layout and design by Bailey McGinn, www.baileydesignsbooks.com
Illustrations by Tauseef Ahmed, www.tauseefahmedart.com
Printed by KDP and IngramSpark
Typeset in Baskerville by Lorna Hendry, www.lornahendry.com

Architectural drawing in Chapter Fourteen, Chemist Shop Renovation in Elwood/St Kilda 1917: State Library of Victoria Archive, Architectural Drawings Collection, Record ID 9939647501107636

Disclaimer
All care has been taken in the preparation of the information herein, but no responsibility can be accepted by the publisher or author for any damages resulting from the misinterpretation of this work.

For my parents, Liesbeth and Yves, who have a good marriage, I think, though who but the individuals inside a relationship can truly know.

SUMMER

CHAPTER ONE

What if she died here, thought Emma. What if her body was found, two days later, suffocated, somewhere under all these colored cushions. Would he mourn her? Or would he just "get over it" and go back to work.

At least this part of the IKEA warehouse was quiet. Rob was less likely to wander off, "get away from the mob," as he liked to say. He didn't like shopping. Right now, Emma didn't either.

There were too many living rooms all at once. She scanned the contents of another showroom, this one staged as a tidy home office. In there was a white desk, with only a cardboard laptop on it. To the side of the desk was a high-backed chair with an artfully crumpled blanket slung over the arm, flanked by a side table, a green teapot, and a newspaper open to an untouched Sudoku.

These spaces were life-sized dioramas of Nordic domesticity. Each display left Emma with the impression that the studious, pragmatic people who lived here had just left the room moments before. She might find them if she kept wandering, discovering clues to their whereabouts in every karate-chopped throw pillow or whiskey tumbler left on a sideboard. Perhaps they had just been here, sitting on this plush blue sofa, playing chess on the glass coffee table. Maybe they'd moved over there, by the vertical herb garden in the oak-trimmed kitchen. Breadcrumbs guided shoppers ever closer to the ghostly residents whose elusive, bohemian chic left its trace on every item, in every room of this warehouse, where no glass rings stained the coffee tables and no cat hair stuck to the furniture.

Emma could appreciate the marketing genius of this living catalog, but she was done with IKEA.

"Aw, bullshit!" a woman's voice snapped behind her. Emma half turned as a young mom hurried past, a toddler bouncing up and down in the shopping cart, piled high with kitchen bric-a-brac and a tangle of plastic plants. The mom glared back at the dad, trailing several unhurried steps behind them. "Because it was *your* fucken' turn," she spat, and stormed off toward Bedrooms, her pink flip-flops thwacking on the gray linoleum floor.

"Was not," the dad muttered to himself, slowly following the cart's general direction.

Emma was *so* over IKEA. Why would a builder like Rob buy a table from here?

Her husband ran his meaty hand along the thin edge of an eight-seater Rönninge dining table, set as if ready for a three-course meal with dinner plates, small plates and soup bowls. Beside them, the lazy dad had stopped following his wife to peer inside a display cabinet, staged with candlesticks and cookbooks.

Rob squatted to look under the table. Emma had been asking him to build them a proper dining table for years, something solid and beautiful, a piece of forever furniture, an heirloom with a story, their story.

It's a different kind of building, he'd say. Was it, though? Or could he just not be bothered?

Emma had stopped asking about it, but when the old laminate table got water damage from a burst pipe upstairs, the touchy subject of a new dining table ended with them at the IKEA superstore, where they'd spent the last hour browsing the showrooms; Skogsta, Vedbo, Voxlöv, Ekedalen, the product range like names in a Viking cemetery.

"This'll do," said Rob, tapping his finger on the cold Nordic Pine of the Rönninge table, dressed with a piano-key table runner and towering salt and pepper shakers, pale as icicles. "Decent piece of timber," he said.

Emma wanted *her* table, not this cheap thing. Something beautiful, made to last. Made with love. She wanted the big table she'd always imagined having, encircled with hardwood chairs where friends and family would sit and talk into the night about things happening in the world. The table where they'd have Sunday dinners and birthday dinners and Christmas dinners in the presence of extended family and the interesting friends they'd accumulated over the years, like the souvenirs they collected from the exotic places they'd been.

"I'm not putting *that* in my house," she said.

Rob was taken aback. He thought this was exactly the kind of thing Emma was looking for. She was always bugging him for a new table, had shown him pictures of the things she liked, tables that looked pretty much like this one. Now it was all wrong? "It's an eight-seater," he added, tilting his head to look at the angled legs. "Ten, if you put chairs on the ends and people don't mind banging a few knees."

Emma felt a flame grow inside her. She was just some problem to him, now. Like one of the clients he eye-rolled about while talking on the phone.

Rob crouched down to have a closer look at the Rönninge table. It was a lot of money for flatpack furniture. "Do we even need one this big?" he said, his back twinging as he straightened up. "We'd probably be alright with one of those smaller ones from over there," he pointed to a section of the shop they'd passed earlier.

Emma knew the area he meant, the one with the cheap, laminate furniture that didn't get its own showroom.

Rob shrugged. "A smaller table could make the dining room feel bigger."

Was he *trying* to be cruel, or did he really have no idea? This was worse than cutting the vacation short, worse than forgetting her birthday. "You know," she said squinting, unable to even look at him right now, "maybe you're right."

Rob's lips tightened. Here we go. Couldn't go more than a few hours without pissing her off these days. When did she get so uptight?

"Maybe we don't even need a table at all," she said, her eyes getting larger.

Rob scratched his chin. It calmed him, kept him from making a face she'd get mad about. There were a lot of places he'd rather be on a Sunday. But he was *here*, wasn't he? "Why are you being all weird?" he said, trying to quieten things down.

"I mean," she continued as if she hadn't heard what he said, "it's not like we really *need* a table, right?"

Oh, thought Rob. She wasn't going to let this go. It was going to be one of her lines in the sand.

He knew Emma had some fantasy about him building them a dining table. Did she have any idea how long it took to make one? A properly handmade wooden table? Solid wood, no metal, not even screws? Thirty to fifty hours, he calculated, and that was after you sourced the timber, not including time to varnish and dry. Who had that kind of time? Or space? His backyard shed couldn't hold a slab of wood that size. Besides, she always had a precise idea of what she wanted. He'd get it wrong. Jesus Christ, it's not like he was Jesus Christ – a literal carpenter. He wasn't a joiner or a furniture maker. He was a commercial builder; a high-end table wasn't just something he could magic up. She always assumed everything was easier than it was.

"Could you please lower your voice?" he said, moving closer. "You're getting a little—"

"No, I don't think I will, Rob! Thanks all the same." She was not about to be hushed. "I think I might even have to get louder," she said, raising her voice and making jazz hands.

Rob sensed people slowing down to look at them. He felt self-conscious; shoppers were stealing glances at them with a kind of amused superiority, the way tourists cringe-watched drunk Australians in Bali.

"Emma," he said sharply. "Please!"

"No," she continued. "Really. I mean it. Why bother with a table? I'm asking seriously. I mean, why not just get hospital trays? Then we can finally eat right *in front* of the TV, and not just look at it from the sides of our faces."

"Okay, can you settle down?"

"Ooooh. Am I making you uncomfortable, Rob? Touching a nerve?"

Rob glanced behind him. People were looking. "Emma," he pleaded.

Emma saw she'd pushed him too far. Rob valued composure and she almost felt guilty using it against him.

"Right," she nodded. "Let's just go."

"Em," he said, but she wasn't even looking at him anymore. They started walking, Emma half a pace in front.

She couldn't look at him. He really thought this was just about the table, didn't he? Emma was haunted by a vision of them, wordlessly shuffling around in a house that no one came to visit, unable to escape this man who resembled her husband, but had grown fatter and grumpier and more distant by the day.

They used to dream and do things. Now they just walked past each other, spoke only of what was necessary: of schedules and bills, shopping lists, or about their son, Will, and what *he* needed, for school, for camp, from the pharmacy, for university. And Emma felt certain that if she did nothing, if she kept living as they had been, that Rob would eventually smother her, consume her, and sap whatever spark and ambition remained in her with his proselytizing, his disapproval and negativity. If she said nothing, did nothing, for one more day, he would suffocate in her the very essence of her being as sure as if it were consumed by flame.

Rob slowed his pace. Why try to catch up. There was no bringing her round from this mood.

He was tired. Tired of fighting, tired of work. He'd spent a lifetime in construction only to end up with a bad back and two blown knees. There was more time, somehow, back when he was younger. At least you'd get a weekend. Nowadays, people wanted everything yesterday, didn't care about quality, just wanted it now, cheap and fast. Even Emma, with her table. It took time, the things she wanted. And he was always pushed for time.

Emma stopped in her tracks. "I'm not going home," she said.

"What?" Rob caught up to her, mindful of people in his peripheral vision. "What do you mean?"

She turned to face him. "I can't do this anymore."

"Do what? What are you talking about? We're looking at tables because—"

"I need space." She breathed audibly, closed her eyes.

"Space? What for? What kind of space?"

She opened her eyes. Everything looked gray under the fluorescent lights. "I don't know. I just can't…"

He shifted his weight to his other leg. "What are you saying?"

"I don't know!" She dragged her palm slowly down her face. "Christ. This is not how I wanted this to come out."

"What to come out?" He moved closer. "What's going on?"

"It's…" She was already second-guessing what she wanted, less certain than she was this morning. "I just need time. I need some space. I need a break, a gap, like…a gap year!"

"Gap year? What, like a trip?"

Emma rubbed her eyelids. "I don't know," she sighed. "I just know I need—"

"Well, why don't you just—"

"I don't want to hear it, Rob. Sorry, that sounded harsh." She looked at him at last. He was a fight-or-flight kind of guy and she couldn't tell from his frown which way he was leaning. "I need to remember who I am, other than someone's wife and someone's mom."

Two women walked past, canvas IKEA bags slung over their shoulders. They both gave her and Rob a wide berth.

"Didn't you ever want to take a gap year?"

"No."

"Didn't want to see the world?"

"I've traveled."

"We went to Fiji one time for a wedding. That doesn't count."

"Well, I didn't like it."

"That's not what I'm talking about."

"What *are* you talking about?"

"Don't you ever wonder *what if?*"

"If what?

"I mean, don't you ever just wonder what it might be like, if we'd never met. How things might've been different. How our lives might have worked out."

"What are you saying?" He moved closer. "You want a divorce?"

"No." The word came out like a reflex. "Don't be so dramatic."

"Well, you just said—"

"Look, I don't know. I think what I'm asking is, what if we just took some time off?"

Rob looked puzzled, the crease between his eyes deepening. "Like, what if we took some time out for a year and lived apart for a while, just to see what it was like?"

"A year?"

He stood like a big kid who'd been told to stay back after class. Emma softened toward him. This must have hit him hard. She had been thinking about this for ages, the deep and empty space between them.

It was out now. This thing she'd rehearsed so many times. But it was happening differently from what she'd expected. She'd expected to feel relief. And she did. But she'd not expected fear.

Rob looked over his shoulder before leaning toward her. "What are you really saying, Emma? You want to see other people?"

"I don't know…maybe."

"Maybe?"

"Yes, maybe. That's not what this is about though." She blinked repeatedly. There, she'd said it. She needed change.

"Fucking hell." Rob shook his head and headed for the quick exit that skipped all the displays.

"Rob." Emma trotted behind him. "I'm not saying I want out of our relationship."

"Right." He glanced back over his shoulder and kept walking.

"I'm not." She stopped following him. "Can you please just stop?"

He did and stood in the aisle with his back to her.

Emma walked over. "I get it." Emma took a breath. This had all sounded more reasonable when she'd rehearsed it in her mind. "I just want see what it's like if I'm by myself for a while."

"By yourself, but also fucking other people?"

"Rob—"

"Jesus Christ, Emma. You're forty-eight, not some fucking teenager."

"Well, maybe that's it then? I never got to *be* a teenager. I didn't have boyfriends or go out to parties. I was too busy working to help my parents out and putting myself through university."

"Oh, here we go." He set off again.

"What do you mean, *here we go*?" She sped up behind him. "Fuck you, Rob. I had to take care of myself."

"Oh please. I took care of plenty." He pushed open the door to the carpark. "Who paid off your student loans? Who kept the lights on and food on the table when you couldn't get a job? Or when you wanted to stay home with Will for two years."

"*Wanted*? I didn't see *you* volunteering."

"Em, you're not a victim here, okay."

"Oh, so I should be grateful, is that it? Just stay quiet?"

"Enough with the drama!" He fished his keys out of his pocket as they got to their car. "What have I done exactly? What have I done that was *so* bad?"

"Nothing," she sighed, and got in the passenger seat, the vinyl uncomfortably hot on her backside. It was boiling in here. She fanned herself with her hands.

The car wobbled as it took Rob's weight.

"Well then, what the fuck, Em? You tell me you want to sow your wild oats or whatever and I'm supposed to be happy about that?"

"Can we please just stop."

"Stop what?"

"All of this. The fighting, the treating each other like shit. I'm not even sure you're mad right now."

"What are you talking about?"

"I thought you might actually be relieved I said something."

He scrunched up his face.

"This," she said, as she moved her hand between them. "This whole situation, there's no love in here. It's like we don't even like each other anymore. Am I a burden to you? Is that it? Like one of your clients who just needs to be put off for a while, placated? I asked you for a table—"

"Christ, enough about the table."

"It's not about the table!" She breathed heavily. "It's that you've stopped trying."

"Whatever." He started the car. The whirr of the air conditioning came to life. Rob pulled out of the parking space.

"It's true," said Emma, more calmly. "It's like you don't want to share a life, don't want to try anything new. Like you're done investing in us."

They whizzed by parked cars, the tires squealing in the steep, narrow circuit to the exit.

"You say you love me," she said. "But do you love me enough to let me go?"

"Oh fuck!" He stopped the car and thumped the steering wheel with the palm of his hand.

"What?"

"Forgot to validate the fucking parking ticket."

Emma spent the car ride home trying to control her breathing. It was out there now, this thing she had thought about so often. Rehearsed. She'd lit the fuse but didn't yet know what it was attached to.

Rob stopped the car outside their house. The little Victorian terrace already looked different. Small.

"Geez," Emma said.

But Rob was already getting out of the car. He strode toward the house and she watched him until he disappeared inside, slamming the screen door shut.

Emma scanned the street for neighbors and pulled the vanity mirror down. She traced the bags under her eyes with the tips of her fingers, sighed, and flipped the vanity mirror back up. Her fingers massaged the roots of her hair. She looked up when she heard the whine of a saw coming from inside the house.

Emma raced up the steps and opened the screen door to see Rob perched over the living room table, revving the motor on a cordless circular saw.

"Hey," she called over the screech. "Have you lost your fucking mind?"

Rob brought the saw down on the dining room table, spewing plumes of sawdust as the teeth gnawed a line through the middle of the tabletop. He lifted the saw in triumph and the table collapsed in a heap on the living room floor. "There," he said, stepping over the fallen timbers. "One less thing to move."

CHAPTER TWO

Don't cry Emma told herself. It'll only confuse him. She ordered herself a latte and waited for Rob to arrive. She wouldn't usually order before he got there, but things were different now and she tingled with a disproportionate sense of joy in this first act of freedom. It'd been a tense month working out the details of their arrangement but today was the day they made it official.

She put down her phone on the table and looked out the window. Already patches of rust were spreading in the trees. She wasn't ready for summer to end.

Lygon Street used to be more edgy, didn't it? Full of cheap restaurants and little hole-in-the-wall bars and cafes that students used to hang out in. This was before the neon noodle-chains moved in, alongside the clean, bright cafes with their Scandinavian color palette of white marble and blond wood: warm enough to invite you in, but not cozy enough to make you want to stay. A transactional environment.

Or perhaps nothing had really changed on Lygon Street. Maybe it was just her. Maybe she was less cool than she used to be. Or maybe she'd been vanilla all along.

"Flat white?" said the bony waiter, swimming in his leather apron.

"Thanks."

"Just the coffee then?" He leaned over the table and scooped up the menu. "Cool. Enjoy."

Emma cupped the glass with both hands and gently blew on the top of her coffee. She took a sip. This was going to be okay, wasn't it? This wasn't a ridiculous mid-life crisis thing? It's what they both needed. Didn't they?

She took a longer drink and felt her brain fog recede. She spied Rob walking toward her before *he* saw her. She watched him stop under the awning of a shopfront and absently browse the window display while talking to someone on his wireless earbuds. Why was he holding a takeout cup? He knew they were meeting for coffee.

She picked up her own phone and, even though she'd taken a few days off, scrolled through her work emails. She knew it wasn't good for her wellbeing. Work–life balance and all that. Still, if it helped her get on top of the workflow it was worth it. Besides, she didn't want to look like she was just waiting for Rob with nothing else to do.

The cafe door opened. Emma briefly feigned not noticing and remained focused on her phone, but the ruse soon felt silly, juvenile, so she looked up and offered Rob a weak smile. He raised his finger and pointed to his ear and mouthed the word *sorry*. Emma returned to her emails. Annual report stuff. Ugh. Was it that time of year again already? The unsexiest part of working in communications. She winced at Rob's too-loud voice, which pierced the cafe's lazy calm. "Yep. Okay. Yep," he spoke into the earpiece. "We can probably sort that out tomorrow…okay. Talk then. Bye."

Emma crinkled her nose as the fruity, yeasty waft of stale beer and coffee oozed from Rob and lingered in the no-man's land between them. The tension around alcohol had got worse over the years, creating fault lines waiting to erupt. How many last night?

Three stubbies? Five? Ten? Did the scotch come out? She knew the routine, the sequence between rounds. Needy. Sad. Incensed. Looking for a fight.

It's not that he raged and smashed windows or anything, but alcohol changed the mood in the house. Sometimes he'd just go quiet and fall asleep on the couch. Other times, he'd fixate on something, a mean client, a bad interaction at work, something *she'd* neglected to do, and he'd prosecute the injustice over and over, wounding himself anew until she gave up trying to help him move past whatever it was and just went to bed. So went this predictable spiral of accusation, self-pity, and apology for "going off" the night before. Those evenings inflicted thousands of injuries on their marriage and she'd been unsure what it all meant, or *how* or *if* she could continue to endure them.

There was no intimacy between them anymore. The sex, when it happened, was quick and perfunctory, an item on a to-do list.

She waited for him to speak before she looked up from her email. "Nice place," he said, and sat down, the little chair creaking beneath him.

The aproned waiter returned. "Can I get you something?"

"Oh, hey mate. Yeah, you got anything bready back there, like a sweet or salty bready type thing?"

"I can bring you the food menu if you—"

"Ah, just wondering if you got anything like a sausage roll, maybe, or a sticky bun or something?

"A bun?"

"Yeah, like a hot cross bun or…"

"I've got a crab-apple Danish or an almond croissant." The waiter fluttered his eyelashes.

"Okay, I'll take the Danish." He pointed at Emma. "You want anything?" She shook her head.

"Coffee?" the waiter asked, his head tilted to the side, almost parallel to the floor, as if he were looking under something.

"All good, mate. Still got this one on the go." Rob held up his takeout coffee, daring the waiter to take exception.

The waiter nodded and retreated to his counter.

Rob turned to face Emma. The table tilted slightly as he leaned his heavy arm on it. Emma looked away from his round belly. It shouldn't matter. But it did. And she felt ashamed about that. A better person would look past that as superficial. But there was other stuff too. Remember that.

"So, thanks for coming." Emma looked down at the table. "Sorry, that sounds stupid. I mean…I'm glad you're here to…" She sighed. "I'm just saying it's good we're moving forward with this now. God, I don't know why I'm getting so tongue-tied." She took a long drink of her coffee. They never made them hot enough.

Rob laced his big fingers together on the table. "You having second thoughts?"

Emma shook her head.

"Okay then," said Rob, adjusting himself on the creaky little chair. "Everything's pretty much set to go."

Emma briefly looked her husband in the eye before adjusting her gaze to the window behind him, where two passing dog walkers allowed their "oodle-mixes" to sniff each other. What had she expected? That he'd cry? Would it have made a difference?

Emma cleared her throat and looked back at him. "You find a place to stay?"

Rob unclasped his fingers and dug his cell phone out of his pocket. He held it at some distance from his face as he scrolled with big flicks of his finger. "Here," he said, angling the phone toward Emma. "Syed's letting me use one of the display homes at Wattle Point." He flipped through interior photos of a new house:

white walls, charcoal carpet, cream blinds. Emma allowed Rob to scroll through the photos more slowly than *she* would have. Let him pretend to be chipper. Managing. Unaffected. She owed him that.

She looked down at the images. They saddened her, these pictures. It was one of those cookie-cutter homes in the outer suburbs of Melbourne. Clean, big and soulless, even with the benefit of furniture to stage it for sale. Emma felt a pang of guilt imagining Rob holed up in a small section of this large house, a warm patch in this cold building. "Looks nice," she said.

"It's right on site," he said, shutting the phone off and stuffing it into his pocket. "So that's the commute gone. All I have to do is keep the place clean and clear out if Syed needs to show it. Doesn't bother me none. I'll be on the job most days anyway." Rob lifted the takeout coffee to his lips and tilted his head way back to finish the dregs at the bottom of the cup. "Saw you got your apartment sorted," he said, wiping his lips with the back of his hand. "In the city, yeah?"

Emma nodded. "Near work," she said. "I always wanted to be able to walk to work."

"Good," Rob coughed. "Well, the renters are moving into our place next week, so if there's anything else you need from the attic, you'll have to let the agent know."

Emma turned to look out the window. She tried to push back tears, but they were already coming.

"And here's your Danish," came the waiter's voice, the clink of a plate on the table. Emma twisted her head further away, toward the view out the window. She wiped at the tears with her knuckle.

"Emma?" Rob's voice drew her back from the distractions outside. She didn't want to be like this, all flushed and red-eyed and snotty. She turned back to face Rob and picked up one of the napkins that had been placed in front of her, unsure if it was Rob or the waiter who'd put them there. She found herself unwilling to gift the gesture to Rob.

His face was at once deeply lined and boyish, the mischief in his blue eyes had dimmed. "This is what you wanted. Isn't it?" he said.

"I know." She blew her nose. "But I can still feel sad about it."

Rob leaned forward. "Because it's not too late, you know? We can undo it all."

Emma shook her head. "No," she said. "This has to happen, one way or another. I don't want us to end up hating each other and that's where this is going."

He leaned back in his chair, rubbed his chin. "What are you expecting from this Emma? What are you going to do, fly off to Tuscany to find yourself? This isn't a movie." He crossed his arms and looked up at the ceiling.

"It's a year, Rob. That's the deal. We set each other free for a year."

He sighed. "Free from what, Em? No one's in your way. I told you, if you want to quit your job, just quit. I'll take care of us."

"Look, thanks for getting the house sorted with the tenants and everything. I appreciate it, but I don't want to go over all this again. That you don't get why I need – why *we* need – time apart is exactly the problem."

Rob scratched his stubbled cheek.

"It's a twelve-month lease, Emma. You going to do your whole life over in that time?"

Emma looked at the tree outside, its gnarled bark wrapped by a wrought-iron skirt.

"We've been through this," she said. "You agreed."

"So what? We can un-agree. Nothing's set in stone."

She closed her eyes and took a slow, deep breath. "I know it's scary—"

"I'm not scared. I just think this is stupid."

She looked at him, drew her lips tight.

"What?" said Rob. "No calls, not even texts? For a year? It's weird, like a reality TV show or something. I know you like drama, but this just feels…childish."

She swallowed. "You still don't get it, do you?"

"I guess not," he said, blinking.

"I don't know if I love you anymore."

Rob sat back, the bulk of him leaned against the thin wing of the cafe chair. "Okay," he nodded and rose to his feet.

"Rob," she said, but he held up his hand.

"Fine." He opened his wallet. "I'll get out of your way then." He dropped a ten-dollar bill on the table. "Guess I'll talk to you in a year."

"Rob," she called after him.

"No, really. Knock yourself out." He left the cafe, pulling the door closed with a thud.

Emma looked down at his untouched Danish. Who did that?

CHAPTER THREE

Emma lay in the unfamiliar bed scrolling through an overwhelming list of "wellness" podcasts. How was she supposed to find the right one for her? *A Passion for Marriage*? No, she was not about to spend this time trying to work directly on her marriage. This time was about her. The soothing green-field thumbnail art of *Alive and Well* drew her in, but the blurb sounded like the show was just vegan propaganda. More guilt is not what she needed. God, the choices were endless. She scrolled quickly, hoping one of the titles would catch her attention: *All's Well, Be Well, Being Well, Cut the Crap, Dream Big, Feel Good, Meditation Nation*. This was only making her feel more anxious.

Emma closed her eyes and stabbed randomly at the screen. She opened her eyes to reveal what she'd landed on. Something called *Presence*, hosted by Eli Jacobs. She started the episode, but the sound was echoey, like it had been recorded in a garage, plus Eli's voice was whiny and annoying. Emma decided she didn't want to listen to a male voice at all. That would help cut down the options.

New plan. She'd flick her finger five times and then pick the first female name that came on screen. And the winner is…Dr Priya Saanvi, host of *Whose Life Is It Anyway?*

Emma appreciated the quiet cheer in Dr Priya's voice. Dr Priya wasn't talking down to her or using the podcast to read from her book, she sounded like she was just on for a chat, sharing ideas as if the thoughts had just come to her in that moment. *If you're looking for a guru or a spirit guide, you've come to the wrong place. I haven't got the answers you're looking for. But you know what? You do. So stick around, and maybe, just maybe, I can help you find them.*

This was good, thought Emma, lying here, listening to her podcast, not having to explain herself, or risk getting interrupted, or think about sounds she might not hear with her headphones on. She sank into the pillow and closed her eyes. Dr Priya asked her to look past whatever she was expecting to get from this podcast, to ignore any voice in her head or impulse in her body that felt critical or competitive.

You know the one, said Dr Priya. *It's the one telling you that you've got more important things to do right now. That you should be doing something else. Just turn the volume down on that voice. It's okay. It'll be back. We just want to give the other voices a go. The quiet ones. The hesitant ones. Let's give them the floor for a minute. What have they got to say? You might not hear them right away. They might be a bit shy, you see. Or scared. They're used to getting shouted down.*

Emma lay back, waiting to hear something, to feel something, but there was nothing. Not even a stillness. She wriggled on the mattress, which suddenly felt too hard; the new paint smell in the room asserted itself.

You're no good at this, she thought. You're not the meditating type. Give up. Do something constructive. She was about to turn off the podcast when Dr Priya interrupted.

If you thought this was going to be easy, my lovelies, think again. Getting in touch with yourself is hard. That's why most people don't do it. That's why they walk around like zombies, thinking other people's thoughts, striving for other people's dreams. Forget about everyone else. What do you *want? Maybe you know what it is. And maybe you don't. This actually doesn't matter. What matters is thinking about it, getting in touch with it. Maybe you'll come up with a list, a feeling, a photo gallery of what's important to you. Whatever. As long as it's yours. Now, I'd love to have you back for episode two, but not if you haven't done your homework. I want you to go on a speed date with yourself. And ask yourself: What do I want? What's my idea of a better life?*

Emma opened her eyes as the peaceful piano music faded out. She stared at the ceiling and thought about all those floors above her and all the floors below, filled with unseen, unheard people going about their business. She'd get used to it. This building had a gym and a swimming pool, the ritual use of which she mentally added to her list of lifestyle changes. She liked Dr Priya and this concept of a speed date with yourself. The session emboldened Emma to start a note on her phone:

A better life is being more connected…body, mind and spirit
To do:
Exercise more (start running)
Reconnect with self
Reconnect with friends
Help Will find independence
Savor beauty, the arts, music.
Be spontaneous
Have more orgasms
Find out if I still love Rob

It wasn't exactly the homework Dr Priya had set, but it was a start.

Invigorated by the thought of her list, Emma peeled herself out of bed and walked the few short steps to the kitchen. It felt strange, tiptoeing on the cold tiles as if she were a guest in someone else's house, like she might accidentally wake someone still sleeping in this unfamiliar apartment. The Uber Eats bag sitting on the counter, which had contained last night's green chicken curry, was oddly reassuring, a reminder that this was her place and that everything would remain exactly as she left it.

She'd added some personal touches to this gleaming cube of an apartment: a throw rug, a baby rubber plant, and some colorful couch cushions, all of which she'd got at the Queen Victoria Market.

Oddly comforting, too, was the sight of her dishwashing wand, sitting clean and dry and upright in a tall mug on the wiped kitchen counter, a fresh sponge twisted onto the handle. Rob always chastised her for changing the heads on those brushes too often; "wasteful and unnecessary," he'd say. But this from a man who thought nothing of letting a sponge sit in the sink for days, until the green, scrubby side was all chewed up and peeling off, while the yellow, spongy part was sodden with muck. How could a man so meticulous at work be such a slob everywhere else? Emma had bought a value pack of those replaceable sponge heads and would change them whenever she damn well liked. It was an insignificant thing, but she found great joy in this small measure of freedom.

She caught her reflection in the window and ran her hand down the back of her head, where she caressed the fluffy tufts of mousy hair growing at the back of her neck. She was done with this hairdo, finished with keeping it short because it was "practical" and "respectable" like all the other graying bobs. She'd grow it out.

Beyond the window, the city of Melbourne stretched to the horizon, a patchwork quilt of every suburb she'd ever lived in, visible in one eyeful. It made the city feel smaller, more manageable, to see it assembled below her like that, as if her own life story could be traced by moving her finger on the window. Heading north was the suburb of Reservoir where she'd grown up. All those moves, from a house to successively smaller apartments, were contained in that parcel of land in the distance where the sun now sparkled off glass buildings she'd never seen before. From there she followed the lines of the familiar arterial roads that had carried her through her early life. There was Northcote Plaza, where she'd had her first job in the sandwich shop. The Westgarth Cinema, where she had her first date. And there was the campus of Melbourne University, where she did her BA. Heading south was that ratty apartment in St Kilda she moved to after graduation, the year she decided to live near the beach. And way over west, behind the rising steam pipes of the industrial precinct, was the suburb of Altona, where Rob grew up. Only an arm's length of unfamiliar suburbs had separated him from her before they met. What parallel lives were being lived out there right now? There were probably people down there she hadn't met yet but would.

The coffee machine gurgled and hissed as it finished steaming the milk. The coffee didn't taste right. Stale and bland. Not as good as what she made at home. It wasn't helpful to think like that. Or maybe it was? She promised herself to allow every thought to exist, to make room for it, even if it felt uncomfortable. Today was the day she would start running.

Emma looked at the three suitcases in the bedroom and promised herself she would put the stuff in them away before she went to bed. She opened one and rifled through the clothes, looking for something suitable to run in. She picked through half a dozen dresses, some of which she hadn't worn in years. She couldn't remember why she'd packed some of these things, but it'd seemed important to have them.

She didn't own anything lycra and settled on a pair of board shorts she hadn't worn since the summer after she'd given birth to Will. She was relieved to find she needed to cinch the drawstring to keep the shorts from falling. But there it was, the doughy little paunch that spilled over the waistband. Emma ran her fingers along the squishy band of fat – pale and saggy, like the soft edge of an uncooked pie crust.

She sighed and put on a loose shirt, a promo from a startup that hadn't made it. She paused again at the full-length mirror. The red and yellow board shorts puckered in the crotch and the T-shirt hung like a drape, the cuffs almost down to her elbows. She looked like a rodeo clown. Even the little gap between her front teeth, which Rob used to say was sexy, felt like a defect again. Christ, she needed a do-over, not a makeover.

Emma had a love–hate relationship with her body. On the one hand, it was through her physical body that she experienced the world: her pleasure, her pain, the unique combination of both that was being a mother. On the other, her body felt out of proportion: smaller up top, but then bulging from the hips down. Her figure cast a silhouette like a butternut pumpkin.

Come on Emma, be kind to yourself, she thought. She promised herself that if she was still running a week from now, she'd buy herself a better outfit. For now, she pulled the brim of her ballcap down low on her forehead. Time to face the world.

The track that circled the Botanical Gardens was already bustling with an intimidating procession of beautiful people. Even the moms running while pushing strollers seemed impossibly fit. Sure, she worked with younger people who probably looked like this under their smart-casual wear, but she never had to *see* their bodies. The people out here all looked so confident. Was it just as simple as putting one foot in front of the other? She came here to run and she was going to do so, even if she looked foolish. Emma couldn't bear the thought of returning to her apartment with this one easy thing on her list left undone. It would be a bad omen. What hope was there for the other goals if she couldn't tick this one off?

She trotted onto the track and looked down, focused on the rhythm of her own feet striking the gravel path. People passed her in brisk strides, their bodies spring-loaded. She wobbled along like a bus on a potholed mountain road. Her boobs jostled around under the baggy T-shirt – she needed a new bra. She'd always been short, but these beautiful people made her feel stumpy, like a quokka sent to run an Olympic track and field event. But she was running. And doing so gave life to the possibility of achieving the other goals on her list. She was outside, on a warm morning, with the freedom and momentum to become the best version of herself. She was part of this now, this flow of people, the runners, who charted their own course and never took their eyes off the horizon.

A persistent smell of shit soon broke the spell. She stopped and lifted her foot. Sure enough, the sole of her running shoe was densely packed with dog turd. Emma hobbled over to the grassy edge of the running track and found a stick with which to scrape the brown mess out of the complex, swirly pattern on the sole of her shoe.

"Oh dear," said an old woman seated on a nearby bench. She was draped in a tartan blanket and wearing a beanie, despite the warm morning sun. Emma couldn't decide if the woman was an old hippie or homeless. "Now you've done it." Emma ignored the woman and continued stabbing at the dog turd with the stick she now decided was too flimsy for the job. "Filthy animals," said the woman.

"Yeah," said Emma, dropping the stick in the grass.

"What you running around for anyway?"

Emma leaned forward, hands on her knees, stretching. "Honestly not sure myself right now," she said, hanging her head, still breathing hard.

"Cuz I watch 'em, you know," said the old woman, drawing circles with her finger. "And they just keep going round. How can they stand it? Makes me dizzy."

"Yeah." Emma felt vaguely nauseous, still struggling to control her breathing. "Well, have a nice day," said Emma and trotted on, trying to ignore the smell wafting from her left foot.

CHAPTER FOUR

A saw whined in the distance and multiple nail guns banged out of sequence. At Wattle Point Estates a whole neighborhood was under construction. Both sides of the street were lined with suburban houses in various stages of production. Some homes were nearly finished, with roofers busy laying tiles and designers fitting interiors. Other house plots were little more than holes in the ground or churned up earth with small fluorescent flags marking out where the plumbing and power had been laid underground.

A heavy-set laborer, frizzy hair spilling out from under his hard hat, poked his head into the dark recess of one of the houses. "Oi, Rob!" he bellowed. Rob looked over from the empty cavity that would soon be a kitchen. He was surrounded by three men wearing spotless hard hats and fluorescent orange safety vests over their suits. "Big boss wants to see you."

"What for?" said Rob.

"Dunno." The laborer shrugged. "I'm just the messenger," he said, and left.

Rob apologized to the suits, inviting them to look around in his absence.

He squinted in the harsh sun outside, shielding his eyes as he made his way to the demountable office on the hill.

Inside Syed was hunched over his laptop analyzing dates and costs on a color-coded spreadsheet. He was wiping his neck and balding head with a white handkerchief.

Rob strode in, white hard hat tucked under his arm. Syed barely looked up from his screen.

"Geez, Sy, it's boiling in here. Why don't you switch on the aircon? It's cooler outside than in."

Syed looked up at the split system mounted on the wall. "Nah," he said, dismissing it with a wave of his hand.

"Suit yourself. You could also join me out there, mate, do some real work for a change." Rob grinned.

Syed cracked a smile and looked up from his screen. "You know, I did build something once."

"Yeah, what?"

"A rabbit house." Syed nodded and closed the screen of his laptop. "Yes, when my daughter was small, she always wanted a rabbit. So, I said why not build a house for the rabbit. How hard can it be? So, I build the house. But it was a bad house. Terrible," he chuckled. "I think maybe the rabbit is scared to move in. Because he knows the construction is bad. He lived a nervous life."

Rob smiled. "I'm sure your daughter was happy with it though." He felt a pang of regret at never letting Will have a pet. There'd always been a good reason to say no.

"She's twenty-five now. Married. Her happiness is out of my hands." Syed leaned back in his chair and laced his fingers together. He cleared his throat. "Rob, I have a proposal."

"Oh?" Rob leaned against the wall.

"A renovation."

"Sy, I've got my hands full here."

Syed shook his head. "This is different. I take you off *this* project to do a new one." Rob frowned. "Don't look so worried," said Syed. "Look at my face. Do I look worried? The project here is like a coloring book. You just fill in the lines. I need you to do something else. Something better."

"Sy, I've got three loads of trusses coming in next week…"

Syed waived the air as if shooing away a bad smell. "Who cares, man. Fucking trusses. You take them off a truck and put them on the roof. Is coloring book." He leaned forward and tapped his finger on a manilla folder on his desk. "With this project, I need you to be an artist. Here," he said, handing Rob the folder.

"What's this?"

"A blank canvas."

Rob opened the folder and scanned the application for a building permit.

"Whose project is this?"

Syed leaned back in his chair. "Mine."

Rob cocked an eyebrow. "Well, what is it? What do you need done?"

"That's what I want you to tell me."

Rob scratched at the base of his neck. "Why don't you get an architect?"

Syed waived away the suggestion. "I have architect. Most of these papers are architect. But architect is bullshit," he said. "They make a sculpture. You," he pointed his finger at Rob, "you make a home."

Rob shifted from side to side. "I'm just a builder, mate."

Syed laughed. "Sure, and David Beckham's just a soccer player."

Rob flicked through a few pages in the folder. "Nah, this is beyond me, mate."

"Not beyond. You have what you need here. Soil tests, engineer report, drawings. It's just design and build." Rob leaned in to look at the drawings. "Just go see it," said Syed. "I know you will understand."

"What? You mean, like, now?"

"Why not?" Syed raised his palms. "It's still early." Rob frowned.

"You'll like it," said Syed. "Ocean view." He spread his open hands as if stretching a banner in the sky. "Australian dream," he laughed.

"Right," said Rob. "I'll check it out next week mate. Just don't trust the boys with those trusses."

"Okay man." Syed rose from behind his desk with some effort. "You pack your crayons away then."

Rob rolled his eyes and turned toward the door. Syed followed and put his hand on Rob's shoulder. "Stop waiting for tomorrow, my friend."

"You sound like my wife."

"She sounds very wise."

"Right." Rob put his hard hat back on. "I'm still babysitting the investors out there. I'll send them your way now so, seriously, put the cooler on, mate. It's hotter than fuck in here. You don't want them thinking you're a cheapskate."

Syed nodded. "I'll freeze their balls off."

Rob smiled as he made his way down the rickety steps. His phone buzzed in his pocket. He pulled it out, hoping it was Emma. It was a text from Will.

This is your fault.

He knew something like this would happen. This stupid gap year was already placing a wedge between him and his son.

CHAPTER FIVE

Across the city, Emma sat in her kitchen and read the same message from Will.

This is your fault.

How dare he! Emma stood up from the stool in her breakfast nook and looked out the window but the view didn't hold her attention.

She looked back at the text.

This is your fault.

What was? Was he talking about her and Rob? Or was there something else?

No, it had to be his way of turning the knife.

Emma had to work hard not to respond to Will's text. It was hot headed. He'd write back soon and apologize.

Dr Priya was still talking, telling her to reflect on her list of her values. She'd written *Honesty* on a notepad she'd stolen from work.

What business did Emma have writing a list like this? What was she thinking? How could she self-actualize when she couldn't even keep her family together? She looked at Will's text again. It was just mean and she resisted telling him so. It would only make things worse.

God, she was imploding, wasn't she? This podcast was for people who were just tinkering with their lives. People who needed a refresher to get them back on track to perfection. Not people who blew up their families on purpose. She probably needed more serious help.

What would Dr Priya say if she met Emma and knew how selfish she was, sitting here in her own apartment, sealed off from the world, up in the clouds. Dr Priya would tell her she was dreaming. That she was stalling. That she had to stop hiding from her problems.

But she *wasn't* hiding. She'd made the hard decision and spoken up, took what she needed.

Except she hadn't given proper thought to how this gap year might affect Will. But he wasn't a little kid anymore. He was at university, for godsakes.

Still, maybe she just wanted him to be more mature than he was. He kept telling her to stop catastrophizing the impact of those Covid years, but how could it *not* screw up a kid to spend his two final years of high school in his bedroom, on a screen. Will was still a child in so many ways. He was tall, sure, but he was lanky and delicate, hadn't filled out like they thought he would. He procrastinated and daydreamed, his tussled hair half covering his eyes, like he was hiding.

She'd pushed him too far now, hadn't she? She said it'd be good for him to live in the dorms, meet other people, see what life was like when you had to do things for yourself. But it was obviously too much too soon. Those years of isolation had messed him up in ways that would plague him for years to come, maybe for the rest of his life. It wasn't her fault, the pandemic, but she still felt guilty. What more could she have done to help him?

Emma turned Dr Priya off and slipped the phone into her bag. Here she was, living in an apartment only a twenty-minute walk from the office and she'd somehow been running even later than usual.

Emma couldn't deal with this now, this heaviness. Not this morning. She had to get to work. She could focus on something else there. Maybe there, things would feel more normal.

The Catch offices were in Docklands, one of Melbourne's newer corporate suburbs. The buildings here, like her apartment block, were all steel and glass, wrapped in brightly colored zinc trim, full of early noughties optimism. Emma reckoned it was all meant to feel playful and fresh, but twenty years later the aesthetic felt a little more desperate, a token splash of color on the cover page of an otherwise boring government report. No one was fooled, not even the architects or city planners who must now see it for what it was: a ghost city, like the ones they built in China, waiting for people to move in who never showed up.

And yet, this morning she willed herself to see Docklands differently. Rather than the streets being deserted, she tried to see them as undiscovered. The neighborhood wasn't empty, it was just waiting, laying the groundwork for what was to come. This newish suburb was a startup and she an early adopter, already a part of what would one day become the heartbeat of Melbourne. She was the new Emma. The single Emma. The one who jogs. The one who was going to be closer to her son. The Emma who was allowed to be ambitious.

The elevator doors opened like a parting curtain, revealing the Catch logo: a smiling catfish looking knowingly at a dangling fishhook. Under that was the company slogan: *Big Fish, Big Pond*. Emma shook her head as she got out of the elevator. It was a bizarre slogan, didn't really make sense. Wasn't a big fish in a big pond just a fish? She never liked the "Big Fish" part either, thought it confused the main aspect of this business, which was about finding little fish small jobs. Anyway, such decisions were not hers to make.

The office struck her as especially bright this morning, the white tops of the tidy stand-up desks like shelves of ice reflecting the sharp light outside. The popular minimalist decor of offices like this one always seemed to discount people's stuff. Where were they supposed to put it? Emma smiled at the few people gathered in the waiting area, people whose names she didn't (and would never) know as she walked across the floor to her desk in the open-plan space, nestled within summoning distance of the executives who lived in glass offices that surrounded the floor. At least she had her own desk and had been spared banishment to the "hot desks" where temp workers sat, an endless cycle of Catch clients doing compulsory office training or work experience. Their smiles were always so needy.

Emma saw her desk as a warm patch in this frosty place. She kept a teapot there and an assortment of loose-leaf teas that she stored in small metal canisters. Beside her computer was a discreet picture of Will, not a shrine, just a small photo, the last of his school pictures before he'd graduated from high school. Beside the image of Will was a small peace lily in a pot and a mason jar of sour candies. The Himalayan-pink-salt lamp was supposed to ionize the air. She didn't care if it did or not, she just liked its soothing peach glow. A green woolen blankie was draped over the back of her chair: cozy in winter, when her legs and feet grew cold, and essential in summer, when the aircon blasted down from the ceiling vents. Emma had bookends, too, between which were copies of all the work she was proud of. Not the stuff she'd done for Catch – most of their material was online – but the printed magazines and glossy reports she'd produced back when companies used to send people things they could hold in their hands.

"Welcome back."

Emma turned and noticed French-manicured lavender nails wrapped around the largest phone she'd ever seen. "Oh, hey Mish."

"How was your time off?"

"It was okay."

"Good. Uhm, you got a sec?

"Sure. What's up?" Emma spun her chair all the way round to face Mish.

"I wanted to talk to you before the stand-up meeting," said Mish, moving closer.

"Okay." Emma made a serious face. "What's up?"

"Uhm. I don't want to blab or anything, but…" Mish looked over her shoulder. "Jarod was acting weird all week."

"Oh?"

Mish lowered her voice to a whisper. "He was in there yesterday," she said, pointing at the glass cube of Isabella's office. "For, like, an hour. And when he came out, he was going around to the rest of us, saying stuff like 'So, what are you working on? What have you been up to?' It was a bit cringy."

"That's weird."

"It is, right? I mean, has he got a reason to swagger around like that?"

Emma sighed. "I just got here."

Mish's facial features spread in concern. "Oh, sorry. You're just putting down your stuff and I'm all like blah, blah, blah. I just thought you should know he was acting weird. Could just be him, though, right?"

"We'll see," said Emma taking off her shawl. "Or we could all get fired before lunch." Mish's face gathered in concern. "I'm kidding," said Emma, remembering that Mish sent money to help support her parents overseas. "Seriously, Mish, I'm sure it's fine. They were probably just talking about the annual report. Okay?"

Mish seemed reassured and nodded sympathetically. "Okay thanks," she said, and turned back toward her station. "Nice to have you back," she said over her shoulder.

Emma made a cup of tea and checked her phone. Her text to Will stared back unanswered: *Let's have lunch. What day suits? I can meet you at uni.*

Her thumbs hovered over the screen. She was poised to write something comforting, something supportive, but she hesitated. She didn't know what to write, feared botching the message and putting Will off. What did he expect her to say? Sorry? She had spent a lifetime apologizing, often for things that weren't even her fault. It was her way of keeping the peace. Absorbing responsibility had become her way of looking after her family and, at some point, it's what Will and Rob expected her to do. Looking after everyone else's needs before her own had become normal. But it wasn't right, and it shouldn't be, and this new Emma wasn't going to do that anymore.

Still, this gap year was obviously causing Will stress. How had she not foreseen that? Or had she ignored his feelings, precisely because considering them might have prevented her from doing the very thing she knew she must. She needed to reinforce the boundary between what she needed and what others expected from her.

Emma scrolled through her work emails as a distraction before the team meeting. Most of them were from Mish. Emma's inbox often looked like this. Mish was the hardest working member of her team. By a wide margin.

Nothing from Jarod. Or Isabella. Emma glanced over her partition to the frosted glass cube of Isabella's office, waiting for her to emerge and shed light on Jarod's sudden confidence. It didn't look like Isabella was even in there.

Setting a meeting on a Friday was cruel, but Emma wanted to catch up on what she'd missed this week.

"Hey Em," said Angie, already in the meeting room, her curly hair dangling just above the surface of the meeting table. "Welcome back."

"Geez, I was only gone a few days," said Emma, playfully. "People are welcoming me back like I spent two weeks in Noosa." She sat down on the white faux-leather swivel chair. "Hey Liam." Liam gave a meek little wave from across the table, his hand barely moving from side to side.

"Oh, two weeks in Noosa sounds *amazing*," said Angie, drooping her head in mock sadness, her hair spilling onto the table. Mish nodded. Liam grinned uncomfortably, as if to suggest he'd not been to Noosa and so had no right to an opinion.

Emma leaned forward to peek out the open door. "Anyone seen Jarod?" she asked, turning back to face the group.

"He was around earlier," said Liam. "He should be coming."

"Oh well, that's good of him," said Emma, adding a snorty laugh to indicate she was joking.

"There he is," said Liam.

"Hey Jarod," said Angie, sitting up.

Jarod strode in, holding a takeout coffee. "Sorry," he said. "Had to wait forever for this." He circled the table and sat at the opposite head from Emma. What was that? Some kind of "power" move?

"Okay," said Emma. "Let's make a start. First off, the big news is I'm back in the office after a few days off."

"Woo," said Angie. "Do anything fun?"

Emma took a deep breath. "I went running for the first time in forever."

"Oh, cool," said Angie.

"Nice one," said Mish. Even Liam gave Emma a little thumbs up.

"We should get an office team together," said Jarod. "Relay event or something."

Emma tittered. "Yeah, well, I'll let you all know when I can do a lap of the park without wanting to barf." This drew hardy laughter from Mish and Angie. Liam smiled. Jarod took a sip of his coffee.

"Okay," said Emma, leaning forward, her elbows on the table. "Shall we talk about work?" She scanned the room. "I've only got two things, really. One is that I'm going to meet with you all individually next week so we can go over your workplans, so if you guys could all flick them through to me. Okay?" Blank faces stared back. Only Mish nodded. Jarod looked down at the table. Emma cleared her throat. "The second thing I want to say is: it's annual report time again." She made jazz hands. "So, yay! I'll need some help wrangling stuff from the other departments."

"I've got some news about the report," said Jarod. "I signed a new designer for it yesterday." He looked at Liam as he said this. That's what he'd done in his interview too. Even though Emma and Isabella were the hiring managers, Jarod had directed his answers to their questions to Liam, the most junior member of the team. Emma had taken an instant dislike to Jarod, but Isabella said he was the one, so Emma had to swallow the hiring decision.

Emma shook her head. "Sorry, you signed a designer for the-what-now?"

"Yeah. There was an opportunity to use a new supplier and, since you weren't here, Isabella signed off on it yesterday. It's done."

"But what about Nat?" said Emma.

"She's been doing it for the last three years. Time to give someone else a go, I reckon."

"Sure, except Nat already knows our style guides. She can hit the ground running. We don't have to go through that awkward part where a new designer tries to impress us with funky design ideas we're never going to use."

Jarod cocked his head. "Sorry, are you suggesting we *shouldn't* try to improve what we do?"

Emma sighed. "Did you at least get quotes?"

"Got *a* quote. They're an awesome crew. They're called Anchor Men. Small team. Big ideas."

"Anchor Men?" Emma scowled. "Sounds like a gay musical." She scanned the others for reassurance, expecting at least a medium chuckle at her joke but only Mish offered a nervous smile.

"Wait." Angie's eyes rolled up to her forehead. "Oh," she said, "like anchors in a website."

Emma resented Angie's attempt to defuse the tension. Jarod needed to be shut down. Emma hoped her face was not reddening. She turned to Jarod. "Where'd you find them, the anchor men?"

"My network," he said too quickly.

"So, what you're saying is you know them personally?"

"Not personally. I mean, I know who they are——"

"Come on, Jarod."

"What?"

"You can't just dish out work to mates."

"They're not mates, they're just people I know who do good work. And even if they were, why not? I mean, that's how the world works. Isn't the whole Catch algorithm based on connecting workers with employers based on networks?"

"Yeah, but people still need to get hired on merit, Jarod, through a transparent recruitment process. When they don't, it's what internal audits are designed to find. It's how people get fired."

"Seriously? It's not like we work for the government, I'm pretty sure we can hire whoever we want."

"Well, it's not a good look."

Jarod leaned forward, the bulging shoulder pads under his suit comically askew. "I don't really appreciate the tone you're using with me in front of the team."

"What?" Emma was taken aback. Was her response unreasonable? "Jarod, seriously. I'm not…I'm trying to protect *you.*"

Jarod slouched back in his chair. She'd wounded his pride and he was now in that volatile state between implosion and explosion. A bomb either way. He was liable to say something irreversibly bad if she pressed the issue further. "Let's just park this for now," she said. "We'll take it offline."

Emma forced herself to move on to the next agenda item. Mish gave an update on fixing bugs in the auto chat feature of the website, but Emma felt herself disengaged from the summary, overly self-aware of the uncertain footing she was on after her interaction with Jarod. He was certainly talking about her to the team behind her back. What would he be saying? She could see out the corner of her eye that he was leaning back in his chair and looking up at the ceiling, making a real show of being elsewhere. She mentally prepared herself to say something, especially if he upped the ante and started looking at his phone or something during the staff meeting. What would she say? Something playful? "We keeping you from something, Jarod?" Or maybe the situation called for something more direct: "Can you put the phone away, please Jarod." Too mommy? Neither version seemed right and soon all the possible combinations of words and phrases she could assemble to put Jarod in his place overwhelmed her. She'd stopped listening and had to find her way back into what Mish was saying about the customer experience of the chatbot. Emma waited for a pause and found her way back into the conversation.

"So, a question," she said, turning to avoid even a peripheral vision of Jarod. His face seemed to channel the loudest voices in her head: you're out of touch, you're weak, you don't know what you're talking about.

She pushed her glasses to the bridge of her nose. "In a word, how would you characterize the user experiences you've assembled so far?"

Mish bit her bottom lip. "Uhm, the word 'grumpy' comes to mind."

Emma had to assert herself here, say something that would remind Jarod why *she* oversaw this team and not him. She wished she'd listened more closely and retained some detail from Mish's presentation. "So," Emma continued, relying on what she'd absorbed, "clients are coming to the website. They chat to the bot, who, whatever the clients ask for, encourages them to upload their résumés, and you're saying the clients are responding with words we interpret as grumpy. Does that sum it up?" She looked around, Mish and Liam nodded. Phew.

"Pretty much," said Angie.

"Well, let me ask you all something." Emma scanned the room. Jarod was looking down at the table. "How do you usually feel when you're looking for a job?"

Mish looked down at her hands. "Nervous," she said, the whites of her eyes showing.

"I always feel kinda needy," said Angie. "A little pathetic." Liam nodded in agreement.

"Right," said Emma, before Jarod had a chance to say anything. "So, maybe the question for us is: are people sounding edgy because of something the chatbot said? Or are they grumpy because they're looking for work?"

Emma looked at Jarod. Was he squirming? She had to do it, put him in his place. She almost felt bad for him, but someone had to be the jerk who got things done.

CHAPTER SIX

Rob almost missed the turn-off. He braked hard and steered his truck onto a narrow dirt track off the highway, obscured by overgrown bushes. The vehicle shuddered on the uneven surface, sending a collection of crumpled paper bags and an empty can of Red Bull falling from the dash. He slowed to absorb the potholes filled with muddy water and drove until he reached a dilapidated wooden gate blocking the road.

The faded words *Private Drive* were still discernible on a graying piece of wood nailed to the front of the gate. The sign was mounted at an irritatingly unlevel angle, hanging askew. Two nails would've fixed that. Instead of just one in the middle. Lazy. Judging from the shape and size of the nail, the person who'd hammered it in was not the same person who'd built the gate. A generation of craftmanship separated the two and Rob hoped that whoever built this gate was also the person who constructed the house beyond it, not whoever put up that wonky sign.

Rob heaved himself out of the truck and walked up to the gate. There was no lock or chain keeping it in place, so he squatted and lifted the sagging structure off the ground. He dragged it sideways, rusty hinges fighting him the whole way, and he was relieved to drop the thing in the weeds growing on either side of the track. He dusted his hands and climbed back in the cab of his truck. What was Syed getting him into?

Rob drove slowly, following the winding track up a steep hill. He noted the logistical challenges of this site. Big rigs would struggle to get up this road and a crane might not clear the pine tree branches that overhung the path. He hadn't seen the house yet, but Rob was already wondering if this project was worth doing. Whatever Syed had in mind for this place, renovating it wouldn't be cheap. Maybe the best advice he could give was to sell the house and pick a location with more manageable terrain. He drove on, surveying the land around him, wondering how and when Syed had managed to accumulate such an estate. What did he say he did in Iran before he came to Australia? Whatever. People made their own luck.

At the top of the hill, the gloomy forest track ended abruptly. Sunlight streamed through the windshield, so bright that Rob stopped the truck and groped around for his sunglasses. His vision adjusted, he could now take in the view, how the hill sloped gently toward acres of green fields. They ended at the edge of a cliff. Beyond that lay the limitless horizon of Bass Strait. Next stop, Tasmania.

Perched in the middle of this postcard setting was a squat stone building that looked like it'd been plucked straight from an English farm two hundred years ago. As he approached from the side, the stonework became clearer, the slats of the shutters. The hazy outline of a distant freighter heading out to sea was the only clue this scene belonged to the same world Rob had come from this morning. It was magic.

You'd almost expect to see a lighthouse on a spot like this, a green slope atop a rocky cliff overlooking a vast body of water.

He'd worked on a lot of high-end homes with ocean views. Many of them were beautiful creations, ball gowns, made to twirl and glitter for all to see.

This was different. As he pulled up to the front of the house, he could see the full state of the place. It was no more than a two-story stone cottage with a sagging roof and rotting windows, but this house had something those high-end places didn't. Mansions were about self-confidence. Bragging. This house was about humility. The people who moved here all those years ago would've been perched on the edge of the world. They would've seen an unforgiving ocean in front of them and a wilderness behind. There was no going back. This wasn't just a house. It was a monument to survival.

He parked, and the breath of the ocean filled the quiet.

Rob stepped out. A chill ocean breeze evinced the changing season. Summer would end soon. Not great for building.

He got his bearings. Behind him lay the city of Melbourne. Straight ahead was Tasmania, both too far to see. The stone building sat between them, watching the ships pass.

Rob thought back to the cheap housing commission flat he'd grown up in, the way the damp rose up through the floor in winter and the heat rolled in all summer, and how, from behind the thin walls of his bedroom, he could hear the squeaking and scrabbling of rats.

Rob pulled open the old timber door to the stone house. The stillness of those dense walls embraced him. It was as if time had stopped.

The old floorboards creaked under foot. Above him, slivers of daylight shone through broken roof tiles. Birds had nested in the rafters, leaving piles of bird shit everywhere.

Rob looked at his watch.

He'd just come to have a look, get Syed off his back, but Rob found himself wanting to stay. The place was a mess, but it had a hold on him. Emma would love it too.

FALL

CHAPTER SEVEN

Emma moved her head to the cheerful opening piano music of Dr Priya's show, briefly using her foamy toothbrush as a conductor's wand before popping it back in her mouth and continuing to brush her teeth.

Hey. Dr Priya sounded young and fun. *Welcome back. Now, I don't want to be the strict one, but how's your homework going? You doing it?*

Emma smiled to herself as she undid her bathrobe to put on deodorant. She *had* done the homework and spared a thought for those less driven, less committed people feeling guilty at this point in the podcast. It was always like that, wasn't it? Whether it was school, or work, or a journey of self-discovery, you just couldn't count on everyone doing the work. People were so unreliable. She put the deodorant back in the vanity and looked at herself in the mirror, turning her face from side to side. Was one nostril bigger than the other?

She thought about her aspirations, her path to a better life: doing exercise (okay she hadn't run for a few days, but that was because she was sore from all the running she *had* done, so check); reconnecting with self (she was listening to this podcast wasn't she, and let's not forget this gap year was a profound measure of her commitment to reconnecting with herself, so check again); helping her son to find independence (big check, she was meeting Will that very afternoon).

She did her hair and makeup and listened to Dr Priya talk about goal setting. Emma even felt charitable toward those people who'd probably keep listening even though *they* hadn't written *their* lists. Emma always did her homework.

So, said Dr Priya. *You reckon you've got a sense of what you want?* Emma nodded to herself as she rubbed in her face moisturizer. *If so, that's great. If not, don't stress.*

Hey, wait a minute. Why was Dr Priya letting the slackers off the hook? I mean, this episode was called "Doing the Work," for god sake.

Here's what I want you to do this week, this month or this year. It's not a race, my lovelies. Do it whenever you can. But do it.

Dr Priya took a long breath as if she were about to disclose something profound.

I want you to take some time out to reconnect with yourself. Now, I'm not talking about having a drink out with your girls. No, I want you to reach out to your more dreamy, more hopeful, more optimistic self. For some people, it helps to go back to places you haven't been in a while. Maybe the family home or a place you used to go to when you were young, a playground maybe or a park. The aim is to get out of the rut of everyday life.

But maybe you don't like the idea of returning to your past. That's fine. Not everyone's past is a nice place. If that's you, then go somewhere new. Some place you have no history. Some place where you can be alone, without expectations, a place that invites you to think and feel with abandon. Think nature. Maybe trees are your thing, or the beach. Or maybe just crack out the colored pencils somewhere and do some drawing, something creative. The point is to just go there with no agenda, no expectation of what success looks like. Just wander or draw or look at the sky and take note of what happens inside. That's your homework for this week, my lovelies. Until next time, be yourself, whoever that is.

Well, thought Emma. What a coincidence. She'd already arranged to meet Will at a place that fitted Dr Priya's description. Her path to wisdom was opening. The universe was recognizing her years of self-criticism as credit toward the self-acceptance that was her due.

This feeling of being blessed stayed with Emma as she strolled down one of the tree-lined paths at Melbourne University. Above her head, expanding patches of red and brown in the leaf canopy announced the fall, even if the cooler days seemed to come later every year.

She couldn't believe it had been nearly thirty years since she first walked this same route, back when she was a student here. The campus looked the same, sort of. It was glossier now, more corporate than she remembered, echoing the same steel and glass structures in her new neighborhood. It all felt a bit colder than the warm embrace of the sandstone buildings she'd adored, the ones that made her feel part of something worthy and serious.

She turned the corner into the old quadrangle. Here, the Oxford aesthetic of the original buildings that had so impressed her twenty-year-old self still enchanted her. Through the ups and downs of her life, and whatever happened out there in the world, these buildings had remained unchanged. There was comfort in that.

As she strolled, she mentally traveled back and forth on her personal timeline, braiding it with her son's. The overlaps were confronting. Was it possible that Will was now only three years younger than she had been when she first met Rob? It seemed only yesterday that her son was a baby. The whole experience of parenthood – of changing him, of teaching him to walk and talk, of childcare, elementary school and high school – all of it was summonable in one short montage. Such a show was life and she choked up at the beauty and brevity of it.

Groups of students walked around the campus, sleeveless tops and jackets tied around waists in this sudden burst of warmth. They walked close together, still cliquey but beginning their adult lives. She thought of Will and of Mish and Angie. Young people today grew up faster than her generation did. This group of young women passing her now, for instance. They already looked more sophisticated, determined and self-confident than her gang had been, when they were lounging around on that very lawn, back in the fall of 1994.

"Hey." Will's voice startled her.

"Oh sweetheart," she said, reaching up and putting her hands on his cheeks. She pulled him close. Will bent down at an awkward angle. "Come on," she said, "you hug your mom. Don't be all cool about it."

"I'm hugging," he said.

She patted his back. "You're so big."

"Ma, come on. I've been this size for a while now."

"I know," she said. He pulled away. She looked him up and down. "It's just…" Emma choked up. "Sorry," she sniffed.

Will stuffed his hands in his pockets and looked over his shoulder. "You want to walk around a bit? Get a coffee or something?"

Dr Priya was right. Places like this were important, the ones that brought past, present and future together. She could connect to the idea of herself as the center of her life, that middle dot where tree rings begin. She smiled at her son, "Yeah, I do."

"Come on," said Will in a gentle voice. "I'll show you around the village."

They strolled back the way she'd come, through the stone buildings to the old quadrangle with its courtyard of unblemished grass.

"Soak up the wizard-school vibes," said Will.

Emma frowned. "I think it's pretty."

Will and Emma walked along the brick laneway toward the student village.

Emma had been the one to push Will to live on campus. Rob had seen it as a needless expense, but she'd insisted. Living with other students, she reckoned, was the best way of getting the most out of the university experience. Plus, he'd just mope around if he stayed at home. All this talk about social anxiety was fine, but in the end, you had to do something about it. He needed a push. If he couldn't handle shared accommodation, this was the next best thing.

"Oh wow," she said as they walked through the main door of the student accommodation. The place had been virtually empty when they'd first visited months ago. It now felt like an upmarket youth hostel, with young people purposefully coming and going from the various communal areas: the kitchen, the gym, the games room, the outdoor pool. It was more resort than dorm, several steps up from the grungy house in Brunswick that Emma had shared with three other girls and a guy whose body odor Emma still recalled every time she smelled a kitty litter box. "This is great," she said, absorbing the bright airiness of the common areas in these student dorms.

She noted her son was nodding to a few people as they walked through the hallway. *He had friends!* This evidence of a social life vindicated the staunchness with which she'd advocated for Will's right to live here. It would do him good, was already doing him good, and she'd been right to fight and win that battle with Rob.

Having options. Isn't that what money was for? Rob never wanted to spend any of it. And never seemed to recognize the rainy day he said they were saving for.

"This one's mine," said Will, opening the door.

"Oh, it's cute," said Emma, walking inside. The studio apartment had seemed luxurious the first time she'd seen it, new and modern. But the self-contained space, with its small kitchen and ensuite bathroom felt different now that Will's stuff was scattered inside it. There was a sour odor of burned toast and unwashed clothes. She cast her mind back to the kitchen of her student share house where leftover pasta competed for space in the communal fridge.

"Do you ever go downstairs to the dining area?"

"Not really."

"How come?"

Will gave her a blank look. "Got everything I need here, I guess."

Perhaps this room hadn't been the best idea after all. How was he supposed to learn how to live with other people if he was shielded from them?

"You going okay, though," she said.

He nodded.

"You sure?" Emma straightened and smoothed the pillow on Will's bed. He looked at her and she stopped. "You can tell me if you're not."

He looked away. "Look, it's just…I know university was, like, *the* thing for you, but I'm just not sure I feel that."

"What do you mean?"

"I don't know. I can't get into it. It just feels like a waste of time. And money."

"Will—"

"It's true." He swallowed. "I keep thinking if everything's as fucked as it seems, if the world's really burning, then why bother?

Maybe I should just live for now, and not wait for some mythical future."

"Bit dramatic, don't you think?"

"Is it? I'm not sure. I don't know what to believe."

"Well, that's why you go to university."

Will rolled his eyes. "The people here don't know anything either. The professors and that, you can learn half the shit they teach on YouTube. A degree isn't a golden ticket anymore. And universities?" He shook his head. "Their days are numbered. But everyone just keeps pretending the world's not crumbling around them."

"Oh." Emma shut her eyes tight. "I remember being your age. But that just sounds stupid." She rubbed her temples. "Look," she said, softening her voice, "I want you to go to university. I just do. And not because I think it's the only way to get a job. It isn't. But the more you learn, the more aware you are of how much you *don't* know. It helps stop people from becoming too cocky. Plus, the world outside isn't pretty. It's about "productivity" and "cost cutting," and it's soul-destroying. I want you to experience something else."

"But that's *your* experience you're talking about, Mom, not mine."

"It will be." She tried to look him in the eye, but he wouldn't meet her gaze. "Will," she pleaded. "You've just started. Give it a chance."

Her son turned away. Emma sat at the foot of the unmade bed and traced the valleys of the wrinkled bedspread with her fingers. "About that text," she said. "I tried not saying anything, but I have to."

"Yeah, sorry, I was a bit drunk when I sent that."

"Is it true?" she said. "That you think it's all my fault?"

He turned toward her but looked at the ground. "I don't know." He paced and flattened the hair at the back of his head. He'd always done that when he was nervous.

"Say what you want to say, Will."

He sighed and squinted into the light of the tiny high window above the bed. "I want to be supportive and everything, but I can't help think this whole situation is a waste of time."

"What do you mean?"

"I mean you and Dad. I mean, you're either going to get back together or you're not. Why do the whole year apart thing? It's cringy. Just prolongs things. I don't see the point."

Emma scoffed.

Will furrowed his brow. "What's to figure out? You've basically been estranged, or whatever, for years."

"Estranged?"

"Well, strained. It's been awkward for a while. You guys don't even sit on the same couch anymore. You think I don't notice?"

"It's your dad's fault too, you know."

"What? Did he cheat on you?"

"No."

"Well then what?"

It was that simple for him, wasn't it? Two sides. No middle ground. She almost envied the simplicity of his perspective if it didn't irritate her so much. Will always took his father's side.

"Right, *I* have no idea, said Will."

"Hey! Watch it. You think this whole set up here just happens? Ta da! Well, it doesn't. It takes sacrifices, Will. Years of 'em. And you have no idea what that means."

"Okay, threats. Nice, mom."

"It's not a threat, Will. I'm *sharing* with you. And I'm saying that I worked damn hard so you didn't have to."

She reached out her hand and guided him to sit next to her on the unmade bed. He did, but he looked rigid and distracted. "Look," she said, resting her hand on his knee. "I'm sorry to hear things have been weird for you. I honestly thought we were doing a pretty good job of hiding it from you, but I was wrong. But you have to understand that I'm in a strange place right now."

"What, are you sick or something?"

"No, I'm just feeling lost. When I see an ad or something that says *follow your dreams*, I don't have any. I've become this person who's just sort of…there. I never thought I'd be like that. And it scares me. It feels like I'm disappearing. Does this make any sense to you?"

Will smiled as if to himself.

"What?"

"It's just funny. You grow up thinking all these people around you, the adults or whatever, that they have some idea of what's going on, like they're living their lives based on some kind of plan. But no one has a clue."

Emma gave Will a hug, and as his arms tightened around her shoulders, she felt a surge of love.

CHAPTER EIGHT

Rob stepped from the shade of the stone house into bright sunshine. Inside, the place had been silent as a church. Outside, the crash of distant waves met the rustling of leaves stirred by the offshore breeze. He breathed in the sea air. This was a good spot. It was good to be back here. Syed was a lucky bugger.

Sitting in the flatbed of his truck, Rob finished checking his own measurements against the architectural drawings Syed had given him. Dimensions, footings, load bearings. It all checked out.

Whoever built this place knew what they were doing. Whatever architectural know-how they lacked, they made up for in grit and over-engineering. These walls were thick and the foundations deep. This house had withstood whatever time and the elements had thrown at it. It was built to last. Rob silently praised its builder, some migrant, desperate to rebuild his memory of the English coast a world away from home. It wasn't just a house, it was a life raft, and he felt himself ever more drawn to the idea of honoring this place. It was a project he could pour himself into. Being out here, on this spot, would do him good.

Rob could've been an architect. He'd seriously thought about it.

Even got some drafting certifications. But that was a dream from years ago. He couldn't get past the building part. In the end Rob was a doer, and no two-dimensional drawing or computer render could substitute the feeling of putting something together, a real building, a place you could walk through and live in, something you made. Maybe Emma recognized this in him when she'd pressed him about the table.

That feeling of creating something with your own hands was probably familiar to whoever built this place. Built like a fortress, its solid walls testified to hardship, a need to fortify oneself against the world outside. Rob pulled out his notepad and sketched swift pen strokes that quickly took the shape of the building in front of him.

Rob continued to draw, needlessly shading, cross-hatching the grass, the slope of the hill. He was enjoying the repetitive motion and the sense of dimension it added to his sketch of the house, imagining the bigger windows he'd put in, and all the sunlight that would pour through them.

Rob used to draw like this all the time. He'd spend hours in his bedroom, drawing cross sections of cars and houses and boats, loving the soothing sense of order he could create on the page. Even if perfect space only existed in two dimensions, it wouldn't stop him trying to build it in real life.

As a kid, Rob would keep his best drawings tucked inside the pages of an old phone book. He didn't like how the edge of his illustrations would stick out from the book, curling and fraying his drawings over time. But it kept them hidden from his dad, who'd scolded him for taping a drawing to his bedroom wall. "You going to pay for the repainting?" he'd said. "Use your head."

It felt good to draw, and Rob did his best to capture the weathered blocks of granite, stained by years of water runoff from the roof tiles, sagging under the weight of time.

He stopped sketching, wedged the pen between his teeth and held the notepad at arm's length, considering his drawing against the real thing. The pages of the notebook quivered in the sea breeze, but the clamp of Rob's calloused thumb kept the pages from turning. He smiled and brought the pad back to his lap.

Rob cocked his head to admire his creation when something in the distance caught his attention. A growing dust plume on the dirt road. It was a truck coming down the hill. Who the hell was that?

CHAPTER NINE

The flashing lights of Crown Casino caught Emma's attention as she jogged past. Cabs were lining up outside the entrance, their red taillights blinking in the violet dawn.

Six years ago, she and Rob had spent a night at Crown Towers for their twentieth wedding anniversary – pool, massages, buffet dinner *and* breakfast. They'd even had a flutter at the slots and the blackjack table. Emma didn't usually drink much but joined Rob that night, and their shared abandon to the booze, the posh room and the twinkling city views allowed them to surrender to their wilder sides. They had sex three times in twenty-four hours, something they hadn't done since Will came along.

In the morning, they'd waited for a cab, right over there, where the honeymooners, the out-of-towners and the people who'd been up all night gambling shuffled toward their ride back to normal.

A determination to succeed was part of Rob's appeal from the beginning. They met in a bar in Brunswick, at the start of her third year of university. He was the only one of his mates who wasn't slobbering drunk and he came over to apologize to her and her friends for the boys' rude behavior. They got talking and Emma was immediately impressed by Rob's maturity. While Emma was still waiting to have a career, to become a proper adult, Rob was already there. He was working for a large construction firm in the city, building malls and high-rise towers. "Get in, get out, get paid." That was his mantra.

He'd gone straight to trade school and bought his first investment property when he was nineteen. He was smart too, not book smart but street smart. He had an opinion on things, especially the political subjects that Emma and her university friends liked to talk about, even though he didn't use the same language they did to express his views. Like when he told them Australia should remain a monarchy because traditions made people feel like they were part of something. All her friends had shouted him down. But he wouldn't budge. She was impressed by that, the way he stood his ground.

It was reassuring to be around Rob. He was more like the people in the neighborhood she grew up in than most of the people in her university crowd. He was a real person, not one of those private school jerks who looked down at her because she came from a public school in a lowly neighborhood.

Rob's clear-eyed orientation toward the future also felt like a tacit promise that they would avoid the bickering of her own parents about money. She and Rob were realists, ready to reap the rewards of hard work.

He was attractive but not intimidatingly so, more cute than handsome, but he was tall and strong, and she liked that. Nagged by Germaine Greer and Gertrude Stein to feel suspicious of feeling safe around Rob, these intellectual reservations collapsed under the weight of her physical and emotional needs. She felt protected by his imposing size.

Over the course of the next few years, the contours of the life Emma could foresee with Rob took shape against the backdrop of cultural expectations and her own social and professional disappointments. Her best friend from high school, Chloe Mathers, had already become Chloe Zevelekakis, exerting the pressure of new measures of maturity and success.

Emma turned to look in the other direction, toward the Yarra River, which seemed to flow at the pace of the clouds drifting in the mottled sky. Her pace slowed to a shuffle as she fiddled with her phone, switching from music to a podcast. The peaceful jingle of Dr Priya's theme music suited the scene. Along the promenade, restaurateurs swept their patios and wiped down their tables. This episode was called "Who Do You Think You Are," and Dr Priya began with a personal story about how she was bullied at school and how it got worse the more she tried to fit in, say the right things, wear the right clothes.

Emma ran faster, fighting back tears that sprang from nowhere.

A boy on a skateboard cruised past, standing like Michelangelo's David, leather jacket slung over his shoulder. A young woman riding an electric scooter also whirred passed, trailing a wake of fluttering blonde hair. Emma ran faster, trying to catch up to them, but they disappeared into the maw of the underpass at Princes Bridge.

Emma was crying now and willed herself to keep going. Under the bridge, she pulled out her headphones and propped herself against the wall, supported by the dark heavy stones. Her chest tightened and she struggled to gulp a full breath. The rhythmic thump of unseen traffic passed on the bridge overhead.

A fit couple ran past. The woman looked back.

"You right?" she said, and stopped. The man said nothing, only turned and jogged on the spot.

"I'm fine." Emma fanned herself with her hand.

"You sure?" The woman approached, hands out.

"I'm okay." Emma braced herself against the stone wall and straightened. "Just went a little hard, that's all."

The woman remained concerned.

"All good?" said her stony-faced partner, giving a thumb's up, his eyes hidden behind mirrored sunglasses.

Emma nodded and waived them on their way.

The pair continued their run, no doubt congratulating themselves on their fitness, leaving Emma behind as a cautionary tale. She put her earbuds back in.

What's your excuse? said Dr Priya. *How do you get in the way of your own success?* Emma walked, catching her breath as she went.

Why are you afraid? What are you worried about? Why do you have doubts? If you knew the answers to these questions, you probably wouldn't be here.

A cyclist sped past and a boat full of rowers sliced through the river, heaving their oars in unison.

Let me ask you another question, maybe a more approachable one. Whose life do you use a model for your own?

Dr Priya paused, as if willing Emma to answer. A succession of names and images in Emma's mind filled the silence: Mom? Dad? Mrs Burton, her Year 9 English teacher? Frida Kahlo? Ruth Bader Ginsberg? This wasn't working. She couldn't even do a wellness podcast right. Emma was relieved when Priya spoke again.

Come on, my lovelies! We all do it. Maybe your model's a celebrity, or someone in your family. Or maybe it's some more perfect version of yourself. Maybe that person's got more money, a bigger house or a flashier job. And maybe being with them feels good on one level, but on another, it can leave you feeling flat, like a bit of a failure.

Emma was thankful to have her breath back.

Or maybe you use someone's life as a warning, an example to avoid. Maybe you know someone who's hanging onto a job they hate, or a bad relationship because they're afraid of being lonely. Or maybe they're using drugs or alcohol or food or gambling to cope with negative feelings.

Emma made a mental note to catch up with her friend Kendry.

The point is whose life choices do you strive to emulate and whose do you avoid? And is their example (for better or worse) what you really want? Because maybe their example is confusing you, maybe it's holding you back. What I'm asking is…what do you want? Whose life are you living?

Emma thought of her father and how his stubbornness about not getting tied down by a regular job had driven a wedge between her parents. Her mother thought making stained glass windows was basically the same as being a glazier and couldn't understand why Bill didn't just get on with it, hustle more, take an ad out in the paper, sell his services like the handyman he was.

Dad said he needed freedom to create. Mom learned not to roll her eyes in front of him when he said that. But when he wasn't around, she made it clear her husband was a slacker, who valued a beer and a bet on the football game as much as he did his "art."

Emma didn't see it that way. Her father was his best self when he was in his shed. He was quiet in there. His movements were smooth and self-assured as he reached for the right mallet, pliers, or twisty bit of lead tubing that he kept upright in a wooden pail, tubes that fanned out like a bouquet of metal flower stems with the tops pulled off.

Time didn't exist in that shed the way it did elsewhere. It sped up and slowed down and Emma spent her happiest moments with her father in there, where he made things. He loved working with his hands, a tangible skill that she later valued in Rob. Thinking on it now, she wondered whether she had driven Rob the way her mother had driven her father.

Her father was happy to take the odd commission to fix a church window after a hailstorm or repair a smashed glass panel at a sailing club, usually when his old Mustang needed fixing, but he relied more on his networks at the local bar for work than he did on advertising his services or pounding the pavement.

After her parents fought (always about money), Dad would go out and get a "proper job," like Mom wanted him to. It was usually a spit-and-handshake deal between him and one of his mates, like the time he sold terracotta pots at a nursery in Lilydale with his friend Massimo. Or the stint at a thrift store in Carlton. These jobs never lasted more than a few months. Dad would eventually insult a customer or break one too many pots, or just stop showing up altogether in protest of some perceived slight against him.

Mom would get angry, Dad would get angrier, and Emma would stay quiet. She loved her parents separately but steeled herself whenever they were together. Occupying the no-man's-land between them for all those years was heartbreaking.

When her parents eventually divorced, Emma could see it was good for them both. Mom now lived in a one-bedroom unit in Bairnsdale and said she was glad to be out of Melbourne, which had become "too big, too crowded and too snobby" for her liking.

Even though Mom's grumpiness was draining, Emma thought she should call her more. She must be lonely, all by herself. More than she let on. But it was work calling her mother and Emma didn't often feel up to it.

Dad was remarried now and living in Brisbane, and she didn't see much of him beside what he posted of his new family on Facebook.

You are not these people, said Dr Priya. *You are not destined to live by their example or their expectations of you.*

Emma picked up the pace. She trotted, then jogged, then ran, past the boats on their moorings, past the burning in her chest. She would *not* feel embarrassed, she would *not* feel frumpy, she was *not* old. She ran the rest of the way to work, grateful for the air that flowed to her lungs.

The floor numbers lit up as she ascended in the elevator, the glow of those numbers helping her feel present, tracking where she was in this moment. Floor 7, 8, 9. She was here. She was in control.

It wasn't her plan to go to the office in her new workout gear, but her panic attack, or whatever that was, meant she'd taken longer than she intended and didn't change. It's not like she was wearing a spandex onesie. The new tracksuit was perfectly respectable and would do fine until she cooled down enough to shower and change in the staff facilities. At least she had the elevator to herself. Then the elevator stopped. The doors opened and Jarod got in. Did he just avert his eyes? What was he doing on the eleventh floor?

"I went for a run," she said.

He raised his eyebrows. "Great."

"Yeah," said Emma, and dabbed her forehead with the gym towel that hung around her neck. Why was she doing that? She didn't need to validate her exercise. So what if she only managed to do three kilometers? She was starting out. And, besides, she didn't need Jarod's approval. Emma let the sweat trickle down her neck in little rivers, which gave her a pleasant shiver and pooled at the small of her back.

"Good for you." Jarod smiled. Condescending little prick. "How far did you go?"

"I didn't really keep track." Emma dabbed her forehead with the towel.

The elevator doors opened. She and Jarod both moved to exit first and bumped shoulders in the doorway.

"Sorry," said Jarod. He stepped back, held the door open and leaned forward in a kind of awkward, exaggerated bow. "Ladies first."

"Thanks," said Emma, sliding past him. "Do you mind swiping me in," she said, rummaging in her backpack. "My card's in here somewhere."

"Sure." He reached for the swipe card at the end of his lanyard and hovered it over the security pad with a needless flourish. The frosted doors with the Catch logo opened with a mechanical whoosh. They both walked in and headed to their desks in the open-plan office.

"Oh, hey," said Jarod. Emma turned around. "We should catch up later."

"Sure," she said, turning away. "You know where to find me." She hoisted the shoulder strap of her backpack further up on her shoulder and waved to Angie and Mish as she walked past them, both on their phones behind the low partitions of their workspace. They smiled and waved back as Emma walked past. Mish's shiny lavender nails were like candies on her fingertips.

Maybe it was the exhilaration of the run, or the residual glow of her honest talk with Will the other day, but Emma felt a welcome sense of comfort and reassurance at the sight of her desk – the u-shape arrangement of books and folders drew her in like an embrace. This was her little base in this sprawling office, a spot put aside just for her, a place where she could be useful and productive in ways that were entirely independent of her identity as a wife and mother. She'd spent many years convincing herself that her career was second to her family. And it was. But life didn't really work that way. Before her family, work was everything. Home life helped put things into perspective. Maybe that's what Dr Priya meant by bringing your "whole self" to your job. Work-Emma reinvigorated home-Emma and she was grateful for both. Maybe work and life were never meant to balance at all. Maybe they were supposed to blend and marble, like cake ingredients.

She put her backpack on the floor and plonked down on her office chair – the weight off her feet soothed the oddly pleasant muscle fatigue tingling in her legs. It had been so long since she'd exercised regularly, not since high school, so young and full of dreams.

She'd been going to be a "businessperson," someone who wore nice clothes to work. She would be a trailblazer, work in advertising, for Oxfam and the United Nations. She'd make money to give it back. She would be a role model, an entrepreneur, and wherever she went, she'd hear the cracking of glass ceilings. Her life would be full of interesting people who devoted their lives to worthy causes, people who would enrich her in ways she did not yet know existed.

There would be lovers and tousled sheets in exotic hotels with views of the Eiffel Tower, the pyramids of Giza, the World Trade Center. She would be awakened by the garbled chorus of unfamiliar birds outside her window, or sober calls to prayer from distant minarets. An open spirit would bring her a life of adventure. It would all just happen.

As the end of high school loomed, lack of money was front of mind when Emma declared a career path. She enjoyed her art classes, the screen-printed T-shirts, the linocuts and the shoebox pinhole cameras, but Mr Blundell's art studio, with its drying racks and paint-splattered walls came to feel more like a guilty pleasure than a realistic vocation, a distraction from Maths, English and Computer Studies. She had helped put together the school yearbook but eventually dismissed "graphic design" as whimsy and soberly directed herself toward a job in "business and communications." That felt suitably grown-up.

Emma had left university energized and emboldened, only to discover the world of work had little interest in what she'd learned. She had no professional network and no experience outside of working at Mr Leung's sandwich shop, which had helped put her through school. When potential employers bothered to call her back, they all told her versions of the same thing: "we're looking for someone with more experience."

Her first job was as an office temp. The feminist theory she'd absorbed at university ran against the entrenched, male conservatism of Melbourne's old boy network. She worked in a series of consulting firms doing general office duties, preparing spreadsheets, proofreading copy, only to have the paperwork thanklessly snatched up by a succession of young men in suits who'd graduated from the "right" schools, captained the "right" teams and whose fathers had, no doubt, laid solid foundations for their sons' success. The patriarchy was not a mythological thing – it was an invisible hand directing traffic inside this network of glass office towers.

Being an adult meant making rational choices, and Emma had been in a hurry to become an adult. She was keen to become a person whose sound decisions would correct the bohemian laxness of her upbringing. She'd grown up in a house with few rules, a place where she sometimes woke to find her dad's mate Massimo asleep on the living room couch as she left for school, the coffee table full of empty bottles and the hubcap ashtray still smoldering with cigarette butts.

When the time came, she would offer her own family a more stable environment. Rob was part of that stability. But now she'd gone and blown it apart. In the end, she was just as selfish and impulsive as her father.

Emma dabbed her temples with the gym towel and turned on her computer. She glanced up at the spines of her publications on the bookshelf above her desk. There was solid work there and she was proud of it. Those publications offered a career timeline, a testament to how she'd balanced work and motherhood by squeezing out friends and hobbies to make room for part-time work through most of Will's childhood. Emma's transition from full-time work to casualized labor was visible on that bookshelf – in the transition from the thick government reports and glossy magazines with professional photographs, to the thin stapled booklets she'd produced for small-time clients as a freelancer. She'd made those sacrifices for her family, but she had not, until now, appreciated how this shift in priorities had plateaued her career. By contrast, Rob's clients had kept getting bigger and better, his career an upward trajectory.

What happened to all her ambitions? Turns out they were dreams enough for five lives, not one.

Emma picked up the tin of green tea with jasmine and dried pear, and lightly shook it. Enough left to make a small pot. She opened the lid and sniffed its contents. Summer in Japan. She'd never been to Japan, but this floral odor is how she imagined it. When she opened her eyes, Isabella was looking down at her from behind the partition, tall, blonde and statuesque with a cell phone phone in her hand. "Got a sec?" she said.

"Sure," Emma said. "Should I bring a notepad or a cardboard box?"

Isabella looked momentarily confused. "Oh, don't be silly," she said, getting the joke and brushing away the suggestion. "It's nothing bad."

The only decor in Isabella's office was a display shelf of Catch-branded merchandise. There were keychains and stress balls and T-shirts, all with that stupid smiling catfish on them. *Big Fish, Big Pond*. The slogan was on everything. There was even a Catch umbrella open in the corner of the room, designed on the premise that office workers would glimpse the logo when wistfully gazing down at the street from their office windows. *Time for something new,* they'd say to themselves. But office windows didn't open. Dumb idea.

"Have a seat," Isabella said.

Emma eased herself onto one of the plastic office chairs draped in a faux-fur throw. "Ooh, this is all a bit formal now that I'm in here. Getting a little nervous."

"Emma, you're not going anywhere."

"Oh, good. Because, I had this feeling of—"

"But there's going to be a restructure."

"Oh?"

"Yeah, the rest of the staff don't know yet. Except people who'll be directly affected."

"Okaaay."

"You're keeping comms, Emma. You're staying exactly where you are."

"Uh huh."

Isabella glanced down at the phone on her desk and looked up again. "It's just that communications is now going to be under the umbrella of a division called 'strategic messages, partnerships and alumni relations'."

"Okaaay."

"And Jarod, from your team, is going to oversee that division."

"Seriously?"

Isabella nodded. "Yes."

"Really?" Emma shook her head and searched inside her skull for words. "Jarod? He's going to – sorry, what is it again? Strategic…"

"Messages, partnerships and alumni relations."

Emma frowned. "Those aren't even real things, though. They're just different words to describe what comms does." Her breathing was shallow.

"Emma, you get to keep playing to your strengths. Nobody does comms better."

Emma's face felt hot. She knew her neck would be getting blotchy now and resisted the urge to do up the zipper on her tracksuit. "Can I…?" Emma took a breath to compose herself. Her stomach lurched. "Excuse me," she said, bolting for the exit.

Emma strode across the office floor to the bathrooms. She tore open the cubicle door, dropped to her knees and dry-retched into the toilet bowl until a string of snot hung from her nose. She blind-groped the wall beside her and pulled out a wad of toilet paper. She blew her nose and tried to muffle her crying. Her life was falling apart. This is how it happened. Bit by bit, the foundations of your life just crumbled.

Why had she been so cavalier with Rob? He wasn't perfect but at least he was there. What was she to other people? Just another grumpy middle-aged woman, growing more invisible by the day. A cliché. She stiffened.

Fuck that. She sniffed, stood, wiped her face and tossed the wads of paper into the toilet. Fine. If she was going to be treated like a discarded rag, she wasn't going to make it easy. She flushed again and left the cubicle. She had things to say, and Isabella would hear them. She splashed cold water on her face, straightened her tracksuit and strode back toward Isabella's office.

Isabella looked up. She was leaning over her phone, which lay on her spotless desk. "Peter, I'm going to have to call you back. Something's come up." She stabbed the hang-up button on her phone and took a breath. "I swear, sometimes it's like you have to lead them each step of the way." Isabella shook her head and closed the door to her office. "Have a seat, Emma. You need some water or something?"

Emma shook her head. She did want water but didn't want to have it in her shaky hands. Besides, she wouldn't be able to swallow past the lump in her throat.

Isabella sighed as she sat down. "Look, I know this restructure is probably a bit of a surprise—"

"A surprise? No, why? An underqualified male, a kid, getting recklessly promoted to a job he's not ready for? Why would that come as a surprise, Isabella?"

Isabella laced her fingers together and leaned forward over her desk. "I don't think you're being fair. Jarod's got credit that you're not giving him."

"Really?"

"Yes. He does things cheaper. The board likes that. Hell, *I* like that."

"Cheaper," said Emma, "but not better. I put together great stuff."

Isabella sighed. "You do, Emma. But you've never accepted that a big part of your job is making the people *above you* look good."

"Right, so I don't suck up enough?"

Isabella's unblinking eyes were unnerving as they locked on to Emma's, who felt certain her own eyelids were fluttering like bee wings.

"Look," said Isabella, "maybe you need the afternoon to—"

"No." Emma shook her head. "Pretty sure 'the afternoon' isn't going to help me feel better about this."

"Emma." Isabella put her palms down on the desk and stood up. "This was a unanimous decision at the executive level. It's out of my hands."

"No, I get it. The tribe has spoken. I mean, why should I get upset about not getting a job I didn't know existed? That'd be crazy."

"Emma."

"It's fine." Emma put both hands on the arms of the chair and stood abruptly. "Seriously. It's just…" She closed her eyes. *Don't cry.* She tried to draw breath into her belly.

"Emma, I can see you're upset. Maybe you should talk to someone. The employee assistance program—"

"Yes, definitely," Emma said, nodding furiously. "By all means, let's outsource this. Great idea." She turned and reached for the door handle.

"He claims you bullied him, Emma."

Emma's hand froze on the door handle. "What?" She turned.

"Sit down," Isabella said, coming out from behind her desk.

"What did he say?" Emma crossed her arms.

Isabella cleared her throat. "He said that you favor Mish and Angie, and that you get him to do all the shit jobs. He says you call him out in meetings and shame him in front of the team."

"What, so you're promoting him?"

"Is it true?"

Emma shook her head. "No. I mean, we banter at team meetings and stuff. We make a few jokes, but it's not bullying. I thought I was meeting him halfway. Being playful. He said that?"

"It's not just what *he* said, Emma."

"So, you're saying the others agreed?"

"Not all of them. He says he feels threatened by you, that you discriminate against him."

Emma crinkled her nose. "What?"

"Yes, Jarod identifies as queer."

"Well, I didn't even know he was gay or whatever. And, anyway, so what, that doesn't make him special. You can be queer and still be an asshole."

"Em—"

"So, what now? The whole team's against me?"

Emma retraced her steps, replayed conversations with her team, searched for that instant, that rupture where she had definitively crossed a line. She came up empty, which was worrying. She'd always thought of herself as self-aware and self-effacing, a good judge of character, including her own. This accusation was blindsiding. Was it bullshit or was there something to it? Had she been so preoccupied with her relationship that she'd lost sense of how she was coming across at work?

"Liam," she said. That little prick. She always knew he didn't like her, no matter how nice she tried to be. "It was Liam, wasn't it?"

Isabella remained expressionless. What a poker face. There was power in saying nothing.

"Look," said Isabella, softening her tone. She came and sat down on the other chair next to Emma. "This isn't actually a big deal."

A contagion of self-doubt spread inside Emma.

"Feels like a big deal to me," she said.

Isabella sighed. "I know it feels huge. But try to look at this in perspective. It's a weak claim, Emma. I can't tell you the details, but I can tell you there's nothing solid in this. And nothing's going to happen because of it. The board just wants the problem to go away quietly."

"Oh my god. The board knows? This is insane."

"Emma," said Isabella softly. "The board wants this to float away on a little cloud, avoid anything that even *looks* like bad press. We were planning this restructure anyway, so with a few tweaks, the problem's gone. Poof. And, even though he has nothing to do with what we've been talking about" – she winked – "Liam will be in a different team altogether from next week."

Emma appreciated Isabella's tacit confirmation about Liam as co-conspirator, but she wasn't prepared to accept the broader injustice of Jarod's promotion. "So, I should be thankful, is that what you're saying?"

"No," said Isabella immediately. "If I were you, I'd be pissed. I'd want to go on the warpath. But that's only going to support this claim. Hard as it is, it's better for you to stay quiet. Suck it up."

Emma scoffed. "Right."

Isabella crossed her arms, framing her thick, braided gold necklace. "You know, these young people, they want stuff from their jobs that we never thought of. They want their workplaces to be supportive."

"Right," said Emma. "Like a 'family'?" She rolled her eyes and air quoted.

"No, they want the opposite. They just want to parcel up the job, make it as small a part of their life as they can, but for maximum pay and benefits. It's awe-inspiring if it wasn't such a pain. Whatever the job is, it's got to fit around *their* life, not the other way around. They want to be able to log in to a meeting while paddleboarding in Broome."

"A lot of sharks in Broome," Emma said.

"The pizzazz of an office doesn't cut it anymore," said Isabella, as if Emma had said nothing. "A paycheck and a coffee machine is not enough. They want to *be* themselves." Isabella flashed both hands as if miming small explosions on either side of her head. "I had a girl walk in here last week – nineteen years old, just started with us. You know what she wanted? An office. Know why? Because she felt anxious making business calls with other people listening. True story."

Emma scanned the display shelf of Catch-branded merchandise. The keychain had been Angie's idea; the stress ball, Liam's. The umbrella was no one's to claim. They'd come up with that one together, in a crazy brainstorming session that had gone well into the evening. Emma couldn't remember how it got started, but it was late, and everyone was delirious. For a laugh, people started pitching absurdly niche and impractical stuff to brand: a truffle grater, an all-you-can eat shrimp canon, Sergey Brin's baby teeth. The umbrella was the first "normal" suggestion after that, and everyone jumped at it.

Had she read that vibe completely wrong? Was she that hard to deal with at work? Prickly and stubborn, like her father?

Or was she deluding herself? Maybe she had no business running this team. Maybe she wasn't smart enough, or cool enough, or patient or good or empathetic enough to be anyone's boss. She couldn't make a marriage work after all.

Mom used to say to her, "You're good. You don't have to be great." Emma suddenly wondered if she'd spent her life refuting that advice or heeding it.

CHAPTER TEN

The purple Ford Raptor lurched over some bumps on the dirt road, rattling the heavy contents of the aluminum toolboxes that flashed in the sun. Rob closed his sketch pad and leaned his arm on the tray of his own pickup as the truck pulled up, dwarfing his own vehicle.

The windows were tinted; Rob could barely make out the shape of the person moving around inside. Who the fuck was this? And whoever they were, the doof-doof beat of their music was unwelcome noise. Could they at least turn off their engine so he could stop breathing diesel fumes?

The engine cut and the music stopped abruptly, restoring the silence that had preceded this intrusion. The driver's side door opened. The crunch of boots on gravel. A nest of dark, frizzy hair hovered just above the roof of the truck. A tall bugger. Rob remained seated and absorbed the truck's personalized number plate: P1ES. First the doof-doof music and now this: a Collingwood supporter. Of all the football clubs. It was getting worse by the minute.

Rob looked down at the ground, pretending to be distracted when a pair of legs moved into view. It took him a second to recognize them as a woman's legs. He looked up. Definitely a woman. Not bad looking either, with a mane of curly dark hair.

"Hey," she said. "You must be Rob."

"Nice truck," he said, nodding in the vehicle's direction. "Pity about the number plate."

She glanced back at her car, and laughed. "Not a fan then?"

Rob shook his head and tapped his own chest. "Bulldogs."

"Oh yeah. They're alright. If you like self-punishment." She grinned and stuck out her hand. "I'm Sareena." Rob shook her hand, a little more gently than he would if she were a guy. Her grip was tighter than most. Rough hands too.

"So, this is it," said Sareena, shielding her eyes to gaze up at the roofline of the stone building. "Nice lines on the gable. It's that classic barn shape." She turned back toward him and steepled her fingertips. Sareena lined the shape of her hands up against the silhouette of the building's roof line. "Sweet," she said. "This is going to look sick."

Rob slipped his drawing pen into the front pocket of his shirt. Sareena's eyes lit up when she saw the stack of papers in his hands.

"Oooh, those the drawings?"

Rob nodded once.

"Can I have a look?"

He tucked the papers under his arm. "No offense," he said, scratching his eyebrow with his thumb, "but I don't know who you are."

Sareena drew a long breath through her teeth. "Seriously. That little fucker." She cocked her head to one side. "So, Syed never told you I was coming?"

"Nah."

"Well, that's a shit introduction then?"

Rob shrugged.

Sareena squinted in the sunlight and shielded her eyes with her hand. "He asked me if I could drop whatever I was doing and head over here to help you out."

"Do I look like I need help?"

Sareena's eyes widened. "I mean, no disrespect or nothing, but I was expecting a bunch of people, some kind of crew working on a house. Instead, I see one dude in the back of a truck looking up at a building. I mean, inspiring and all, but this project's not where I thought it was at and, I got to be honest" – she moved her hands between herself and Rob – "I'm not really feeling this."

Rob stepped out the back of his truck. He was used to standing taller than most people, but Sareena looked him straight in the eye. He stood up straight, tried to speak but something caught in his throat. He coughed. "I'm sure you're good at whatever it is you do, but this place isn't like a normal house. It's old, and there's all kinds of rules around it, heritage stuff, so you have to be careful because it's easy to muck it up. I have guys, a crew—"

"I've got guys too." Sareena grinned and flicked a bushel of hair off her shoulder. "But okay," she said, turning back toward her truck. "I get it. You sound like a man who's made up his mind."

Rob raised both his palms. "Sorry, darl."

Sareena nodded. "Sure." She stooped and climbed back inside her truck. The engine roared and the doof-doof music thumped back to life. She spun truck round so it was facing up the hill and backed up until the driver's side window lined up to where Rob was standing. It had taken all his nerve not to step out of the way. The tinted window lowered. The base beat of the music poured out of the cab. Sareena turned it down but not off.

"Just thought you should know," she said, putting on a pair of pink-wraparound sunglasses. "Before you get stuck in. The building's not just 'old.' It was built in 1891. And made of solid granite blocks that came from a quarry in Cape Woolamai, just a few miles from here. It's solid as a lighthouse cuz it's made of the same stuff as the cliff it's standing on." She pointed at the house, and he noticed that two of her fingernails were black from bruising. "The stone in *that* house is the same stuff that used to be in some of the nicest buildings in Melbourne before some dickhead tore them all down. It's not just a *house* you're restoring, it's a piece of history." She aggressively shifted the truck into gear and leaned out the window. "Oh, and my name's not *darl*, champ." Sareena spun the tires and left Rob in a cloud of fresh dust.

He watched the Ford carve its way up the dirt track, leaving a dust plume and a steady base beat in its wake.

CHAPTER ELEVEN

Emma didn't need to check the map on her phone to know this was the right place. The vibe was exactly what Mish and Angie liked. An old building that used to be a car garage zhuzh'd up in that retro-chic that was Melbourne's specialty. The place, like Mish and Angie, was effortlessly fashionable.

The glint of shimmery material drew Emma's attention to a pair of young women vaping outside the venue. The too-sweet scent of artificial cherry wafted over. Their dresses had cut-out sections around their hips and arms, the very areas of Emma's own body that most disappointed her. She admired these young women with their youth and confidence but wished they had the sense to put on a coat. It was cold out here, and this priority for warmth left Emma feeling conspicuously middle-aged. She hadn't even opened the door and already she felt intimidated by the stylishness of this place. It left her wondering if any of the things she thought were cool were still considered cool. Jazz mixed with some kind of electronic music spilled out of the building, uncontained. How this squat brick building in the formerly working-class suburb of Northcote had become the latest high-water mark of Melbourne cool was unknown to Emma. She didn't much care to know either. She was just happy to be out.

Emma pushed open the heavy metal door and was enveloped by music that went straight to her bones. Her eyes rose to ornate chandeliers that hovered in the darkness of the high ceiling like UFOs. Their dim light fell on round tables, plush chairs and overstuffed couches scattered in the middle of the venue. At the back were bed-like platforms with multiple people lounging on them. These nooks could be sealed off by drawing vast purple curtains hanging from metal rafters. Some of the curtains were already shut. Was this just a place to grab a drink and a bite to eat or were there other options here?

A stunning girl with a powdered white face stood ready to greet Emma, who now felt certain she was the daggiest person here. Her loose black skirt and nice red blazer no longer felt enough. "Hey," said the girl, her voice higher and younger than Emma expected. In the semi-darkness a disembodied hand waved at Emma. She was relieved to recognize the candy-colored fingernails. "Em," Mish called out and beckoned her over.

The powder-faced sentinel with cat-eye makeup noticed Mish too. "Have fun," she said, and stood aside to let Emma through. It was the kind of thing a parent says to a child.

As Emma approached the table, she smiled widely to mask her disappointment at seeing a guy there as well. This was supposed to be a girls night out. "Hey guys," she said, approaching the empty seat. "Hey Em," said Angie, standing to peck Emma on the cheek. "This is Erik, my brother. He had an early gig around the corner, so I asked him to pop by."

"Oh, nice," said Emma. He had a distant, brooding look, this Erik, and lean veiny forearms. "Singer?"

"Musician mostly. Mixed media."

"Great." Emma could think of nothing further to say and was relieved when an elaborately tattooed waitress appeared and asked if they needed more drinks. "What are you guys having?" said Emma, resting her hand on Mish's shoulder.

"These are hanky-pankys," said Mish, twirling the little raft of orange rind floating in brown liquid at the bottom of her glass."

"Do we all want more of those?" said Emma.

"Oh, don't Em," said Angie. "You don't have to be the sugar mama."

"I never get to go out with you guys, at least let me spoil you a bit."

"So, four pankys?" said the waitress, stabbing the order onto the screen of her tablet, lighting the stem of a floral tattoo that wound up her thin forearm.

"Sure," said Emma. "Let's live a little."

The waitress held out her tablet. Emma's eyes widened at the total. She never knew four drinks could cost this much. She scanned the items on the bill. Four special cocktails. Nothing more. Emma tried to soften her expression, but the awkwardness was already tangible. She fumbled inside her bag for her credit card, which only prolonged the collective discomfort.

"Thanks Em," said Mish cheerily, as if to break the uneasy silence.

Emma retrieved the card and quickly tapped it against the screen. "Cool," said the waitress. "I'll bring them out when they're ready."

"Grab a seat." Angie pushed the extra chair out from under the table with her foot.

"Great place," said Emma, lowering herself onto the pink velvet seat. She resisted the impulse to thread one of the chair legs through the handle of her bag so it would be harder for someone to grab and run of with. That'd be daggy. Trust people more. That's what Dr Priya said.

"Hey guys," said Angie with a cheeky grin. "We should totally have the staff Christmas party here, right?"

"Hmmm, yeah," said Mish, smiling into her martini glass as she finished her drink. "Those beds over there would be super cozy." Angie and Mish sniggered. How much had they already had to drink?

"You guys," said Erik. "You promised you'd keep the work talk to a minimum."

"Oh, come on," said Angie. "Em just got here so we get to start over. Besides, I think I saw Jarod over there earlier, stretched out on one of those beds wearing a pair of leather chaps."

Mish burst out laughing. She fanned herself, flapping her hands as if to compose herself. The laughter was contagious, and Emma joined in.

"Who's Jarod?" asked Erik, confused, and the three women erupted in laughter.

The expensive cocktails arrived. Emma lifted hers as if to propose a toast and spilled a little on the table. Whatever. Emma no longer cared about how much they cost. Their value was greater than money.

"To leather pants," said Angie, and bent down to slurp from the rim of her glass. They drank and it felt good to know they were all drinking the same thing, as if there was a pact in it, the warmth spreading inside them like the heat of a communal fire that drew them closer.

Was it just an impression, or was Erik glancing at her more than was normal? Don't flatter yourself, she thought. He probably thinks of you as the adult in the room and is looking over to see if you've understood a cultural reference.

Emma tried to relax, absorb the flow of easy conversation, uninterrupted by time demands. She didn't feel like a bully. She felt like a cool boss. She couldn't help it if she liked some of her team members more than others. That was just human nature.

They didn't talk about work. Much. They mostly talked about places they'd been and the countries they still wanted to visit. Emma kept quiet at first, not wanting her life experience to widen the age gap between them, but she soon found it was *their* life experience that widened the gap more than her own. They'd traveled more, done more, had more relationships than she had. Each experience they shared deepened Emma's impression of these young people as having lived their lives more deliberately than she ever had. They could articulate what they wanted out of life in a way she had rarely done, or felt entitled to. She had spent entire years wavering and uncertain, pouring herself into completing to-do lists where her needs came last. It was invigorating to be in such company and the age difference seemed to evaporate into the high ceilings of this place.

Erik *was* looking at her, stealing glances when he thought she wasn't looking. Emma pretended not to notice and lured his gaze by looking squarely at whoever she was talking to while keeping him in her peripheral vision. He was a good-looking guy, and the persistence of his attention gave wings to the pleasant flutter rising in her stomach. *How old was he though? Was he even thirty?*

Fancy cocktails in different shapes and sizes came and went as the night wore on. There was a Daiquiri, plus a bunch of other drinks with exotic names that Emma could barely remember. A Howitzer? A Monkey Gland? Many rounds later, Mish left, something about yoga in the morning. Then Angie was called away, drawn by text to some nightclub. You want to come? No. Emma was fine here.

She stayed and talked to Erik about music. "Who's your favorite band?" she asked, her lips close to his ear, pulling back to give him her full attention, curling a stray lock of hair behind her ear and feeling his eyes all over her even though he didn't break his gaze. She was in control, and she liked it.

He listed a bunch of artists that meant nothing to her, Olafur something, and other foreign-sounding names. Maybe Erik was one of those music snobs who liked something the more niche it was. The only band she recognized was Sigur Rós. But she let him talk about them all. He was so excited about them and his enthusiasm was contagious. She was flirting, wasn't she? And she liked it. The drinks made her bold and trusting of her impulses. What was the big deal? She was allowed to have fun. Wasn't that also what this gap year was about?

Emma liked his face. The way the stubble on his cheeks accentuated the sharpness of his jawline. She liked his fingers, too, long and delicate. It made sense when he told her his favorite instrument to play was the piano.

"You want to grab an Uber or something?" he said, when they stepped into the crisp night air. He stuffed his hands into the front pockets of his jeans. "You live far from here?"

It was that easy. All she had to do was go along.

"I'll get us an Uber." Erik pulled out his phone.

This was all happening fast. Did she really want this? Or was she just letting it happen? She'd imagined a moment like this, many times, had dreamed up scenarios like this one. The static charge of a sudden encounter, the thrill of a shared attraction, the intoxicating promise of an unfamiliar touch.

She gave him the address and Erik's leather jacket squeaked in the cool night air as he tapped his phone. "Hey, look," he said, pointing up. "The Southern Cross."

"Oh yeah." Emma saw the constellation behind the flashing lights of a passing airplane.

Did she really want him? She'd been drinking, but not enough to blunt her appraisal of the situation. It could end her marriage.

But it could also save it. What if this dalliance satisfied her curiosity, delivered the excitement she was looking for? She'd only slept with three people in her life, and they were from a time before she knew what she liked or felt too ashamed to ask for it.

Maybe it wouldn't be so much a betrayal as a settling of accounts, retribution for Rob's lack of tenderness and affection, his *not* desiring her, *not* sleeping with her, unless *she* made it happen.

Or was she just using Erik to push her marriage beyond the point of no return? And did this brinkmanship feel necessary only because she was too weak or callous to find the words to say what she truly felt? Did words even exist for what she needed?

If she didn't do this, she'd always wonder.

Erik was distracted, hammering on his phone. Emma stared at the firm, roundness of his butt through the worn fabric of his jeans. He was the sudden plummet of a roller coaster, the shrieking, sparking wheels of a runaway train. Only she could make it stop. But she let go, surrendering to the momentum of her abandon.

"Kadir's on his way." He held up his phone. "Three minutes."

Emma turned to him, slid her hand inside his unzipped leather jacket, felt his stomach tense at the touch of her fingers. Could he feel her hands shaking? She moved up his torso, his ribs, the warmth of him like breath on her skin. Her doubts and reservations melted at the thought of his mouth on hers.

He hesitated, but relaxed into it, his lips gentle and soft.

They tumbled through the doorway of her apartment. Emma drew in the freshness of his skin, felt the soft tousles of his hair between her fingers. The unfamiliar shape and taste of his mouth excited her. She pushed Erik up against the front door and pulled off his leather jacket. It fell away behind him and dropped to the floor with a thud. He kicked off his shoes and, together, they peeled him out of his tight black T-shirt. Erik stood there, his swimmer's body exposed. She hooked a finger into the belt loop of his jeans and pulled him to her, feeling the heat of his body, the closeness of his belly against her body, the firmness of his chest against the softness of her own.

He reached behind her and rubbed her backside, the part of her body she disliked most. She took his hand and gently guided it away. He stroked her hip, her back and brushed his other hand against her breast, tingling with goosebumps.

Emma guided his hand downward, placed it between her legs and sank the weight of her body into the pressured caress of his fingertips. She rested her forehead on his shoulder, groped at the front of his pants and was taken aback by the stiffness of the bulge that gathered there. When had Rob last been hard like this?

She unzipped Erik and slid her hands in, felt the jut of his pelvic bones, mindful of her cold fingers. His dick bounced out the top of his boxers. She'd forgotten the insistence of a man's desire.

She stroked him, too thick to fully wrap her fingers around. He slipped his hand inside her pants too and they looked at each other, flushed and dazed, and kissed with the urgency of breath. Emma no longer cared what he might think of her body. She gasped and pushed down against his fingertips, desperate to cross over and abandon herself to the weightless giddiness of her pleasure. She moaned and clasped the hair at the back of his head. "Fuck me," she whispered in his ear. Erik kissed her and she moved him backward toward the bed.

When they reached the foot of the bed, he lay back and shimmied toward the headboard, his underwear slipping further down his waist. Emma crouched on the bed and crawled toward him, peeled off his boxers. He was throbbing and he shuddered when she touched him.

"In my jacket," he said.

"What? Oh, right."

"Hold on." He slipped out of bed to fossick in his crumpled jacket on the floor. Emma watched him hunch over, his butt cheeks as round and smooth as brioche buns.

He returned to bed and lay beside her, the cold sliminess of the condom brushed against her leg. The chemical whiff of lube briefly took the heat out of her. The moment oscillated between something spontaneous and something transactional. But then he touched her, slowly at first, then, gathering pace, his fingers built and released her orgasm.

She squeezed Erik's forearms as he moved on top of her, easing himself in with short, fluid movements. Sex with Rob was a rhythmic and dutiful pounding that reminded her of someone plunging a blocked drain. This was different.

Emma lost and found herself in a maze of sensations: the warmth and limberness of his body and her own; the vulnerability and exhilaration of being beneath this man she'd only just met; the luxurious feel of dense muscles in his arms, his chest, his back, vibrating beneath smooth skin. The feather bedding flattened beneath them as the groans and the slap of their colliding bodies grew louder, each body taking what it needed.

He gasped, shuddered, pulled out and curled up next to her, trembling with aftershocks.

"Sorry," he said, running his fingers through his hair. "That was really hot."

"It's okay," she smiled. But it wasn't. And Emma couldn't decide if that was because she'd crossed a threshold or because of how quickly and easily she'd done so. And still she wanted more.

She got up and went to the bathroom, grateful she only had to pee. She felt tender as she dabbed herself with the paper. Her rawness and slipperiness made real what had just happened, and the scale of her transgression grew in the silence of the unlit bathroom where she sat, still feeling the lingering pressure of his girth inside her.

She emerged from the bathroom to find him naked on top of the bed.

"Want to go again?" he smiled, still hard.

CHAPTER TWELVE

The microwave beeped. Rob opened the door and carefully pulled out the steaming tray of Irish stew. He hurried across the kitchen tiles in his wool socks and fleece bathrobe, adjusting his grip on the hot plastic tray. "Fuck." He dropped the container onto the table and shook the heat from his hands. He picked up his can of pale ale, which eased the stinging in his fingers. He chugged a third of it and sat down, the metal chair scraping on the tile floor. Rob leaned over to inspect the tiles. No marks. It was a display home. He had to be more careful, kept forgetting to pick up some rubber caps for the chair legs. This place was staged with furniture, but it didn't have actual people in mind.

He burped and stirred the stew with one of the new spoons he'd bought at the supermarket earlier that day, along with garbage bags and a toilet brush, the ugly necessities you don't find in a display home. The stew was unevenly cooked – scalding in patches, tepid in others – but he couldn't be bothered heating it again, so he kept swirling the mixture around, hoping the heat would distribute itself. He ate a mouthful. *Good enough, but nothing like Emma's.*

It was still light outside, but the sun had already dropped out of view. He looked down at his phone and scrolled through an article about changes to his football team's coaching panel. A lot of the league's senior coaches had stepped down in recent years. Who knew what really went on behind closed doors, away from the cameras?

He got to the end of the article without really reading it, absently chewing the beef stew. He wondered what Emma was doing right now, how long it'd be before things could go back to the way they were.

Was this an "empty nest" thing? Will going to university had hit Emma hard. But then, why was she so keen to get him into that student accommodation? It's like she was pushing him out the door.

Women's changes might be different to men's changes as they got older; he could appreciate that. But why did Emma have to take her anger and disappointment out on him? He'd always provided, always supported her. What more did she want? Life wasn't all beer and skittles. She'd be better off expecting less from life and saving herself the disappointment. What they had was fine. Good enough. Better than a lot of people. And that was pretty good, all things considered. But Emma always wanted more. She was always planning, looking to change things. He never expected one of those things would be him. This was temporary, though? She just needed some time. Some "space," like she'd said. She'd soon see that he was right. That they had it good. As good as it got after twenty-six years.

The phone lit up with a text. Syed.

Make it work!

www.heritage.vic.gov.au/conservationguides/media/

Rob clicked on the link.

Sareena Samad, a master builder and stone mason, has been appointed to Heritage Victoria's Board of Directors, the youngest member in the organization's history. Board Chair Peter McCormack says the appointment of Samad (33) signals a generational shift for the heritage institution. "Samad is a young, capable woman whose commitment to preserving Victoria's heritage shows in everything she does. The future of our work relies on people like her to help preserve our past."

Samad, whose family migrated to Australia from war-torn Lebanon, says her family's experiences are part of her drive for conservation. "I've seen what it's like when a society falls apart," says Samad. "When the future isn't safe, the past isn't either. Progress is about making the past and the future reinforce each other."

Well, fuck me.

CHAPTER THIRTEEN

Emma twitched as she became aware of the chill spreading up her bare leg. She woke, groggy, and pulled her exposed limb back inside the nest of warm covers. Her eyes opened and took in the empty space beside her. She rolled onto her back and slowly rubbed her face and temples, at once disappointed and relieved to see Erik gone.

The muffled flush of the toilet in the other room came through the wall. She turned toward the closed bedroom door, listening for movement in the living room. She half expected to hear the clunk of the lock on the front door opening, almost wanted it to end that way. It would be easier if he just left. It would save them the awkwardness. She could pretend it never happened. It would also avoid the moment when he realized what she looked like in the sober light of day.

Then she heard footsteps and the rustling of a paper bag. She sat up and arranged some pillows behind her, smoothed out her hair. The footsteps drew closer until his shadow dimmed the light streaming in from the gap under the door. The door opened slowly, and Erik walked in, carrying a box of fresh pastries. Emma was slightly nauseated by their sweet, doughy aroma.

"Hey," he said, putting the baked goods down on the bed. "Didn't know what you liked, so I got a bunch of stuff."

"Thanks," she said, patting down the bed covers in front of her.

"And here's your swipe card for the door." He handed her the card. "It was on the counter. I didn't want to wake you."

She nodded and put the security card on her nightstand. He took off his shirt and tossed it on the floor. His skin, smooth and taut. Emma felt her eyes follow the pleasing outline of his torso, from the roundness of his muscular shoulders down to the narrowness of his waist. He undid his jeans, let them fall to the floor and lay down on the bed. It was an odd thing, presumptuous and intimate, as if he was already more comfortable around her than she was around him. How could he be so cool and collected? Was it habit?

"You want one of these?" He held out the box of pastries.

"Maybe in a minute. You go ahead."

"Okay," he said, and picked out a glazed doughnut from the box. How could he look like that and eat this stuff? She might as well staple that doughnut right onto her hips. She tore a small piece off the top of a blueberry muffin. The oily dough soothed her nausea. "Hmmm," she said, more to make him happy than in appreciation of the muffin. She sucked the purple smudge of blueberry juice from her thumb, saving herself from having to wash the stain out of the sheets.

"Want to do something today?" he said through a mouth full of food. "It's okay if you don't."

She wanted him gone. And she needed him to be less nice to make it easier to ask him to leave. This was sweet and everything, but she needed space to figure out how she felt about what had happened, without having to consider him and his needs. "What time is it?"

"About 9:30." He stretched out on the bed.

She groaned.

"You okay?" he said earnestly.

She closed her eyes. "Feel like shit. You don't?"

"Not really," he yawned.

Emma glanced at him sideways. "Well, that sounds nice." She flopped back on the bed, put her arm across her face to shield her from the flash of sunlight under the blind.

"I'll get going." He sat up, slowly. "Give you some space."

"Sorry, I'm not –"

"It's okay." He smiled. "Honestly." He fished around for his stuff, which was strewn on the floor: a sock over here, another over there. He took his time, as if he knew she was watching his round muscular butt with its fading tan lines as he bundled together the scattered clothes. "You mind if I have a quick shower though?"

"Sure," she said. "I'll make some coffee."

"Oh, I don't drink coffee." He scooped up his jeans. "Got any matcha powder?"

She shook her head.

"No worries. I just need a shower and some sunlight." He stretched and padded out of the room.

Emma rested her head on the pillows, looked up at the ceiling.

"Mind if I use your towel?" his voice echoed from the bathroom.

"There's more in the cupboard in there."

Some shuffling and the switching of lights. The whirring of the exhaust fan.

"What cupboard?"

She rolled her eyes. "The one behind the big mirror." She listened for movement.

"Okay, got it."

Emma lightly banged the back of her head against the padded headboard. "Oh my god," she groaned. He was sweet, and last night was a thrill, the softness of his touch and the hardness of him inside her. But this morning she just wanted to be alone, to figure out what this meant and what to do next. His being here made everything feel more involved and complicated than she wanted it to be.

The hiss and trickle of the shower came through the thin walls.

Would she tell Rob about this? She wanted to. Why was that? To hurt him? To absolve her guilt? Maybe both. But also because last night had been a new experience for her and she was used to sharing new experiences with Rob. She pulled the covers aside and swung her legs out of bed.

Sitting up, she squinted in the shaft of daylight shining through a gap in the blinds, which made this situation feel real, as in the things that happened in here had consequences out there.

She was shaking, a twitch in her hand, her legs. It wasn't the booze. She hadn't had *that* much. It was fear. There was no coming back from this. What had seemed fun and adventurous last night now felt reckless in the sharp light of day.

Emma was a bad person. She'd cheated on her husband and used Erik. Neither of them deserved to get pulled into the messiness of her life. She was a basket case. Dr Priya would disapprove of her behavior too.

Emma needed to talk to Kendry. She always had a way of putting things into perspective. She'd know what to do.

The bedroom door opened a crack and Erik stuck his head in. It was strange and intimate to recognize the floral waft of her own shampoo coming off him.

"Hey," he smiled. "Mind if I use some of your deodorant?"

"It's there," she said, pointing to the dresser. He walked in, trousered, but shirtless.

God, he looked good.

CHAPTER FOURTEEN

Rob signed onto the register at the building site. He didn't get to the beachside suburb of St Kilda much anymore. Even so, he had no idea this mansion existed, tucked away behind a high stone wall so close to Fitzroy Street where backpackers cruised all summer long.

The front of the house had that solid ornateness of a Federation trophy home. It was probably built from old gold rush money, yesterday's bitcoin. Scaffolding spanned the width of the place where a couple of women were fixing the wooden fretwork.

Rob stopped a guy who was shouldering a thick beam of oak and asked where he could find Sareena Samad. He was pretty sure he mispronounced the last name.

"Inside," said the guy, pointing to the archway of the main entrance. Was this some kind of trade school project? Everybody on this site seemed at least twenty years younger than Rob.

Inside the building were more women in hard hats, way more than he was used to seeing on a job site. It was oddly quiet in here too. There was a distant banging and buzzing coming from outside, but in here the screech of power tools was absent. Rob walked past a drop sheet where old-fashioned woodworking tools were neatly laid out: a hatchet, an awl, an assortment of wooden mallets, a leather roll of chiseling tools. At the end of the drop sheet, a young guy with a long beard hand-chiseled a wooden peg, thick as a rolling pin. Rob hadn't seen a treenail in years. The bearded guy blew sawdust off his creation and turned the peg around in his fingers, holding it up to the light as if it were a rare jewel.

"Looking good, mate," said Rob. The beard nodded gravely as Rob walked past. Without the hard hat and work boots, this guy would've looked at home in the 1800s with his collared shirt and woolen trousers with suspenders. A lot of people in here were dressed like that. Like craft beer people.

Over in the corner, he spotted Sareena, hunched over a trestle table, pinching her fingers to zoom in and out of whatever was on her tablet. She noticed him but kept talking to someone on her earbuds. She raised her index finger. How did she get all that hair to fit under a hard hat?

Rob walked over anyway, his eyes wandering over the woodwork on the ceiling. Nice details. Someone had a sore neck from laying all those timber planks. Long thin parallel lines, like the underbelly of a gray whale. Would've taken someone weeks.

Sareena's conversation ended and Rob moved a little closer, his head still tilted up at the ceiling. "Hmm, stained pine for the ceiling beams?"

"They're decorative," she said. "Not load bearing."

"Still, would've thought oak was better. Or cedar? Spiders don't build webs on cedar wood."

"Yeah, well, there's always the dream and the budget. Even rich people get tight-assed about stuff like that." Rob nodded. "So, what's up, Rob? As you can see, I'm kinda busy."

"Got a text from Syed."

"Hmm." Sareena kept looking down and zooming in and out of the architectural drawing on her iPad.

"Have a look at this." She zoomed in. The building plans were old, hand-drawn and delicately shaded in green, purple and blue. Notations were written in calligraphy:

Front Elevation.
Section AB.
Back Elevation.

The penmanship was exquisite. The whole thing was a work of art, ready to put in a frame.

Sareena zoomed in on the base of the building. "Here," she said, moving aside to let Rob position himself over the screen. "You see?" She scrolled between drawings of the front and back of the building. "It says the ground floor elevation on the front is six inches lower than it is in the back. Now why do you reckon that is?"

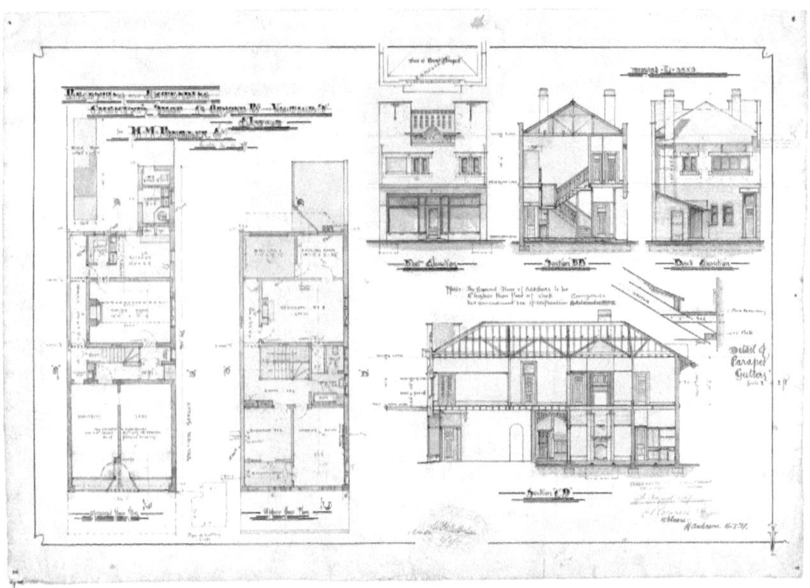

Rob leaned down for a closer look at the drawing on the iPad.

"It's weird, right?" said Sareena. "A drainage thing, maybe?"

Rob looked up from the screen and around the open space he was standing in, getting his bearings. He pointed at a large brick wall in the distance. "This drawing is that bit over there, right?"

"Mmm hmm." Sareena nodded.

Rob got out from behind the trestle table and walked over to the far wall. He ran his hands over the bricks, his fingers tracing the troughs of mortar between them. Sareena came up behind him. Rob kneeled on the floor. He rapped his knuckles on the bricks about shoulder height. "I reckon there's a fireplace behind here."

Sareena smiled. "Why do you think that?"

"Makes sense. I mean, six-inch elevation. Sounds about right for a hearth. Plus, you got some cracking in the mortar here. Probably moisture coming through from behind the wall. Chimney makes sense of that too."

Sareena nodded. "Not bad, Rob. There's no fireplace in the drawing though. And no chimney on the roof."

Rob stood up, slowly, hand on the brick wall to hoist himself up, then dusted his knees. "Don't know why that would be. Fireplace still makes sense."

Sareena smiled. "It does. They used to leave them off the drawings sometimes, cuz each fireplace cost more in taxes. Once the drawings got approved, they'd whack in some more fireplaces. The balls, right? But the city guys eventually caught on to the six-inch elevation thing, realized it was as good as saying *fireplace*." She laughed. "Cheeky, eh?"

Rob grinned. "Yeah." He dusted the front of his fleece even though there was nothing there. "So, what was that, a test?"

"Maybe."

"Did I pass?"

"Nah." She smiled. "But you were right about the fireplace."

Rob blushed. "Look…" He scanned the floor. "About the other day. I didn't like how we left it."

"Oh, are we a 'we' now?"

"Okay, how *I* left it, then." He cleared his throat. "Not my best moment. But Syed's keen on us both working together on that house."

"Oh, Syed is." She cocked her head. "And what about you, Rob? Are you okay with that?"

Rob looked around the place, the drop sheets with the old tools, the fine woodwork on the ceiling. "You got an impressive set up here, obviously know what you're doing."

"Thank you." She smiled.

Rob shifted his weight. "Is that a yes?"

"It's a maybe." Sareena put her hands on her hips. "I've got conditions."

Rob raised his eyebrows. "Like what?"

"You get the permitting and materials ordered, but we use *my* crew."

Rob grimaced. He looked over the construction site, the guy with the Ned Kelly beard still chiseling away over Sareena's shoulder, making pegs for a wooden frame that wouldn't have a single piece of metal in it. It'd outlast them all. Quality work.

"Fine." He extended his hand. "But I'm not cheering for the Pies." He smiled. "If that's a condition, the deal's off."

She laughed and shook his hand.

CHAPTER FIFTEEN

Emma waved at Kendry from across the street. She was as tall and elegant as ever, wrapped in a sleek wool coat and a silk scarf. Her red hair tumbled past her shoulders like Boudica, the warrior queen. Emma took a step onto the road. A car honked and she stepped back onto the curb as it sped past. She looked both ways and crossed the road into Kendry's outstretched arms.

"Oh, darling," Kendry said, pulling Emma into the soft and fragrant bundle of material around her neck. "Don't tell me things have got so bad you're jumping into traffic." She rubbed Emma's back as they hugged. "It's good to see you."

"So good." Emma let herself melt into Kendry's embrace. "It's been way too long."

Kendry pulled back, but held Emma by the shoulders. "The only good thing about a crisis is that it brings people together." Emma sniffed and dabbed at her nose with the sleeve of her coat. "Come on," said Kendry, looping her arm in Emma's. "Let's go have some fun." They walked down the fancy end of Collins Street, the cars swishing past in the damp streets after morning rain.

"It's not a crisis," said Emma.

"Okay, what do you want to call it?"

"I don't know, it's more like time out."

"Hmmm."

Emma looked up at her friend and frowned dramatically. "What do you mean, *hmmm*? Don't give me hmmm."

Kendry squeezed Emma's arm and patted her hand. "Remember when I was with Alistair?"

"Oh god."

"I know. But do you remember what you told me when everything was unraveling, after I found out about his trips to Palm Cove?" Emma shook her head. "You said – and I remember this clear as if it were yesterday – you said I was better off creating the future I wanted on my own than settling for a compromise with someone else."

Emma frowned. "I said that?"

"You did." Kendry brushed a strand of hair from her face. "And I remember thinking it sounded stupid, like the kind of thing someone puts on the back of a cereal box for adults, some self-help, high-fiber mush. And I was so mad at you when you said that."

"I had no idea." Emma squeezed Kendry's arm. "You should have told me."

"I couldn't have. I was too pissed off. I thought it was an easy thing for you to say, what with your husband and family. I thought you were wrong, too. I thought I *could* fix things. If only *I* worked hard enough, got counseling, couples therapy, whatever it took. But – and it pains me to say this – you were right."

"I was?"

"Yeah, turns out it's not enough for *one* person to compromise, the other person has to as well. Who knew, right?" Kendry smiled and leaned her body into Emma's. "I never understood that. Could have saved myself a stack of money, not to mention time."

Their matched footsteps found a pleasant rhythm on the sidewalk. "You know," Emma said, "all that stuff about compromise…I'm not sure I got that either."

"Great," said Kendry, smiling. "Neither of us know what we're doing. We're both fucked."

They passed a building site where the machine-gun rattle of some massive drill interrupted their chat. "Where are we going?" Emma shouted.

"Trust me."

That was Kendry's catchphrase. She was the queen of out-of-the-way places, always knew that little restaurant no one had heard of yet, always befriended the owner, knew the head chef. She'd been that way since university and it was no surprise that she managed to turn her gregarious nature into a lucrative public relations career. Kendry never tired of openings, soirees and galas, and treated every event as a new opportunity to satisfy her genuine curiosity about what made people tick. She asked people questions and cared about their answers. Other people might assume Kendry was just a persona. They might dismiss her expensive clothes and elongated vowels as an affectation, an act, but it was all genuine, or had been so practiced as to become authentic.

When they got to the Louis Vuitton boutique, Emma stopped and peered into the display window of purses. Kendry joined her. "Do you think I'm a bully?" said Emma.

"Whatever gave you *that* idea?"

"At work. Apparently, some people think I'm a bully. Not sure how I'm supposed to respond to that."

Kendry turned her head and looked skywards, as if in deep contemplation.

"Shit, Kendry, if you have to think about it."

"I'm giving it careful consideration." Kendry took a deep breath.

"Okay, the answer's no," she said decisively. "You speak your mind, there's a difference. Bullies only hear their own voices, no one else's."

"I guess that's good." They strolled on again, a little further apart.

"Your problem's not about listening," said Kendry, "it's about doing."

"Christ, I don't need more self-help shit right now, Ken, I just need you to be a friend!"

"You okay?" said Kendry, concerned. She took a few steps closer.

Emma turned her face away and felt the first contortions of an ugly cry.

"Honey, what's the matter?" Kendry put an arm on Emma's shoulder.

Emma shook her head and wiped her eyes with the palms of her hand. "I cheated on Rob," she said quietly.

"Oh sweetie." Kendry pulled her friend close and put her arms around her. "God, you *have* been busy." Emma snorted and Kendry held her friend as she cried. "You didn't cheat. Not in my books. You were on a break. It's different." She rubbed Emma's back.

"You're going to get through this," said Kendry, her head behind Emma's ear. "No matter what it is." Kendry pulled away and looked Emma in the face. "You know why?"

Emma shook her head.

"Because you don't have a choice."

Emma smiled.

"Plus," said Kendry, patting her on the shoulder, "you don't have to do it alone." Kendry looped her arm through Emma's again and they walked on, turning down a side street that was more of an alley, where commercial dumpsters stood against water-stained concrete walls.

"The good news is the surprise I had in mind is even better now." Kendry dropped Emma's arm to push open a large wooden door that was easy to walk past without noticing and disappeared inside. But Emma felt a bit wounded and raw, less inclined to follow Kendry on one of her off-the-beaten-track adventures.

Kendry popped out again from behind the door. "Come on. This'll be good for you."

Emma took a breath. Kendry could be pushy. It's how she got what she wanted. Her way was the best way. Problems were solved whenever *she* decided they were. Alistair's affairs were inexcusable, but, on some level, Emma conceded that her friend must have been difficult to live with day-to-day. She'd never say that to her face, of course, felt guilty just thinking it. But thinking it helped Emma feel somewhat better about her own situation. Nobody's life was perfect.

Emma pushed open the heavy door, expelling her residual frustration with Kendry. She stepped inside the hushed elegance of a boutique spa. Soft light fell on walls of recycled wood paneling. Different-sized niches were cut into the wood and filled with bonsai trees. These miniature trees left Emma feeling like a giant striding through a manicured vertical forest. Kendry was at a counter under a blue fabric banner with Japanese writing on it and the words Kazuki Day Spa. She was taking possession of two white robes from a young woman with skin so tight it looked stretched across her face like a canvas. She probably had a chic spa-worthy name like Bella or Chantelle. Emma walked over on the stone floor, which radiated a soothing warmth that rose up her legs. The soft glow of light poured in like radiant mist.

"What is this place?" said Emma, still feeling a little drained. No doubt her eyes were bloodshot from crying. She'd look a mess.

"We're going to shut out the noise for a while, hon." Kendry handed Emma one of the robes. "Whatever plans you had, cancel them. We'll be here for a while."

Emma hesitated when Kendry handed her a glass of champagne.

"Drink up," said Kendry, taking a sip from her own glass, followed by a gulp. "We've got a full agenda: halo therapy, salt-and-oil scrub, but first, we clear out the clutter with sensory deprivation. Sixty minutes of just you. No light, no sound, no gravity." Kendry closed her eyes and hugged herself.

"Like in one of those tubs?" Emma took a sip of champagne; she didn't like a buzz this early in the day.

Kendry nodded as she filled in some form at the counter. "Mmhmm," she said, scribbling her signature with a flourish.

"You should've said something before. I didn't bring a bathing suit or anything."

"So what?" Kendry grimaced. "We'll just get some here." She turned to the spa attendant – Arabella, it turns out. "You guys sell swimsuits here, right?" The attendant nodded. "There you go, just pick something you like and strap it on. Me, I prefer to go in the nude. You didn't hear that," she added, smiling at Arabella, who nodded demurely.

Emma scrunched up her face. "Are there going to be other people in there?"

"No. Relax. You're in there by yourself. That's kind of the point, darl. It's just you. In the dark. Alone." Kendry leaned in close. "Back to the womb."

Emma crinkled her nose, then leaned into her friend and whispered, "Kendry, this place looks…high end. I'm not sure I can—"

"You're right, you can't," said Kendry, finishing her champagne. "Which is why it's my treat. And don't go getting all weird and guilty about it. I have money, hon. It's about all I've got, so at least let me enjoy using it to spoil the people I love without them feeling bad about it. Deal?"

"Okay," Emma smiled. "It's just weird."

"What's weird?"

"I don't know. We used to do this, going to some kooky place you'd found. Back then they were nightclubs, now they're day spas."

"Ha. Darling, nothing's changed." Kendry tucked the folded bathrobe under her arm. "We just need to cleanse our bodies to make room for the devils who desire them."

Arabella spoke in a monotone whisper. "Have you both done this before?"

Kendry's hand shot up. "I'm a veteran. She's a first timer."

"Okay. Come through and I'll show you how it works."

"I'm in this room here, right darl?" said Kendry, pointing, already heading down the hallway. "Em, I'll see you in the heated charcoal room in about an hour. Bliss out. Don't worry about creating your future in there. Just be in the now." Kendry disappeared behind a frosted glass door, leaving behind a sudden quiet which the pan flutes drifting down from overhead speakers could not fill.

Emma followed Arabella into a square, tiled room. The sensory deprivation tank in the middle sat like an open clamshell. Emma approached the pod as she might an open casket, peering over the ledge, ready to spring back at the sight of whatever lay inside. The still water glowed with colored lights. The effect was mesmerizing, and Emma paid little attention to Arabella's instructions on how to use the various buttons inside the cocoon to adjust lights, sounds and whatever else.

"Pure darkness and silence is best to quiet the mind," purred Arabella. "Though many people have to work up to complete darkness." So, Emma thought, there were levels to this contraption. She vowed to show the tank she could handle being alone in the dark.

"If you have any issues, press the emergency button inside the tank." The need for such a button fueled Emma's anxiety, but she was determined to be mindful. She needed Arabella to leave now, so she could approach the sensory deprivation tank in her own way.

"How long do I stay in there?"

"One hour. Some gentle music and lights will let you know when time is up."

Arabella padded to the door and bowed before leaving. Emma checked the door was locked and undressed.

Once inside, Emma closed the lid and floated in the salt water, slowly spinning in the warm darkness of her cocoon. "Pretend you are a lily pad floating in the primordial soup," Arabella had suggested. Emma soon got bored of being a lily pad and farted in the primordial soup. Instantly she felt safer in there, as if the echo made the pod belong to her somehow, erasing whoever had been in here before.

Try as she might to "empty her mind," to "accept the now," none of Dr Priya's incantations seemed to work. Images of Erik's shirtless torso, her hands squeezing his ropey forearms, the litheness of his body on top of hers invaded the false stillness of this place. The warmth and silkiness of the water, the steamy air, the steady drips of condensation sliding off the lid of this contraption now all felt sexy. Emma moved her hands over herself, but it felt weird. Too public. What if there were cameras? For safety or whatever?

Plus, there was Rob, now a victim in the situation she'd created. What was *he* doing right now? Probably not trying to baptize away his guilt in a sensory deprivation tank. How was she supposed to get a sense of what to do if she was always asking herself if *he* was okay? Was it right to be tethered to someone this way?

How long had it been since she closed the lid? She'd felt good at first in the strange buoyancy of the warm water. But it wasn't long (or was it?) before she found herself working hard to chase all these thoughts from her mind. She wondered how clean this water was. Whether the solution was drained after every use, or just filtered. How forgiving was the filter? And when had the tub itself last been cleaned? What if being naked in here made an infection more likely?

This was meant to be calming and restorative, and yet here she was coming up with reasons to abort the experience, disconnecting from the very tranquility she was meant to enjoy, squandering the expensive serenity that Kendry had so generously paid for. Emma's thoughts resembled an Escher drawing, leading everywhere and nowhere, a fluid cycle of confusion and anxiety.

Her fingertips creased with water wrinkles, and she caressed the skin of her belly, made soft and slick by the kilos of dissolved salt that kept her afloat. She caressed the stretch marks on her hips and tried, as Dr Priya suggested, to think of her scars as rings on the inside of a tree, lines of growth and wisdom.

She wouldn't tell Rob about the other night with Erik. It would do no good. Besides, if Will found out, he wouldn't understand. Maybe a relationship needed a few secrets to keep it afloat.

CHAPTER SIXTEEN

The dim morning sun rose from behind a still pink ocean. Slow waves slapped the base of the cliffs, the only disturbance in the breathless dawn. Rob shifted uneasily from one foot to the other on a dewy patch of grass near the edge of the cliff. He blew on his hands and rubbed them together. There was work to do, but Sareena was still sitting in the back of her truck. She lifted her phone above her head, adjusted a few strands of hair that poked out from under her beanie and snapped a selfie. Rob raised his eyebrows. Sareena adjusted the collar of her puffy down vest and took another picture.

Rob checked the clock on his phone. "It's nearly eight."

"They'll be here," said Sareena, without looking up.

Rob scratched the back of his neck.

Sareena kept tapping the screen, zooming in and out of her photo. "Relax. This isn't my first rodeo."

"Yeah, well, I don't like the look of the bull."

"Uhm." She turned her head toward him. "Am I supposed to be the bull in this scenario?"

"What? No. I meant the project and the f—"

"Rob." Sareena hopped from the back of her truck. "Chill, mate. I'm fucking with you. Look!" She pointed at the hill. "Here they come now."

Rob looked up and saw three pairs of headlights moving around on the bumpy road.

The cars descended the steep track and moved into a growing shaft of morning light. They were old-looking vehicles, vintage and restored, painted in deep, luscious colors you just didn't see on the road anymore. There was a bottle-green truck with polished wood paneling, a canary-yellow flatbed with curvy almost bulbous fenders, and a candy-apple red fire truck with a chrome grill that sparkled in the sun like a disco ball. They certainly made an entrance, these trucks, but why use showpiece vehicles on a worksite where bumps and scrapes were part of the job. Were the owners of these fancy trucks too precious for the work that lay ahead? They had a lot of gutting and repointing to do today to keep the build on schedule. Still, it was cool to see these old cars. They looked impractical, but they made him happy.

Rob's old man had been a long-haul trucker, but he had spent a life on the roads taking notes on the cars he most often saw broken down in a ditch. "Don't get a Holden," he said. He was a man of few words, as if each one cost him something.

But there was a Holden now, an orange 1970s Sandman panel van. And it looked bizarre coming down the hill, as if emerging from the wormhole of time. The only thing missing was the surfboards. Rob smiled just looking at it.

He surveyed the loads these vintage trucks were hauling, anxious to see gear that was fit for purpose, and was relieved to identify the components of aluminum scaffolding, piled high in the back of the old green truck. The whole load was tied down with ratchet straps, neat and prim as Christmas wrapping. Whoever that guy was, he knew what he was doing. You could tell a lot about a person from his attention to detail.

He turned to Sareena. "How come you don't have one of these?"

"Who says I don't?"

Rob smiled.

The vehicles fanned out and parked on the open field next to the house. Sareena put on her hard hat and walked over, with Rob following slowly behind. Doors opened and Sareena hugged the occupants of the vehicles as they emerged, each one a woman.

Rob planted himself beside Sareena and the group sort of gathered, even if they were still spread out, propped here and there, leaning on their cars. It wasn't the tight semi-circle Rob preferred for a morning briefing.

"Everyone," said Sareena, "this is Rob. Rob, everyone." Sareena pointed down the line. "This here is Jemma." She gestured toward a round woman whose facial features seemed to gather in the center of her face. "Jemma's a – what would you say, Jem? – a woodworking, landscape designing—"

"Just chippie will do. Nothing fancy. Good to meet you, Rob."

"Okay," said Sareena, "next there, in the flannel, is Jacqui. Jacq's a stonemason and so is Kim over there – hey Kim." Sareena waved.

"Hi," said a woman small enough to be mistaken for a child.

"So," Sareena continued, "the three of us are going to work on the exterior wall today, which is why…" Sareena scanned the assembled group. "Alex? Where's Alex? I just saw her?"

"Up here." Alex popped out above the pile of scaffolding, a ratchet strap tight in her wiry, tattooed arms.

"Oh, hey," said Sareena. "I was just going to say it'd be great if you could give us a hand putting the stage up before joining the demo team, but you're already onto it."

"Yep, on it."

"Sweet. Okay, well that leaves Steph and Dani over there in the – what are those girls? – prison jumpsuits?"

Steph posed like a model. "They're coveralls."

"Well, they *are* a bit *orange*," said Dani.

"Mega orange," said Steph. "Super hi-vis."

Dani put both hands on her hips and did a little twirl like a catwalk model. "At least we won't get shot by hunters."

"I like it," said Sareena. "Safety first. Plus, extra points for style." She motioned to Rob. "Like I said, this is Rob. If you're working and he asks you for something…check with me first." Sareena laughed, turned to Rob and put a hand on his shoulder. "Just kidding, mate," she chuckled. "Your face, though. Classic. Seriously, guys, this is Rob's project, we're just here to make sure it gets done right. The client who owns this place is a major property developer, so if we do this well, it could mean a fuck ton of work for us, so let's put in our best?"

The group murmured in agreement. "Couldn't hear you," said Sareena. "I said, are you ready to put in your best?"

"Yes," they shouted in unison.

"Good," said Sareena. "Remember, you're only here for a few months. But this house has been here a hundred years, and if you do your job right, it'll be here long after you're gone. So, let's do our best to honor the house and this amazing place. I mean just take a moment to look around and feel it." They all turned and took in their surroundings. A chilly ocean breeze raised goosebumps on exposed skin. The lapping waves stirred up a milky haze of salt spray that floated deep into the trees, alive with birdsong. The moist sea air seemed to help them breathe deeper and longer than normal air, as if each breathe were a sigh.

"Okay," said Sareena quietly. "Rob, did you want to add anything?"

Rob rubbed his palms together. "No, you pretty much said everything I was going to say," he said, laughing. The others chuckled with him supportively. "Look, I'm not much of a public speaker, but I just want to say that I'm excited to see what you can do."

"Okay, everyone," said Sareena quickly, almost cutting him off. "Steph and Dani, you can get started with the internal demo, start working out what the plumbing situation is. The rest of us, let's get that scaffold up. Have a great day, people." Sareena clapped them out. The team dispersed and went about their work with military precision.

Sareena turned to Rob and raised her eyebrows. "I want to see what you can do?" she said quietly.

"What?"

"Seriously? You don't see the problem? Like, not at all?"

"What?"

"Is that what you would've said if it was a bunch of guys?"

Rob shrugged. "I don't know, probably."

"Uh, huh." Sareena turned and began to walk away.

"Not sure what I've done wrong here," said Rob, puzzled.

Sareena looked back over her shoulder. "I believe that, Rob." She looked him up and down. "Doesn't make it right, though." She put on her sunglasses and walked away.

Geez. Everyone was so sensitive nowadays. Why did everything he said have to *mean* something. Just because you read into something that wasn't there, that didn't make it true. Not everything was a man or woman thing. He was talking about craftsmanship. Skills. You had 'em or you didn't. Simple as that. That's all he meant. He wasn't talking about sex or gender or whatever. He'd worked with plenty of good female tradies and never had a problem with them. He'd have to watch this chip on Sareena's shoulder. It could get a guy in trouble.

WINTER

CHAPTER SEVENTEEN

The Catch office was quiet. No phones rang, no one spoke, even the staff kitchen was free of rummagers and water-cooler prattle. Everyone was already at the general staff meeting.

Emma sipped her tea and put the finishing touches on her PowerPoint presentation. It was nearly perfect, cool infographics, clever headings, a lot of images. This would show Jarod and Isabella that she knew exactly what they meant by "adding value." Ugh, that phrase.

The USB twinkled as it saved her presentation. Emma checked the time, at least another fifteen minutes before she was scheduled to give her comms update. She didn't want to be in there from the start; presentations made her anxious, even when she was as well prepared as she was for this one. Emma wore her best suit, the one she wore for interviews, her I-can-do-anything suit, and it put her in the right headspace. She'd stay here for a bit longer, calm and quiet. Mountain pose. Then go in. She was getting hot though, and flustered. She hated presentations. Always had. The spotlight. All those eyes judging her. She was getting fidgety, and uncomfortably warm.

Emma tried to breathe and calm down, and absently scrolled through a list of approved courses for professional development.

Manage Performance Effectively

Making Difficult Conversations Work

Wellbeing Works

The course titles were like banners announcing her failings. A passing colleague glancing at her screen would assume she was incompetent.

She kept scrolling. Free training was one of the perks of working for a company and she'd always taken it up. But the person now responsible for approving her courses was Jarod. She couldn't bear the idea of his smug face considering a request for this training. *How to Build a Winning Team.* Indeed. It'd be like admitting Jarod was right to file that bullying complaint she wasn't supposed to know about. The prick.

Maybe there was another course here, something benign. Emma's phone buzzed an incoming text. It was Mish.

Where are you?

My desk.

Mtg rm 4. You're on next!

Emma's insides dropped inside her body. She stood abruptly and spilled her tea. "Fuck." She uselessly brushed her hand against the milky stain spreading on the front of her skirt, grabbed the USB and headed for Meeting Room 4, scanning all the empty desks behind the partitions. She thought she had more time.

Emma's footsteps echoed along the uncarpeted hallway that led to the big meeting rooms. She took a deep breath and opened the door.

Half the staff was assembled inside, eighty people or so. A few of them turned as the pneumatic door hissed slowly and closed with a metallic thud. She stood there, in her "power suit," while everyone else was wearing casual clothes. Had she missed something?

People were gathered in a semicircle around a low stage at the front of the room. On it was living room furniture arranged like the set of a talk show. Jarod was seated on a plush green lounge chair opposite Amanda from HR. They both seemed very pleased with themselves, smiles, bright teeth, basking in the theater lights and the dying murmurs of a group chuckle about something said before Emma arrived.

Where was the podium? The projector? The thing she was supposed to plug her USB into? This looked more like the set of a celebrity interview than a meeting. She locked eyes with Mish, grinning nervously at her from the side of the stage.

Jarod looked through the gathering and found Emma. "Oh, hey Em, thanks for coming." He waved his fingers at her.

Another murmur from the staff.

"Hi." She cleared her throat. "Did you want me to come back?" She breathed heavily. Her heart pounded.

"No, no. Stay, stay. As you can see, we're doing something new, everyone's presenting together, no more silos, going for a kind of fireside chat thing. You're in the hot seat next. In fact," he said, turning to Amanda, "we've pretty much covered what you wanted to say, right?" Amanda nodded. "Cool. Well then, everyone, please thank Amanda and welcome Emma from comms." Jarod clapped energetically. People joined in. Amanda nodded and blew air kisses as she made her way down the steps, a beauty queen exit, confident of her heels on the wooden dais.

What was this scene? It felt contrived, American, like something out of the management playbook at *Google* or *WeWork*. Who did Jarod think he was?

Emma stumbled on the last step up the stage, caught her footing, and dropped into the chair, which was still warm from Amanda from HR. Jarod's assertive aftershave smelled like a barrel of wet moss.

"You alright?" Jarod leaned in and touched the arm of her chair. Emma nodded. "I've got a PowerPoint." She held up her USB stick. Jarod brushed it away.

"Don't worry about that. We don't need a formal presentation. This is more of a get-to-know-you session." Jarod cleared his throat.

Emma was in free fall, totally unprepared.

"So, first off," said Jarod, "on a personal note. And I hope you don't mind me sharing this, but you told me a while ago that you started running."

This was like being on *The Biggest Loser*.

Emma leaned back in her chair. Her eyes narrowed. "Mmmm."

Jarod turned to everyone. "Isn't that great." A few people clapped. Emma blushed.

"So," said Jarod, "how's it all going?"

Emma squinted. "What? You mean the running?"

"Yeah." He slapped his knee. "How's it all going?"

"Uh, fine." She turned sideways in her chair to keep the milky tea stain in shadow as best she could. "I don't know, it's sort of a weird question, like, how's shaving going?"

A few people chuckled.

"Now, now," said Jarod, smoothing his shiny tie. "I just think everyone likes hearing about their colleagues, their hobbies and talents. Like, we just learned that Amanda's taking salsa lessons."

"Wooo," yelled one of the silhouetted bodies in the darkness, which drew a low rumble of subdued laughter.

Emma adjusted herself in her seat. "Okaaay."

Everyone else always seemed to have a ready-made list of personal anecdotes that were vetted for public consumption. She had no repository of stories to air, there was no salsa lesson to mention, no quirky celebrity sighting to recount. She didn't have the knack for distilling life experiences into "sharable" vignettes on social media.

For Emma, work was work and personal was personal; opening the barrier between the two meant inviting colleagues into everything. Other people seemed to have a filter that sensibly blended work and personal life. She didn't have that. It was all or nothing.

Jarod tilted his head and pursed his lips. "D'you want to start over? Maybe that's the best thing?" He looked to the audience, raised his hands like a conductor and encouraged the employees to clap. They did, and the vigor with which they hooped and hollered felt disingenuous, ironic, like Emma was the butt of a joke.

Jarod turned back toward her, a wry smile. "So, Emma, how *are* you?" Emma reddened, couldn't swallow. Jarod leaned in close, "What's something we don't know about you yet?"

She shifted uncomfortably in her chair, crossed and uncrossed her arms over the tea stain. "I don't know. I'm not that interesting."

"Oh, come on. Of course you are," he beamed. "There must be *something*." He tapped the arm of her chair with his rolled-up piece of paper.

She squinted in the glare of the overhead lights that heated her exposed skin. She was hot, boiling, and had a sudden need to peel off clothing. Her dad used to call a job a ransom. "One day I'll be free," he'd say.

"Do I have to?" she said.

Jarod blinked. "Of course not." His eyelids fluttered. "It's just supposed to be fun."

"Okay. Sorry." She was sure the skin on her neck and face was red and blotchy now. People looked away. She was probably making them anxious, fumbling like this. Public speaking just wasn't her thing. The darkened silhouettes in her peripheral vision were judging her. Just another "privileged" middle-aged white lady taking up space, a nuisance, a "Karen." People, jobs, economy, power. It was a vicious circle. A trap. And she was sick of getting baited.

"It's okay," said Jarod, with a needless enthusiasm that signaled it was not. He cleared his throat and sat upright in his chair.

Emma glared at him. The sum of the workplace injustices she'd suffered in her life rose up in her. Every "darl" and "sweetheart," every time she'd been overlooked, underestimated, or denied the benefit of the doubt. Every idea she'd had repackaged, rephrased or plain stolen by a male colleague over the years now seemed embodied in Jarod – this kid – with his too-tight suit, too-short trouser cuffs and bright socks. He was a caricature, a bro in a wedding party, dressing the part of a gentleman.

"It's not okay," she said. It just came out.

Jarod overdid his puzzled expression.

"It's not." Emma adjusted herself in her seat. "Even when I do my best it's not good enough."

"Em——"

"I know it was you." She glared at him.

"Okay." Jarod smiled and sat forward in his seat. "This is interesting. Me what?"

Emma wanted to slap him, wipe the smirk off his face.

"You made a bullshit bullying claim against me. I know it was you."

"Boooo," yelled someone from the darkness. "Kick his ass," said someone else, which drew a ripple of laugher.

Jarod sat there, blinking. He jutted his chin out as if to look down at her, grimaced and turned briefly to the audience. He turned back, half facing her. "Em, I don't know what you're talking about but it's highly inappropriate to——"

"Oh, shove it, Jarod." She stood up.

"Ooooooh," came the disembodied voices.

"Fight," yelled some guy. People laughed.

"Em, seriously."

"You know what, fuck off. You *and* your fucking fluoro socks. Learn how to wear a suit. What are you, twelve?"

The audience gasped and guffawed. A few people cheered.

"No, said Emma turning to the audience. "Fuck you all too. Fuckin' enablers."

People booed.

Jarod panned between her and the unruly crowd. "Em, this is totally unacceptable, like, way off—"

"You know what," Emma picked up the glass of water on the little side table and threw its contents in Jarod's face. "Fuck off," she spat. "I quit."

"What the hell!" he wiped his face with his hands and nervously scanned the silhouettes. More people joined the clapping, someone whistled. Someone else tried to start a chant. "Em! Em! Em!"

The staff cheered and booed and parted, creating a narrow channel for her to walk through. Emma felt dizzy. She might puke, but kept it together to make a graceful exit, the heavy door closing behind her like an air lock.

In the corridor, she almost turned back to apologize. No, not this time.

She hurried to her desk, grabbed an empty photocopy paper box and collected her things. She just snatched up the photo of Will when Mish blew in. "Oh my god, are you okay?"

"I'm fine." Emma started adding publications from her trophy wall into the box.

"So, you're serious?"

"Yup."

"Because I'm sure you could—"

"No, I'm done."

The door burst open and Angie came in. "Fuck, that was sick! Are you okay?"

"I'm fine."

"That was nuts," said Angie.

"I don't even care." Emma wedged the last booklets onto the pile of stuff in her box.

"It's a shit show in there," said Angie. "Like, full on damage control."

"Some people are saying you're a legend, others are, like, *what the fuck*? Em, what the fuck *was* that?"

Emma threw one hand up in air. "I don't care anymore."

Angie looked at Emma's cardboard box. "So wait, you're just going?"

"I am," said Emma. "I'd say that was definitive. I'm not staying here another minute. Are people coming back?"

"Yeah, they're heading back now."

Mish looked concerned.

"Shit," said Emma, throwing her puffy coat on top of the box. "I've got to get out of here."

"Take the emergency exit," said Angie, shepherding her toward the back of the office. Emma moved quickly, holding her sagging cardboard box. She pushed her back against the bar on the heavy fire door, half expecting an alarm to go off. Mish looked stricken. "It'll be okay," said Emma reassuringly.

"You're a vigilante, Emma Connors. A hero," said Angie, holding the door open.

"Heroes leave through the front door," said Emma, as she navigated the closing fire door with her box. It shut with a thump, leaving her in the quiet stairwell that led to the world outside. She took a big breath before finding her footing on the steps, her toes obscured by the box and the bulk of the puffy coat piled inside it. Her footsteps echoed as she made her way down. Emma felt banished.

She didn't cry until she was halfway down. There was relief in crying. Not because of what she'd lost, but because it was over. In the echoey stillness of that fire escape, she realized how much she'd hated this job. It was like a bad relationship. The wrong fit. Hadn't been right for years. Or maybe from the start. How had she not acted sooner?

When she reached the ground floor, she stopped. "Fuck it," she said out aloud. "I'm going out the front door."

The world beyond the fire escape felt unreal, like a movie set. A man in a suit with a wheelie suitcase, a passing woman in heels, the ding of a tram outside, it all seemed choreographed, her life as a musical where the songs never began.

She walked to the front of the building, her tea tins rattling inside the cardboard box, and hoped there'd be no colleagues milling about near the cab rank. As she reached the end of the lobby, she spotted Erik, sauntering toward her from the revolving glass door of the office tower, holding a guitar case in his hand. He turned and smiled. "Hey."

"What are you doing here?" said Emma, still adjusting to the brightness of the lobby.

"Just finished a gig, around the corner." He pointed out the window with his guitar case. "I was coming to see Ange, but she's not picking up."

She felt foolish thinking he might have been there for her. It made sense, he and Angie were siblings.

But then, why *couldn't* he be there for her? Not in a stalkerish way, but in recognition of what had happened between them. She'd seen him naked, held him in her hands. He had touched her in ways that no one had in years. It'd feel dishonest to watch him pass by as if he were no more than an acquaintance. How did people separate feeling casual from feeling expendable?

"You were at a gig now? Who goes to a show at eleven in the morning?"

Erik smiled. "It didn't start then, just finished then."

"Oh, right." She blushed.

He gestured at her cardboard box. "You get fired or something?"

Emma bit her lip. "No," she swallowed. "I quit."

"What, just now?"

"Yeah."

"You just stormed out?"

She nodded.

"That's badass." He smiled.

"You reckon?"

"Definitely."

"Well, I don't feel badass."

"No?"

She shook her head. "I feel kind of crazy. Do I seem crazy?"

He looked her up and down, glanced at the high ceiling of the lobby, the glass elevator to the mezzanine and smiled. "Not wanting to work in here seems pretty sane to me." Erik smiled again. He had dimples!

Emma adjusted her grip on the box. "Did you really come here to see Ange?"

He blushed.

"Right." She briefly looked away. "Okay."

He moved in as if to kiss her, but Emma moved her head back. He looked disappointed before she even said anything.

"I'm not sure that's a good idea," she said.

"I was thinking you could use a proper send off."

"Huh?"

"A badass exit, a little *fuck you* to this place." He looked around as if scoping out the joint. "Is there a place we could go down here?"

Emma glanced over her shoulder. "You serious?"

He smiled. "Why not? It's not like they can fire you, right?"

The disaster of the fireside chat flashed in her mind. The unfairness of it all, getting blindsided like that. The fucking PowerPoint presentation she'd spent days putting together. For nothing. A fire grew inside her. She guided Erik toward the disabled washroom in the foyer and he locked the door behind them.

Emma dumped her stuff on the floor and moved toward Erik. He put down his guitar case and pressed her up against the door, kissed her neck. It was Emma's first time in a public place. She was self-conscious as she kissed him, her eyes open, watchful. His mouth was soft and his stubble rough on her lips, cheeks, fingertips. Her heart beat fast.

He opened her shirt, unclipped her bra and cupped her breasts. She groped for the zip of his pants. It was a button fly. She tore it open. She reached over the waistband of his boxers, and as she pulled out his dick, he moaned. She gave him a few slow tugs and bent down to lubricate him with her mouth. The slurp and pop echoed off the cold tiles, and he grew harder.

"Oh fuck," he moaned. She stood to kiss him again. He bent down and got a condom from his guitar case while Emma leaned against the low sink. Erik's hands slid up the sides of her legs and pulled down her panties. He lifted her onto the sink and slowly entered her. Emma braced herself against the mirror as he sped up. She leaned into his ear. "Slower," she whispered and kissed his ear, cupping the back of his head. He adjusted his stance, changing the angle, going deeper, until the pressure was just right. "Further up," she said, guiding his hand and surrendering herself to pure pleasure.

Unable to take any more, he shuddered and stopped, resting his warm forehead on her shoulder, spent and breathless. They smiled, then laughed.

A loud metallic rapping at the door broke the mood. They both looked at each other with alarm and Erik mouthed the words *what the fuck*. They hurried to dress and compose themselves. Erik handed Emma her box of stuff, picked up his guitar and opened the door.

An enormous man on a three-wheel scooter was outside the disabled washroom. He glared at them from under his fisherman's cap.

"You people are disgusting."

"Sorry mate," said Erik, picking up his guitar case.

"Yeah," said Emma from behind her cardboard box. "But totally worth it." The two of them giggled and ran from the building like teenagers.

They walked outside for a while within view of the Yarra River, the residual thrill of their encounter wearing off. They made vague plans and hugged goodbye before Erik headed home to sleep.

Emma walked down to the boardwalk along the river where she found a park bench on a wedge of grass. She zipped up her jacket and sat there for a long while, her cardboard box next to her. She watched people, couples, kids in school uniforms, a homeless person draped in blankets as they walked past. Then she looked beyond them, feeling more connected to the gentle flow of the river than the people who walked beside it. The days were short now, the sun already behind the tallest buildings, casting shadows of office towers on the grass. She stood up, leaving her cardboard box on the bench, taking only the picture of her son.

It was nearly dark when Emma reached her apartment. She opened the door and found it as generic and soulless as a hotel room. She'd resisted the urge to stop for Ramen noodles on the way home and had to convince herself all over again not to order them from Uber Eats. She hadn't been running the last few days and couldn't justify another cheat day. Plus, she had to save money now.

The apartment was too quiet. And empty. And the nothingness of Emma's life deepened the void inside her. She put Dr Priya on. It was an episode about the relationship between fear and setting boundaries, but Emma wasn't in the mood. She usually liked the way Dr Priya talked, the chirpy casualness of her voice. But tonight, she found Dr Priya irritating. It was too much talking to listen to when she felt this way. Emma felt numb, too disoriented to examine whatever that feeling was. She put on soothing chakra music and instantly felt calmer.

She opened the fridge. Three giant bags of pre-made salads. The carrots, celery and spinach stared back, daring her to keep her promise to "eat well." She found no joy in contemplating their watery crunch. Emma wanted something salty and fatty, something she could savor.

Fuck it. She went to the bedroom and retrieved the kitchen footstool she'd stuffed in the closet and used it to reach the high cupboard above the fridge. She pulled down a family-sized bag of salt and vinegar chips, poured herself a glass of rosé.

There had been no wine, cookies or chips when she was growing up. Dinner was whatever Mom boiled up in the stockpot, which was so blackened that Emma could never scrub it clean. Dinner was often breakfast too, and lunch, if the soggy vegetables and beans stretched that far.

As a kid, she had assumed it was normal for people to have toast and jam for dinner a couple of nights a week, or to move house every year or so. It wasn't until she was in high school that Emma properly understood that her mother's part-time job as an elementary school admin assistant was steady work to support the family and pay for her husband's hobby/business of making custom leadlight windows. Abstract designs, his squares and triangles, suited a modernist church, while his ornate floral patterns were at home in grand Victorian mansions, the kind she visited on school fieldtrips. Her father's work was beautiful, superbly detailed.

"Your dad's futzing in the shed," her mother used to say. Did Mom not see the beauty of his work, or did she just refuse to? Emma herself had been awe-struck by her father's designs. Anyway, she wasn't about to broach this topic with her mother and bring up the past. She felt she'd had been fairer with Rob than her mother had been with her father, hadn't she?

Emma wanted to talk to Rob, or to her mother, and she would have called them, if she thought they'd be there for her, that they'd listen, and give her the benefit of the doubt and say the right things. She needed to hear soothing words that would make her feel heard and safe, like they supported her, no matter what. But she knew what they'd say. They'd say the situation would blow over. To just give it time. She couldn't hear that, not tonight. Emma needed love, not an empty promise, a cliché. She needed someone to hear her, to accept her messy, complicated life as a human being. Mom's brand of "tough love" was just code for her unwillingness to enter the realm of feelings.

Emma gulped her wine and refilled the glass. The frigid newness of this apartment made her long for home. Her place. Their place. The little Victorian terrace that she and Rob had bought and renovated, when Clifton Hill was affordable and their house was the worst one on the street. She missed the old place, with its oak-frame windows and the little rooms off the main corridor. There was always somewhere else you could be in that house. This apartment, besides the bedroom, was open plan, meant to be experienced all at once. There was no discovery here, no secrecy.

Memories felt closer in the old house and, tonight, Emma suddenly missed being close to them. She mentally roamed the rooms, cataloging the traces they'd left behind: the bruised patch on the living room ceiling caused by a leak after that crazy winter storm; the cracked tile on the kitchen floor where she dropped the mortar and pestle during her curry-making phase; and the swirly shaped burn mark on the wooden floor of the bedroom left by a cheap oil heater they'd bought that cold winter after they first moved in, before central heating, before air conditioning, before Will.

This apartment was not her home. Nor would it ever be. Not just because she was here alone, but because this place didn't contain the physical evidence of what had come before, the things that corroborated the life she'd built, the one she and Rob shared. The apartment was bright and shiny and new. Like Erik.

The family now renting her house cooked in *her* kitchen, sat in *her* loungeroom, slept in *her* bedroom. She knew only that it was a couple with young children. She suddenly dreaded the idea they might want to buy the house and knock it down. She preferred to imagine the traces of her former life remaining there, the defects, perhaps embalmed in fresh paint or entombed under stiff new carpet, but not erased completely.

She went to bed. The darkness of the bedroom was a void, which frightened her as it had when she was a child, this blackness crowded with unseen monsters.

Dr Priya said you weren't supposed to define yourself through your work. It wasn't your job but how you did it that expressed who you were. Nice idea, but what about the bills, the rent? Without a job, she'd run out of money fast. But how was she supposed to get another job if she'd quit this one in a huff? Who'd want a cranky middle-aged woman with limited social media skills?

Emma couldn't afford to keep living here. Now what?

CHAPTER EIGHTEEN

Rob reached past the takeout containers in the fridge and palmed two cans of pale ale. He stuffed one into the front pouch of his hoodie, opened the other beer and meandered around the display home, turning on lights as he went. He'd thought being here would be like staying in a hotel, but it was stranger than he expected. He was more like a ghost than a guest, haunting the five empty bedrooms with their identical furniture: beige lamp, wooden bed, mound of colorful pillows.

He flicked on the light in the fifth bedroom. It was dressed like a little kid's room with bunk beds and a wooden toy train set assembled on the floor. Will's room had never looked like this. It was all too neat in here. Contained. Real life was messier.

As he roamed the house, Rob turned all the lights on, even the LED strips under the cupboards and in the closets. He stood back and felt weird, like he was living on a movie set, as if just being here interfered with the job this display home was meant to perform. Every footprint he pressed into the deep carpet was a trespass, a betrayal of this fairytale version of family life. He thought of his mom and that he hadn't visited her in a while. But she'd ask him about Emma, and he couldn't lie to her. She'd only worry.

With all the house lights blazing, Rob eased himself down onto the wooden bench on the front veranda. The steam of his breath expelled like cigarette smoke into the cool night air. Outside, it felt less like he was living in a real-estate brochure, even if there were colorful pillows out here too. This glowing house was the only sign of life in the expansive darkness of the unfinished suburb. It would be a nice neighborhood, one day, with lawnmowers going and kids playing cricket in the quiet street at the end of the drive. Did kids still do that?

Rob watched the fumes of his breath disintegrate into the night and wished he still smoked. The burn of a smoke, that steely pang at the back of the throat, that'd feel good right now. Fortifying. He didn't usually miss the cancer sticks. Even when the younger guys lit up on a break, he could smell their smoke and feel no craving, but tonight he yearned for a cigarette like he'd just quit smoking yesterday. He rubbed his leg. Who was he kidding? It'd been years. He'd probably cough and splutter like a teenager taking his first drag. Nah, that time was behind him. He had to take better care of himself now. He swallowed the rest of his beer and opened a fresh can. "Chug the first, sip the second," his old man used to say. "Two cans, per man, per day." A rule they both struggled to live by.

Rob used his sleeve to wipe the cloudy grime of sunscreen and sweat that had gathered on the screen of his phone. He scrolled, if only to keep his fingers busy. The usual pics of some hot girl or videos of someone doing something stupid, or videos of hot girls doing stupid things. The daily funnies. Random texts from mates. He wasn't in the mood. He didn't know what he was in the mood for exactly, but whatever it was, it wasn't here. Even the beer bored him.

He thought of calling Emma, but she wouldn't be happy to hear from him. It would break her rules. But the rules were stupid. He wanted to talk to someone who knew him, didn't assume the worst of him. He was a good guy. Sareena was harsh with him, always showing off in front of her crew. *You go girl.* Were all men bad suddenly? How was *that* okay? He wasn't a saint, but he was alright. Wasn't he?

He wanted Emma to get over herself and take his phone call. This silent treatment was giving him the shits. He didn't deserve it. All he'd ever done was provide for her and Will. He'd done his duty. Never had an affair. Was always a good dad, better than the one he had. She didn't know how good she had it. He'd never hit her, never would. If she knew even half the stories he'd heard from guys on site, she'd realize how lucky she was. But nowadays everyone had to be some kind of victim. If you weren't, you were automatically the attacker. People today were just a bunch of open toes, looking to be walked on. Emma wasn't like that. She had some steam to blow off, but she was in *his* corner. She'd come good. He tapped out a text – *Can I call you?* – and held the phone in his palm, waiting to send it. He scratched the stubble on his chin and then backspaced what he'd typed, erasing the letters, slowly at first and then rapidly.

No sooner had he put the phone down than he picked it up again and called Will. It rang for a long time, then Will answered.

"Willie…Geez, mate, Where are you? Sounds loud…Oh, right… What kind of mu– Right…nice…Nah, everything's fine, mate, just checking in. You good?…I understand, you're working…It's fine… Hey, you should check out this place I'm working on…Eh?…Okay, you better run then…No worries…Bye."

Rob chugged the rest of his beer. He burped and blew the steam of his breath into the dark and empty suburban street that stretched beyond the reach of his porch light. Here row upon row of empty blocks, blank concrete slabs and framed houses waited to come alive. For now, even the metal streetlights were dark and hollow, their arched silhouettes hanging over the road like an avenue of burned trees.

CHAPTER NINETEEN

Emma heaved another large suitcase over the threshold of Kendry's front door.

"Christ, Em, so much for traveling light." Kendry stood to the side of the doorway, keeping her antique leadlight door open as wide as it would go. "How many more you got?"

"I know, sorry." Emma took care to avoid bumping her suitcase against the wainscotting.

"Here." Kendry's manicured fingers pulled the suitcase into the hallway and parked it next to the others.

"This is it," said Emma, picking up the last wheely suitcase, the small one she'd bought for work trips that never eventuated. "Thanks again, Ken. I promise it's just for a bit."

"Oh, just get in here." Kendry stood aside, waved her in.

"Seriously," said Emma, placing the carry-on bag next to the others. "Couple weeks. A month tops."

"Whatever," Kendry said, opening her arms. Emma melted into the hug, comforted by the squeeze of her friend's arms and the faint odor of expensive perfume that lingered in her shawl. Kendry had her shit together. She had a job, a house, a spare room; she was an adult.

"Come on," said Kendry, grabbing the handle on one of Emma's suitcases. "I've made up Mom's old room." She set off down the long hallway, the suitcase wheels clunking rhythmically on the parquetry floor.

Margaret's old bedroom was spacious and clean, but not polished and pretty like the rest of the house. The simple, metal-frame bed and faded striped wallpaper felt almost austere, and the too-tall pedestal lamp on the bedside table made the room feel lopsided.

"If it's weird in here, I've got another room upstairs."

"No no—"

"This way we get our own floors."

"It's great."

"Yeah," Kendry said glumly. "I keep meaning to tackle this room, but…" Emma squeezed Kendry's arm. She smiled softly. "Seriously, if it's creepy," said Kendry.

"It's fine." Emma put a hand on Kendry's shoulder. "It's great. Thank you."

Kendry smiled, her eyes dewy. "You hungry?" Emma shook her head. "Well, just help yourself to whatever's in the kitchen." Kendry touched Emma's shoulder and left her to settle into her new room.

Emma brought all her bags together and lined them up against the far wall, ducking to avoid hitting her head on the old-style box television that was bolted to the wall on a metal arm. The little red light turned on when she touched the power button, but the screen remained black. Emma turned the TV off.

The fan in the ensuite bathroom rattled as Emma sat down to pee. She scanned the room, pausing on the metal handrails affixed to the walls near the toilet and the bathtub. Poor Margaret.

Emma felt guilty for not calling her own mother more often than a few times a year. But it was always so draining. Her mom was so bitter.

Back in the bedroom, Emma found some space in the closet, among the collection of shoes and hangers draped with black garment bags.

She couldn't deal with her stuff again. Maybe later. Emma lay on the bed and stared up at the ornate ceiling rose, the swirly floral pattern where tufts of broken spider webs fluttered in a current of air. She closed her eyes.

"Hey sleepy head," said Kendry as Emma padded into the lounge room. "You okay?"

"Yeah." Emma yawned. "I don't know what happened. I just crashed."

"Well," said Kendry, turning off the TV. "Good news is you haven't missed dinner." She motioned to a platter of crackers, cheese, cut veggies and a large bowl of chocolate almonds.

"Hmm, I'm starving." Emma picked up some crackers and sat on the other end of the couch. "Thanks again, Ken."

"Would you stop already. You don't have to keep thanking me." Kendry leaned forward and picked a chocolate almond from the bowl. "I'm glad you quit." She popped the almond in her mouth and crunched. "You're so much better than that place."

"I don't know," said Emma. "Everything's a fucking mess." She ate a cracker, reached for some cheese.

"Well, you've certainly gone all in on shaking things up, haven't you?"

Emma popped a square of cheese in her mouth and slowly massaged her own temples. "Hmm," she said, a faint smile appearing on her lips. "If you're going to fuck up, why not go big, right?" She reached for a chocolate almond.

"Does it really feel like fucking up, Em?"

"I don't know." Emma lay down, her head on Kendry's lap.

"I just thought it would be easier, you know. But it's not."

"No, it's not." Kendry stroked Emma's hair.

"It's like" – Emma closed her eyes as if to remember – "it's like we're all tangled up. I'll hear something funny and want to tell Rob about it. Or I'll be going through a magazine and see a picture of a cool restaurant and think that looks like a nice place, and then I ask myself, wait, do I think that? Or is this what Rob would think? And I can't be sure if it's because we have the same taste, or because I'm so used to thinking about 'us' that I can't tell the difference between me and we. Sorry, I'm, like, blah."

"It's okay, you're going through a lot of stuff."

"It's not okay, though." Emma sat up and faced Kendry. "When you were going through all this with Alistair, I don't reckon I was there for you."

"That was different," said Kendry.

"Different how? The only difference is that I'm the one having the affair."

"Em—"

"I'm sorry, Ken. I didn't know what you were going through."

Kendry cupped her friend's cheeks with her hands. "You done? Look, the situation with Alistair was complicated. Let's just say we both made mistakes." Kendry crossed her arms. "I'm just hoping you're only making a little one with this boy."

"I don't know why you keep calling him that. He's twenty-nine."

"Okay then. And *you're* gushing like you're fifteen."

"It's pathetic. I know." Emma rubbed her temples again. "I'm having fun and that feels important."

Kendry looked at Emma for a long while. Then her face softened. "Let me tell you something. If you're really going to hang out with these young people, try not to be so hung up on everything."

"I'm not *hung* up."

"So *keen*, then. They're all just cool with everything. It's like everything's all okay. Just do your thing."

"What, so nothing's uncool?

"No, only people who think stuff is uncool are uncool. Just be open is what I'm saying. You can be a little—"

"I have standards, Ken. Integrity."

"I was going to say you have a stick up your ass."

Emma smiled, slapped Kendry's arm. "Fuck off."

"I'm just saying, if you want to hang out with twenty-year-olds, luv, you can't be judgey, you've just got to roll with it."

"*It?*"

"Whatever they're in to. You can't look down on any of it. No matter how dumb it is. They're convinced they're changing the world one open heart at a time."

Emma pretended to think about it. Kendry brushed her hands of crumbs, leaned forward. "I'm going to say something, and I don't want it to sound mean." Emma raised her eyebrows. "Fucking someone younger doesn't make *you* younger."

"Gross."

"There, I said it." Kendry wrung her hands, as if washing them.

"I'm not, I'm just…trying to have fun."

"I know. And that's great, but I also know that you take things super seriously, like everything's a mission. What if you just let go a little? Stopped worrying so much about what it all *means*."

Emma smiled. "When have I ever done *that?*"

Kendry cocked her head, and they erupted in laughter.

"Well," said Kendry, adjusting the collar of her bathrobe that framed her thin neck, "if you're going all in on this, then you're going to have to do something about your shrubbery."

"Huh?"

"Your bush, luv. It's going to need some attention."

Emma glanced down at her lap. "What's wrong with it?"

"I'm sure it's fine, hon. But girls today…they keep things tidy."

"I'm tidy." Emma feigned insult.

"When's the last time you waxed?"

Emma shook her head. "Nah, not turning myself into some pre-pubescent girl. Not happening."

"Easy, Germaine Greer. No one's turning you into Lolita. I'm just saying you might want to do a little maintenance down there."

"I maintain."

"Fine. I'm not going to argue about your bush. It's *your* mid-life crisis."

"Thank you."

They laughed. Emma put a hand on Kendry's knee. "But seriously, Ken, thank you. For letting me stay. I know you like your own space."

Kendry squeezed Emma's hand. "Don't worry about it," she said, getting up. "Space is something I've got plenty of." She motioned toward the large, empty rooms beyond the lounge room. "I know you won't take it, but if you need money, just ask." Emma opened her mouth to speak, but Kendry put her hand up. "I know you couldn't possibly, blah, blah, but I have it if you need it. I'm not going to mention it again." She yawned. "Now, I'm going to head up."

Emma smiled and looked over at the antique clock on the mantle. "Really? It's, like, eight-thirty."

"I've got a big day tomorrow. A soft opening for a nightclub next month. You should come."

Emma cringed.

"Come on, it'll be good for you. You can even bring your toy boy."

"I'll see."

"Yeah, we'll see. Goodnight luv." Kendry adjusted the collar of her robe again. "Ugh, it's fucking freezing in here. Aren't you cold?"

Emma shook her head.

Kendry tucked her hands under her armpits. "I've got a hot date with my electric blanket. Just help yourself to whatever." She yawned again and padded across the Persian rugs on the herringbone floor toward the staircase in the hallway.

Emma lay on the sofa, listening to the creak of floorboards grow faint until she was alone with the slow tick of the antique clock.

There was a deliberate oldness to this house that felt comforting, as if it had already seen many lives in this leafy suburb of Hawthorn. Kendry had spared no expense to renovate and kit out the place. The decor wasn't period specific, just high-end luxury antique, pastiche. There was a baroque-looking secretaire against the wall that was all inlaid wood and curves. The desk probably cost more than all of Emma's furniture combined. Next to the desk was an antique Japanese room divider, decorated with flower blossoms and flying cranes. On the wall hung an oil painting of a little girl with sad eyes, wearing a blue smock and holding a small oval needlepoint.

The whole place was both tasteful and outrageous. Cherry blossom wallpaper and little side tables and pedestals that supported bouquets of pink and purple flowers, and the copper statue of an ostrich in full stride. Part Victorian parlor, part quirky tearoom, this lounge room would look random and cluttered if it weren't so meticulously arranged.

Emma moved around the room, ran her hand across the milky surface of an old marble tabletop. She picked up a framed etching of a woman wearing a high wig and one of those frilly, poofy dresses with the whale bones in them. Whatever possessed Kendry to furnish the house this way, Emma was certain that every piece in here had a story. She put the gilded frame down and walked over to the buffet and opened the drawers.

Inside the first were pink boxes of macaroons from La Belle Miette patisserie on Collins Street, the boxes embossed in gold lettering, like jewelry cases. Emma shook them lightly. They were empty. The drawer below contained a full set of silverware, darkened by moldy streaks of tarnish. The third was full of crumpled blister packs and boxes upon boxes of pills for Valium, pethidine and oxycodone.

CHAPTER TWENTY

The truck engine groaned as it backed over loose stones. The beeping of the reversing flatbed almost drowned out the metallic whir of the circular saw echoing from inside the stone house. Rob guided the truck with its load of timber, signaling the driver toward the back wall of the house where deliveries were received and offloaded. He'd always enjoyed waving a truck into position. There was something satisfying about moving a big thing just by waving your hands. He recognized the self-satisfied expression on guys who guided commercial aircraft into position on the airport tarmac.

"Whoa," he called out, and the driver hit the brakes. Rob gave him a thumbs up.

Dani and Steph materialized behind Rob. They were still wearing those high-vis orange coveralls even though the others had been rubbishing them about this for weeks. The crew had started calling them "lollipop ladies" and the nickname stuck enough for everyone on site to know that "Lolli" meant Dani, Steph or the two of them together.

"Will," said Rob, as his son walked past. "You need to put your hard hat on, mate."

Will reluctantly put the thing on. It was too big and the brim of the hat sunk below his eyebrows. He looked like a kid in a costume, but Rob didn't want to embarrass his son by telling him to adjust the fit in front of the girls. He was just happy Will was here, even if it was only to help for the day. Rob was paying him of course, because that was the honorable thing to do, but also because he was unwilling to test if Will would've done it for nothing, just to spend time with his old man. Having him on site seemed like a win–win situation.

"What are these anyway?" said Will, picking up squares of plywood edged with fluorescent plastic tubing.

"It's subfloor," said Dani, stacking three squares onto Steph's forearms.

"Heavier than a dead dog, eh?" said Steph, and carried her load to the shipping container they used as lock-up storage.

Will fumbled with his two squares of plywood, trying to find a comfortable grip.

"Maybe put your gloves on," said Dani. "These things'll tear your hands up."

"I'll be alright." Will clamped a square in each hand like hand luggage and walked uneasily toward the shipping container, the plywood sheets bumping his knees with every step. Rob and Dani shared a smile behind Will's back.

Inside the house, Alex and Jem were pulling up the old floorboards and stacking them against the far wall. For someone built more like a jockey than a tradie, Alex got the job done. What she lacked in strength, she made up for in speed, prying up the floorboards and ferrying them to the far wall in quick, short strides, like she was in competition with Jemma, who was more of a plodder, examining each board she lifted out of the floor.

"You're numbering them, right Al?" said Jemma, cradling one board like a rifle across her chest.

"Yeah," said Alex, annoyed, tucking a board under each veiny arm.

Rob smiled. Every site had its tensions. People who worked too fast butting heads with people who worked too slow. Crew bosses overeager to assert their authority over junior team members. It didn't matter how fancy the build was, by the time the owners moved in, the house had already hosted plenty of bad blood. In fact, the more prestigious the build, the more precious the crew and the more intense these little squabbles could become. Rob recalled a job in a Toorak mansion where he had to yank a painter off an apprentice who had sanded in a room with fresh paint. The poor kid was crying and walked off the job. Never saw either of them on a site again.

You never knew what people were dealing with at home. It might be money troubles, a dying parent or a bad breakup. The problem was a lot of these guys brought their troubles to work. As a foreman, Rob also had to be policeman, judge and counselor. He was relieved that whatever was going on between Alex and Jemma was Sareena's problem. It was *her* crew and Rob found some pleasure in seeing her mob exhibit the same personality clashes and dysfunctions that played out on any worksite. They weren't perfect.

Rob walked over to where the floorboards were stacked against the wall and ran his thumb along the spine of one of the water-stained boards, each one numbered with chalk.

"They're staying," came Sareena's muffled voice behind him. Rob turned and searched the room. "Down here." Sareena's torso poked up from a trench dug into the living room floor where a large section of floorboards had been removed. "The boards are in pretty good condition, considering." She wiped dust off her nose with the back of her hand.

Rob considered the numbered timber boards leaning up against the wall. "They're a bit bowed, don't you think?" Rob held up a board and turned it on its side, pointing out a discernible curve in its length.

"It's fine," said Sareena. "I can brace it from underneath. It'll be good-as-new timber and no one'll even know when I put it back together. Then we can keep as many of the originals as we can. Look at those lines, the patination." She pointed at the floorboards all scuffed and worn. "You can't fake that shit. We gotta keep 'em. It'll look sweet. Way better than new boards."

"Hmm." Rob leaned the curved board back against the wall.

"Don't fuck up my numbering system," said Sareena, her hands resting on the floor, the rest of her body submerged under the house.

Rob wiped his hands on his jeans. "How are the joists down there?"

"Come take a look." Sareena looked down into the hole she was in.

Rob peered into the void beyond the floorboards.

"Well, come on, get in here," said Sareena, "I want to show you something cool."

Rob sat on the floor, dangled his legs into the trench and lowered himself under the floor. He steadied himself, gripping the rough beams of the floor joists. They were old-growth mountain ash, a timber he hadn't seen in a long time, not since he was an apprentice.

"Look," said Sareena, pointing under one of the floorboards.

Rob ducked and turned to look up. A palm-sized date was written there, neat and precise, like calligraphy, chalked onto the rough wood.

1891

Sareena shone her phone torch onto the writing, the white chalk, fine as sifted flour, clung to the wood grain. "Pretty cool, eh?"

Rob nodded, squinted to take a closer look.

"And look." Sareena pointed at the bottom of the nine. "There. You see that?" Her finger traced the dandy flourish at the end of the number. "The chalk's still dry, like it's about to flake off. See?" Rob nodded. "That tells me it's been dry as down here for more than a hundred years. I thought for sure this'd be rotted out, what with water coming through the missing roof tiles, but it looks alright. Looks fucking amazing. Better than you'd get if you pulled up the floor in a random house in Melbourne." She held her phone close to the writing and took a photo, the "click" of her phone camera an otherworldly sound in this earthy, muted tomb below the house.

"I love finding shit like this," said Sareena, tapping and scrolling on her phone.

Rob leaned in to have a closer look at the chalk lines. "Who'd have put that there?"

"Who knows," said Sareena, looking at her phone, thumbs hammering. "Maybe the owner. Or the builder. Could've been the guy who put the floor in, if he could write. You sometimes find old stuff like this, clay pipes, chicken bones from someone's lunch. Found a champagne bottle once. Empty." Sareena's phone whooshed.

"You posting that?" said Rob.

"Yeah. People love shit like this."

"Yeah?"

"It's house porn," she said, smiling. "People can't get enough."

"Really?" Rob shook his head. "How many people you reckon'll look at that?"

"By when?"

Rob thought for a moment. "I don't know, say, next week?"

Sareena looked down at her post, considered it. "I don't know. Three thousand, maybe."

"Yeah?" said Rob.

"Yeah. I'll bet we get a thousand views before the day's through." She held out her hand.

"What are we betting?"

Sareena turned her head toward the hole in the floor above them. "If I win, you have to number the rest of these boards."

Rob's eyes scanned the dark expanse of floor that had yet to be cataloged so each board could return to its original position. There was a fair bit of work in it. "Yeah, and what do I get if *I* win?"

"What do you want?"

Rob looked down at the earth beneath his feet and rubbed the back of his neck, avoiding Sareena's gaze. He didn't like asking for stuff. He thought about Will and how he wasn't as close to his son as he wanted to be. The boy was more like his mother, into artsy stuff, and Rob always felt like he disappointed his son somehow by not being smart the way he and his mom were. It's partly why he'd offered Will more than apprentice wages for basic labor. Rob couldn't have taken Will saying no. He was worried about his son, what he thought about this gap year nonsense, but was pretty sure he'd screw up the conversation if he tried to talk to Will about it. What if he did blame him for what his mother had done. It was Emma who wanted the gap year, not him. Not him.

Sareena was younger and neutral in this thing, maybe she could help.

"Maybe you could just have a conversation with Will," he said.

"About what?"

"I don't know," he said. "Just want to know if he's doing okay."

"Why don't you ask him yourself?"

Rob's eyes wandered across the floor above them, half looking for defects. "He won't talk to me, not really."

"Well, that figures, you're not the most approachable guy."

She laughed and touched his arm. "Sorry, but it's kinda true." Sareena comically furrowed her brow and pursed her lips so her whole face got tense and wrinkled. "You always got this stern look on your face that is like 'Uhm, I don't approve. Grrr.' Doesn't exactly make someone want to spill their guts to you."

Rob frowned.

Sareena smiled. "Oh, *that's it*, that's the look right there. Grrr."

"Hmm." Rob stood up and moved toward the hole in the floor. He didn't crawl down here to be ridiculed.

"Oh, come on, don't get mad."

"I'm not." Rob braced his hands on the floor to lift himself out. "Just got work to do."

"Okay."

Rob pulled himself up from the subfloor. That's what happened when you talked to people about stuff like this. They just cut you down. He should've kept his mouth shut.

"Remember our bet though," Sareena called up. "I'll get the chalk ready."

"Yeah," said Rob. He dusted off his knees and headed back outside.

He was dismayed to see his son alone and sitting on the big portable cooler next to the shipping container, looking at his phone. You never sit on a jobsite unless you're on a designated break. That was a rule. A law. He had to be delicate here, though, didn't want Will to feel singled out or to scare him off. He tried to soften his face and smile as he walked over.

"Hey, mate. Where'd Dani and Steph go?" He looked around.

Will slipped the phone into his pocket. "They went around front, something about stones."

"Right." Rob glanced at the parked truck. There was still a stack of subfloor sheets in the back. That driver was getting paid until the load was emptied and would happily sit there all day until it was. Didn't Will understand how his sitting there, dicking around on his phone was fucking up the supply chain, the schedule, the budget? Rob could've kicked the cooler out from under him. "Well," Rob took a breath. "I've got a minute. Maybe we can unload the rest of that subfloor, get this truckie on his way."

"Sure," said Will. He got up, slowly, put his gloves on and walked toward the back of the truck. At least the kid had learned the value of a pair of gloves.

"So, how's school going?" It felt like a safe question.

His son waived it away.

"What, no good?"

"It's fine."

"Well, that's good."

"It's just…"

"What?"

"It's just a bit preachy, you know."

"No, not really."

They reached the back of the truck and each grabbed two sheets of subfloor. It was a smaller load than was efficient, but Rob let it slide. He matched Will's pace too, ambling back toward the shipping container. The twitch in his back flared up and he was quietly grateful for the smaller load he was carrying.

"Unis are an antiquated system," Will continued. Rob snapped back into the conversation. Will looked up at the sky. "The whole concept of a university used to be about making worldly citizens. But now it's just about money. It's not really about values or anything, it's just a business trying to stay relevant in a world that's moving faster than it can keep up with. Like, it's nice, I'm grateful and everything, but it's kind of old-fashioned."

"Hmmm." Rob looked down at his steel-toed boots. Geez for all that, it was costing a bundle. "So, you going to stay, then?"

Will put his load of subfloor down in the container, dropping the materials a little more heavily than was ideal. "I dunno," he said. "For now, yeah. Probably." Will dusted his hands off.

"You know," said Rob, gently placing his load on the pile and suppressing a wince at the twinge in his back. "I got a lot out of my study."

Will wiped his forehead. "No offense but building and drafting certifications aren't really the same as doing a degree."

"Maybe, I wouldn't know about that." He breathed through the pain in his back. "You'd have to ask your mom." Rob straightened the stack of subfloor. He shouldn't have mentioned Emma. It could get weird. How was he supposed to have a nice conversation with his son when there was this thing, this gap year, between them? He backpedaled to safer ground. "You could always come over to my side of the fence. Start making some coin."

Will scratched the side of his face. "I don't know."

"It's up to you, mate," said Rob encouragingly. "A man's got to make his own decisions."

"Hmmm." Will kicked a stone that hit the side of the shipping container with an echoing thud. "When's lunch?" he said, shielding his eyes from the sun that had broken through a cloud.

"Not till noon."

"Is there a cafe or something around here?"

"Nah, mate. You're out bush here. Didn't you bring anything?"

"Nope."

Rob and Will walked back to the truck to grab the last load. Rob patted Will's shoulder. "I've got loads, so you can have some of mine."

"Thanks, Dad."

He'd screwed up, hadn't he, mentioning Emma like that? The weight of that situation now sat between him and Will, real as a brick wall. Rob had to say something. His own father never said much, especially the night before he'd leave on a long haul with the semi, out Darwin way, or Perth or Cairns. He'd be gone weeks then. And his dad always clammed up before those long stints, as if silence could change the unwanted truth of his departure. Silence never worked, and Rob didn't want Will to worry, to wonder if he was responsible for whatever was going on between his parents.

"Hey," said Rob casually. He straightened his back. "This thing with me and your mom. It's temporary. You know that, right?"

Will frowned and looked at the ground. "I don't know. It's up to you guys."

"Well, don't worry is what I'm saying." Rob pulled the two remaining sheets of subfloor from the back of the truck. "She'll come around. She always does. We all need to blow off steam sometimes, so don't stress." He handed the planks to Will.

"I'm not stressed," said Will, taking the load.

"Good." Rob dusted his hands off. "That's good." He lifted the tailgate on the truck. "Take those sheets back to the container. I'm just going to have a quick word with this guy." He gestured toward the truck driver.

Will turned without saying anything. Rob watched his son shuffle back toward the shipping container before walking to the driver's side window of the truck. "How ya going? I'm Rob. Not sure we've met before."

The guy adjusted his BHP-branded ballcap and scratched at the tuft of hair that stuck out from under the brim. "Andy," he said, without looking up from his phone.

Rob leaned in closer to the open truck window and noticed the takeout containers littering the floor. "Well, Andy...Travis usually does my deliveries from you guys.

"He's sick."

"That's fine, but the thing is…Travis usually helps out with the unloading, saves billing me for the truck just sitting here."

Andy was already shaking his head vigorously. "Yeah, not doing that. Not insured for it."

"Come on mate, I wasn't born yesterday."

Andy cleared his throat, craned his neck to look out the window and pointed at Will, now halfway between the truck and the shipping container. "Look, that little prick's been sitting there just watching me for about twenty minutes. Why don't you get that lazy little shit to do it?"

"Oi! Pull up." Rob leaned against the door of the truck, put his face nearer the open window.

"What are you shitcanning me for? I just deliver this stuff. Why are you climbing up my ass? It's not my problem you've got a shit crew, mate. Not my problem."

"Hey," Rob barked, his grip tightening on the ledge between the door and the roof. "Travis's guys help. They at least get out of the truck. How long were you going to sit here doing fuck all and charging me for the time?"

"Oh, fuck this." Andy threw his cap onto the passenger seat. "I do not need to take shit from you. Why don't you haul the load yourself, ya fat fuck?"

Rob's chest danced with excitement. He visualized reaching through the open window and grabbing hold of this guy by the neck, pulling him from the cab, kicking and screaming, legs flailing, boots cracking the windshield, all that trash raining off the dash. His eyes widened at the thought of it.

A good thump. That's the only thing a guy like this understood. You weren't allowed to give 'em one. Not anymore. There'd be consequences. And people wondered why guys like this behaved as they did. It was because no one knocked them back into place.

The women gathered behind him to see what the commotion was.

"That's it." Rob threw up his arms and backed away from the truck. "You're gone. I see you on my site again, I'm sending the load back and you can explain it to Travis."

"Go on then, get fucked."

Rob took a step toward the vehicle.

Andy revved the engine and the truck growled.

Out the corner of his eye, Rob spied Sareena in the arch of the doorway. He turned back to Andy and pointed down the road. "Fuck off, you fuckwit."

Andy revved the engine again and sent black diesel fumes billowing in everyone's direction. Sareena held Alex back, whose fists were clenched at her sides.

Andy stuck his middle finger out the window. "Youse can all get fucked!" He stared Sareena down. "Yeah, look at me again you fuckin' bitch."

"That's it." Rob marched toward the car.

"Rob!" Sareena shook her head.

The truck spun its tires in the dirt, spitting pebbles that ricocheted off the stone walls or landed in the tall grass with a thud. Rob turned and covered his head. The truck lurched forward, spraying dust into the air and took off, the cage and chains rattling as the vehicle shot up the unsealed road at a ludicrous speed. They all watched the roadrunner plume of dust forming in its wake.

"What the fuck was that all about?" said Sareena approaching Rob, hands on her hips, her gaze still following the dust cloud spreading from the hill.

Rob spat into the dirt. "Nothing. Guy's a dick."

Sareena looked over at Will. "You okay, hon?"

"I'm okay," he looked at his father. "Just a dick."

Sareena adjusted her hard hat, slid it further to the back of her head. She looked over at Rob. "Well," she said, "can we please make sure that grumpy motherfucker never comes back here again. It's bad juju." She walked closer to Rob and looked him in the eye. "You okay?"

He swallowed and nodded.

"Good. Because I don't like this macho bullshit. If that's the way it's going to be, this isn't going to work."

Rob's limbs still buzzed with adrenaline. "The guy was being a fuckwit—"

"Yeah, and so were you." She crossed her arms. "I don't need you to save me, mate. I just need you to build this fucken house."

Rob nodded slowly.

"Okay?" said Sareena, her hands dropping to her hips. "We cool?"

Rob nodded. "You alright?"

Sareena shrugged. "This shit comes with the territory."

Rob looked over his shoulder at the trail of dust spreading on the hill. "It's not right. I'm going to tell Travis to get rid of that guy."

"Whatever," said Sareena. "Those guys are like weeds, you chop 'em back and they pop up again." She turned to address the others who were now looking down from windows and the tops of ladders. "Okay, show's over," she said. "Let's get another thirty minutes done before lunch. Go on." The others dispersed, except Alex, who lingered a moment and seemed unhappy about getting moved on. "Go on, Al," said Sareena. "It's over." Alex, still glaring up the hill, reluctantly returned to the stone house.

"Okay," said Sareena cheerfully to Will. "The good news is you're both here because…" She reached into the pocket of her vest and pulled out her phone. "Ta da, I want to show you something. Check it out." She danced the screen from side to side before handing the phone to Will.

Will took the phone and leaned in to have a closer look at the Instagram post, the picture of the 1891 date she'd found written in white chalk under the floorboards. He looked up. "What's this?"

"*That?*" Sareena bobbed around and swayed from side to side as if she was dancing to a beat only she could hear. "I'll tell you what that is." She raised her open palms in the air. "*That* is two thousand and seventy views." Sareena pumped her fists and looked over at Rob. "People are digging it." She snapped her fingers.

"What is that?" said Will, handing the phone back.

"*That* means I just won a bet with your dad." Sareena smiled at Rob. "He has to crawl on his hands knees under the house now, getting all gross and cobwebby and number all those fucking floorboards by himself." She danced a little more on the spot.

"Yeah, yeah." Rob rolled his eyes and turned to Will. "You want to give me a hand?"

"Nah." Will dragged his forearm across his mouth. "You can have that one. Think I'll go help Dani and Steph with those stones." Will shoved his hands in his pockets and loped to the side of the house.

Sareena turned toward Rob. "Tough break," she said, handing Rob a piece of chalk. "Don't worry." She patted his shoulder. "I'll still talk to the kid."

CHAPTER TWENTY-ONE

Emma stood outside the beauty salon, her heart pounding. "This is where you want to go," Kendry had said. "Lina's amazing."

From what Emma could see beyond the glass door, the reception area didn't look so flash, not what she'd expected. She looked up at the sign above the door again. *Sleek and Chic*. This was it.

Emma pushed open the door, the tinkling bell announcing her arrival. The receptionist, a beautiful girl with a nose ring and purple hair, smiled warmly. "Hey," she said, her voice gentle and soothing.

"Hi." Emma fidgeted with her hands. "I'm here for a wax."

"Ah, you're Emma." The receptionist's eyes softened. "Kendry told me."

"Right." Emma nodded.

"Don't worry." The receptionist came out from behind the counter. "I'll make it quick."

"Oh, *you're* doing it?"

"Yeah, I'm Lina. It's my shop," she laughed. "You'll see, it's not like in the movies. Just a sting and it's over."

Emma followed Lina to the waxing room with its soft lighting and soothing scents of lavender and oils.

"Take your bottoms off and lie down here," said Lina, motioning toward the waxing table, draped in white towels.

Emma hooked her thumbs into the waist of the loose skirt she'd worn to avoid getting fully naked in front of a stranger.

"Here," she said, handing Emma a towel, "put this on your lap."

Emma wriggled out of her skirt and undies, and felt the chill in the room on her bare skin. She cautiously positioned herself on the table and covered herself with the towel, soft and warm. Emma's apprehension grew as Lina moved around behind her.

"You seem young to have your own business."

"I've been doing this for a long time. Ten years."

"Wow," said Emma, "that's a lot of pubic hair."

Lina laughed, "I guess so." She came to the foot of the examination table with a rice-cooker sized tub of wax.

"You must get all sorts of people in here."

"Oh yeah. A lot of men too." Lina swirled a wooden paddle in the tub of wax.

Emma couldn't imagine Rob coming to a place like this. He wasn't the manscaping type. Lina would need a whipper snipper to find his penis.

"I don't want everything off," said Emma.

Lina smiled reassuringly. Emma lay back. The first strip of warm wax touched her skin. "I expected it to be hotter." Emma pushed her shoulder into the cushioned bench. A sharp tug and the sound of Velcro ripping.

"You okay?" said Lina.

Emma grimaced, bit her lip, nodded.

"Good," said Lina, and applied another layer of wax. Rip. "See, not so bad." She tugged off the third strip, the fourth. Emma felt that one more and exhaled sharply.

Lina smiled. "Nearly finished," she said, her voice calm and gentle.

Rip. Emma winced.

"All done," said Lina. "Have a look."

Emma lifted the towel. Shorn but for a neat strip of hair.

"Oh god," she frowned. "It looks like a mustache."

"It's a French bikini. Too much?"

"I don't know. Now that I see it, I wonder if it's not enough. It's like a slug just sitting there."

"We don't want that," Lina chortled. "You want me to take it off?" She paddled the wax.

"Yes, please." Emma bit her lip, lay back and winced in anticipation. "Ooof!" Her hand shot up to her face as Lina tore the last strip. "That was the worst one." Emma sat up and looked down at herself, pale as raw chicken.

The aesthetic was strangely exhilarating. The sudden absence of pubic hair was a shock. It reminded her that she hadn't really thought about her vagina for a long time. Or, more accurately, she'd only thought about the vagina that was about birth and pelvic floor exercises, the one of medical interest, poked and prodded, the one prone to dryness and bladder infections, the one that needed pap smears. She used to get so much pleasure from her vagina. Seeing herself exposed like this was confronting, like seeing a long-lost relative to find them suddenly aged, sagging and liver spotted.

"Oh god," said Emma. "Can you put it back?"

Lina laughed. "You'll get used to it."

"If you say so."

"You want to turn over and we do the back," said Lina.

"What, my butt?"

Lina nodded.

"Nah," said Emma, peeling off the towel. "I'm good. This is plenty."

Emma left the spa feeling sleek and oddly limber, her skirt swishing around her as she walked.

Her phone chimed.

Hi Emma,

Click https://automedsystem.com.au/fmg/bookings

to confirm/cancel your appointment.

12:45PM appt at Fitzroy Medical Group.

Dr Nguyen

Or reply YES/NO

Aw shit. It wasn't like her to flake on appointments like this. She responded YES and checked the time. She'd have to get on a tram quick smart if she was going to reach the clinic in time.

Emma ran to board a packed tram, standing room only, and grabbed onto the nearest pole. She shifted her weight, feeling little bits of wax sticking to her undies and moved her hips to unstick them, pulling at the waist of her skirt. Her gaze landed on an old woman, whose handbag was perched on her knees.

In the consulting room Dr Nguyen sat across from Emma and adjusted her glasses with the back of her hand. "How are things?"

"Good," Emma said. "Well, I'm feeling bloated and hot all the time. Like, suddenly stifling and I can't take my clothes off fast enough. It's like I'm suffocating."

Dr Nguyen turned to look at her computer screen.

Emma peered at the screen as well, a blur of text boxes. "Is there anything we can do? It's driving me crazy." She cleared her throat. "I've been reading about hormone replacement therapy and—"

"It's probably too early for that."

"Oh, really? Because—"

"The next time you come, make a longer appointment, and we can talk about the risks and rewards of HRT. Until then, let's explore some other interventions, like over-the-counter remedies and lifestyle changes. You still don't smoke?

"No."

"That's good." Dr Nguyen glanced at her screen again and clicked the mouse. "Hot flushes are common."

"So that's it?"

"There are things you can try," said Dr Nguyen. "I'll give you some information before you go and next time we can make a more solid plan."

"No magic bullet then?"

Nguyen smiled through tight lips.

"You know," said Emma, "I bet there'd be a cure if men had to go through it."

"You may be right." Doctor Nguyen stood up and started putting on latex gloves. "Hop up on the table so I can check the bloating." Dr Nguyen motioned for Emma to lay down. Emma loosened and lowered her skirt and submitted to the doctor's hands pressing on her abdomen. "How long have you felt bloated?"

"Months."

Dr Nguyen tapped her belly. "You still have an IUD, right?" Emma nodded. Dr Nguyen continued pressing on Emma's tummy. "Ginger tea is good for bloating." Then the doctor paused, her gaze below Emma's belly button. Emma looked down too. Her skirt sat below her hips and the elastic of her underwear had slid down just enough to show some of the pink chicken skin below her abdomen. In the twelve years she'd been coming here, Emma had never waxed.

"Just trying something new," she said.

Dr Nguyen offered a wry smile. "It looks a bit irritated. Put on some aloe vera, that should calm it down." Dr Nguyen smiled and finished the examination, then peeled off her gloves. "Otherwise, all good?" she said, tossing the gloves in the trash and sanitizing her hands. Emma smiled and nodded.

"And the family are good?"

"Yep, all good." Emma stood and rebuttoned her skirt. She pulled her shirt down over her belly and sat down again on the chair. "Actually, I wanted to ask you something. You'd know about drugs."

Dr Nguyen's brow furrowed. "Hmm," she said, curious, possibly suspicious.

"I've got a friend—"

"Hmmm—"

"No, I'm serious, I mean, an actual friend. And I found a bunch of pills in her drawer the other day and I don't know what to make of them." Emma sat up and reached for the phone in her purse.

Dr Nguyen raised an eyebrow. "So, you are snooping in your friend's house?"

"No. Well, yes. It's out of concern. I'm living there, and I found a bunch of stuff and I'm worried about her."

"Maybe it's better we respect your friend's privacy."

"I know." Emma had her face down in her phone, scrolling photos for the image she took of the pill boxes in Kendry's loungeroom. "I don't need a medical opinion or anything." Emma scrolled madly. "Here." She held the phone out for Dr Nguyen to see. "I just need you to help me understand what this stuff is. I've googled it but, it didn't help, you always just end up with cancer."

Dr Nguyen held Emma's gaze, unwilling to look down at the phone. "Please," Emma pleaded.

Dr Nguyen's face softened, and she looked down at the image on screen. "Okay, so these are pain medications. Pretty serious."

"Why would someone take those?"

Dr Nguyen scrunched her face. "A lot of reasons. Maybe your friend had surgery?" Emma shook her head. "They can also be used in treatments for other conditions, like cancer." Emma's eyes widened. "But I don't know," said Dr Nguyen quickly. "It's only hypothetical. I don't know your friend."

Emma looked down at the phone. "Yeah, maybe I don't either."

CHAPTER TWENTY-TWO

Sareena and Will sat on a pair of fold-out chairs in the front yard drinking kombucha. Rob shook his head as he walked toward them on his way to the portaloo.

"Bit early for a break," he said, pretending to look at a wristwatch.

"Excuse me." Sareena lowered her chin and glared at him from under raised eyebrows. "We just smashed out both bedrooms, so yeah, we're taking a little break." She raised her bottle to Will's and they clinked them together.

Rob barely broke his stride. "Plenty more to do." He disappeared inside the portaloo, the plastic door clapping shut behind him.

Will and Sareena grinned at each other, got up and crept to the sides of the loo, brandishing rolls of duct tape. As they approached, Steph and Dani came out of the house.

"Hey—" called Dani, but Sareena put her finger to her lips to shush her. Sareena winked, held up the duct tape and motioned toward the toilet cubicle. The girls grinned as they understood the plan.

The four of them crept up on the sides of the toilet. Sareena nodded, and the three of began taping up the door.

"What's going on out there," called Rob from inside. They kept taping. "Oi!" he said, and banged on the door. "Oi!"

Their laughter grew louder as they circled the loo. The door shook with an occasional thump until they stepped back, admiring their work.

"Okay, ha ha," said Rob, his voice echoey from inside. "You got me." They struggled to control their laughter as he fumbled with the door, trying to push it open. "Come on," he pleaded. "It stinks."

They erupted in laughter. The ramshackle loose strands of duct tape hanging off the door only seemed to make it funnier. Will wiped tears of laughter with the sleeve of his shirt.

"I hear you out there, Will," came Rob's muffled voice. "So much for your inheritance."

Sareena doubled over, her eyes watering.

Steph finally cut the duct tape holding the door closed.

"Gotcha!" said Sareena, as Rob emerged. "Stuck in the shit shack," she said, wiping her eyes. "Classic. Gets me every time."

Rob shook his head, but even he couldn't resist smiling.

"You guys are assholes," he said, and walked back toward the house.

Work continued and, by the afternoon, they'd made good progress. It was nice having Will on site. He seemed better for it, more relaxed, even seemed to have picked up a few skills.

Sareena looked up from her phone as Steph walked over. "I'm going to run out and get a new drill," said Steph.

"Why?" said Sareena. "What's wrong with it?"

"Think it's the motor, it's just shuddering."

Sareena rolled her eyes. "Cuz, if you leave now the sheeting doesn't get done until tomorrow. I need it today. You gotta check your tools, Steph."

"I did."

"Let's have a look." Sareena hopped down from the window ledge. "Maybe just jammed, yeah." Steph shrugged.

"If it *is* busted," said Sareena, "just borrow one."

Sareena strode through to where Steph's hammer drill lay on the floor. "Look," said Sareena, bending to pick up the power tool. "You've got it on the wrong gear ya dufus." She held it up. "How the fuck you going to hammer into granite with this weak ass thing here." She flicked a switch on the handle. "Now you can blast a mountain." She pulled the trigger and white powder erupted from inside the tool, forming a dense cloud that enveloped Sareena. She smiled, wiped her lips and blew a raspberry sending puffs of white flour airborne.

Rob and Steph laughed and the others joined in. Steph and Rob high-fived.

"You motherfuckers." Sareena smiled. "It's on." She wiped her face with her sleeve. "Okay. Fuck you all and get back to work."

CHAPTER TWENTY-THREE

Emma stepped from hard concrete onto the soft cushioning of red carpet rolled out onto the sidewalk. She wasn't sure she could get herself into the mood for this gala opening. She still hadn't asked Kendry about the pills. There was always an excuse not to; they had a nice vibe going. Emma was a guest at her house, plus Kendry was always so defensive. You had to be ready for a confrontation with her. And Kendry *did* seem to have her shit together.

Emma's life was the disaster, marriage on the brink, no job, unable to afford her own rent, mooching off a friend. What a loser she was. Hustling backward. Dr Priya said it's not what you do, it's about who you are. Sounded nice but offered little comfort.

Who Emma was, is forty-eight! What the hell was she doing standing in the cold outside a cocktail lounge, surrounded by all these young and fabulous people? Everyone else inside these velvet ropes was part of a couple or a group. She was the only one standing here by herself. Christ, her life was such a fucking mess.

She checked her phone to appear busy (no messages) and looked up when the line of well-dressed people shuffled ever closer to the front steps of the cocktail lounge. A waft of electronica escaped the venue every time the doorman opened the solid brass door.

The doorman was an older gentleman, sixty-something, and his white mustache had been waxed so the tips pointed up toward the shiny brim of his black cap. He struck Emma as rather splendid in his red coat with gold embroidering and epaulets. She didn't know if his look was meant to be ironically old-fashioned or a deadly serious recreation of the past. Whatever it was, she liked the way this older man seemed to inhabit his uniform; the way it gave him a style and gravitas was comforting. He looked…dignified. The somber, dutiful way he welcomed guests into the place with a slight bow made Emma feel a little silly about going in there to face the absurdity of introducing her oldest friend to the younger man she was seeing. Butterfly wings of anxiety fluttered in her chest, her throat, her stomach. This was pathetic, wasn't it? She was out of place here. And yet, when the doorman finally doffed his cap at her, she felt reassured, emboldened, as if he'd opened the door to possibility itself.

Inside, the music thumped a little louder, the bass jostled her guts. She recognized the electronic jungle beats of *Papa New Guinea*. That band transported her back to the early 1990s, drinking cider at a house party and pashing a boy on the veranda. Did these people realize they were listening to old music? Or did these young people appreciate it with that sentimental irony that seemed to move them to buy obsolete stuff like old tape decks and roller skates. When did her life become a vintage curiosity?

Emma scanned the room. The decor was kooky, Victorian gentleman scientist meets art nouveau chic. Hanging plants cascaded down from wall to wall; floor-to-ceiling bookshelves displaying antique medical instruments, microscopes, beakers and specimen jars filled with swirling-colored liquids. Pedestal lamps of female nudes lit framed displays of taxidermic insects. Emma's gaze followed the Rorschach patterns on pinned butterfly wings and the shimmering rainbow exoskeletons of giant beetles. This place had Kendry's touch all over it.

Emma looked for her friend, a welcome ally in this sea of young faces. She searched the room twice before noticing Kendry's long, braceleted arms waving at her from the wraparound bar where backlit bottles of booze glowed in a mosaic of colors, solemn and penitent as a cathedral's stained glass.

Kendry patted the empty bar stool next to her. Emma didn't want to sit at the bar. Erik would join them soon and the bar would be awkward. It would leave at least one of them on the outer, struggling to join the conversation. She didn't want to be the one stuck in the middle, bridging the conversation. She wanted a booth, but they were all taken.

"Grab a saddle," said Kendry, kissing Emma on the cheek.

"Hey, Ken. Any chance we can—"

"Watch this." Kendry tapped Emma's knee and turned on her stool to watch the three bartenders pumping out fresh cocktails. They looked serious in their blue shirts with the sleeves rolled up, burlap ties tucked under the bib of their aprons. "I'm loving just watching these guys work. Oh, check this one." Kendry nudged her, and turned again to focus on one of the bartenders whose face was all jawbone. "Watch this." The jawbone poured a trickle of Kirsch into the frosty silver sleeve of a martini shaker. He slid the glass onto the metal sleeve and raised the shaker over his head. He shook it like he was dancing to the beat of the music that filled the place, throwing his whole body into the rhythm of the action. He then held the shaker low and gyrated, throwing his pelvis into the motion, splintering the ice inside the shaker.

"Well, I'm stirred," said Kendry, and laughed at her own joke.

The hint of a smile curled at the edge of the bartender's mouth as he poured the frothy, pink mixture into a pair of frosted martini glasses. He pushed the stems toward them.

Kendry saluted him. He winked.

"Been here a while?" said Emma.

Kendry picked up her martini glass. "I've been here all week." She raised her glass. "I did my job. It's the soft opening and the place is full." She clinked Emma's glass and took a gulp from her drink. "So," Kendry said, licking her lip, "what do you think?"

Emma looked around. The moody lighting, the music, the chatter of people in dark clothes, the crunch of scooped ice. "It's nice," said Emma, picking up her martini glass.

"Nice?" Kendry's forehead wrinkled. "Babes, this is the premiere event in Melbourne tonight but, hey, who cares? Cheers to nice." Kendry toasted the air and slurped her martini.

Emma wanted to bring up the pills, but it didn't seem fair. She didn't want to ruin the opening. Kendry had worked so hard. Plus, she'd already had one too many. Things could get ugly. "You okay?" said Emma. It was a neutral-ish question.

Kendry put her drink down a little heavily and adjusted the peacock patterned shawl unfurling itself from her neck. "I'm fine." She moved the stem of her glass around in a little puddle of condensation on the bar. "Just been working too much is all." She leaned in close. "The guy who owns this place has deep pockets, but he's got no idea what he's doing. Most of what you see here is my idea." She took another drink.

"I'm sorry, Ken. If you want, I can call Erik and tell him not to come if it's going to—"

"No! Are you kidding?" She licked froth from the top of her lip. "What, and miss the boy wonder? That's the only part of tonight I'm looking forward to. No way." She took another slurp of her drink. "Besides, Syed would be pissed. You should've seen how happy he was when I told him we put Erik's name on the VIP guest list. You didn't tell me he was famous."

Emma took a sip of her drink.

Kendry's eyes widened. "Oh my god." She gave Emma a playful shove. "You don't even know, do you?" She laughed. "Oh, that is *so* you."

"He is *not* famous."

"Maybe not to *you*," said Kendry. "But if you were into *this* kind of music…" – she pointed up at the ceiling where the speakers now rained down something that sounded like the thump and squeal of a train on rusty tracks mixed with the bleeping of an '80s video game – "you'd think he was the bee's knees."

"Seriously?"

"Oh yeah. He's not, like, mauled-by-fans famous, but in his own scene he is definitely a thing."

"I really didn't—"

"Well, I guess you two don't spend a lot of time talking."

"Are you going to be nice when he gets here? You're not going to be all weird?"

"Why would I be weird just because I'm meeting your little man muffin?"

Emma shot Kendry a disapproving look as a stout little man in a shiny black V-neck T-shirt came up behind her and put his hairy-knuckled hands on Kendry's shoulders.

Kendry turned. "Oh hey."

The man briefly massaged Kendry's shoulders and leaned toward her ear. "Having fun?"

"All in a night's work," said Kendry, twirling her straw in the near empty glass. "Syed, this is my friend, Emma."

Syed looked up and his eyebrows arched with recognition.

"It's you," he said, pointing a stubby finger at Emma. "I know you."

Emma's eyes narrowed as she placed Syed, recalled the endless string of insults Rob had hurled at this man over the years. She mentally tallied the hours Rob had spent on the phone with him. It didn't matter if it was a weekend, their vacation, Mother's Day, their anniversary, however sacred the occasion, it always came second to whatever this man wanted. She would know it was Syed calling before Rob even answered the call. He'd look at his phone and a crease would appear on his forehead, a hidden scar drawn out by the sound of a ringtone. Then Rob would say "Sorry, gotta take this," and walk into another room. It was the same every time. Syed wasn't responsible for the state of her marriage, but he was a symptom of what was wrong with it. Rob was married to his work. Maybe he got that crease on his forehead when *she* called him too?

"I know you," Syed repeated, still stabbing his pudgy little finger at her.

"You work with my husband, Rob."

"Ah," said Syed, raising his index finger in the air. "He works for me."

"Sure, okay." Emma was keen to turn the conversation away from Rob. "So," she leaned in to be heard over the music. "You do this too." She motioned toward the ceiling.

Syed nodded. "Yes," he smiled. "In Australia, there's a lot of money in construction and alcohol. I bring them together." He laughed and looked at Kendry, who smiled encouragingly.

"Yeah," she said, "Syed's Australia's answer to Mark Cuban. Hospitality, booze and hot property. The trifecta." She rolled her eyes for Emma.

Syed shook his head. "No, no, I'm too old to be the boss here. Needs someone younger. More pretty. My nephew will do it. I just invest. And party."

Emma nodded and smiled politely, hoping her silence would give Syed the hint. She was increasingly desperate for him to leave but she couldn't be overtly rude. He was Kendry's client, another guy in a long line of self-absorbed B-listers looking to make it big. How Kendry managed their egos over the years was beyond her. She said she didn't want children, but that wasn't entirely true. She had hundreds of them, a week, a month at a time. Emma picked up her drink and felt a hand on her shoulder.

"Hey." Erik leaned in and they exchanged an awkward peck on the cheek. "You good?" She nodded.

Erik withdrew his hand from her shoulder, and she sensed an airy vacancy where it had been.

"You're Kendry, right?" Erik held out his hand. Kendry got up from her barstool. "Handshakes are for strangers and politicians, luv." She leaned in for a hug. Erik embraced her. Emma took a sip of her drink. Kendry folded into the hug and then pulled away, a long strand of her hair trailing on Erik's shoulder as they separated. "You give good hugs," she said.

"Thanks."

Syed shot out his hand. "I don't give hugs," he laughed, and looked to the others to join him. "But it's nice to meet you. Maybe you can play here," he said, rocking back on his heels. "The sound system is best on the market."

Erik followed Syed's gaze up to the ceiling and nodded back. "I'm sure we can work something out. Not tonight though."

"No, no. Now you relax. Enjoy." Syed patted Erik's shoulder like he was a dog. Syed looked over at the bartenders and gave them a little twirl of his finger. The bartender nodded. "Okay," said Syed. "You enjoy."

"Sure thing," Erik stuffed his hands into the pockets of his leather jacket. Syed whispered something in Kendry's ears and walked away, receding until he was absorbed by the dark silhouettes gathering in his night club.

"Geez," said Erik. "That guy's keen."

"Well," said Kendry, "maybe he knows quality when he sees it." She winked. Kendry handed Erik one of the fresh martinis on the bar. "A toast," she said, holding her glass high above her head. The contents dribbled. "To life in the middle ages!"

Emma gave Kendry a stern look. Kendry slurped her drink. Erik took a small sip of his and put it down on the bar. Emma gave Erik an apologetic look.

"Sorry, mate." Kendry placed a limp hand on Erik's chest. "I've asked her, but she won't tell me." She leaned in as if to whisper in Erik's ear but spoke loudly. "She doesn't tell me anything anymore. You don't have to say exactly, just gimme a ballpark. When were you born? You don't have to say the year. Just tell me, was it pre- or post-9/11?"

Emma mimed the words *what the fuck*.

"Sorry." Kendry waved her arms, the jangling of her bracelets swallowed up by the thump of the electronic beats. "My friend's telling me I'm embarrassing her."

Erik smiled nervously. "No, it's cool. I guess I don't really think about age that much."

"Hmm, is that right?" Kendry stroked her chin theatrically. "Must be nice."

"Lay off, Ken," said Emma.

Kendry wrapped her arm around Erik's arm. "Erik's a big boy, he can take care of himself." She patted his arm. "He doesn't need you to protect him from the nasty lady. Does he?"

"Look, it's fine," said Erik. "Honestly. I don't know what the big deal is. I'm twenty-nine, not that it matters. I just think there's way too much emphasis on age. Especially for you guys."

"*Us* guys?" Kendry gestured to her and Emma. "Totally, thanks for standing up for us." She gave Erik a playful jostle. "Oh, what's this," said Kendry, turning to look as two grinning young women in short skirts and tight tops shyly approached Erik. "Hello girls," Kendry beamed. "Can we help you?"

"Uhm, hi. Sorry to butt in," said the brunette, her polished little face framed by bangs cut sharp as a Lego minifigure's. "Aren't you Erik Braun?"

"Uh, yep." Erik smiled and slid his hands into the back pockets of his jeans.

The girl held up her phone. "Could we take a selfie?"

"Oh, we can do better than that," said Kendry, plucking the phone from the young girl's hand. "What's your name, dear?"

"Vanessa."

"Okay, Vanessa. And you are?"

"Phoebe."

"Well, Vanessa and Phoebe, why don't you go over there and snuggle up next to Erik and I'll take a photo of the three of you."

The girls sheepishly approached Erik.

"Hey," he said, and smiled. Those dimples. The girls glanced at him, blushed and turned to look at each other before facing the camera. Erik rested his arms on their shoulders. They leaned their bodies toward him and smiled on cue.

Kendry moved around taking pictures from different angles. "A little closer, girls. You look scared of him."

The girls reddened, nudged closer and smiled at each other. Phoebe bit her glossy bottom lip. They wrapped their arms around Erik's waist. Kendry circled them taking photos and then handed the phone back. Erik said something to them that Emma couldn't hear and the girls covered their mouths as they laughed.

They were almost children, thought Emma. And yet their gushing over Erik made her uncomfortable, not because they were young and pretty – okay, maybe a little – but mostly because the three of them were organically part of a scene she knew nothing about.

She thought of Rob and missed the security of knowing that he was on her side, that they aligned in age and experience. They shared a child, friends, cultural references; they were comfortable, could fart in each other's presence. These things mattered.

Emma's daydream was interrupted by a bartender handing her a shot glass of some clear liquid. She took it apprehensively and saw that everyone had lifted theirs, including Erik, Vanessa and Phoebe. They all shot their drinks and grimaced. Emma sipped the concoction, enduring the cold and citrusy vodka thing, whatever it was.

Erik walked over with his hands in his jacket pockets. "Hey."

"Hey." Emma put the half-empty shot glass back on the bar.

"Sorry about this," he said. "It's stupid. I know."

"No, it's okay."

Erik scratched behind his ear. "Apparently there's a whole bunch of people at a table back there." He nodded toward the back of the venue. "It's a Discord group or something. I know it's annoying, but I should probably go say hi. Do you want to head over there for just a bit? Say hello?"

Here it was. One of those moments that betrayed the age gap between them. A table of young people, his fans, and her, some hanger-on. It'd be embarrassing for them both. "Why don't you just go," she said, as softly and genuinely as she could.

"Really?"

She nodded.

"Sorry," he said. "I didn't mean for it to get weird or anything. I don't really know how to act in situations like this. It's not like it happens all the time."

"You *should* go," she said, patting him on the chest. "It's part of what you do."

"Then why do I feel like a dick doing it?"

"I don't know. You're not a dick."

He slid his arm around the small of her back. "Thanks for being cool about this."

"Of course."

He kissed her on the cheek and walked toward Phoebe and Vanessa. The three of them disappeared into the depths of the club, toward whatever happened next. Her pang of jealousy felt juvenile and perplexing. The only dignified move was to leave.

Emma walked tentatively back toward Kendry who sat there, glassy-eyed and twirling her straw inside the icy mush that remained of her drink. "What the fuck was that?" said Emma.

"What?" Kendry held the glass to her lips and used the straw to shovel pink slush into her mouth.

"Nuzzle up girls," Emma mocked. "I'll take your picture."

"I was being playful."

Emma rolled her eyes. "You were obnoxious."

"Oh please."

"Well, I think I'm going to get going." Emma stood.

Kendry put her glass down on the bar and slid it away from her reach. The bartender eyed her. She shook her head no. Kendry dabbed at her mouth with a napkin. "Sit down," she said.

"Excuse me?"

"Sit down," she said gravely. "I need to show you something."

Emma lowered herself back onto the barstool like an obedient dog.

Kendry pulled out her phone and put it face down on the bar, her golden phone case glowed under the bar lights. "I found this photo." Kendry's French manicured nails hovered over the phone case. "I don't know if I should show you, but I also think you need to see it."

Emma threw up her hands. "Now you *have* to show me."

"A warning. It's bad."

"Just let me see it." Emma reached for the phone. Kendry turned it over.

On it was a picture of Rob standing next to a tall, young woman in a hard hat. Behind them was a stone wall with the ocean visible in the distance.

"Any idea who *that* is?" said Kendry.

Emma zoomed in on the photo and shook her head. The young woman was striking. Beautiful, in a rugged sort of way, dressed in jeans and work boots, her crimpy dark hair flowing out the back of her hard hat.

The most remarkable part of the photograph was Rob. His face. Emma zoomed in and out on her husband's expression several times. He looked relaxed, younger, as if a great weight had been lifted from him. He looked happy.

"He is *so* banging her." Kendry picked up her drink, saw it was empty and put it down again.

"What do you know about it?" Emma zoomed out of the photo to frame Rob and the young woman together. You could tell she had a nice body, even though it was hidden under a puffy orange vest.

"Just telling you the truth," said Kendry.

"No, you're just being shitty now." Emma hated when Kendry got like this. There was such a fine line between her being the life of the party and being a mean drunk. Why couldn't she just stay on the wagon once and for all?

Emma took a last look at the photograph of the woman. How was she supposed to compete with that? If that's what he wanted, good luck to him. She handed the phone back to Kendry.

"Hey, you can't be that surprised," said Kendry. "And you can't really blame him. I mean, what's good for the goose is good for the gander?"

"You know what?" Emma stood. "I don't need this tonight."

Kendry chuckled. "Oh, come on, Em. There's no need to be so fucking dramatic. Sit down."

Emma gathered her purse from the hook under the bar.

"You're actually leaving?" Kendry woozily leaned back on her stool. "Okay, that's cool. Did I 'offend' you?" she air quoted. "Seriously, grow up."

"Me?" Emma hissed. "You know what, get your shit together, Ken. I mean it."

"Ha." Kendry's head drooped as if it suddenly got heavier. "Pot. Meet kettle. You're just mad because your toy boy found a younger kitten to paw."

Emma grabbed her coat. "You can be such a cow."

"And *you* can be *sooo* needy."

"You're pushing it, Ken. Don't act like I'll always come back."

"Pffft. Sweetheart, I don't know if you've noticed, but I'm all you have left."

Emma slung her bag over her shoulder. "Dry up, would ya." She brushed past Kendry, and pushed through the bodies now mashed together in the venue. Erik was in there someplace, with his harem. It'd been so easy for him to abandon her. She stormed out of the club, past the glorious doorman in his gold embroidery and the well-groomed people waiting for permission to come inside.

Emma lay in Kendry's mom's old bed trying to fall asleep. Margaret hadn't died here. She passed in hospital. But this is where she suffered. Emma switched on the too-tall pedestal lamp on the bedside table and it cast sinister double shadows on the wall. Why didn't that bloody TV work? She just wanted to flip channels, anything to fill the silence of Kendry's empty house, but the knot of dusty cables at the back of the TV/DVD unit was too daunting. Rob always handled that kind of stuff. She flicked off the light, pulled the blankets up to her chin, hugged the second pillow and soon drifted into a shallow sleep.

Emma woke to rattling and rustling in the kitchen, the clinking of glass bottles, the thump of the refrigerator door. She squinted at the digital clock. 3:27.

Kendry was out there, shuffling around, opening and closing cupboards. The murmur of voices on the TV soon came through the wall. Emma turned onto her side, put the pillow over her head, then turned over on her other side. She closed her eyes but sleep felt impossible. She pushed the quilt off and put on her dressing gown.

The blue light of the television glowed on the cream walls of the hallway. The house was cold and Emma balled her hands inside the pockets of her dressing gown.

She found Kendry in the loungeroom, her head flopped back on the arm of the sofa, the flicker of the TV like a strobe light in the dark room. Some cooking show. Cutting onions.

Kendry snored, an open bottle of white wine on the coffee table. Emma found a blanket and draped it over Kendry and her eyes opened suddenly, dark and vacant as a shark's. She murmured something unintelligible before her eyeballs rolled back into her head and she passed out again.

Emma took the bottle of wine from the coffee table and returned it to the fridge. She left Kendry with a large glass of water, just as she used to do for her father. It was hard to let people be themselves.

CHAPTER TWENTY-FOUR

The table saw screeched and the spinning blade shuddered to a halt. Rob looked up from the timber he was leaning over. Across the spiky edges of the circular blade, he could see Sareena ambling toward him from the long grass at the cliff's edge. She was on her phone, laughing in an exaggerated way, tilting her head back, hand circling as she spoke. He could only faintly hear what she was saying, but it sounded cheerful. If it wasn't for the hard hat, she might be someone out for a walk in the park.

Rob replayed his recent conversations with Syed. He didn't like keeping Sareena in the dark. But Syed held the purse strings. What he said is how it went. That's just how the world worked.

Sareena looked over at Rob as she drew closer and gave him a thumbs up and pointed to her phone.

Why take a call now? There was shit to do. He straightened himself and leaned back, kneading the small of his back where the kinks gathered.

Sareena smiled again and pointed at her phone. "Oh, that's so awesome…," she said to whoever was on the other end. "No, really, *so* great."

It seemed most things were "awesome" to Sareena, whether it was a sunset, a mitered edge or a vegetarian pizza. She nodded again and gave Rob an enthusiastic thumbs up. Rob was only half listening to what she was saying. It set a bad example for her to be on her phone all the time. No phones outside break times. That was another rule.

"Really," she grinned, still engrossed in her conversation. "Yup… No, you've made my day, seriously… You're going to love it… That's fine, whatever works for you guys."

Rob picked up a plank of LVL timber and dropped it on the saw plate, letting her know that *he* was working while *she* was on the phone.

"Yeah…," she said, turning her back to him. "Yeah…yeah… yeah…No, totally…Okay. Awesome. Thanks so much…Okay… Bye." She turned back to face Rob, hunched over his plank of wood. "Guess who that was?"

Rob gave her a sideways glance.

"That was the editor of *Home Design*! They want to do an article for the magazine." She fist pumped the air.

"An article about what?"

She gave him a playful shove. "About the build, ya nob. I reached out and they said yes."

Rob straightened the plank of wood on the table. "Yeah, but I mean what about it? What do they want to know?"

"Do you seriously *not* know this magazine? They're all about the journey. Before. After," she said. "They'll want to get some of the history of the place, find out how we're restoring it, get some before-and-after shots. It's a big deal!" She pumped her fist again. "You should be proud."

Rob placed his aluminum speed square against the piece of timber for the door frame he was building. Sareena said the tool was "old school," that it looked like some pyramid-looking contraption he'd stolen from a masonic lodge or something, it was so old and scuffed. But it was one of the few useful things he'd inherited from the old man. It felt substantial in his hands and was stamped *Made in Australia,* as things used to be. Young tradies never properly understood the value of the thing. He knew they privately mocked him for the way he wandered around site using his speed square to check angles on freshly laid timber. Even though Sareena joked about it too, Rob knew she appreciated its value. She may not have been as fanatical as he was about plumb lines and sharp edges, but she had her own obsessions: salvaging, repurposing, period accuracy. It sometimes gave him the shits the way she clung to materials he thought were well past their use-by date, but he could respect her devotion to doing things right as she saw them.

Rob slid his speed square up the side of a fresh plank of timber and fished out the chewed-up pencil that lived behind his ear. He licked his pencil and scribed a sharp line on the wood. "I don't really like people poking around in my business until the work's done."

"Oh, stop being a fusspot. It's a nice story and we're doing good work here." Sareena looked up at the repointed stone facade of the house. "It's going to look fucking ace. Plus, to be a little selfish about it, me and the girls could use the exposure. I haven't been in the game as long as you and if I can't close deals, my crew don't eat."

Why was that suddenly *his* problem? He didn't want some magazine poking around here. He'd told her that. That should have been the end of discussion. Did Syed know about this *Home Design* article thing? What would he say? It was *him* that insisted on Sareena being part of this project. *He's* the one who gave her more control than Rob was comfortable with. Now some magazine was prying around. They'd want to see the building plans. This couldn't end well.

Rob had been ready to treat this job like any other. Sareena and her crew were making that difficult, the way they poured themselves into the work. It was admirable, but they were too invested in the outcome of this project, the way they personified the house as "Marge," the fine old lady who lives by the sea, who was growing old gracefully but needed some attention. The way they joked about "her" needing a facelift, how "she" needed a chiropractor, a new frock, a hat. It all suggested they'd grown too attached to what they were doing here, and Rob knew from experience that it would cost them time and money in the end. *Get in. Get out. Get paid.* That's how this business worked.

For all her expertise, Sareena was still naive, and treated this project like she was personally invested in every detail, reviewing each decision made at any stage of the build, regardless of what it meant for the schedule and the budget. Some decisions you lived with. Once you built them, you didn't go back and undo the work you'd done for a change of heart. Decisions led you to a certain point and you worked with where you got to from then on. Forward momentum, that's what got the job done on time and on budget.

He could respect Sareena's fastidiousness. It was her creativity that worried him. The way she kept adding extras to the brief: a hand-carved lintel here, a commissioned sculpture there by some stonemason she knew who could carve a "cute little gargoyle," as if construction was something entirely organic, grown at the pace of her imagination. She had to learn to separate herself from her client, otherwise she'd burn bridges, that is if she didn't burn herself out first. Keep money in the budget and fuel in your tank, he'd tell her. There was a fine line between pride in your work and wasting time chasing perfection. Knowing the difference was the key to success and self-preservation.

"Well," he said, "if you're struggling to make ends meet, then maybe you should do some more commercial stuff, not just these handmade jobbies. I could put a word in with some of the developers—"

"Nah." Her hands slid into the back pockets of her jeans. "Look, thanks, I get what you're saying, but I'm trying to do something here. Trying to change some of the ways this industry works." She put her hands on her hips and looked at the building trash piled high in the dumpster. "There's just too much fucking waste." She shook her head.

Rob smiled.

"What?" said Sareena. "You probably think that's naive."

"Well, it's fine. It's good. It's just…you ever work with one of those big building consortiums?" He wiped his forehead with the back of his hand. "They don't even look at materials, you know, just spreadsheets. They don't build, really. They account. Pick battles you can win."

She sighed. "I just want to make shit that lasts. Buildings that mean something to people. Even if it sinks me, I need to know I tried."

It all sounded young and idealistic to Rob, a speech by someone who had little to lose and time on their side. But he didn't want to hurt Sareena's feelings. He looked up at Jacqui and Kim, high on their ladders, scraping mortar from the hanging plastic buckets that bumped against the stone as they finished repointing the facade of the house. "And what about them?" he said. "I mean, they've got to eat."

Sareena rubbed her hands to warm them. "They're with me," she said, without looking at him."

Rob hunched back over his circular saw and winced, put his hand on the small of his back.

"You right?" said Sareena.

"Fine," said Rob, digging his thumb into his lower back.

"You should get that looked at."

"It'll sort itself out."

"Hasn't so far. Go to a physio, get a massage or something. No use groaning and hobbling around. That's not tough, man, that's stupid."

"I'll be right." Rob leaned over the table saw again.

Sareena's phone chimed. She fished it out of her pocket and frowned. "You got to take care of yourself," she said, typing without looking up. "A man your age." She walked off in her puffy orange vest, into the house where Rob's new wall frame was up, the studs arranged neat and symmetrical as fish bones.

Rob adjusted the piece of timber. The saw screamed back to life.

He spent the morning in his comfort zone, marking and framing timber planks. A burst of warmth from the sun drew sweat from his brow and coaxed out the sharp medicinal fragrance of freshly cut timber as he snipped and shaped it with a chisel and saw. Whenever the machine stopped whirring, the ambient sound yielded to the distant murmur of the ocean and the scraping of metal trowels against stone as Jacqui and Kim, small as dolls way up their scaffold, wedged the last bits of mortar into the stone facade. Over there, by the overgrown lawn, Alex's veiny arms carried plastic buckets, heavy with wet cement, to reinforce the house's ancient foundations. Jemma leisurely raked gravel into a drip edge along the exterior walls. The house was coming back to life and he appreciated the earnestness with which Sareena's team committed themselves to their tasks.

An icy wind blasted in from the sea. Rob shielded his eyes and looked up at the flapping plastic tarp that still covered the roof. He'd soon have to explain to Sareena why he'd knocked back her roofer for another three weeks. She deserved to know.

CHAPTER TWENTY-FIVE

Erik joined Emma in his bed, wrapping the sheets loosely around himself. Emma turned toward him. "Thanks for letting me stay, it'll only be a couple of days."

"It's all good." Erik smiled. "I like to help the homeless."

"Fuck off," she said playfully. "I'm not homeless. I'm just giving Kendry some space. I can go someplace else if it's too much. I'm not here to cramp your style or whatever. It's just a short term—"

"It's okay," he cooed. "Seriously, it's not a big deal. Stay as long as you need. I've got gigs coming up anyway, I'm barely here when I'm touring."

Emma looked around at the studio apartment, even smaller than her place, and extra cramped from all the metal storage boxes he kept his music stuff in. Erik moved onto his side, propped himself on his elbow. "So, what happened?

"Ugh, it just wasn't bearable at the house with her. She's just − well, you met her."

Erik smiled. "She seemed okay, kind of kooky, but nice."

Well, she's… I don't know. I don't want to talk about her right now, it's taking up too much headspace."

"Okay." Erik lay back. "Why don't you tell me more about, Rob," he said, stretching his arm behind his back, the skin taught over his biceps, his chest.

"What for?" She looked away.

"Because…" He shuffled toward her, his weight barely making the bedsprings move. "You don't talk about him much."

"Why would I?" she glanced at him. "That'd be kind of weird."

"Isn't it more weird *not* to talk about him? Besides," he yawned, "I'm curious."

Emma sat up. "Okay, what do you want to know?"

Erik moved closer. "I don't know. The usual stuff. Like, where'd you meet, how'd you get together."

Emma looked at Erik with surprise.

"What?" he smiled. "I'm just interested, it's not a conspiracy."

Emma's face tensed. She sank down into the mattress, turned away from Erik and teared up, disoriented by feelings of fear and guilt. Could she still do right by Rob? Or Will? Or Erik? All three of them if that was still possible? Or had she let things go too far, miscalculated the cost of her desire? If she could just lie here and do nothing, then maybe everything could still be okay.

"You alright?" Erik's voice restored Emma's need for composure.

She hastily wiped her eyes with her hand. "I'm okay," she sniffed. "I just…ah," she sighed, pressed her palms against her eyes.

He shuffled closer, put his hand on her arm. "You sure you're okay?"

Emma turned to face Erik. He looked so nice, lying there with his fresh, smooth skin and his warm, earnest eyes, longing for connection. He didn't deserve to be pulled into the messiness of her life. It was greedy and irresponsible of her to draw him in like this. It had already gone further than it should have. And yet it felt so good to be looked at this way, to be desired, to feel someone trying. "What is this?" she said, softly.

"What do you mean?"

"This," she said, waving her hand between them. "Like, what are we doing?"

"We're talking."

Emma shot him a look that said, *seriously*.

"What?" he smiled. "Why does it matter so much?" Erik looked at her quizzically. "Like, why is defining this so important to you?"

"Because." She looked up at the ceiling. "Maybe when you're a twenty-nine-year-old guy it doesn't matter, but when you're a forty-something woman it really does."

"Why?"

"You know, asking *why* after I say something doesn't automatically make it a meaningful question."

"Okaaay."

"It just matters. Trust me." She pulled the sheet up to her chest.

"No, why?" He sniggered.

"It's not funny." She playfully slapped his shoulder.

"Well, it's *kind of* funny."

"What is?"

"You getting bent out of shape because you can't accept that I just like being with you."

"I'm not bent out of shape."

"Oh, okay."

"It's a fair question right? I mean, what *can* this be, really?"

He moved closer toward her, his hand, his arm a soothing weight on her hip. "Why does it have to *be* something? Like, why can't it just be what it is?"

"What is that? One of your song lyrics? I'm serious."

"Me too." Erik shuffled even closer, until she could feel the heat of him against the back of her thigh. "Look, I like you. That's something. It feels real. And I know that whatever else happens it's—"

"Yes, but *why* do you like me. Is it some weird fetish? Are you into moms or something?"

Erik laughed. "I'm not into *moms*." He shimmied closer, pressed up against her. "Look, do you like hanging out with me?"

Surely this was the moment to end things. It had been fun. But it was going too far now. When Dr Priya talked about finding ways of feeling beautiful, feeling sexy, she'd meant it rhetorically. She didn't mean this. This was dangerous. It risked destroying everything she'd built in her life.

But Emma *did* feel sexy. She felt alive, the tingle in her body, animated by the same life force that made trees grow and bee wings flutter, the same power that set the universe in motion stirred in her.

"Gee, that's taking a long time to answer," he joshed.

"Sorry." She turned to face him. "This *is* fun."

"Okay, so why can't we just let that ride?"

"Yeah," she said, too quickly. "Wait." She sat up. "What does that mean?" His expression looked puzzled. She closed her eyes, tried to form words from the jumbled thoughts in her head. "I'm not saying I want to be your…whatever…ah, fuck, the words are coming out all wrong. Look, I'm married, so I'm not looking for a thing. I guess I'm trying to figure out what this means for you. Like, are you seeing other people at the same time or are we not supposed to? Help me out here, I don't know what the rules are. This isn't something I've done for a really long time."

Erik grinned. "The *rules*?" He chuckled.

"You know what I mean. The social convention or whatever."

"Well," he said, rubbing her leg, "I usually like to ask a girl to a ball and then seal the deal with a romantic horse-drawn carriage ride through the park before meeting her parents—"

"Shut up." She teasingly slapped his arm. "I'm serious. I'm just trying to figure out what's going on here. Why would you want to be with me?"

He rubbed his hand over his face. "Why ask me that? Because I'm younger, I need a special reason to want to be here?"

She pretended to think about it. "Yeah, kind of."

He smiled wider. "That's so fucked up." He propped himself on his side, elbow on the mattress, head in the palm of his hand. "But if *you* were the younger one, then it wouldn't be a question."

"Probably not."

"That's so sexist." He grinned.

"Is it?" She scrunched up her face, playfully mocking him. "Yes, I'm taking advantage of an unfair double standard." She moved her face closer to his.

"You are." He blinked rapidly in mock indignation. "And frankly, I'm offended."

"Well," she said, moving close enough to feel his breath on her skin, "that's just tough shit then, isn't it?"

She kissed him and felt the cool spaces in the bed where the tousled sheets had kept their skin from touching. He rubbed his feet against hers, transferring the warmth of his body into the chilliness of her own.

"Is it really so hard," he whispered, "for you to believe that when I look at you, I like what I see." He kissed her shoulder. "That I like you because you're funny." He kissed her neck. "Because you're thoughtful." He kissed her cheek. "Because you know what you want." He kissed her mouth. "And because you're this intense ball of energy just waiting to explode."

"A ball of energy?" She craned her neck to look at him "Well, I guess it's better than me reminding you of your mom."

"What's with the moms?" He smiled. "You're the one with the

mom fetish, I reckon."

"I'm not."

"You should know…" He kissed her shoulder. "My mom teaches art history at Monash." He kissed her neck. "She drinks too much, works too hard and we get along great for a day or so, and then we start giving each other the shits."

Emma turned to face him. "No mommy issues?"

"No mommy issues." He kissed her on the mouth and laced his fingers in hers, his hands so soft and smooth against her skin compared to Rob's calloused hands. Erik held her fingers against his own cheek. "Hey, I've been meaning to ask you something."

"What?"

"I've got a gig in Melbourne next month. I'd like you to come."

"Oh." She untangled her fingers from his hand and rubbed her face, then sank back into the pillow and threw her arm across her forehead. "I can't go to a concert," she sighed. "I'm not groupie material."

Erik sat up on his knees and gently peeled Emma's arm off her face. "Hey," he said quietly. "It's not a groupie thing." He stroked her hair and tucked it behind her ear. "It's a fun thing." He traced her lips with his thumb. "You remember fun?" He kissed her forehead, her nose, her mouth. Emma softened.

Erik lifted the sheets. "Now, what's this?"

The Brazilian, which had seemed fun and playful, now seemed kind of desperate and presumptuous. She felt vulnerable, compounding the anxiousness she already felt about her body.

"It's sexy. But I liked you before too."

"Well," she said lightheartedly. "I didn't do it for you."

"No?"

"No, I did it for me." She rolled onto her side, facing away from him. "So, it doesn't matter if you don't like it."

"I do like it." He shuffled up behind her, rubbed her shoulder, the side of her arm. "Hey," he whispered. "What do you want me to do right now? What's some crazy shit you've always wanted to try but were afraid to ask for?"

Emma craned her neck and squinted. "You know what I really want?"

"Tell me." He moved closer, spooning her.

"Just to lie here."

"Okay." He held her close, burrowed his face into the back of Emma's neck.

"No." She tapped his legs behind her. "I want you to face me. Like this," she turned around and pulled him toward her. "That's it." He shuffled back. "Don't squirm away," she said. "Just lie here and look at me."

"Okay," he swallowed.

"Feel a bit weird?" she said.

He nodded, adjusted his head on the pillow. "This is some freaky shit."

"Just give it a second," she said.

He made googly eyes before settling into her gaze.

"See," she said. "Isn't that nice?"

"Hmmm."

She laughed.

"What?" He blushed.

"Well," she smiled. "It's hard to concentrate with your dick poking into my leg."

He grinned, peeled back the sheets and disappeared under the covers.

CHAPTER TWENTY-SIX

Rob noticed the snarling bear tattoo before he noticed the kid's face. He tried not to be obvious about it, but he couldn't help staring at the huge head of a grizzly bear that took up the whole of the kid's muscly front leg. It was an impressive sight walking toward him in the gloom of the stone house at dawn, almost as if the bear was charging toward him from the hallway. As he approached, Rob could see the guy and the bear more clearly. The beast's snarling teeth and open jaws were centered on his knee, so the animal's muzzle protruded like an actual snout. Rob didn't much like tattoos, but he had to admit this one was a work of art. The "kid," now that he walked into the relative brightness of the open living room, was probably in his mid-twenties, and he was checking out the wall framing Rob had completed a few days ago. "Nice," he said, nodding in appreciation. "Not everyone uses LVL for wall studs."

"Well," said Rob, "I wouldn't use anything else."

"No, totally," said the bear guy. "I'd go engineered timber every time."

"Stronger," they both said at the same time.

"Jinx," said the guy.

"Rob," said Sareena, coming up the dark hallway and slipping her phone into the pocket of her puffy vest. "This is Aaron. The electrician I was telling you about."

"How are you, mate." Rob stuck out his hand and Aaron shook it, a good firm grip. "That's some tattoo," said Rob, letting go of Aaron's hand.

"Thanks." Aaron looked down at himself, as if appreciating the bear for the first time. "Took ages. And hurt like hell."

"I bet." Rob grimaced, though he had no real sense of how much pain a tattoo represented.

"So," Sareena interjected. "What do you reckon, Rob? I was thinking Aaron could start laying cable downstairs, even though I'm not happy with the state of the roof yet."

"I know," said Rob. "We'll sort it out today."

"Good," she said, and turned back to face Aaron. "So, Aaron, we won't do upstairs today, but just cable down here like it's going upstairs, yeah. I know it's a bit ass backward, but that's how we're doing it."

"Yup, no worries." Aaron looked around, hands on his hips. "Geez, it's bigger than you think from the outside."

"Ninety-four square," said Rob.

"Yeah," said Sareena. "Well, it's twice as big as your average miner's cottage back then, but still way smaller than your average house today. Go figure."

"I can see what you're doing here, opening it up and that," Aaron said, scanning the stonework up to the high ceiling. "Looks sweet." He ran his fingers down the face of the speckled granite blocks. "Definitely don't make them like this anymore." His head swiveled around, taking the place in. "It's beautiful." Aaron then clapped his hands. "So, where's the circuit board?"

"It's out back," said Sareena. "In the shed. Come on, I'll show you."

"Sweet. You reckon I can park me truck back there?"

"Tons of room," said Sareena. "Just pull up next to the storage container. You can't miss it."

"Too easy." Aaron trotted to the front door. His heavy footsteps crunched on the gravel outside.

"Seems like a good kid," said Rob.

"Yeah, he's good. You'll like him, he lays cable symmetrically." She made a "peace sign" with her fingers and brought them together until they touched. "Even if the wire's going behind a wall, it's got to be neat. He can't have a crease or a wonky line in them. Bit OCD, like you."

Rob nodded in approval.

"So," said Sareena. "Can we finally talk out this roof thing or what?"

Rob put up his hands. "Let me frame up these last internal walls first, then we'll talk about it."

"Rob," she said impatiently.

"Just give me the afternoon. I need to get this done, especially if Aaron's laying cable down here. He's going to want to go through the stud work."

"Fine. You really are a pain in the ass, mate. You know that?" she half joked.

"I know. I get that a lot."

"Yeah, well." She walked off, fished her phone out of her vest pocket, the blue light illuminating the dim hallway as her silhouette receded. "I want that roof sealed," she called over her shoulder.

"I know." He called after her. "And you'll get it."

She raised her middle finger over the back of her shoulder.

Rob smiled, picked his tool belt off the floor and buckled it around his waist. He looked up at the cavity of the second floor through the naked floor joists, where patches of subfloor on the second story served as a walkway. He picked up his screw gun and started putting up the wall for what would be the downstairs bedroom, eyeing the chalk mark on the stonework where the engineer would install the steel beam next week. He couldn't keep Sareena in the dark anymore. Syed was the real boss. He got what he wanted.

Aaron's van revved outside, the engine growling as he backed over the lumpy soil to the soggy dirt patch out back. Things were happening.

Rob turned the music up on the boom box. He liked Tom Petty. That guy played the kind of happy–sad music Rob liked. Why didn't people make music like *that* anymore?

Rob took a deep, cleansing breath. The weight of the tool belt around his waist, the shape of the screw gun's trigger, firm against his finger, these things made Rob feel like a warrior, a man with a calling. The crack of the screw gun, the clomp of hard timber under his feet and the voice of Tom Petty, whatever else was going on, in this moment, right here, everything was okay.

He thought of Emma and hoped that she was doing okay too, wherever she was at this moment, and that she was finding whatever it was she was looking for. He felt saddened by the possibility that she was out there, thinking ill of him, when all he wanted was for her to be happy. But what if *her* happiness depended on their being apart? It didn't bear thinking about and so he poured himself into his work.

The morning passed and the wall went up, just as he'd planned it. The downstairs floor plan made sense now. Gone were the dinky little rooms, replaced by open spaces, a good-sized kitchen, a bathroom and a bedroom, all of which could now drink in the ocean view.

At lunch Rob sat out front, slicing wedges off an apple with his pocketknife. Will was rubbing his hands on the legs of his jeans, wiping off the grease from his toasted sandwich when Sareena pulled up in her truck. "Oi," she said to Will. "Get in." Will shot Rob a quizzical look. Rob nodded.

Will turned to Sareena. "Where we going?"

"Down to San Remo," she said. "Picking up an antique copper basin I found online. I need a hand getting it in the truck." Will stepped up into the vehicle, the big truck registering the addition of his weight. He was getting bigger, stronger.

"Need anything else while we're out there," called Sareena through the open window. "Timber screws or what not?"

Rob shook his head. "Thanks. I've got what I need."

"Sweet," said Sareena. "See you in a bit."

Rob waved them off. The site seemed emptier with them gone.

He finished his lunch and got back to work. He noticed a few of the women making unusual and unnecessary trips inside the house. Jacqui and Kim, who'd been on their ladders, outside, almost the whole time they'd been on the job, suddenly found reasons to poke around the inside of the building for "color matching" or to "get out of the wind." But Rob knew they were really in there to have a peek at Aaron, bending and stretching to lay cable in his short shorts. He let them have their fun and they eventually returned to their posts. It'd been a long time since anyone looked at him the way those women looked at Aaron.

Will returned from the village of San Remo excited. Sareena showed Rob the beaten copper wash basin, which he conceded would look *awesome* in the kitchen. Handcrafted, built to last.

Sareena was chummy with his son, put her arm around his shoulder as she told the story of how Will had spotted an old barn door outside a thrift shop that he thought would look cool on the wooden shed out back. Rob cast an eye over the solid door, strapped down in the back of the truck. It was heavily patinaed with layers of ancient paint, chipped and peeling so you could almost see all the different colors at once. The timber had been smoothed by generations of hands opening and closing that door.

"He's got a good eye," said Sareena, patting Will on the back. He blushed.

Rob was pleased. It was a great day, the kind where the crew hummed like a machine, where work got done and people took pride in their labors. It's days like these when loads felt lighter, progress seemed faster, and their team was tighter than it had been when they started a few months ago. The job had a sense of momentum now, and the comradery was palpable, even as people started peeling away for the weekend, waving from the windows of their vintage trucks, their mirror shine no longer visible as they made their way up the hill in the early dusk.

"Any of youse going back to Melbourne?" said Aaron, sliding his toolbox into the back of his van.

"How far you going?" said Will.

"Well, where d'you live?"

"Uh, Carlton."

"Hop in."

"You sure? It's a bit of a way."

"It's all good. I'm going past there anyway. Hey, Rob," said Aaron, "d'you need a hand getting that villaboard upstairs or—"

"Nah, thanks, Aaron. It's all in the container, right?"

"Yup."

"Good, said Rob. "Just leave it there. We'll deal with it later."

"Sweet." Aaron took his hard hat off and tossed it in the back of his van. "So," he wiped his brow, "you want me back next week then, start roughing in upstairs?"

Rob could almost feel the collective desire of the women wishing he'd say yes.

"Not going to need you next week, mate. We've got a few things to sort out up there. How you looking a few weeks from now?"

Aaron nodded. "Should be right."

"Okay. I'll give you a call."

Aaron got into the white van, which looked a little plain and small next to Sareena's giant purple Ford with its knobbly tire treads.

"See you next week," said Will, getting in the passenger side.

"Take care, mate," said Rob. "Be good."

The van pulled out of the field, its headlights illuminating the sparse trees on either side of the path up the hill.

Apart from Sareena and Rob, only Alex was left, piling usable bits of stray timber into the shipping container.

"Beer, Al?" said Sareena.

"Nah, just going to finish up here and get going, but youse go ahead."

"Sure?"

"Yeah, honestly just want to get home, have a shower."

"Cool. Well thanks for this week, darl," said Sareena. "You have a good weekend."

The place felt quiet inside now that nearly everyone had gone. Rob and Sareena looked up at the ceiling beams. He'd make something beautiful of this place.

This part of a build, where the full scale of the project came together, always made him grateful for the order taking shape within the chaos. It made him think back to his childhood home, a crooked unit at the bottom of a long, sloped driveway where the rain collected. The main sewer point for the whole complex converged into the narrow courtyard at the back of his place, where the sewer pipes connected to the city's main waste point. The wastewater from every flush and bath and sink in the whole complex ran to that sewer point. From his bedroom, he could hear the evening flushes slithering down the pipes, the constant flow of hidden turds streaming toward his house like an army of legless ants. His home was where the shit collected. And he resented it. It made him feel poor.

"Get over it," his dad would say when he complained about the stink, and then tell him again about how, when *he* was a boy, he used the pages of a telephone book hanging off a hook in the backyard outhouse to wipe *his* ass.

Whatever. Dad would be on the road again soon, on his way to Perth or Darwin or wherever. "What are you hauling this time, Dad?" Rob would ask.

But his father always said the same thing, "I'm haulin' ass son, that's what."

Mom worried about Bill out there, catnapping on the side of the road. "It's not right," she'd say. But Rob liked thinking of his dad out there, someplace, driving through the night while Rob lay in bed. It felt better, somehow, knowing someone was out there, awake, keeping an eye on things. "Whatever you do," the old man used to say, "do it right."

What about his marriage? Had the old man done that right? Had Rob?

Sareena plopped down next to Rob and handed him a can of cold beer.

"Thanks." Rob held the can way out in front of him. "Montgomery's Pale Ale," he read aloud, turning the beer in his hands. "Never heard of it." He cracked the tab, hoisted the can to his lips and tipped it back, the cool froth refreshing after a long day. "Hmm, don't mind that." He licked his lips. "That's nice."

"Reckon we deserve it."

"Fuck yeah we do." Rob took another swallow and leaned his head against the wall.

Sareena took a gulp of her own beer. "I reckon you got a good kid there, mister."

"Yeah?"

Sareena nodded, adjusted herself on the floor, crossed and uncrossed her legs. "It's just hard being young. You remember?"

Rob frowned. "What are you talking about? I had a great time."

"Hmm." Sareena gave him a wry smile. "I bet you did."

Rob sipped his Montgomery's. "What was yours like?" he said. "Your childhood?"

Sareena rested her back against the wall. "It was short, you know. I grew up in Lebanon, so…" She nodded slowly, somberly.

"Right," said Rob, vaguely remembering Lebanon had been in the news. He couldn't recall why, exactly. *Something to do with a war?* He felt dumb asking. "That must have been tough," he said, ashamed to know so little about the hardships she'd probably endured. Whatever they were, she didn't deserve them.

"What makes you stronger, right?" she said.

Rob tried to look at Sareena, but she was looking down at the floor. "I hope that's true," he said.

Sareena looked up. "Me too," she smiled, and toasted the air with her beer can.

They drank, the glugs of Montgomery's Pale Ale audible in the quiet room.

Rob wiped his mouth with his sleeve. "So, you reckon Will's alright?"

Sareena wiped her mouth with the back of her hand. "I think so. I'm not the kid's therapist or anything." She stretched her legs out, the sole of her work boots kicked at some building detritus on the floor. "Think he's got a crush is all."

"Oh yeah?" Rob smiled to himself. "Good for him. Anyone I know?"

"Uhm." Sareena pulled her knees toward her torso, rested her arms on her knees. "Not sure it's for me to say. My bad for bringing it up."

"Don't sweat it." Rob looked down at his beer can, wiped his finger at sawdust floating in the trough of the rim. He looked over at Sareena from the side of his face. She was taking a long drink. "Think I know who it might be," he said. "The crush."

"Oh." Her eyes widened.

Rob looked at Sareena, cleared his throat. "Any chance it's that boy, Aaron?"

Sareena looked away, made a grimace. "You didn't hear nothing from me."

Rob sank the last of his Montgomery's and nodded to himself. "Well, okay." He wiped his mouth, lightly squeezed the aluminum can so the metal clicked in his hands.

"Does that freak you out?" said Sareena.

Rob stopped clicking the can. He pulled his legs up close to his body and glanced up at the ceiling beams. "No." He twirled the empty can in his palm. "His mom thought it might be the case, so I'm not shocked."

Sareena nodded slowly. "So, you alright?"

"Yeah," he sighed. "I just feel bad for him, you know." He looked down at the label on his beer, the mustachioed ship captain. "Life's tough enough as is. You throw that on top…"

Sareena's looked down at the ground. "That's a decent thing to say," she said. She shook her head slowly. "Wish I'd had a dad like you is all I'm going to say."

"I wouldn't go that far," he smiled. "I've had my moments." He burped. "Believe me."

"Oh, I believe you. I definitely believe that shit."

He smiled, mentally replaying some of the moments he was least proud of. How he'd resented Emma, back when Will was a baby, the way she'd hold him up the minute he walked in the door from work and say "Your turn" after he'd just spent a day in the muck of a construction site and all he wanted was to have a shower. Rob thought of the cruel way he'd made fun of Emma's salt lamps, her herbal teas, yoga mats or diet fads, the stuff he lumped together as her "new age shit" when she was just trying to get through the day as much as he was.

This rift between him and Emma seemed more real, somehow, with new and harsh dimensions. It wasn't just Emma he'd lose, but the entirety of the life they'd built together, everything he thought he'd worked so hard to gain for them both. Rob still could not pinpoint the moment when things had started to go wrong between them. Could it still be put right? He looked up at the dark void of the roof.

Sareena followed Rob's gaze along the ceiling beams. "You get hard on wood, eh?"

He looked at her, puzzled.

"Timber," she said. "It's, like, your thing."

"Oh, right." He stretched his legs out and leaned his head back against the wall, looking up at the roughly hewn timber rafters above them. "I like that you can't do whatever you want to it. Timber's not a fiber glass mold, you can't just make whatever shape you want out of it. It's more like a puzzle. To work it you have to understand it. Is it hard, like jarrah? Or soft wood, like hoop pine? You start by asking yourself, what do I *need* it to be? Do I need it to hold something up? Like a lintel. If so, you need to make that piece of wood comfortable enough to carry that load for a long time, couple hundred years, maybe. So, you start by looking at the wood. Run your hand along it. How does the grain flow? Are there notches? What part of the tree did it come from? And that wood, it'll talk to you. Not in words, but in its own language. You tap on it, you smell it, and decide if it's the right piece. Is it too young, too old, too wet, too dry? What does *it* want to be? And does what it *is* match what you *need*? It's a conversation. Here, look." He reached over and handed Sareena an offcut from an original floor joist. "Any idiot can saw that in half or screw a metal bracket onto it. But that's not letting that piece of wood be itself. To do that you need to understand it, work with what it'll give you. Those castles and temples out there, still standing on their original timbers…that's how they do it. Because someone spoke wood."

Sareena raised her eyebrows. "Wow," she said. "That was kinda deep." She smiled.

"Yep," said Rob, pulling himself back up to his feet, "I'm full of surprises."

"Hey, hold up," said Sareena, reaching for her phone. "Let me snap you."

"Nah, come on."

"No, it looks cool with the beams behind you and everything."

Rob looked up at the roof, his eyes tracing the lines of the beams. "They're nice. But they're coming out."

"Wait. What do you mean they're coming out?"

"They're no good." He pointed at the roof line. "Rot's gone through them. Can't hold up much longer."

"Since when?"

"Ages."

"What the fuck are you talking about? The wood's fine. It's the soul of the building. If some is water damaged, we'll just use reclaimed timber to fill the gaps. I've got loads of the stuff."

"Not using wood at all."

"No?" She frowned.

"Nah," he said. "Glass roof. Well, glass cube, really. Cantilevered. Plan's approved."

"Since when?"

"Before you got here."

"Bullshit."

"No, it's true."

Sareena crossed her arms. "I've seen a lot of plans for this place. Not one of them mentioned a glass motherfucking roof."

"Late addition. It wasn't part of the original plan." He handed Sareena a bundle of crinkled architectural paperwork.

She flipped pages, scanning subsections and amendments as she went. "This here is bullshit. No fucking way this got approved."

"Well, it did."

"Oh yeah?" She stood up. "We'll see about that."

"This isn't *your* place." Rob got up off the floor. "We don't tell the architect his job. Or the owner. We just build the fucking thing."

"Oh, is that how you see it? Really. See, I don't get that from you. I thought you were all quality."

"Look," Rob said, putting put his hands up in surrender, "doing good work is one thing. But we don't call the shots. The sooner you get that, the better this goes. Less headaches."

"Nah." She shook her head. "This doesn't feel right."

"*Feel* right? What's feeling got to do with it? This is a fucking business."

"This is wrong, mate. Fucked up. It'll destroy this place, rip the heritage right out of it."

Rob took the plans back and rolled them up. "Look, we tried the conservation thing. And it worked, okay, the bottom's original, but the top of the building was just too far gone. It's not your fault the roof was collapsing."

"It's *not* collapsing though. That's bullshit. It's totally salvageable. Who made that call?"

Rob rubbed his chin.

"Ah, I see. You motherfuckers." Sareena put her hands on her hips. "*You* did this."

"Look," said Rob. "I work for a *client*. *We* work for a *client*. The *client* gets what he wants. Full stop."

"Fuck that!" Sareena spat. "That's weak as piss."

Rob leaned in. "Syed wanted it this way. I thought you should know but—"

"Oh, but you're telling me now so everything's okay. Great, thanks. That's awesome. Way to have my back, you're a fucking hero."

"What's the big deal? At the end of the day, the bottom part's original. The top's something new. I thought you'd think that was cool. A mix of old and new. It'll look ace."

"*At the end of the day*," she said, "you and Syed are assholes. Show me the fucking plans. The real ones, not this bullshit."

Rob hesitated but could see she would not let this go. He reached into his bag and handed her the manilla folder of paperwork and drawings. She flipped pages and stopped at the full view.

"It's going to be a landmark building," he said. "Just like you wanted. And every ship in the strait's going to see it. The sun sparkling off this glass like a lighthouse. It's the kind of project they put in that magazine of yours. And you'll have built it."

"Nah, mate." She handed the paperwork back. "You'll build it. Because I'm not doing it. Not this."

"Grow up, for Chrissake. You signed a fucking contract. You're building the goddamned thing."

Sareena leaned in close, near enough for Rob to see the pores on her face. "You don't need me for this," she said. "If this is what you want, you can get any Toorak McMansion fuckwit to put it up for you." She looked at Rob sideways. "Wait a second." Her attention returned to the documents, she turned pages quickly, her index finger hovering over the text as she scanned sections of the paperwork. "When did you file these?" she said without looking up.

"Can't remember. Doesn't it say?"

"No, it does *not* say. And it *should* say." Her eyes looked at Rob from the open document. "What the fuck is going on?" She squinted. "Did you play me? Did you submit this paperwork before or *after* my name was on this project?"

The muscles in Rob's jaw twitched as he ground his teeth.

"You fuckers," Sareena said, glaring.

"What?"

"You know what. You and Syed. You wanted me on this project just so it'd look like I endorsed whatever fucked up plan you had for this place."

"No, it wasn't like that. I always——"

"Bull. Shit." She threw the papers onto a pile of building trash.

"I wanted to tell you."

"Oh, but you're telling me now," she said sarcastically. "Thanks. Yeah, that's great," She shot Rob a disgusted look.

Alex came in. "Uh, there's some guy outside, says he wants to see you."

"Who?" said Sareena, irritated. "What guy?"

"I don't know," said Alex. "Some guy in a suit. Says he wants to talk to you."

"Talk to who?" said Sareena.

"Whoever's in charge." Alex scowled. "I thought that was you."

"Send him in," said Rob. Alex glared at him.

A pale guy in a pinstriped suit came through the doorway. "Are you Robert Connors?"

Rob nodded and averted his eyes from the man, whose tousled, thinning hair looked like something scooped out of a drain.

"My name's Jerome Kent. I'm an attorney at Willison's. I'm here to inform you that my client, the Bass Coast Shire, is demanding immediate cessation of construction on these premises for breaching sections 12 and 33 of the Heritage Protection Act 2007."

"What?" said Rob. "The job's already been approved."

"Well, this is an order for the immediate cessation of works. The filed plans fail to conserve the heritage of the building, nor do they provide adequate protections for the flora and fauna of this environment. Details are all in here." Jerome Kent handed Rob a thick white envelope.

Sareena looked over her shoulder as she passed Rob. "Well, good luck with that." She threw up her hands and walked out the front door.

CHAPTER TWENTY-SEVEN

Emma turned the key and pushed open the heavy door, wheeling her small suitcase behind her. The door thumped shut, sealing her within the dim chambers of Kendry's big house. The silence was thick. She called out, but the stillness swallowed her voice. Not a word in reply, only the distant whir of a power tool.

Something wasn't right. The faint scent of something sharp and medicinal lingered in the air, growing stronger as she moved toward the kitchen.

As Emma approached, her footsteps slowed to an apprehensive shuffle. Her blood ran cold. Kendry lay sprawled on the tile floor, a tangle of hair and limbs, face down in a stew of vomit that disappeared under the refrigerator.

Emma dropped onto all fours. "Ken." Emma felt for a pulse. Didn't know if she found one or not, didn't know what she was doing. Was that Kendry's heart she felt beating or her own?

"Ken!" Emma's voice broke. "Wake up!" She shook Kendry. "Fuck!"

She fumbled for her phone and dialed 000, her hand shaking. She relayed the address and the urgency of the situation. The woman had questions. "I don't know, I don't know," Emma kept saying. "Just get here. Please."

"The ambulance is on its way."

"I don't want her to die!"

"We're on our way."

Emma opened Kendry's mouth like the lady on the phone told her to, swirled her finger around in there. It was clear of obstacles. Kendry's face was gray but she *was* breathing, you could hear it when you got up close. Emma brushed the hair from her friend's face. It seemed important.

Sirens pierced the air, growing louder and closer. Emma leaped up and let the paramedics in. Two solid women strode through the door with their medical kits, expressions masked with professional concern. Emma led the way. "I found her like this," she stammered, her voice fraying. "I think she took pills."

"What kind of pills?" said the older one, the leader, putting her kit down, kneeling beside Kendry. They moved with practiced efficiency, assessing her vitals.

"I'm not sure," said Emma. "There's a bunch of them."

The women worked around each other with a self-assured, fluid urgency. Their mission was clear: to salvage life, no matter how broken. "It really helps if we know what she took."

"It was oxy and Valium and...I don't remember the other one."

"Right," said the older paramedic – Jan, her name on her shirt. She looked at her partner who was already rummaging inside her kit. "You do it." said Jan. Her partner put a nasal spray up Kendry's nose and pushed the trigger, a wet spritz of air.

Jan kneeled at Kendry's side, put her hands on Kendry's hip and rocked her gently. "What's her name?"

"Kendry."

"Okay, Kendry, we need you back now." Jan stroked Kendry's

cheek, tickled under her chin.

"Come on Kendry," said the younger paramedic, retrieving another nasal spray from her kit.

"Yeah, give her another one," said Jan. Another spritz up the nostrils.

"Stay clear of her legs," said Jan, pushing her glasses up the bridge of her nose. "She's going to wake up in a second and she's not going to be happy."

Emma's mind whirled. Kendry's hand twitched.

"There you go," said Jan. "You're coming round."

"Come on, Kendry, you can do it," said the younger paramedic.

Kendry's body twitched. She blinked and sat bolt upright, head swaying. The paramedics put their hands out as if to catch her from falling and cradled her head.

"Kendry, you've been unconscious," said Jan. "We know you've taken some pills. We need to know exactly what you took and how much."

Kendry swayed, eyes rolling to the back of her head.

Emma got up and marched to the buffet in the loungeroom. She pulled open the bottom drawer and inside found torn blister packs and empty medicine bottles. Emma brought samples back to the kitchen and showed Jan who leaned in to have a closer look at the labels. "Right," Jan nodded. "She's not mucking around." Jan looked down at Kendry. "How many pills did you take and when did you take them?" She spoke loudly, enunciating each word. Kendry was unresponsive, her head wobbled as if suspended in liquid.

"What pills and how many?" Jan repeated.

Kendry's eyes opened, she wriggled. "Stay still, Kendry. We've got you." Jan gave her protégé instructions. "Better get the chair, Loz, I don't reckon she'll walk out on her own legs." The young paramedic left and returned with a wheelchair.

The paramedics eased Kendry onto the chair and wheeled her out of the house. She was groggy, her head falling forward. "You're alright," repeated Jan.

The sound of the ambulance doors closing sent a shiver down Emma's spine.

"You right?" said Jan.

Emma nodded. "Do I go with you guys?"

"You family?"

"I'm a friend."

"And a good friend too. I reckon that spew in the kitchen and you coming home might've saved her life."

Emma's face contorted.

"You can follow us," said Jan. "But I got to be honest, it's going to take her a while to get right."

"Is she going to be okay?"

Jan nodded. "Look, it's good we found her when we did. We'll get her to hospital. Then the doctors will take over and they'll be able to give you some more answers." Jan checked her watch. "You could be sitting at St Vinnie's all night before you see her." She turned toward the ambulance; her partner inside gave her a thumbs up. Jan nodded and turned back to Emma. "I know you want to be helpful. You could clean up here," said Jan, turning to reach for the door. "Head in later, or you can follow us." Jan climbed into the driver's seat.

Emma glanced back at the open door of the house. "No, you guys go. I don't want to hold you up. I don't have a car. I'll come after."

"Okay." Jan gave a thumbs up. "It's good you were here," she said, and closed the door. The ambulance pulled away, its siren wailing in the cold blue sky. Emma stood motionless, a profound sense of responsibility and indecision settled on her. She would collect some things and take them to St Vincent's.

Emma stopped in the kitchen doorway and took in the scene the paramedics had left behind, the footprints, discarded tissues, the plastic packaging from the nasal sprays, the puddle of vomit streaked with skid marks.

What would've happened if she hadn't got home when she did?

Emma cleaned up, then mopped and scrubbed the floor with vigor as if doing so could erase what happened. She threw all the sponges away and took the trash bag straight to the outside garbage can.

According to the St Vincent's website, visiting hours were over. She called but the patient inquiry line couldn't give out any information, only that Kendry had been admitted.

Emma couldn't bear to sleep in Margaret's old room, not tonight. Emma swore she could feel a slight depression in the mattress, the shape of Margaret herself. It was a bad omen.

Emma summoned an Uber and headed to the hospital, grateful that the older man behind the wheel was not a talker.

The emergency ward at St Vincent's was crowded; people waited on plastic chairs facing the glassed-in box of the reception office, a waterless aquarium in which a round woman with rectangular glasses shifted her attention between multiple screens. Outside her refuge, paramedics in their dark blue uniforms stood talking with colleagues or calmy wheeled their patients down corridors to other parts of the hospital.

Emma was told to take a seat and wait. The child in front of her repeatedly turned around to stare at her until the kid's mother, a baby in her arms, told him off in a language Emma didn't recognize. The mom smiled apologetically. Emma smiled back. Poor mom.

The receptionist gestured for Emma to approach.

"Your friend's been moved to an observation room," she said. "You can wait in there if you like. Might be more comfortable."

Emma nodded and followed the woman's instructions, turning to have a last look at the mom, again settling her son who now stood in his seat. She coaxed him down with one arm, her crying baby in the other.

After some twists and turns, Emma found Kendry, asleep in a wheely hospital bed parked in an alcove. She looked gray but peaceful. Alive. Emma stuck her head out into the hallway, looking for someone to flag down. What was happening? Why wasn't her friend being looked after? But there was no one there.

She sat on one of the two vinyl lounge chairs and kept vigil. Kendry slept, snoring lightly.

Emma pulled out her phone, no messages. She fidgeted with the device, turning it over in her hands, scratched at some gunk stuck to the screen and wiped it with her sleeve. She scrolled her contacts, paused on Rob's name, her thumb hovered over the call button. She switched the device off and put it in her jacket.

Emma pushed the two chairs together and dozed in fits, awakened sometime later as a team bustled in to move Kendry elsewhere, wheeling her bed into the hallway.

Visiting hours started at 10am. Emma spent ages drinking bad coffee in the hospital cafeteria and picking at a banana muffin until she asked a new stern receptionist if she could finally see her friend.

The maze of corridors had her asking someone for directions at every turn. Eventually she found Kendry sitting up in bed, propped up on pillows and hooked up to wires and tubes, the only patient in a room with three empty beds.

"Hey, sunshine," she said.

"Ken," said Emma, approaching.

"Oh, don't look at me like that."

"Like what?" Emma stood by the bed.

"Like I've disappointed you."

"Not disappointed. Worried."

"Well don't be."

"Pfft."

"I overdid it. It was an accident."

"Right."

"I did."

"You could've died."

"Don't be so dramatic." Kendry swatted the air, flashing her hospital bracelet.

"You see where you are?"

"They're just being cautious. You know how they are, don't want to get sued. I just got the mix wrong."

Emma raised her eyebrows.

"What?" said Kendry. "I'm not your afterschool special. I don't need saving. It was a mistake. I'm fine. It wasn't a cry for help or whatever. Worry about your own life."

"Ken, you were a corpse."

Kendry frowned, then sighed. "Look, I'm sorry you found me like that. It wasn't the plan. There *was* no plan, I just…" She took a breath. "I've got to remember it's pills *or* wine, *not* both. I screwed up. Simple as that."

Emma took her frustrations to the window. Traffic moved noiselessly on the street below. "It's not simple, Ken." She sighed and turned back to face the bed. "What am I going to do with you?" She looked down at Kendry's hands. They were thin, creased and papery, an old person's hands.

"You're in the will, you know."

Emma put her hands on her hips, "What?" she snapped. "Why say that?"

"Just saying."

"Well unsay it."

Kendry ran her fingers through her hair. "I just wanted you to know."

"Well, change it. I don't want it. You're only two years older than me and you're probably going to live to a hundred. You're going to need every penny."

"You done?"

"Maybe. I don't know. I'm pissed off at you." Emma crossed her arms.

Kendry sat up, winced. "You remember when we went to that Radiohead concert, what was it, 2004?"

Emma nodded.

"We were early thirties."

"I was twenty-seven," said Emma.

"Fuck." Kendry shook her head slowly. "We thought we were so old."

"Yeah, and we'll probably feel the same way about us now in twenty years."

"God," Kendry sighed. "I'll be nearly the age Mom was when she moved in with me." Her eyes widened. "That's a trip."

"Yeah," said Emma. "That music didn't age though, hey?"

"How *is* the boy wonder?" Kendry laughed.

Emma gave Kendry a dirty look.

"What? Just making conversation."

"I was supposed to go to his show tonight, but I'm not going."

"Why not?" Kendry waved her hand dismissively. "Go."

Emma shook her head.

"What are you going to do?" said Kendry. "Stay here and watch me watch TV? I'm not going to top myself if that's what you're worried about."

Emma glowered.

"*Go*," Kendry shood her, the tube in her arm jiggling. "For

Chrissake. If you stay here, I *will* kill myself."

Emma made a face.

"What?" said Kendry. "Too soon?"

Emma nodded. "Yeah."

"Seriously, though," said Kendry, "It was a mistake, Em. I don't want to die." She brushed the hair out of her eyes. "I'm too interested to find out what happens next in your life to go anywhere." She smiled. "Go out. Please. I'm fine."

The nurse came in, a young woman in blue scrubs and chunky white sneakers.

Kendry perked up. "There, see," she said. "Nurse Ratchet's here, Em. You're free to go."

The young nurse smiled; she had a friendly, open face. "Someone's got their energy back."

"I was just telling my friend that she doesn't need to chaperone me or do anything heroic like sleep on a chair."

"We're going to keep you in until at least tomorrow," said the nurse, scribbling on a form.

"Oh, great," said Kendry.

"Doctor's going to want to see you again in the morning."

"I'll set my alarm."

The nurse checked Kendry's tubes and wires. "She always this feisty?" she said to Emma and thumbed the valve on the IV bag.

"Yep," said Emma. "She's always been a stubborn pain in the ass."

"Hey," said Kendry, "when you're good at something, you can't help but show off a little."

"You guys been friends for a long time?" The nurse adjusted the bedding.

"Too long," said Kendry, then fake whispered and pointed her thumb at Emma. "Had to say it before *she* did."

Emma rolled her eyes.

The nurse smiled. "It's good you've got support," she said. "It'll get you discharged faster."

"Oh, don't say that." Kendry lay back on the pillow. "I could get used to this." She twiddled her fingers. "Maybe you can convince my friend it's okay to go out tonight. She's got a hot date."

Emma frowned.

The nurse pushed buttons on the patient monitor. "You can go," she said over her shoulder. "She's not going anywhere. We've got her."

Emma hesitated. "You want me to bring you anything from home?"

"Yes," said Kendry. "Something cashmere. Honestly, what are these hospital gowns made of?" She chuckled, lay back and fell silent, leaving only the beeping of the monitor, its flashing numbers and squiggly lines.

"Is she okay?"

"She's been dropping off like that. It's normal. She's been through a bit.

"I can still hear you guys talking about me," Kendry said, eyes still closed.

"You're a sneaky one," said the nurse.

"Hmm," said Kendry wearily, and sunk into her pillow, her dry lips frozen in a weird expression.

The nurse motioned toward the outside corridor and Emma followed her out.

"Is she going to be alright?"

"Yeah," said the nurse. She was in bad shape when she got here, but she's had charcoal and it looks like it did the job. We're waiting for it to pass.

"But she's going to be okay?"

The nurse hesitated. "Well, she's going to need a psych consult before she goes. She's lucky."

"Right."

The nurse scanned the corridor and leaned in. "It's not my place, but my mom went through this." She swallowed. "Kendry's got to *want* to get better."

Emma nodded. The nurse took her leave, her chunky white sneakers squeaking in the hallway.

Emma couldn't go to a concert. Not tonight. There was too much on her mind. She wanted to be outside, just watch the moon pass across the sky or something. There'd be a lot of people at a concert.

But then she didn't want to be alone at Kendry's house either. It felt vacant and haunted in here, all those trinkets, cold and unknowable, like museum pieces.

Kendry wanted her to go. She'd want her to dress up and have an adventure. But how was Emma supposed to spend an evening with a bunch of strangers at a show? She already felt old and frumpy, would probably be surrounded by young women like the ones at the club, girls with names like Mimi or Holly. Sha'rae. Why had she agreed to this? And where was this theater anyway? The Quintilian? Never heard of it. Sounded pretentious.

Okay, no talking yourself out of this. She'd go and tell Kendry all about it tomorrow. She'd be full of questions.

Emma went through her closet, the steady squeak of clothes hangers sliding across the rod. Too formal, too conservative, too small, too chilly, too pilly and too…why was there a wetsuit in here? She hadn't worn it in years. Probably didn't fit either. Must have thrown it in the suitcase in an aspirational moment when she first moved out, back when she imagined herself – what? – joining that polar bear club of old ladies who swam daily in the icy waters of

Port Phillip Bay? Who did she think she was? Or was going to be? You couldn't just reinvent yourself like that.

And yet, here she was, heading to her "boyfriend's" concert. It was ridiculous to say "boyfriend," even in her head, such a juvenile word. What were they? Friends? And why did these labels even matter? She was just trying to let loose a little. Have fun. But life had a way of getting serious when you least expected it. Had it always been that way? Or was it something that happened more as you got older?

She hadn't been to a concert in ages. The last time was at a folk festival for one of Kendry's clients, for Chrissake. How were you supposed to dress for An Evening of Contemplative Pop, whatever that was?

Emma googled *what to wear to a concert* and found a list of "Cool, Girl-Approved Outfits":

- Relaxed jeans and a floral top
- Puffy sleeve crop top and midi skirt
- A breezy top and black denim
- Classic band tee and fun pants
- Lather in leather

Ridiculous list. How was this helpful? And what even were "fun pants"? This list was probably written by a seventeen-year-old fashion influencer. Or by AI. Emma couldn't decide which was worse. She searched *what 40-year-old women wear to a rock concert* and cringed at how daggy the outfits were on Pinterest. Rhinestones? Really? Maybe she should cancel after all. It wasn't right to go out while Kendry was in hospital.

She put on her go-to black A-line dress and turned in front of the mirror several times to scrutinize herself from multiple angles. The dress hung nicely, covering the bulges of her hips, but it was sleeveless, and she felt self-conscious about her arms jiggling.

Plus, sleeveless meant cold, which meant she'd need a silk scarf or something, which would be fussy and bundled around her neck, which could make her hot and flustered. She pushed aside the remaining hangers to reveal the jacket she was looking for: a military-cut cashmere jacket by Balmain of Paris, an overly generous forty-fifth birthday gift from Kendry that always seemed too extravagant for the occasion. Her arms slid effortlessly through the luxurious silk lining in the sleeves. The double-breasted blazer had real brass buttons, was fitted at the waist and flared at the bottom, and draped her body with the comforting weight of designer wear. Why had she waited so long to wear this jacket? It was like being with her friend.

Dress with your heart, not your mind, Dr Priya had said. *Because your eyes will deceive you.*

Whatever. This jacket pleased Emma's heart, skin *and* mind. So, take that, Priya.

Emma decided the teenaged AI might have described the outfit as *urbane*. She called it tasteful without being too stuffy, too beige. Kendry would be proud, and Emma felt nearer to her friend just for wearing the jacket, as if her going out was for them both. It gave a sense of mission to Emma's numbness and fatigue. Life was for living.

Emma had vaguely imagined a grungy, bar-like atmosphere, but when the Uber pulled up outside the Quintilian, she had to adjust her expectations. This wasn't some squat, brick building with metal doors. It was a sculptural dome, like a giant ostrich egg lying on its side on a patch of well-mowed grass.

"You sure this is it?" she said to the driver, who nodded and pointed at the car's map display. "Okay, thank you." She got out of the car, still uncertain about whether she'd come to the right place. It looked fancy, like something in a magazine, a sculpture park maybe. But a lot of young people were going in, which was strangely reassuring. A few older ones too, which made her feel more at ease.

Inside, the egg building was roomy, breezy even, a more substantial space than she'd imagined. There was no stage, just a large oval-shaped floor with charcoal carpet. The place was lit only by soft LED strip lights that circled the perimeter of the space at knee level. The curved walls were covered in rich, chestnut-colored wood panels that wrapped all the way around. It felt like the kind of place a Danish furniture designer might have their funeral.

No one looked at her ticket too closely and she now understood why: there were no seat numbers. People were lounging on scattered bean bags, reclining in the flickering light of hundreds of electric candles resting on the floor. People chatted softly and drank craft beer straight out of the can.

Smack-dab in the center of the room was a grand piano, flanked by a keyboard, a trumpet, a guitar, and towers of amplifiers and other electronic gizmos that blinked with colored lights. The whole setup was steampunk meets electronica.

Emma ordered a glass of bubbles from a young woman with spiky hair, who wordlessly poured and slid it across the bar. Emma sipped her sparkling wine (not bad) and looked for a place to sit. A few folding chairs had been arranged along the wall. Some of them were marked "reserved," but Emma didn't want to presume. Besides, she'd only seen truly old people lowering themselves onto those seats, and a person on crutches. She wasn't game to sit too close to those big amplifiers either. She identified an available beanbag further back from the piano, not so close as to feel trapped by the people who'd eventually fill the space behind her.

Emma worried about the conspicuous exercise of getting

herself into the beanbag without rolling off. She gave the thing an experimental tap with her toe and it seemed firm enough. She put her bag and drink down, and lowered herself into the beanbag, comforted by the way it molded itself to her shape. She felt better sitting there in the dim light, nursing her champagne. New people arriving would see her as part of the scenery.

A lot of people seemed to know one another, waving and smiling at each other in recognition from halfway across the room. Some people even brought small children, who ran around playing with the electric candles. This was fun, kind of exciting. Emma hadn't been to a concert in ages. This one felt...friendly.

The lights soon dimmed, and the room slowly filled with the milky haze of incense and dry ice. People settled in their seats or stood at the back, leaning against the wood panels.

A dweeby-looking dude with peach fuzz on his chin and dressed in a too-long T-shirt welcomed everyone, talked about the electronic music scene in Melbourne, blah, blah blah. He introduced the first musician, Briley LaFontaine, who made stern faces while playing a mournful cello piece that seemed to go on forever. This is what became of children whose parents praised them no matter what. She was okay, but seriously, enough.

Next was DJ something or other, who got the crowd rocking with a variety of samples and doof-doof music. A small group danced up front. Maybe the guy's friends. The DJ left and there was longish pause after which a few people began to clap and whistle from the back of the room. Emma turned to where their attention was focused. The noise grew as a silhouette she recognized as Erik walked out and crossed the floor. The crowd of some two hundred people began to cheer in earnest as he reached the light of the candles concentrated in the middle of the room. Emma sank into her beanbag. She was sure that she didn't want Erik to see her and equally certain that she wanted him to look straight at her. He seemed at ease, ready to accept the crowd's adulation, as if it was natural. He was in his element, smiling, bowing, dressed as he might have been in his apartment, black jeans, T-shirt, red high-top shoes and a knitted blue cardigan, absorbing applause like it was air.

He sat at the piano, the creak of wood audible in the silence of the egg-shaped space. Erik wordlessly placed his long fingers on the keys and rested them there. He crouched forward, took a breath and began moving his fingers. The delicate notes, barely audible at first, grew into something sweet and melancholic as he stretched his fingers up and down the length of the keyboard. He moved his head as he played, eyes closed.

Emma had no idea he was this good. She hadn't known what to expect, but any notion she'd had of hearing some dinky garage band evaporated. The tenderness of his playing held the audience captive, save for the occasional cough, or snap of a plastic cup. She was close enough to hear the muted thump of the piano hammers as they moved.

The piece ended and he stayed there, fingers resting on the keys until the last, lingering note disintegrated into the vast silence of the space. As soon as Erik lifted his hands from the piano, the audience erupted in applause. Emma turned in her beanbag to appreciate the shadowy figures shouting and whistling. She'd only been to one piano concert in her life before this one and it was strictly polite golf-clapping, not this football-stadium atmosphere. Emma looked around self-consciously before putting her fingers in her mouth and whistling. She hadn't done that in years. It felt good, like she was more part of this tribe now. She let her weight sink deeper into the beanbag as the clapping subsided.

Erik's smile dropped as he turned to face the piano again.

He played another, livelier tune, followed by a somber one, accompanied by a pre-recorded cello that filled the room at the touch of one of the blinking lights on the audio console beside him.

The audience met each one of these pieces with an enthusiastic applause that left Emma feeling special just for knowing the artist privately.

Erik played on, coaxing music of unsettling beauty from the piano. He then stood up, one hand still holding down a piano chord while his free hand turned dials and switched on one of the blinking electronic gizmos stacked beside the piano. A part of the music he'd been playing now continued through the speakers on a continuous loop.

Unhurried, he shifted some dials on another machine and ambled over to a small synthesizer. He stood behind it and used it to add some synthesized base beats to the ghostly recorded piano track. He jiggled more dials and sauntered over to the trumpet. The brass glowed with the reflected light of all those blinking lights and flickering candles. He brought the trumpet to his lips and played a series of sad notes. More dials and the trumpet now joined the assembled chorus of instruments. Erik then picked up his guitar, the one he'd been carrying in the Catch office lobby that day. Those long, creamy fingers of his plucked the strings, adding a pacy little guitar riff to the layered track he was building in real time. He fiddled with more knobs and dials, so that the music built from a single piano chord culminating in an ocean of sound that filled the space. Every note imaginable now seemed to pulse at once. Emma's brain lit up. Her heart thumped. It seemed possible, probable even, that outside every light in the world now blinked in unison.

The music grew louder, as if gradually revealing a secret. Whatever it was, it began to evaporate as the music grew softer, disintegrating the moment Emma seemed close to grasping whatever the secret was. She felt the certainty of its collapse under the weight of her own self-awareness. Emma glimpsed only the secret's fragments. But they were beautiful. Erik's music was the soundtrack of a film made just for her. And she knew, at that moment, every person in the auditorium felt it was their movie too.

After the performance, Emma lay in her bean bag, misty-eyed, her emotions pulled in multiple directions. She felt worried for Kendry and angry for what could have happened. She felt compassion for Rob, whose emotional limitations were part of his upbringing, comparable to her own mother's, whose parents never taught her to love with an open heart.

The house lights turned back on for intermission and the murmur of voices grew, restoring the contours of her private consciousness.

How had it been so long since she'd gone to a concert? She used to go to them all the time when she was younger. This show reminded her that experiences like this were everywhere. You just had to stop hibernating, *immerse yourself in life*, as Dr Priya liked to say.

Emma took a sip of her champagne, but it had gone flat and warm. She remained in her beanbag, unhurried by the idea of clambering out of it. Indeed, this presented a logistical challenge: she should've worn pants.

She shuffled onto her side and tried to lift herself off the beanbag while keeping her legs together. Flat shoes might have helped too. She kicked off her heels and dug her shoulders into the beanbag, readying herself for lift-off.

Emma took a moment to fortify herself, observing the shadowy figures now fussing about the "stage." They busied themselves packing up instruments, rearranging the towers of blinking lights, coiling and relaying all those black cables.

Two of the shadows walked toward her.

She wriggled her hips, her shoulders, preparing to leave the beanbag. When the figures moved closer, they took on familiar shapes as they moved into the light.

"Mom?"

"Emma."

Will's head panned between her and Erik. "How do you know my mom?"

Erik just raised his eyebrows.

Her son looked her up and down, took in her heels, the fancy jacket and turned to Erik. "What the fuck?" He brought his hands to his face. "Oh, no way."

"Mate," said Erik.

"Are you serious? You're fucking my mom?"

"Dude."

"Oi!" Emma struggled out of the beanbag. "Language."

"What-the, seriously?"

"Will!" She grabbed her son's arm. "What are you getting mad at *him* for?"

"This is fucked up."

"Guys," said Erik, his hands out, conciliatory.

"Take it outside," yelled someone in the auditorium. "Meeoow," came another voice, followed by ripple of laughter.

"Come on," said Erik, and walked toward a door beside the stage. They followed.

The door led to a short corridor that opened into a fenced-off area in the back alley. Judging from all the cigarette butts on the ground, this is where the muzos smoked between sets. There was one now, a guy with a long beard and thick glasses. He acknowledged Erik with a nod of his head, exhaled and flicked the smoke onto the pavement.

"Have a good set, mate," said Erik. The bearded guy left without a word. Now the three of them stood there, their breath steaming in the night air.

"Okay," said Will. "So, what?"

"Dude," said Erik. "This doesn't have to be a big deal."

"Okay. Good to know."

"Why is it bro?

"Uh, because she's fucking married!"

"Dude, it's not—"

"Ah, *hello*," said Emma. "Standing right here."

"Mom, you—"

"No." She waggled her finger to shut him up. "Don't talk about me like I'm not here."

"I'm not. I'm trying to—"

"Well don't. I can speak for myself."

"I feel I should go?" said Erik.

"No," snapped Emma. "You're in this now. You don't get to sneak off."

The backstage door creaked open and another hairy guy in a leather jacket walked out. "We're having a private conversation," said Emma. "Go smoke somewhere else." The man's eyes widened. He held up his hand in apology and turned around.

"Mom," Will said, pointing at the door. "That was the lead singer of Fraztrap!"

"I don't care if it was the Pope!"

Erik laughed.

"You think it's funny?" said Emma.

"It's…kind of funny."

"Well, I'm glad *you* think so."

"I quit school," said Will, and looked away. "There, I said it."

Emma squinted and cocked her head, leaned toward Will as if she hadn't heard him correctly.

"I did." Will turned back toward her. "It's already done, so…"

"Well, what the fuck!" She threw her hands up, couldn't stop blinking. "Why, what happened? Did something happen? Did your father—"

Will shook his head.

Emma glared at Erik. "Did *you* put him up to this?"

Erik raised his hands and shook his head. "It's got nothing to do with me."

"No," snapped Will. "It's my choice."

"I'm going to leave you two," said Erik. Emma frowned and Erik disappeared behind the squeaky metal door.

"Look, I'm sorry," said Will. "Uni's just not the place for me." His eyes finally met hers, briefly, and darted away. She couldn't read them.

"But why not?" said Emma. "I mean, how do you *know* that? You haven't even finished your first year. Give it more time."

She took a long breath, inviting him to seize the quiet space between them. He said nothing and she felt the delicate moment she thought she'd created slipping away. She softened her tone, whispered, "I get that you're confused."

"I'm *not* confused."

"Okay, fine. But I've learned in life it's good to have options. You don't know what it's like to feel you don't have options."

"I know. You've told me a thousand times. But at some point, I need to look at my options and make choices, right?" He looked at her and she glimpsed in his eyes a certainty and maturity she'd not seen there before. He looked back at her without anger, without confusion, without fear. His eyes were calm and self-possessed.

She looked down at his hand and noticed what she'd thought were blood blisters on his fingernails was nail polish. Will let her hold his fingers as she fought back tears.

She'd watched him grow up, but he'd always remained little somehow, in need of her, but she suddenly understood that she needed him now, more than he needed her. She raised her chin to swallow past the lump in her throat. "So," she said, wiping the corner of her eye with the back of her knuckle. "What are you, a groupie now?"

Will smiled nervously and pulled away. He paced and flattened the hair at the back of his head. "Look," he said. "I like it, Mom. I'm not just rolling cables. I'm learning loads about sound and stage design. I like the music. And I like the scene. It's something I want to try for a while. Just see where it goes." He kicked at the ground, the litter of cigarette butts. "So, are you, like, *with* him?"

Emma bit her lip. "Not really." She rubbed her palm on her forehead. "Oh, I don't know. Kind of." She glanced at the floor. "Is that weird? It's weird, isn't it?"

"Kinda."

"Yeah. It's weird." Emma shook out her wrists and sighed. "Look, I don't know." She tried to smile, make light of it, but Will looked away.

He combed his hands through his hair. "I did *not* expect to see you sitting there," he said. "That's for sure."

"Well," she smiled. "I didn't expect to see me there either." She looked at the ground again. "Surprise," she said quietly.

Will smiled, put his hands in his back pockets and briefly looked at her before looking up at the sky. A police siren wailed in the distance. "Pretty good show though, eh?" he said.

Emma exhaled in relief. "So good."

Will turned and looked at her. "He is pretty awesome." Will dragged the toe of his sneaker across a crack in the pavement. "What does this mean?" he said, shyly. "Like, for you and Dad?"

Emma pursed her lips and put her hands on her hips. "I've been thinking about that. I should tell him. It's the right thing to do."

Will considered her response. "What do you think he'll say?"

Emma hesitated. "I don't know. Kendry reckons he's seeing someone, so who knows."

"*Dad?* Seeing someone?"

"Okay, you're going to think it's stupid, but she showed me this picture of him with a young dark-haired woman."

"What, Sareena?" he laughed. "Yeah, no. You guys are way off."

"Oh Christ," said Emma, blushing. "This is bad, isn't it?"

Will was still crushing cigarette butts with the scuffed-up toe of his running shoe.

"Do you love him?" he said.

"Who, your father?"

"No, Erik."

Emma thought of Erik, the smoothness of his skin, taught against his ribs, his chest, his shoulders. She thought of those long, delicate fingers and the things they could do. She thought about how the beauty of his music had transported her, had moved her, but it had also distanced her from him. The show had made Erik seem real to Emma, in a way that he had not been before. He had become someone wholly distinct from her, someone who had abilities and plans, a direction in life that pre-dated her, reminding her that Erik was not just there for her pleasure. He had a life before her, just as certainly as he would have one after. Their relationship could not fulfill the promise of hearing that music for the first time. She'd already known this, the first time she met him, but it was convenient to forget.

It had to end. She had a life. Kendry needed her. And Will needed her too, in ways neither of them could yet understand.

"What are you going to tell Dad?"

"I don't know. Maybe nothing."

Will frowned.

"Does he *need* to know?" She looked down at the scuff marks on Will's running shoe.

"Yes, he does."

"Why?"

"Because…it's shitty not to tell him. You're just looking for an excuse to get away with it."

"I'm not trying to get *away* with anything."

"Right."

"I'm not. And you can wipe that little smirk of your face. You have no idea what you're talking about."

"So you're *not* saying you should lie to Dad about fucking someone else."

"Hey, watch it! I know you're pissed off, but I'm not going let you talk to me like that. Don't be crass. I'm trying to be honest with you. Trying to be an adult. Maybe you can do the same." Will stared back.

Her relationship with Erik, which had felt like a private world, had now infiltrated the rest of her life with consequences beyond her control. Emma softened her voice. "I'm not sorry about Erik. He was amazing. *Is* amazing."

"Gross."

"It's not. He's lovely and I like the person I am with him. I'm adventurous and brave, and I feel like I can ask for things I want, not because he owes them to me, but because he wants to make me happy." Emma wiped her eyes. "I *will* tell your father, when the time's right."

Will opened his mouth as if to speak but Emma stopped him. "It's okay," she said. "You're allowed to keep secrets when they protect people."

Will made a face like he didn't like what he was hearing.

He was so earnest. She'd given him that, the luxury of growing up slowly. It was worth more than he could know.

"You staying for the second part of the show?" said Will.

Emma smiled at him. "You want me to?"

He rolled his eyes. "Come on," he said. "Let's go," and led her back inside.

CHAPTER TWENTY-EIGHT

Rob noticed how his dirty work boots had worn a path of footprints to and from the veranda of the display home. No prospective buyers had visited the place in weeks. That didn't bother him. He welcomed not having to clean up after himself as much. Since work had stopped on the stone house, he'd been sleeping in too, allowing himself to be awakened by the beeping of heavy trucks reversing and the dumping of gravel before he got out of bed. It didn't matter if he was late. He wasn't on the tools out here, it was more of an advisory role. Tell that to his lower back, which twinged as he dodged muddy puddles on the way to Syed's demountable office.

Rob's phone chimed and he stopped on the dirt road to check it. It was a text from Will:

Quit school. Sorry dad. Man's got to make his own decisions.

"Oi!" The blast of a car horn startled Rob, who looked up to see Shane, one of his old apprentices, leaning out the side window of a mud-splattered truck. "No phones unless you're on a break," said Shane grinning. "Don't you know the rules, mate?" Shane smiled, blue eyes on a sunburnt face. "How are ya, Rob? All good?"

"Not bad, mate. Not bad." Rob forced a smile and tucked his phone in the pocket of his jacket. "Know if Syed's up in the bunker?"

They both looked over at the portable office, atop the hill. It was surrounded by chewed up grass, streaked with muddy tire tracks.

"Where else?" said Shane. "Warm and dry in there. Don't blame him, either. Fucken miserable out here." Shane glanced up at the sky, then tapped the steering wheel. "I better get going, mate. These steel frames aren't going to move themselves. Catch ya later, Rob."

"Be good, mate."

"Not so far." Shane smiled, and the truck pulled slowly away.

Rob thought he heard his phone chime. It hadn't.

Inside the portable office, it was even colder than it was outside, even as the heater wheezed on the back wall. Syed was on the phone, pacing around and speaking Persian, which always sounded like whispering, even when he was angry. The sound of that language gave Rob a pleasant shiver.

Syed waved him in. "Okay mate," he said, now speaking English into his phone. "No worries. See you next week." He put his phone down on the desk and looked at Rob with half-closed eyelids. Syed frowned. "You look like shit, man. You sick?"

"Nah, just a crap sleep. I'm good." Rob blew on his hands to warm them.

"You sure?" Rob nodded. Syed lowered himself onto his office chair, manilla folders piled all over his desk. "You know, I saw your wife."

"Oh." Rob's eyebrows arched.

"Yes. At my club in the city. Months ago." Syed cleared his throat. "With her friend."

Rob nodded. Probably Kendry.

Syed just sat there, blinking. "Everything good?" he said.

Rob nodded. "Yeah. Fine. Just a bit worried about this roof, mate. It was supposed to go on two weeks ago. We're still dead in the water."

Syed swatted the comment away.

"Should've told her, Sy," Rob shook his head. "Wasn't right to trick her like that."

Syed screwed up his face. "I should just sell that fucking house for the highest price." He tossed a stray folder onto one of the towers of paper on his desk. "Fucking heritage," he said, slumped back in the creaky chair. "It's just stones. All Australia is stones."

Syed sighed, rubbed his face with his hands and rested his chin on steepled fingers. "That's it." He dropped his hands to his knees and turned to look out the grimy little window. "I'm finished with houses. Going to build apartments now. Australian houses are very expensive. But why so much?" He turned to Rob and raised his palms in the air. "There is so much space. Maybe people they don't want to be married now, they don't want children, maybe not have so much money for a big house. But they still need a home. So, I build apartments. I sell the house."

Rob looked at him sideways. "Yeah, but who's going to buy an unfinished house, mate? That looks dodgy. You should finish it."

Syed swiveled on his chair and looked out the window. "Fucking shit." He smashed his fist on the desk. "Okay. *You* finish it." He stuck his chin out at Rob. "And I sell it."

"Yeah, but we can't, Sy. Not until this legal thing with the Council's sorted."

Syed waved his hand indifferently. "Come on. Council my balls. That's the fucking neighbor."

"Hmm?"

"The neighbor. On the hill, behind the house. He's a jerk.

Doesn't want me to have a nicer, bigger house than him." Syed brought his thumb and forefinger together. "Small penis."

"Well, okay, but I don't reckon Council's going to back down because of that, mate. Bottom line is, we're not building anything until you fix the heritage thing."

"*You* fix it."

"Nah, mate. I'm just the builder. You need a lawyer."

Syed leaned back and rested his hands on his pot belly. "You know, Australian government always try to make like they protect things: the environment, heritage buildings, ladies from a bad man. But you know…if you really want to do something… is difficult." Syed brought his palms together. "You work with others. Together. Help them do *their* things, then they help you with *your* things. It's better but is more work."

"What is that?" Rob sneered. "Wisdom from the old country or something?"

Syed shook his head. "Not cultural wisdom, mate. It's fucking universal law." He grinned. "You can fix it."

"How am *I* supposed to fix it, Sy? Just get your lawyer to give them a call."

Syed closed his eyes and shook his head. "No. Lawyers are always talking. Council. Always talking. It's a game they play to look busy. We spend months talking and say nothing. Very expensive conversation. Call the girl."

"She's pissed at me, and you too."

Syed tut-tutted. "Doesn't matter. She'll want to fix it."

"Wouldn't be too sure, mate. She's ropeable."

"Just think about what *she* is wanting to protect. She loves the house. I think you do too. So…" He smiled and theatrically wiggled his fingers.

"So what, mate?"

"So, make it work."

"How? What am I supposed to tell her?"

Syed frowned. "You don't say anything," he said, and leaned back in his chair to the rubbery squelch of vinyl. "You listen."

CHAPTER TWENTY-NINE

Emma had set herself up permanently on the lounge room sofa, a cocoon of blankets and pillows. Now that Kendry was at her "wellness facility" in Byron Bay, Emma had moved out of Margaret's old bedroom and set up in here. As Dr Priya said, *it is important to be mindful, to recognize patterns in your life.*

Emma's pattern was watching TV while scrolling LinkedIn or jobs.com, half-heartedly applying for positions she was overqualified for. Marketing Consultant, Communications Adviser, Senior Communications Adviser. Ugh. She clicked Apply on another application and looked up at the TV.

It felt good to graze the culture, get lost in a rabbit hole of YouTube clips. Being unproductive felt strangely constructive at first, but it was alarming how quickly a search for videos on manifesting positivity and good mental health opened a gateway to people sharing their crystal therapies and near-death experiences.

Erik was busy doing gigs up in New South Wales. She told herself she didn't care.

Emma flipped TV channels, from cooking show to renovation show to '90s sitcom and back again.

She might go for a walk later. Get some air. She hadn't run in ages. Every time she thought about lacing up her trainers, she talked herself out of it. It was either too dark or too cold or too wet, and besides, she just didn't like running that much.

Emma slept a lot these days, her nest of pillows and blankets like a warm bunker that kept the world at bay. Only the occasional roar of a truck to remind her of the world outside. If the weather was okay, she might go for a walk. If it wasn't, she'd stay in. It'd get late and Emma would eventually drift off to the gentle voices of the shopping channel. Dr Priya did say routines were important.

She worried about Kendry but was hopeful she was getting the care she needed. Emma couldn't go in the kitchen anymore without thinking about how close she'd come to losing her friend.

CHAPTER THIRTY

Rob sat at the kitchen table of the display home and folded another soggy fry into his mouth. He peered into the cardboard box, just the crunchy little bits at the bottom left. He pinched one, popped it in his mouth and his phone rang. Rob quickly licked his fingers and wiped them on his pant leg. He squinted at the display before answering.

"Jimmy," he said, still chewing. "How are you, mate?" Rob worked his tongue, dislodging the bits of potato stuck in his gums. "Good, mate, good…Nothing, just having an early tea. What's that?…Nah, no tandoori for me, mate, just the old fish and chips." He laughed.

"No bad news. I called you earlier because I'm working on this swish project and I thought you might want to give us a hand… Well, I was working with this young bird and, let's just say, we had some creative differences. What do you reckon, can you help us out? It's a good project, well advanced and…What's that?…Nah, next year's no good, I need it now." Rob pushed the takeout box away from him. "Well, what about Tony? He's probably just busy counting money but…You're shitting me…Since when?…So he's

on a cruise ship somewhere…Poor bastard…Nah mate, all good…
No biggie. Just thought I'd check in with you old farts first, see if
you could give us hand…Nah, I hear ya mate…Okay, no worries."

He put the phone down and swished his tongue around his
bottom teeth.

Rob surveyed the mess on the table, the beer cans, the grease-
stained cardboard box, the bitten piece of fish stewing in vinegar
on the crumpled wax paper.

He stood abruptly, knocking the chair down behind him. "Fuck."
He breathed heavily, closed his eyes and opened them, took in the
mess on the table. He swept his arm across the table, knocking
everything to the floor. Rob stepped over the mess and rested both
hands on the edge of the sink.

"Fuck me," he sighed. He couldn't get anything to work out right.
Rob looked out the kitchen window. Another cold and moonless
night.

SPRING

CHAPTER THIRTY-ONE

The rocky outcrop of Phillip Island didn't look like a tourist destination in early spring. That's what Emma liked about it. When the weather was still gray and blustery, fewer tour buses arrived to see the little penguins waddle ashore at night. It was the football semi-finals too, so you didn't have to book a table at a restaurant ahead of time or otherwise deal with crowds and flies.

Kendry and Emma had been doing this spring pilgrimage for years, staying at the same cabin on the beach long before Airbnb had been a thing. They had watched Will crawl, then walk, then run on this narrow strip of sand, and the recurring annual booking ensured this weekend was pre-booked on their calendars, clear for them to escape the city and allow the wind and wine to blow the cobwebs away.

Emma got to the house first, becalmed by the way it never seemed to change. The same daggy beach decor, the wood paneling, the outside shower, screened from the beach by a fence made of old surfboards. They could afford something more glamorous these days, but they always came back to this place. Time had a way of standing still here.

Emma sat down on the mission-brown pull-out sofa with the dip in the mattress. She'd been waiting for this moment to listen to Dr Priya's episode "Old Friends." It was the perfect time to hear it. Emma parted the shade curtain, enough to see the beach and the white caps of surf in the distance. It felt good to blend this familiar view with Dr Priya's soothing voice, as if it helped Dr Priya overhear the years of conversation that Emma and Kendry had shared in this place. *Old friends*, said Dr Priya, *are both simple and complicated. They tend to keep you one of two ways: either they hold you down and prevent you from evolving into someone they don't want you to be; or they hold you accountable to your values, help you stay true to the best of yourself. One friend, my lovelies, is worth keeping*, said Dr Priya. *The other one is for letting go.*

Which was Kendry? Could someone be both?

Even though Kendry said she'd be there, Emma couldn't shake the apprehension that this year might be different, that Kendry would cancel, possibly at the last minute. Why else did she not want to be picked up from the airport, had insisted on meeting her here, rather than driving down together.

But Kendry did arrive, with three bags, four hats and a chessboard-sized box of Koko Black chocolates, which, she said, was their sworn duty to finish before the weekend was through.

She looked thicker, somehow, more substantial. The wrinkles in her cheeks had filled in and her overall complexion was softer, buttery. As soon as Emma had noticed this, she'd looked away, mindful of how sensitive Kendry was about her physical appearance. The changes in her face spoke volumes about how much pain Kendry had gone through in the time they had been apart.

"Where is it?" said Kendry, her head inside one of the low kitchen cupboards. "I have to see it." She rummaged to the clanging of pots and scraping of metal things from deep inside the cupboard.

"Here it is." She pulled out the Dutch mini-pancake pan. "Ta da," she said, straining to hold on to the cast-iron pan with little divots in it.

"I can't believe it's still here," said Emma.

"Look at it." Kendry's wrists strained to hold it. "This thing's indestructible."

"You think anyone's ever used this except us?"

"Of course not!" said Kendry. "Because making little Dutch pancakes is a pain in the ass." She stuffed the pan back in the pantry. "It's like a fondue. Nice idea, not worth the effort."

They unpacked, had a cup of tea and agreed to stroll down the main street where they browsed real estate boards and peeked in shop windows, pretending there was nothing to discuss.

As much as Emma wanted to tell Kendry how concerned she was, she knew her friend well enough to know it was worth holding off until Kendry was in a more serious mood. She'd get all defensive otherwise. Let her get comfortable first, look in the shops, eat a pistachio ice cream. They had the whole weekend to talk.

The weather turned by late afternoon, and they began to regret how far they'd walked away from the house along this wide stretch of beach. The gray water and sudden chilly breeze made it hard to imagine this place in summer, full of beachgoers.

"I'm going stay away for a while, Em," said Kendry, zipping up her coat.

"In Bryon?" said Emma cautiously.

"Yeah." Kendry zipped the jacket up tighter, so the collar was stiff around her neck. "I've just got too much past in Melbourne." She shivered and warmed her hands in her side pockets. "Besides, I want to be somewhere warm."

Emma looked at her friend, the translucent quality of her pale skin was accentuated by the flat gray sky. "So, rehab's going okay then?"

"Fuck no," said Kendry, putting her face into the wind. "It sucks. Plus, it's not goddamn rehab." She ran her fingers through her hair. "It's a wellness center in Byron Bay thank you very much."

Emma turned toward Kendry, who stared down at the sand as she walked. "Well," I'm glad you're going."

Kendry took Emma's hand and held it tight. "How did we get here, Em?" Kendry pulled her friend in close. "It's all going so fast."

"I know."

Kendry squeezed Emma tight and rubbed her shoulder. "Why do this, this gap year? Why not just split?"

"You sound like Will." Emma scooped hair out of her eyes.

"Maybe he's got a point."

Emma shot Kendry an unappreciative look.

"No, I'm serious," Kendry insisted, trying to catch Emma's eye. "What is it, this thing you're doing for yourself?"

Emma turned her back to Kendry and looked down at the sand, mixed with curls of dried seagrass, twisted and knotted like blackened Christmas tinsel.

"Hey," said Kendry, quietly, "do you reckon whatever problem you guys have is as much your fault as his?"

"Oh, please. Haven't you been listening?"

"Em, I'm your oldest friend and so it's my job to tell you these things, because who else will? What if the problem isn't just out there somewhere?" Kendry gestured toward the horizon. "What if it's in here?" She pointed at Emma's chest. "What if it's because you make yourself available to everyone but yourself? What if it has nothing to do with your marriage? Like, what if you married a hundred people and whoever they were, you ended up in the same situation?"

Emma shook her head slowly. She reached down and dug one of the little tufts of dried seagrass up from the sand. "When I was eighteen," she said, the brittle strands of seaweed coming apart in her fingers, "I was at this park in Coburg. It was a dump, car parts in the creek and electricity towers all around, but we all hung out there. Anyway, this one time, I came out from under a tree – it was one of those saggy ones with the branches that hang down."

"A willow."

"Right. Anyway, the branches were hanging down kind of like a curtain, and when I pulled them apart, I saw this guy standing there in the distance. He was a bit older than me, but not in a creepy way. And he was pushing this little kid on a swing. I didn't get the feeling it was *his* kid or anything, maybe his little brother or something, but that part doesn't really matter. Something weird happened after that." Emma wiped her hands of the crushed tuft of seagrass and let the dry shards sprinkle onto the gray sand.

"What?" said Kendry, impatiently.

"I'm not sure," said Emma. "It's hard to describe without it sounding stupid. But, when I looked at him, he looked back. And we had this…almost telepathic connection, like, somehow, I knew we were both thinking the same thing. Except it wasn't thinking, not in words. It was more like pictures. I saw him walk over, with that little boy, and I saw them both take my hand, and we walked back up the street, together, to the house where we all lived, like it was normal, like we'd done it a thousand times before, like it was the most natural thing in the world. He smiled and I did too. And it was as if our whole lives, and not just our lives, but the whole *world* had been slowly tipping us toward this moment of coming together. And it wasn't like I was just thinking these things. I *knew* them. And I *knew* that he knew them too." Emma gazed out at the gray waves. The breeze stiffened, making her nose leak.

"So, what did you do?" said Kendry.

"Nothing." Emma sniffed, wiped her nose with her sleeve. "The whole thing was super fragile, like a smoke ring. Someone kicked a ball and called out and the feeling was gone, it just went away."

"Yeah, but the guy was still standing there, right? It's not like *he* disappeared?"

"He was still there but it was different, somehow. Like the connection was broken."

"You got cold feet?"

"No. It wasn't like that. It was bigger than that. Afterwards, I always thought, maybe that's how love at first sight is supposed to feel like. But no one tells you what to do after you feel it. Like, I thought it should last longer and that's how I'd know for next time. But I never felt that again, for anyone, and I've always wondered, what if *that* was my soulmate?"

Kendry blew a raspberry. "Come on, 'soulmate'? Hon, I know you're kind of a romantic, but you sound like a teenage girl."

"I shouldn't have told you."

"No, I'm glad you did. It's a beautiful story, and I'm glad you had that experience. But…you haven't accepted what love is."

"Oh, and what is it? This should be good. Alright, go ahead, what is love?"

"Well, it's a compromise."

Emma rolled her eyes.

"It *is*," Kendry insisted. "It's a compromise you're both willing to live with."

"Oh, real romantic, Ken. Even for you that's fucking bleak."

"I don't think so. Not from where I sit. From here it sounds mighty peaceful, darl." Kendry put her hand on Emma's shoulder. "It's no fun being alone at our age."

"I thought you liked being single."

Kendry rolled her shoulders. "I do. I'm not going to lie. But it's not nice all the time."

"But what if things aren't right?"

"Is that what you're feeling, really? That it's wrong? Or is it something else?"

Emma kicked at the sand.

Kendry hugged her coat close, shielding herself from the wind. "Can you honestly say that your marriage is no good? What's so bad about Rob? I know he's flabbier than he used to be and he's not the most romantic guy going, but he's good. He loves you. Agreed, he's got a bone-headed way of showing it sometimes, but he does. I've seen it. How he looks at you and Will. Do you have any idea how much I want someone to look at *me* like that? It's great being single, but it's lonely out here too, Em. There's no fairytale perfection, except in a dream or a vision under a willow tree. And as much I like being single, I can't help but feel there's something missing sometimes. There's this hollow space in my heart and I want to fill it with something other than a partner but, deep down, I know that's what I want. I wish I didn't. But I do." She rubbed her hands. "You know, my parents were together for fifty-three years. They weren't all good years. But I also know, whatever happens to me, I'm never going to have that. You've got no idea what that's like. You're risking stuff you don't even realize you have." She pulled a tissue from her pocket and dabbed at her eyes. "Aw fuck." She blew her nose.

Emma looked over at her friend. The tall one. The boisterous one. The strong one, the one who always knew what to say or do, or where to take the party next. Emma could still see the young woman she'd met all those years ago in the quad at Melbourne University. But she could also see the older person she was becoming, breathing through her skin, the image fleeting, a shape in a cloud. "You know, Ken." She cleared her throat. "You could always—"

"Don't!" Kendry blew and wiped her nose again. "I know your heart's in the right place. But don't you dare tell me that it could still happen and that you never know what's around the corner because, hon, I don't even know if I can *do* that anymore." She put her hands in the pockets of her coat. "I just want something comfortable, without having to go through all the hard shit to get there." She sniffed. "I just want a thirty-year relationship out of the box. If they had that on the shelf, I'd buy it. A thirty-year marriage from five to eleven pm every night and then I get to go to sleep and wake up alone. Sold. Where do I sign?"

Emma put her arm around Kendry and rubbed her back. "I'm sorry, Ken. I just want you to be happy."

"Me too." Kendry rested her head on Emma's shoulder, the whole of their shared past summoned to the narrow space between them.

Kendry sniffed and blew her nose again. "Ugh, wet tissue," she said, holding up the soggy Kleenex. "It's coming apart. Christ, it's a fucking symbolic tissue," she sniggered. "You're done," she said to the soggy tissue, balling it up and putting it into her pocket. She fished for a fresh one in her coat. "Did I tell you I've been seeing an escort?"

"What?"

Kendry nodded, tucking her hair behind her ear, but the wind blew it out again. "There's no need to look so shocked. I wasn't even going to tell you."

"I'm not shocked. I'm just…but why?"

"Why not?" Kendry squinted.

Emma raised her eyebrows.

"Because," Kendry said, "guys my age want someone younger. Preferably, a lot younger. So do the math on how old some geezer is before he takes a second look at me. Unless you count the younger ones with mommy issues."

"Oh, please don't start on that again."

Kendry slapped her own wrist. She leaned in close. "I bet it's nice, though, eh?"

She jabbed her elbow into Emma's side.

The two of them laughed. The waves crashed on the empty beach and Kendry's dyed red hair leaped around her scalp in the wind like flames.

"What's that like?" said Emma, looking out to sea.

"The escorts?" said Kendry, her eyes also scanning the horizon. "A bit weird at first, but it gets easier. I kind of like it now. They're like lollipops, I pick a flavor."

"Really?"

"No, not really." Kendry looked at her hands, drained of color and papery dry from the wind. "I'd obviously prefer something a little more intimate, but I am nothing if not practical, a woman of action."

Emma took Kendry's hand.

"So, what happens now?" Kendry squeezed Emma's hand. "With Rob?" They both turned to the horizon, which disappeared and reappeared behind the ocean swell.

Emma thought about the little things that had started her on this journey, how they had become indistinguishable from the bigger things. The way Rob lay in bed, the outline of his body like a quilted mountain range, pulling her into the dent in the mattress, the way he expelled air when he laughed, the way he snorted, and, if he was really laughing, the way it always ended in a coughing fit. The disgust she'd felt when she noticed his sudden growth of ear hair, coarse and wiry, like an animal's. When had such small and seemingly insignificant things begun to annoy her? Or had she always noticed those things and had only stopped forgiving them?

But there was the bigger stuff too. The drinking. The way he'd pretty much given up on sex, always too stressed, too tired or too sore to accept her advances. He was never willing to discuss her concerns, dismissed her worry about the remoteness she perceived growing between them. There was always some reason to explain away his coldness, he had to get up early or he got to bed too late, had a lot on his mind. She could not help but feel that he was avoiding her. Questioning the motives behind his excuses only met with accusations: that she didn't appreciate the stress he was under, how hard he worked, the weight of the "boring but important things" that pressed on his mind. She offered to discuss these things with him, to work them out together, but he always said it was "too hard to get into," "not worth it," or that the issue, whatever it was, would "sort itself out." She came to hate those phrases, hearing in them only that he kept a part of his life separate from her. Was it too much effort to let her help him unravel the frustrations that kept him awake at night? Or was she not worthy of confiding in? In the end, Emma had stopped trying to bridge the gap between them and tried in vain to subdue her own unmet needs.

Weren't men supposed to be insatiable? Or was it just *her* he didn't want? Could he have been cheating? It seemed absurd. But then maybe that's why he seemed to distrust her, tried to control her in a million little ways, like when she was driving, the way he swiveled in the car as if she was bound to crash if he didn't survey the world outside her window. If it was caution that led him to behave this way, it didn't stop *him* from driving after drinking too many beers. Far too many beers.

Dr Priya reminded her to be grateful for the people in her life, to thank them for the gifts they imparted through their actions, both good and bad.

Rob was also passionate. The way he talked about his work, his clients, the way he stood back, arms akimbo, admiring the store of salvaged timbers he kept in their garden shed, treasured like dinosaur eggs. She didn't get it, but she could respect it. He loved Will. Of that, she was sure. He'd do anything for his family.

It felt true what Kendry had said, that things were different now that they had fewer years ahead of them than they had behind them. She could start something new, something serious. But Emma didn't need someone else to save her. She could rely on her own drive and ingenuity the way she used to, the way she'd had to, the way she knew she could.

But she also knew these things were no longer entirely true. They were in the sense that she *could* call on those strengths if she needed to, but she no longer *wanted* to. She just wanted to be happy and comfortable, and if her younger self was inclined to judge her for this, then her younger self did not, could not, understand what life was really like. "Fuck satisfaction," she'd once said. "I want my life to be full, a bonfire of the soul." But that was before she knew how rare contentment was.

Rob knew her in a way that no one else did, that no one else could. He'd known her when she was young, had met friends she no longer kept in touch with. He was one of the few people in her life now who'd had an actual conversation with her father. That stuff mattered. More than ever. They filled out a relationship, those experiences, and made of them a living scrapbook, a midden that would see them through the longest winter. What she and Rob had was irreplaceable. But she wasn't sure she wanted it back.

"You know what," Kendry said, wiping her nose with her sleeve, "maybe all you need to do is disappoint people for once. And not apologize for it. Just own it."

"I'm trying," said Emma.

"And how's that going?"

They laughed.

"You're going to like this," said Emma.

"Oh?"

"Erik's invited me to a music festival."

Kendry smiled, steepled her fingers. "Seriously?"

Emma nodded. "Him and his mates. It's stupid, right?"

"Oh god." Kendry rolled her eyes. "I'd pay to see this. Well," she said, slapping her thigh, "you said you wanted to go all in. That is all in, but seriously, sleeping in a tent on the ground?"

"Oh no, we'd have a cabin."

"Fancy." Kendry tubed her lips.

"I've never been to one."

"Yes, you have."

Emma shook her head.

"You did! Ninety-four, we all went to Meredith."

Emma shook her head.

"You were there," Kendry insisted. "With Mel and Sophie. You don't remember Spiderbait?"

"I didn't go, Ken. I worked that whole summer."

Kendry squinted, remembering. "Really?" Emma nodded. "Well, they were overrated," said Kendry, chuckling.

"I'm not loving the idea," said Emma, "but I should be open to new experiences, right?"

Kendry snorted. "Take clean undies and some cranberry juice, luv. A yeast infection's the price you pay for rooting in the dirt." She stood up. "Come on, Em." Kendry held the collar of her coat tight around her neck. "Let's get inside. It's fucking freezing out here."

They left the beach, past the sand dunes where the green tufts of seagrass bent and swirled in the wind.

CHAPTER THIRTY-TWO

Rob watched Sareena through the chain link fence of a worksite. Beyond it was a wedding-cake of a house, a Victorian jewel with a lot of fretwork and chimneys. She hadn't seen him yet, was too busy zooming in on something on her tablet. Sareena showed it to a stumpy little man, who lifted his glasses and leaned in close to examine whatever it was. The little man smiled, lowered his glasses and said something to Sareena, who playfully slapped him on the shoulder. She saw Rob through the fence, then, and her expression dulled slightly. She raised her index finger.

Rob retreated and leaned back on a pallet of timber, wrapped in plastic and dumped on the boggy nature strip. He waited, moving some gravel pebbles around the stomped grass with the toe of his work boot. He heard the clang of a metal gate and looked up. Sareena didn't approach, just stood there on the outside of the fence.

Rob pointed his thumb at the pallet of wrapped timber behind him. "It's the wrong stuff," he said. "Should've used engineered timber."

Sareena stuffed her hands into the front pockets of her puffy orange vest. "What do you want, Rob?"

He looked at her sideways. A jackhammer started up someplace inside the house. "I was thinking," he said, peeling himself off the pallet of timber, "that, maybe, we could finish what we started."

Sareena shifted her weight onto her hip. "I think I was pretty clear."

"I know." Rob held up his hands in submission. "You were. It's just…"

"I'm not building that Frankenhouse," she said, crossing her arms.

Rob scratched under his chin at the itchy stubble growing down his neck.

"Anyone tell you that you look like shit?" said Sareena, one eyebrow cocked.

"Thanks."

"You're welcome." She shifted her weight onto the other hip. "So, is that it?"

Rob sniffed. "What if…" He looked past Sareena at her construction crew moving around behind the fence. "What if you had more input, more control?"

Sareena sighed. "It's tempting, I'm not going to lie. Thing is," she said, balling up her fists inside the front pockets of her vest, "you weren't straight with me. And I'm not sure I can forgive you for that."

"I know," Rob admitted. "It's just that——"

Sareena held up her hand. "What I'm saying is that nice vibe we had, that flow we all had going on…I don't know if we can get that back." She shook her head. "When you don't let me into your shit, don't put everything out on the table, then I can't do what I do. You can't treat people like they're a project, Rob, something you manage. You've got to let 'em in."

Rob put his hands in his pockets. "Sorry you feel that way."

"Yeah, me too."

"So, what? That's it then?" said Rob.

"Guess it is."

He looked at her, glanced away. "And what if you took over?" he said. "Did it all the way *you* want?"

Sareena smiled. "I'd say that ship's sailed, mate."

"Seriously?" Rob frowned. "I'm offering you *full* creative control."

She smiled. "You still don't get it, do you?"

"What?"

"How I work, mate. Didn't you notice? I'm not about *full control*. I pick my crew because we work together. I pay the bills, but you don't see me bossing them around. You said I'm always on the phone talking," she smirked. "Well, you were half-right about that. What I do mostly is listen, mate. All these people back here" – she motioned over her shoulder, at the crew working behind the fence – "they show up here every day because I respect what they do. I rely on their expertise and ask them to help me with everything. It's not just *me* making the decisions, mate. It's a big, messy discussion, and that shit takes time. Would you make time for that, Rob?" She looked at him sideways.

He took a deep breath. "Not sure. Maybe. I'd have to know where I was meant to start."

She laughed.

"What?" said Rob, encouraged by her response.

"Look at you." She looked him up and down. "Man of action. Always looking to find the thing you can do."

Rob was puzzled. Of course he was looking for what he was supposed to do. Wasn't that what Sareena was doing right now? Telling him what was what? Schooling him? Her turn to gloat. To win.

"Dude," she continued, "I'm not suggesting you *do* anything. Just the opposite. I'm saying you can start by *doing* less and *listening* more."

"I listen."

She slowly shook her head and smiled big, all her teeth showing. "Nah, mate, you hear people out. There's a difference. I've seen you. You make up your mind before the other person's even finished talking. Look!" She pointed at his face. "You're doing it right now."

"I'm not." He blushed.

She smiled wryly and stamped mud off her boots. "I've got to get back," she said, adjusting her hard hat. "You'll be right. Just do what feels right." She turned and walked toward the gate.

"So, is that a definite no, then?" he called out.

"See you, Rob," she said, without looking back. The gate buzzed open and shut behind her with a wiry hiss.

Parking in the city was always a pain in the ass. Too many vigilante cyclists with a grudge against cars, hogging the road and daring you to hit them. It was a pride thing with those people. They'd miss fossil fuels as much as everyone else if they got their way.

Easy Robbie, you're sounding a little too much like the old man.

Rob leaned close to the windshield, looking up at the high-rise buildings to glimpse a street number. Will said the bar was around here someplace, in one of those grungy city laneways that tourists like so much. Rob didn't see the appeal of eating and drinking around trash cans and graffiti, but he wasn't about to miss out on a drink with his son.

Ah, a parking spot. He stopped his truck. Someone beeped behind him. "Yeah, yeah," he said to himself, opening the window to wave the angry driver around him. "There you go."

Rob parallel-parked, gratified by how his truck eased into a spot barely larger than his vehicle, all in one fluid motion. He learned that from the old man too.

Rob balked at the price of parking and grudgingly swiped his credit card on the meter. Everyone was out to fleece you. Banks and governments were the worst.

He found the entrance to Milk Man down the end of an alley, a double steel door between a tattoo parlor and a Nike store, where a group of Asian tourists were taking pictures of each other, posing with their shopping bags. Rob had an urge to jump into one of their photos, but they probably wouldn't like that. Could've been fun though.

It took a moment for Rob's eyes to adjust to the darkness of the bar. There were no windows in here, just pools of dim blue and purple lights that gave the place a permanent sense of night. The room was narrow, but deep, with sculptures of headless male torsos tucked inside niches all the way down, the muscled busts of decapitated Roman gladiators.

On the other side of the room, a huge bar stretched all the way to the back of the room where a few people sat drinking at round tables.

Will sat at the bar, his face lit by his phone. Behind him, a lone barman fed a mountain of glassware through the hissing jets of the glass washer. It was mid-afternoon, but Rob couldn't tell if the place was opening or shutting.

"Nice piece of timber," he said, running his hand along the glossy, varnished bar as he approached. Will looked up, smiled, glanced back at his phone, hammered his thumbs on the screen and sent whatever it was. Will had a whole life Rob knew nothing about. When did that happen?

"Red mahogany." Rob's fingers traced the pleasing curves of wood grain.

"It's nice," said Will, without conviction. He turned his phone upside down on the bar.

"You know," Rob smiled, "this piece of timber probably got to Melbourne on a ship that would've sailed right past our little house on the hill." Rob felt an unspoken tension settle between them at mention of the stone house. "Isn't that something?" he added, trying to clear the air.

"I guess," Will turned on his stool.

"You guess? Well," Rob said, pulling out a bar stool, "I think that's pretty cool." He sat down and a sigh of air escaped the stool's leather upholstery. "Wasn't me," he grinned. "It was the stool." The barman was unmoved by Rob's arrival and continued placing dirty glasses onto the conveyor belt of his washing machine, the clean glasses jamming up at the other end.

Behind the bar, among the bottles of booze, hung framed black-and-white photos of naked men with flaccid penises. Rob looked away and scanned the ceiling. A circus trapeze hung up there.

He turned to his son. "Should we get a beer or something?"

Will grimaced. "I really only drink rum and coke."

"Okay, we'll get that then." Rob waved to get the barman's attention. "Two rum and cokes, mate," he called over.

The barman fished a pair of glasses from the clean side of the washer.

"You mind using glasses that are already on the bar?" said Rob. Will huffed.

"What?" said Rob, turning to Will. "The glasses are all hot when they come out of that thing. Who wants a cold drink out of a hot glass?"

The barman slowly walked over to where the dry glasses were stacked, wiping his hands with a towel that hung out of his pocket. "I don't like it either," said the barman, laying the tumbler glasses in front of them. "Hot glass melts the ice," he said gravely. "Waters down the booze."

"See," said Rob, nudging his son. "He knows."

The poker-faced barman scooped a mound of cubes into the glasses and free poured the rum with a flourish of the wrist. Rob liked the way the ice cracked at the touch of alcohol, made him think of a foundation settling into place.

"Thanks," said Will, accepting the drink from the bartender.

Rob, put a twenty dollar bill on the bar. "There you go, mate."

"It actually comes to thirty-six fifty," said the bartender, pinching the bill between his fingertips. "You can pay by card."

"Here," said Will, holding out his bank card.

"Nah." Rob pushed away Will's card and fossicked in his own pockets, jangling with loose change. "Geez, pretty steep, eh?" The barman opened his hands, palms up. Rob pulled some bills and coins from his pockets and left them on the bar. "All good," said Rob. The barman wordlessly took the money and returned to his dishwasher.

"Cheers," said Rob, holding up his glass.

Will clinked glasses with his father and sipped through the straw. Rob slurped his from the rim, his eyes moving back to the trapeze swing that hung above the bar on a metal wire. He took a long drink and gulped up a piece of ice, crunching it with his back teeth.

"So," he said, "how'd you find this place?"

Will took another sip of his drink. Held it with both hands, elbows resting on the bar. "I don't know, just some friends."

"Yeah?" Rob looked to the back of the room. Some people were playing cards back there. "Anyone I know?"

Will shook his head. "Mostly people from uni."

"Well, that's good. See, university's good for something."

Will smiled, his cheeks rosy. God, he looked like his mother. Lucky for him. "You know," said Rob, without turning to Will, "you didn't need to bring me here."

"What do you mean?"

"You know, to shock me or whatever." Rob slurped his drink.

"Are you shocked?"

Rob looked up, caught a glimpse of the framed pictures of naked men above the bar. He jutted his chin out. "No." He saw Will in his peripheral vision and realized that looking at him directly was sure to make Rob cry. He just wanted Will's life to be easy. And this would make it harder.

God, he looked like his mom. But he also looked like he did when he was a little boy. He was half man, half boy now. Rob would always see him that way. Like right now. He wanted to pick his son up in his arms, like when he was little, make raspberries on his belly and fold his little body into his own. Where did all that time go? And why didn't he savor it more when he had the chance?

This wave of emotion had come from nowhere and Rob didn't know what to say now. He wanted things to be good between him and Will. Easy. The way they used to be. Time had a way of complicating things.

Rob swallowed past the lump in his throat. "What'd you think I was going to say?"

Will turned his drink on the bar.

"I'm still sitting here, Will." He looked at his boy. "That tells you all you need to know, son."

Will nodded, swirled his finger in a puddle of water on the bar.

Rob wiped his face with his hand. "Did I do something to make you think I wouldn't be okay with this?"

Will sighed. "It's not like I thought you'd freak out or anything. I guess I just...I don't know."

Rob absorbed the weird space between them. Didn't Will realize how much he loved him. No matter what. "Will, look at me." Will, head still tilted down, briefly met Rob's gaze. "I just want you to be a good man. Stand by the people you love. And stand up for the things you believe in. You're a good man. This doesn't change that."

Will smiled. Rob looked up at the photos of the naked men above the bar, the muscled busts of those gladiator statues in their niches. "That's a lot of penises in one day though, mate."

Will snickered.

Rob smiled, finished his drink and rattled the ice. "You want another one?"

"Nah," said Will, playing with the puddle on the bar, making a series of connected Olympic rings on the bar with his glass.

"You're probably right," said Rob, drumming his fingers on the bar. "Best stop there. I'm driving." He rubbed his palm on his pant leg. "It wasn't always like this, you know," Rob turned on his stool, looked around the place, the swirly blue lights on the ceiling. "Yeah, we used to have a lot more freedom in this country."

The barman raised an eyebrow as he stacked his glassware. "It's true," said Rob to no one in particular. "Too many rules now, wherever you go. Can't do this. Need a permit for that. It's like a – what do they call it – a nanny state." He snapped his fingers. "That's what it is, mate, a nanny state."

Will pushed his drink away and looked at Rob.

"Ah fuck it," said Rob and nodded at the bartender. "I'm going to have another one. Just a beer, though. Pot of Carlton."

"We've only got Mountain Goat."

"Fine, whatever." Rob turned to Will. "You talk to your mom?"

"No. You?"

"Nope," Rob shook his head slowly. "It's against the rules, mate. You know your mom."

The barman put the beer down in front of Rob. "Eight fifty."

"For a pot? Christ." Rob fished a five dollar bill and some coins from his pocket. The barman scooped the money off the bar and walked back to his glass machine.

Will sighed. "It's a bit fucked up don't you think? I mean… Mom—"

"She just needs to blow off steam, Will." He reached for his beer.

"And what if that doesn't work?"

"It will." Rob sculled the beer and brought the glass down on the bar with a bang. "Now," he searched the room. "Where's the head in this place?" He squinted down the dark corridor. "There it is. Back in a sec." He walked down, past the card players who glanced up from their game.

The toilet door screeched on a wobbly hinge. Someone should fix that. Rob stepped onto the steel grate of the urinal trough and unzipped his pants. He looked down at the yellowed water in the metal trough where barely smoked cigarette butts lay sodden among the broken urinal cakes. As he waited to expel the growing pressure in his bladder, he contemplated the untidy mess of his graying pubic hair and the sad puddle of flesh in the middle. He wasn't the man he used to be.

He'd deflated. It happened sometimes, more often than not. He'd just collapse like the inflatable cactus that flapped outside the discount furniture shop on Hoddle Street. That's how he felt down there. Unpredictable, never sure which direction the wind would bend him. When he *did* get hard, Emma wasn't there, and he couldn't bring himself to jerk off in a portaloo at work like he did when he was twenty.

There were the little blue pills, but he didn't like the idea of side effects. He needed his wits about him. Plus, Rob didn't want to get hooked on those things. Who knew what else was in them. It all seemed artificial. Untrustworthy. No, if this is what nature wanted, he'd have to accept it. You couldn't just turn the hourglass over.

Truth was, he didn't mind as much as he thought he would, this absence of longing. Sex always complicated things, like it had, just now, with Will. Life was easier without it.

Emma got touchy about sex, disappointed, frustrated. She didn't say so, exactly, but he knew he left her wanting, so he did his best to avoid the subject. It was easier that way. Life would probably be better if they could just forget about sex altogether. But it wasn't that easy.

Sometimes, when he woke in the middle of the night, he could feel his wife awake beside him, could hear her quiet panting, feel the rhythmic pulse in the mattress beneath him. He'd pretend to be asleep, didn't want to embarrass her, or disturb the pleasure she deserved. He could hold on, go to the toilet later. He owed her that much.

The wobbly hinge squealed behind him as someone else entered the washroom. Rob looked straight ahead, felt the other man's weight depress the metal grate they both stood on. Geez, this guy stood close, way closer than a guy would normally stand. The unspoken rule of a man apart didn't seem to apply here. Rob now felt weird about holding his cock in his hand in this place, like it signaled something more than nature calling. He wasn't pissing yet either, this guy. What was he doing? Checking him out? Did he like what he saw? Or was Rob just another fat guy waiting to piss?

Could someone still feel that way about him? Desire him the way Rob desired a beautiful woman when he saw one, even if he meant to do nothing about it? He'd never thought of it like that before and gay guys suddenly made more sense to him. Same job, different tools. He smiled.

Relief came at last, a trickle at first, growing into a weak flow. "Phew," said Rob, still looking straight ahead at the shabby green subway tiles. "Pipes don't work the way they used to," he said, almost looking over, breaking the second rule of urinal etiquette. The other man said nothing, just peed in a steady, effortless stream.

Rob zipped up and headed for the door without washing his hands.

Down the end of the long corridor, Rob spied Will talking to the barman, who returned to his glasses as Rob approached. "Ah," said Rob, getting within earshot of his son. "Well, that cleared the pipes."

"Gross," said Will.

"Oh, I don't know." Rob sat down. "At my age it's a blessing." Rob picked up his empty beer glass and downed the last frothy dregs sitting in the bottom. "You know," he said, turning to Will. "Your mom's alright." He put the glass down and pushed it away. "She's just getting older, mate. We both are. It's got a way of messing with you, it's…it's hard to explain."

"Dad."

"Yes, mate."

Will looked at him, hesitated, glanced at the bar taps. "You want another drink?" he said.

"Nah." He thought about it and put his hand on Will's shoulder. "Your money's no good to me, you know that." He stood up and his back twinged. "Besides," he said, digging his thumb into the small of his back, "I'll be over the limit soon. I can't lose me license." Rob searched his pockets, pulled out a crinkled fifty dollar bill and put it on the bar. "Here. Buy yourself one and get one for that guy while you're at it." He nodded toward the bartender. "I've got to get on." Rob patted Will on the shoulder.

"Dad." Will sighed. "I'm sorry work stopped on the house."

Rob blinked. "Me too."

"I was getting into it."

Rob put his hand on Will's shoulder. "Me too."

"So, what happens to the place now?"

"Dunno. Syed might have to sell it. Or change the design. Could be tied up in council for years, mate, with those fuck heads."

Will nodded. "That really sucks."

"It does."

"Hey." Will stood up and put his arms around his father. "Love ya dad."

Rob patted his son's back and blinked back tears. "You too, son."

Outside, Rob felt a little wobbly. Probably should've eaten some food before knocking back those drinks. The booze helped dull his back pain though, which nagged him as he moved. He'd walk around the city for a bit, let the booze pass before getting back in his car.

It'd been ages since he'd wandered around Melbourne like this. Geez, there were a lot of cafes, seemed like a different one every few steps. It wasn't always like this. The CBD was a dead zone when he was growing up. Everyone lived in the suburbs.

His eye caught a flashing sign that read "Massage." He pressed his thumb into his lower back. Why not? When in Rome.

An older Asian lady at the front counter greeted him with a grandmotherly smile.

"Hi," said Rob, and the lady handed him a mandarin orange. "Oh, thanks," he said, and turned it in his hand.

"How long you want massage?" She motioned toward the price list on the wall, which Rob contemplated. Ninety minutes seemed a long time.

"How about thirty minutes," he said, pulling out the cash.

The lady smiled and led Rob to a small, dimly lit room with a large massage table covered in white towels.

"Please," she motioned for him to take off his clothes and lie on the table. Rob turned his back to her and took off his fleece vest.

The grandmother left, gently closing the door behind her.

Rob undressed, all but his underwear, and felt a slight chill in the air on his exposed skin. He crawled under the warm towels and put his head down through the hole in the massage table.

A light tapping on the door. "Yep," said Rob.

The door opened, gently, and Rob looked over his shoulder. A young woman with long black hair smiled. She carried a wicker basket in front of her, filled with little glass jars that clinked as she put the basket down on a side table. "Welcome," she said, leaning across him and gently laying her hand on the towel covering Rob's back. He lay face down. "It's sore here," he said, straining to point his thumb at his lower back.

"Here," she lifted the towel and rubbed her fingers on his skin, giving him goosebumps.

"Christ, I tell ya," he said. "Pain enough to make a grown man cry."

"Sore?" she said, placing her palm firmly on the spot. Rob let out a sigh.

"It's okay?"

"That's the spot."

She spread warm oil on his back and massaged it in, slowly and with increasing pressure. She was strong, dug her knuckles into his back, moved her fists back and forth like a rolling pin. It hurt like hell, but it felt good, like something tough was breaking loose inside him. Cracking the gristle. She pressed harder, dug her elbows into his lower back, and he breathed on, expelling tension with every breath.

Her hands moved to his sides, his hips; she massaged the sides of his butt.

"Can I remove your underwear?" she whispered.

"Uh, sure."

"It's more easy." Her hands slid under the towel, up the sides of his legs and gently pulled his undies down in one, fluid motion. Rob adjusted himself on the table, feeling strange under the towel now, naked and exposed. He tried to relax, to breathe, head down in the face hole. He followed the flowing pattern of the carpet on the floor, but his mind was on her hands, kneading the inside of his thighs, her hands sweeping the gully of his ass crack.

"Is it okay?" she said.

"Yeah," he said to his own surprise. "It's good."

"Thank you."

"Thank *you*," he said, closing his eyes.

She gently parted one of his butt cheeks and dribbled oil between them.

Rob tensed, a dull ache returning to his back.

"Hmm," the woman sighed, and gently rubbed oil on his bum. "Very sore," she said, her voice croaky.

Rob's body tingled and his attention moved to his crotch, the dormant epicenter of his arousal. He was inflating.

Her fingers slowly walked up his spine. She crept closer. Rob could feel her there, by his ear, near enough to hear her breath, to smell her fruity shampoo and to feel a wisp of her hair tickling his neck.

"You want just massage," she whispered, "or something more special?"

Rob's butt cheeks clenched. He brought his face out of the hole in the massage table. She was right there, looking down at him. She smiled, her tongue flicked her bottom lip.

"Ah," he rolled onto his side, aware of the bulge that tee-peed the towel at his crotch.

She noticed it too. "Why not?" She smiled. "Maybe hand job?"

Rob brought his knees toward his stomach, trying to conceal his clumsy erection. "Look, I think there's been a misunderstanding here."

"It's nice," she said, and her eyes widened.

"Look, I'm married, see, and it…well, it doesn't feel right."

She seemed to think about this. "Why you come here, then?"

"Cuz my back hurt," he said.

She looked down at him, sizing him up.

"Eighty dollars," she said.

"No, I don't want it."

"Seventy."

"I don't want it." He shook his head.

"Okay." She got up, briskly tied her hair back in a ponytail and left, closing the door behind her with enough force to shake the wreath of plastic flowers hanging on the wall.

Rob expelled a long breath and sat up in his mess of white towels. He noticed the large mirror in the room, big enough to cover the whole wall. How had he not noticed that? He looked down at his lap. The erection was gone.

Rob got dressed and put a fifty-dollar bill in the young lady's basket of oils. He left the mandarin orange.

CHAPTER THIRTY-THREE

Emma's head listed as Erik pumped the brakes. She peered out the back window of the cramped hatchback, traffic banking up on this narrow stretch of road somewhere near Porcupine Ridge. It was all fields and farmhouses now, rickety fences and scrubland. Hard to believe they were nearing a concert venue.

"Definitely more people than last year," said Erik, tapping the wheel to the beat of the moody techno music.

"Tons more," said Briley, his bassist, whose monolithic cello case was propped next to Emma in the back seat while Briley sat up front on account of her "travel sickness".

"Sweet," said Erik, high-fiving Briley. "So cool that we're the closing set this year. Look at all the people. It's, like, peak party." He raised his head to catch Emma's eyes in the rear-view mirror. "Still okay back there?"

Emma gave a thumbs up and adjusted herself in her seat, bothered by the electric cables and amplifiers and bulky electronic equipment piled around her.

"The festival's catching on," said Erik. "My buddy, Enrique, started this a few years back, rented a field from this old hippie farmer – cool guy." He shook his head and smiled, as if remembering something. "Now look at it." His head swiveled, taking in all the parked cars . "It's blowing up."

Emma nodded politely.

It was too hot in this car. If princess up there was prone to a chill, why didn't she wear a sweater instead of blasting the heater the whole trip up from Melbourne? Wasn't this generation all about fixing climate change?

The car inched forward, past traffic cones and a bored man in an orange trench coat mechanically directing traffic. Emma rechecked her text to Angie and Mish.

You guys there already?

Nah. Hanging at hotel.

You coming tho?

Emma's text just hung there, unanswered. She bumped in her seat as the car veered onto a dirt track. Erik and Briley high-fived each other again, and Emma couldn't help but roll her eyes as they bounced toward the epicenter of the third annual Synth Eclipse Festival of Electronic Music.

Further up the road, a woman in an orange trench coat nodded at the official VIP Pass on the dash and pointed them toward a small service road that ran the length of the field.

They drove on, passed acres of mowed fields, pockmarked by dams round as meteor craters.

The first youthful revelers came into view, a lot of fluoro and colored hair out there, crop tops and flared pants, spandex and a few people in full-body animal costumes – cartoon lions, zebras and giraffes. Emma did a double take at a pair of topless young women with crisscrossed bandaids over their nipples setting up a dome tent near the fence line.

Was she ready to step into this world of carefree spirits? Erik had promised her a swag inside a demountable office, luxury compared to what these women were willing to endure. Angie and Mish's idea of staying at a hotel in town now seemed more appealing than the authentic festival experience Emma was in for. Still, even if the cabin had no plumbing, heating or electricity, at least it had walls.

They parked next to a bunch of cars lined up behind a tin shed filled with rusty farm equipment. Emma surveyed the rickety wooden cabins and absorbed the three portable toilets that made up the VIP area. She was not doing a shit in there.

A goth girl was talking into a headset. She fluttered her fingers at Erik as he stepped out of the car. Briley got out too and hopped around, clapping. "It's twice as big as last year." She danced on the spot. "Paige!" Briley threw her arms around the goth girl.

Emma waited to be released from the hatchback.

Erik stretched then turned suddenly, remembering her. He pulled the driver's seat forward and helped her out of the car. "Sorry," he whispered. She grabbed her wheely suitcase. Briley could get her own shit.

The suitcase wheels struggled on the uneven ground and Emma picked it up, heavy and awkward, bumping against her leg.

"Need a hand?" Erik reached for her suitcase.

"I've got it."

Out in the field, a sea of youthful bodies was forming near an open-air stage. Mellow electronic music pumped from giant speakers. Emma took in the short skirts, crop tops, tube tops, and fashion that seemed to have been plucked straight from a Japanese anime. She felt daggy in her jeans, leather jacket and old Guns N' Roses T-shirt. She was dressed like someone's mom.

There were some middle-aged people here too, and even older, but they looked like people for whom the party had never ended; they danced alone, eyes closed, transported somewhere beyond sight.

"We've got to set up," said Erik. "You can head out there if you want." He ran his hand through his hair. "Or you can hang back here. Might be boring, though."

Emma's spirits threatened to dampen. But she reminded herself that she'd chosen to be here. And not as a tourist; she wanted to get into it. "It's okay," she said. "Just do your thing." She eyed Briley chatting with goth girl Paige, all smiles, laughing as if they were besties. "I'll be fine," said Emma.

Erik brightened. "Okay," he said, taking Emma's suitcase. "We're in cabin three." He pointed his thumb over his shoulder. "There's no shower or anything. Just swags."

Emma glanced at Briley and the goth girl. "She staying with us?"

Erik put a hand on Emma's shoulder. "Briley's staying in there" – he pointed to another cabin – "*with* Paige."

"Oh, right." Emma's face flushed. Her attention returned to the portaloos, the communal water station, the distant thump of music and the growing crowd. She resolved to immerse herself in this experience. As Dr Priya said, age was *not* just a number, it was an accumulation of experience, a sign of rank like military insignia, life training you could rely on. Emma didn't need a babysitter; she was here to make memories.

"You okay?" Erik wrapped an arm around her waist.

"I'm good." She patted his back. "Don't worry about me. I'm a big girl. I'll see you later."

She headed toward the festival grounds, noting secluded spots between trees and bushes where she might pee later, after it got fully dark.

The bass got louder – physical – and snippets of conversation flew around her like speech bubbles in the breeze. A guy on stilts in the distance, dressed like a disco wizard, blew soap blobs that drifted like floating jellyfish over the crowd's outstretched fingers.

Emma marveled at the unapologetic confidence radiating from these young people, the uninhibited crush of their buoyant joy.

She was caught off guard when she felt a hand on her shoulder. "Hey," Briley said, brimming with mischief. "Brought you a present." She held out a tiny pink pill engraved with a picture of a hedgehog.

Emma's mind was a battle of curiosity and caution at the unexpected offer. What if she acted like an idiot, lost control? She declined with a smile. "I'm good," she said.

Briley nodded, as if she'd expected that answer.

Fuck you, thought Emma and continued through the festival grounds, determined to enjoy herself, to revel, unburdened by societal expectations.

Nearer the stage, a layer of dust hung in the air, kicked up by people dancing on the dried grass and hard dirt.

Emma slowly moved to the music, at once dreamy and spooky. She felt unsure how to dance to it and moved tentatively. She closed her eyes. The bass thumped in her guts like a second heartbeat. She swayed, finding her rhythm.

Someone touched her and she opened her eyes to a young woman, dressed in a blue leotard and fuzzy rabbit ears. "Can I take your picture?" she said, holding up her phone.

"Sure," said Emma, leaning back and making a peace sign.

"Oh, so *cute*," said the young woman, angling her phone, taking photos. "You're an inspiration, like our Earth Mother."

"Right." *Little shit.*

Blue leotard receded into the crowd, limbs flailing, a fairy-floss Vishnu with rabbit ears. Emma didn't feel like dancing anymore. She walked back to the sheds in the VIP area.

There were more people around now, hauling gear, vaping. The goth girl with the headset, Paige, directed traffic and hugged people as they stepped out of their cars.

Briley, earmuff headphones on, was leaning against a shipping container, her face in a honeyed wedge of sunset. She opened one eye, squinting as Emma approached.

"Hey," said Briley, sliding one of her earmuffs aside.

Emma nodded. "That pill still on offer?"

A mischievous grin spread on Briley's face. "Emma C on the lollies." She reached into her bag and retrieved a small tin of breath mints. "Here," she said, fishing out the hedgehog and holding it out.

"It's ecstasy, right?" said Emma, nervously. Briley smiled and nodded. Emma took a belly breath and swallowed the pill, grimacing at the bitter tang. She'd expected it to taste like candy.

Briley smirked. "You'll never be the same again." She slid the headphone cup back over her ear and closed her eyes.

Emma tried to smile, like she wasn't fazed by the comment. But the butterflies in her stomach were now freaking out.

"Oh hey," said Briley, sliding the earphone off again. "You want to switch tops?" Emma looked down at Briley's fluorescent camouflage crop top.

"I'm fine," said Emma, briefly looking down at her own chest, the fading print of her Guns N' Roses T-shirt.

"No big deal," said Briley. "Your boobs are amazing if that's what you're worried about."

"Thanks, I'm not."

"I hope *mine* look like that when I'm older."

"Good to know."

Briley tucked a strand of hair behind her ear. "Just trying to help you fit in."

"I'm actually kind of attached to this top. Sentimental value." Emma turned away. "Think I'll keep it," she said over her shoulder, and walked away.

"Fine," said Briley, calling after her. "It's probably not even vintage. And your boobs look saggy."

Emma raised her middle finger and held it up as she disappeared into the crowd.

Out there, she felt incongruous again, an old hag, a chaperone, dulling the edge of this party. What was she doing here? She needed to get away from these people.

She wandered the perimeter of the fence, looked up at the trees, their gnarled trunks and knotted branches where little parakeets played peekaboo from inside their hollows. More time in nature. That's what she needed. It was so simple. A truth.

Emma looked up at the fading blue sky and momentarily sensed herself falling toward it, an airy plunge toward a pale and infinite sea. She braced herself on the fence and the feeling passed. Her pulse beat in her ears and she walked on, slowly, using the fence as support. The grass felt spongy underfoot. Her face tingled.

The music got louder. No, not louder, it came from everywhere, saturating the very atmosphere that held everything together. It was the living voice of this place, as if the trees and the rocks themselves were singing.

Someone dressed as a blue creature from *Avatar* beckoned and she heeded their invitation, joining a group of dancers who moved aside to let her in. She danced, drawing on the kinetic energy of moving bodies around her. Her inhibitions evaporated and she danced with weightless abandon.

Someone placed a tutu on her head like a crown, a headdress, and she laughed, a surge of joy dissolving her being into the very air they breathed, exhaling the night that closed around them. She was now part of this beautiful crush, a blur of feather boas, colored wigs and moving limbs, kinship palpable in the flow of bodies, dancing to the heartbeat of the universe.

Sweat poured off her and the weight of the bass rumbled in her belly, building pressure in her abdomen. She had to poo. Now.

Emma couldn't bring herself to use a portaloo, not even now. She held on. A few people were going off to squat in the scrub along the fence. For Emma, the urge retracted instantly at the thought of going in the woods. Then it returned with a vengeance. This was going to happen, with or without her consent.

She fought through a sappy bush until she found the wire fence, climbed up and over, dropping into the long grass on the other side and rolling down the hill. She stood up, dizzy, and groped in the dark, snapping twigs under foot as she found her balance and level ground on which to relieve herself. The ecstasy of voiding her bowels intensified her communion with her body, releasing a new surge of joy, as if she'd been purified spiritually.

She hiked up her pants and noticed they were wet and soiled with what she hoped was mud. She pulled off her jeans and looked for a place to put them, settling on a tree branch. She looked down at the tutu, her legs appreciating their unbridled freedom. The moon hung low in the sky, close enough to touch.

Emma scrabbled through the bush until she found the dirt road that ran the length of the fence and followed it back to the VIP area where Paige kept vigil, talking with a couple of security guys.

"Well hellooo," said Paige. "Out for a little walk?"

Emma smiled. She'd been too harsh with Briley. Of course she wanted to wear her Guns N' Roses shirt. Who wouldn't? It was awesome. Emma had been selfish keeping it for herself. Hoarding. Sharing mattered, small acts of kindness could yet save the world.

Emma smiled, she'd make things right. Filled with the righteous pleasure of magnanimity, she walked toward the cabins.

That one was Briley's, the little one. She fumbled with the door and opened it.

Inside, Erik stood shirtless, with Briley kneeling in front of him.

"Ah!" Emma screamed like she'd just seen a rat.

"Fuck," Erik pulled away from Briley and turned sideways, fumbling with the crotch of his pants.

"Don't you fucking knock?" said Briley, still kneeling. She wiped her mouth with the back of her hand.

"Oh." Emma laughed, covering her mouth with her hand. "Don't stop. You had some good technique going there."

"Em," said Erik. "It's just—"

"No, it's okay," said Emma. "I was just popping in." She looked at Briley. "I wanted to give you my shirt."

"Okaaay," said Erik, putting his shirt back on.

"It's true," said Emma. "I want to give more."

"What the fuck—"

"She's loved up on pingaz," said Briley.

Emma smiled. "Don't minimize it. We can all do better."

"See what I mean?"

"Are you okay?" said Erik, concerned.

"I'm fine." Emma hugged herself and sighed. "But I'm worried. About you guys. And you," she said, pointing at Briley, "you need to get off your knees. They'll keep you there forever, you know."

Briley scowled.

"Em." Erik held up his hands.

Emma laughed. "Relax. You're free," she said, twirling her hand as if she were a sorceress releasing him from a spell.

"Em," Erik called after her, but she was already leaving. She shut the door behind her and made her way to the other cabin. Their cabin. Her cabin. She grabbed her suitcase and headed toward the tin shed where Paige and the security guys were.

"Hey," said Emma, placing her hand on Paige's shoulder, the suppleness of her buoyant flesh giving way under the stiff velvet of her top. "It's good to stick together."

"Okaay," said Paige, smiling. "You going somewhere, hon?"

Emma nodded, gravely, her hand still on Paige's shoulder, the texture of the velvety black dress alive, like animal fur. "I'm going to find my friends," she said, and lifted her hand from Paige's wing-collared dress.

"You know where you're going?"

Emma nodded. "There," she said, pointing to the forest. "To town," she smiled. "I'm bringing the party to them." She turned toward the security guys and offered them a hundred bucks to drive her the few miles to Daylesford.

Emma sat in the passenger seat grinning and waved goodbye to Paige. As the truck sped up, Emma absorbed the rejuvenating power of the wind from the open window, the earthy wafts of spring.

"You sure you're okay?" said the driver.

"Never better," she said, bringing her head back inside the car.

"Here." The driver handed her a bottle of blue Gatorade. "Drink this."

Emma popped the lid and drank, replenished by its sugary tang. She sipped and nibbled the plastic nozzle, which felt good in her mouth, like a pacifier.

Beyond the high beams, in the darkness, the trees were like sentinels patiently awaiting the extinction of humanity. It wasn't even that big a deal, and she laughed, freed by the beautiful, unavoidable simplicity of it all.

She was dropped off in the middle of Daylesford. "You sure you'll be okay?" said the driver.

"Absolutely."

"The hotel's just there. You want me to wait for you?"

"Nah, I'm good."

"Have a good night then." He rolled up the window and drove off.

Emma walked, grateful for the silence, the rhythmic clomp of her own feet on the pavement, the easy rumble of her wheely suitcase on the smooth sidewalk, reverberating in the palm of her hand.

She had to pee and ducked inside the nearest restaurant. She pushed past the young woman at reception and headed straight for the restrooms.

In the stall, she sat quietly, waiting for the pee to come. She examined the engineering of the cubicle, the way the bolts went into tiles, the way the brackets held up the walls, so straight and neat, defying the force of gravity. It was beautiful.

She jumped at a knock on the stall door. "Em," came a familiar voice.

Emma looked around, wondering if she was hallucinating. "Hello?" she said, unsure if there was anyone there.

"It's Angie."

"What?"

"I'm here, with Mish. What are you doing?"

Emma looked from side to side. The toilet paper dispenser, the graffiti on the cubicle wall. "I'm in the toilet."

She heard giggling.

"We know. Are you okay?" She heard Mish's voice.

"Mish," said Emma. "Mish, Mish, Mishhhhhh."

"Are you okay?"

Emma pulled a long strand of toilet paper, loving the feel of it in her hands, held a wad of it against her face. "I'm great."

More giggling. "You want to come out?"

Emma looked around the cubicle. "Yep." She dabbed at nothing, flushed, stood and opened the door. "Hey," she said, throwing her arms around Mish.

"Oh," said Angie. "Nice outfit, Em."

"I know," said Emma, untangling herself from Mish's embrace "It's beautiful." She stroked the folds of her tutu. "I got it from an angel."

Mish and Angie walked Emma to the sink and helped her wash up.

"You guys are nice," said Emma.

"Well, you're nice too," said Mish.

"You know I *am* nice."

"Good," said Angie. "We're all nice."

"She's off her face," said Angie.

"What did you take?" said Mish.

Emma brought her thumb and forefinger together and held it in front of her eye. "Just one little hedgehog. Hey, your brother" – Emma poked her finger at Angie's shoulder – "has a beautiful cock."

"Oh god," said Angie. Mish looked concerned.

"It's naughty though," said Emma, pouting. "It's a peevish pecker," she smiled. "Pecker," she repeated, emphasizing the P.

"Okay, let's sit you down." Angie put an arm around Emma.

"A pompous penis," Emma laughed. "A petulant prong."

"You want to come sit with us for a bit?"

Emma nodded. "Oh, I do. I really do." She hugged Angie, then snapped her fingers. "A problem prick," she laughed.

They moved out to the restaurant. Emma smiled at patrons as they passed, the beautiful families out for dinner.

"Can I get you anything?" said the waitress.

"You guys got any Gatorade or anything?" said Angie.

The waitress raised her eyebrows, looked at Emma. "How about a Sprite?" she said knowingly.

"Great," said Angie, "and a bowl of fries." The waitress nodded and left.

"She seems nice," said Emma.

"So," said Angie, "what happened?"

Emma's phone dinged and lit up. Emma just sat there.

"Oh, who loves you," said Angie, reaching for Emma's phone.

Emma crinkled her nose. "Probably a scammer."

Angie squinted at the phone. "Hey, you've got a missed call from, like, Friday."

"What the fuck," said Mish, as Angie pressed the phone and held it to her ear, listening to the message. Mish reached for the phone, but Angie leaned sideways to stay out of reach and kept listening. Mish frowned. Angie grinned and held onto Emma's phone. "So," she dropped the phone on her chest. "Not a scammer."

Emma leaned forward.

"You've got an interview tomorrow. Hayman something."

"Ooh," said Mish. "Haimon Young. Prestige."

"You're supposed to click on the link and accept your time slot," said Angie. "Can I click *yes*? I'm going to click yes."

The waitress came back and unceremoniously delivered the Sprite and the bowl of fries.

"Yum," said Angie.

"I'm fucked up," said Emma. "I can't go anywhere."

"You'll be fine tomorrow," said Angie.

"Really?"

"Totally." Angie popped a shoestring fry in her mouth. "We'll drive you."

"Oh fuck," said Emma. "I'm being punished, aren't I? I'm a bad person, right? A bad woman, a bad mother?"

"Em. Seriously. It's all okay," said Angie.

"Ha."

"True," said Mish. "It's not a big deal. No one's died, right?"

"Unless you killed someone in the woods earlier." Angie grinned, picking at the fries.

Emma thought about the evening's events. "I don't think so."

"See, you're fine," said Angie.

Mish nodded.

Angie crunched another French fry, looked Emma up and down. "Might want to wear a different outfit to the interview though."

Angie laughed. As did Emma. Mish joined in and the three of them kept each other going.

"You know," said Emma, pondering the rafters. "I've made a decision." Mish and Angie leaned in. "I think I've sucked my last cock." Emma's head flung back, and she cackled with abandon. "Dick denied."

People turned in their seats to tut-tut them. An old man at a nearby table frowned and shook his head, which only made them laugh more.

CHAPTER THIRTY-FOUR

Rob spent the day picking up fixtures and hardware. He didn't care that work had officially ceased on the house. It wouldn't stop him from making progress. He'd build that house alone in the dead of night if he had to. Whatever it took. He needed it to occupy his body and his mind.

Today was about making the living room look…livable. It was an ass-backward way to build a house, but he didn't care. He needed to see at least one room in that house fulfill the vision in his head.

He could've had the stuff shipped to the site, but he was already in Melbourne and he felt like driving. He headed to the timber and hardware in Clifton Hill. Chris and the boys looked after him there. Plus, he wanted to give Angelo a ribbing about his football team losing the semi-final.

Rob walked through the sliding doors and browsed the aisles. None of the staff looked familiar. The grumpy girl behind the timber counter said Chris didn't work there anymore, didn't know why he left. Angelo was on vacation. She wordlessly scanned his stuff while he peered into the warehouse behind her, searching for a familiar face.

Out in the carpark, Rob caught a whiff of cigarette smoke and tracked the odor to a shaggy guy in paint-splattered coveralls loading tubs of primer into a beat-up hatchback.

"Mind if I bum a smoke, mate?" said Rob, a little loudly.

The paint-splattered guy turned, squinting past the cigarette stub in his mouth. He looked Rob up and down, his gray whiskers stained yellow with nicotine. "Sure." He reached into the breast pocket of his flannel shirt and handed over the pack, crinkled and almost empty, with only a few smokes and a plastic lighter jammed inside.

Rob felt at once exhilarated and nervous about crossing this threshold. What if he couldn't turn back? He needed this, though, some action bold enough to match the storm brewing inside him. He pulled out a ciggie, automatically turned to shield it from the breeze and flicked the lighter. If these instinctive movements made Rob feel young again, the burn of smoke in his lungs did not. He suppressed the urge to cough and closed his watering eyes.

"Thanks, mate." Rob handed the packet back.

"No worries," said the painter, returning the mangled pack to his shirt pocket. He'd sucked his own cigarette down to the filter. "We're a dying breed," he smirked, and then continued loading paint cans into the back of his car.

Rob dumped the new drill bits and tubes of Liquid Nails adhesive onto the passenger seat of his own truck. He sat there in the quiet of his truck, the blue smoke curling in the airless vacuum of the cabin. His hand on the steering wheel, a cigarette nestled between his fingers – this all felt good. Familiar. Safe. The pang of nicotine remembered places his body forgot.

He knew this was temporary, that he was role-playing his younger self. Truthfully, he didn't much like the taste of cigarette smoke anymore, or the burn of it in his chest. He appreciated the ritual, though, and found himself relaxing into a remembered state of calm. Even his back seemed to hurt less.

He took a few more puffs, opened the window and tossed out the butt, drawing a sour look from a middle-aged woman in lycra pants and a puffy jacket. He smiled to himself. Even if someone built a time machine, you couldn't really go back to the past because *you'd* be different.

He started the car, turned on the radio, settled for Bryan Adams mid-chorus and drove to pick up that suspended wood-burning fireplace. It would look great in the living room of the stone house. Sareena's taste was rubbing off on him.

The Schots Home Emporium was in his neighborhood. His house, *their* house was just up the road. Probably not a bad idea to drive past, make sure the tenants hadn't damaged anything.

Rob drove around the back streets, noticing the little differences in the neighborhood since he'd last been there months ago. There was a new cafe on the corner where the 7-11 had been, the bowls club had fresh, white shade sails, and that McMansion with the too-tall pillars and the unusable Juliette balcony was complete.

There'd been so much fury in the neighborhood about that building. Rob agreed it was ugly, the scale was absurd, the proportions were all wrong, the symmetry poor, materials mismatched. It was a dog's breakfast, half White House, half conference center. A total mess. Still, the neighbors were snobs for lobbying council against its construction. *Inappropriate development*, they said. People deserved the right to build whatever house they wanted.

Rob still believed that, but, as he drove past that house, he conceded it was inconsiderate of those people to ignore the wider feelings of the neighborhood in which they'd chosen to live. While the owner should be *allowed* to build this house, it was an unneighbourly thing to do. Hard to make a law against that.

His chest fluttered with nerves as he glimpsed his own house through the branches of the trees. He parked across the street. How many times had he trudged up and down those front steps without really noticing his home? The front porch looked saggy and the cobwebbed weatherboards needed repair. He had a mind to ring the real-estate agent and blast him for not looking after the place, but the wood must have been like that for years. How had he let it go like that, and why hadn't he noticed it before?

A light in their living room flickered with a passing shadow. It felt strange to know that someone else was in there, that he couldn't just open the front door and walk inside. While this might still be *his* house, it was not his home. Rob shifted in his seat, trying to ease the ache returning to his lower back. What if one of the neighbors saw him there, idling his car and staring at his own house? They'd have questions he didn't feel like answering. He didn't relish the hour's drive back to the display home either, only to sit there, staring at the plush carpet and cold walls. He wanted to go out, be someplace different. He'd call his mate Vance, but he had a young kid again and never went anywhere anymore. Rob didn't get on much with any of Syed's other regular guys. Besides, they were all younger and he was their boss. He couldn't let his guard down with them.

He drove on, leaving his street behind.

On his way out of town he picked up a chicken schnitzel roll and pulled into a drive-through liquor store.

"What can I get you?" The attendant leaned into the open car window, a scrappy-looking guy with earrings in his lip, nose *and* eyebrows.

"You got any Montgomery's Pale Ale back there?" Rob tried to look past the kid's nose ring, at the beer fridges inside.

"Nah. Just the usual. Got your Carlton, your VB...Great Northern."

A jacked-up truck pulled up behind Rob, close enough to feel the doof-doof music rumble through his own vehicle. Rob lowered his rear-view mirror to dim the aggressive headlights of the growling truck behind him. "I'll take a Carlton."

"Case?"

Rob scratched his eyebrow with his thumb. "Yeah, give us a case, mate."

"Anything else?"

Rob hesitated. "Better give me a bottle of Johnny Walker too."

"What color?"

"Black's fine." Rob passed three fifty-dollar bills through the open car window.

The pierced shop clerk snatched the money and turned to retrieve the booze.

Rob squinted into the rear-view mirror. The diesel behind him revved its engine. That truck was almost bumper to bumper. A few years ago, Rob would've got out, told that guy to back up or turn his headlights off, but you didn't know who you might be dealing with these days. Some guys even carried weapons.

"Have a good night."

Rob jumped in his seat, startled by the shop attendant handing the booze through the open car window.

"You too," he said, relieved to be heading back to the safety of the open road.

He liked driving at night, the featureless sky, the ordered rows of headlights and taillights. The world seemed more manageable in the dark, less cluttered.

As he drove, Rob became aware of the side roads that fanned out beyond his windshield. Not just the streets he usually took to get where he was going, but all the streets and how they branched out across the city and out of it, feeding highways, roads and dirt tracks that crisscrossed the country, places he'd never see. What would happen if he just veered off and kept driving until he felt like stopping? How long would that take? Where would he end up? And who'd even notice he was gone?

Rob veered onto the South Gippsland Highway toward San Remo. He was glad to be rid of traffic lights for a while and relaxed into his seat, lulled by the smooth highway surface gliding under his tires. He ate his fried chicken sandwich, occasionally brushing away the shredded carrot and breadcrumbs that tumbled onto his knees from the sweating paper bag.

The dry sandwich clogged in his throat. Rob panicked, struggling to breathe past an unswallowed lump of bread. He reached over the passenger seat, cracked open a can of Carlton and chugged it, dislodging the sticky glob of food that dropped to his guts like a stone. Eyes watering, he tossed the empty can of beer onto the floor of the passenger seat where it rattled and rolled. He wanted another, but the risk of getting pulled over by the cops was too high. That bottle of Johnny Black was calling him too. It'd burn off the greasiness of the chicken sandwich, maybe even blast away the furriness of the cigarette smoke that lingered on his tongue.

The turn-off to the stone house felt sinister at night. He'd only *left* the gravel road when it was this gloomy, not entered it. The track felt familiar but empty, the windswept trees bowing over the narrow path like outstretched arms shooing him away. He would not heed their warning. *No cops out here. Safe to crack a can now.*

He almost expected to crest the hill and see the house finished, nestled at the bottom of the valley, aglow with lights, a warm mosaic of lit windows. But the top of the hill descended into ominous darkness. Only a shaft of cold moonlight rippled on the black waters of Bass Strait.

The truck lurched over the potholed dirt, spilling Rob's beer. "Fuck." He wiped his pant leg with his hand and kept driving until his high beams found the corrugated steel sides of the shipping container. He could almost see ghost images of the women still working there, of Sareena walking around with her phone, talking, poking her head around the frames of unfinished walls, of Will loading stuff into the container, his mind elsewhere.

Rob parked next to the container and sat for a moment in the still darkness, pierced by the shimmer of moonlight through gathering clouds and the crash of waves against the rocks at the base of the cliff.

He picked up his beer and stepped into the night. He marched toward the front door, turning briefly to consider the bottle of whiskey still lying on the floor of the truck, but he kept walking.

At the front door, Rob stared down the stop-work order the Bass Coast Shire had posted there.

NOTICE:

Immediate Cessation of Construction Works by Order of…

Rob stuck his middle finger up at the sign and used his shoulder to open the sticky door.

Inside, he cracked a fresh beer, flicked on a few site lamps and walked around, running his hand over the various materials. The herringbone of his studwork felt solid and the equidistant gaps between the timbers pleased him. The coarseness of the granite felt unyielding, real as only something borne of the earth can be. The house cracked and whistled as the wind picked up. Even unfinished, he could feel this structure communing with its surroundings, seeking a truce with the brewing storm.

He cracked another can and laid out insulation sheets he'd use as a mattress, covering them with a bunch of drop sheets. Even if this now seemed like a dumb idea, it was too late. He'd had too much beer to drive. Better to freeze his ass off and fuck up his back than lose his license. Couldn't afford that. Besides, he couldn't go back to that empty display home. At least this place had a soul, a history that felt nearer just for being here.

As he snapped open beers, he expected his craving for cigarettes to return. But it didn't. Maybe the one he had earlier put the cancer sticks behind him for good. Maybe it wasn't the cigarettes he missed after all. It was liking them.

He lay on the stack of insulation pads, trying to get comfortable. He turned onto his back and stared up at the ceiling, listening to the roof tarp flapping outside while he lay under the drop sheets. Beer had been a mistake. He lay there, bloated and burping, the greasy chicken sandwich threatening to return in the acid reflux that welled at the back of his throat. Is this what it would be like on his last day, uncomfortable in a makeshift bed someplace? Alone. The tarp flapped violently, banging against something metallic outside.

He tore the drop sheets off and strode through stinging rain, scanning the roofline. Nothing broken. He headed for the car and sat in the passenger seat, breathing heavily, wiping rain off his forehead. The wind hissed against the car. He reached between his legs and felt around for the bottle of whiskey, instantly soothed by its familiar shape in his hands. He held the bottle in his lap, the rain pelting the windows like hail.

It was him or the bottle, wasn't it?

One of them had to go over the cliff. It couldn't go on. Not like this. He teared up, wishing things could've been different, that *he* could be different, a better person, a better father, a better husband, a better man. They deserved more. Emma. Will. They deserved better.

He picked up the whiskey and opened the car door, the wind beating it back. Rain lashed him as he leaned into the storm.

He opened the front door and strode toward the kitchen. He put the bottle on the floor and prised up one of the old floorboards. Then another and another, tossing them aside. He dangled his legs into the opening and lowered himself into the trench under the floor. His hand surfaced like a periscope and felt around for the Johnny Walker and he pulled it down.

He flicked on his phone flashlight and groped around in the dark, rain dripping from his chin. He searched for that chalked date on the floor joist. His and Sareena's footprints still looked fresh in the dry soil under the house. His narrow light shone on the raw timbers, streamed with cobwebs. The flaky chalk flashed under the cold light of his phone.

1891

Rob fished his pen knife from his pocket and scratched into a neighboring joist, splintering dry timbers that rained onto the powdery dirt until the chunky writing was clear:

Rob 2023

He ran his fingers over the carved writing, dropped to his knees. He looked at the gold lettering on the bottle of Johnny Walker, dragged the back of his hand across his mouth. Rob put the bottle down, turned and scooped out a shallow hole in the dirt with his hands. He placed the whiskey bottle inside and covered it with earth.

He flopped down on the mound and felt for his phone. He dialed and listened to her voicemail with his eyes closed, cleared his throat before he spoke.

"Em, it's me." He shimmied, rearranging himself on the dirt floor. "I know you don't want to hear from me, but I wanted to call. I had to. I…" He licked his dry lips. "I don't really know what to say…I didn't plan this, just sort of did it…I think maybe because I just wanted to hear your voice." He took a long, deep breath and swallowed.

"You should see this house, Em." He looked up at the floorboards above his head. "I want you to." He breathed into the phone, puffs of static into the night. "I've had a few. But I know you already know that. You can always tell. And I know you don't like it…" He shifted his weight, making a more level crevice for himself in the dirt. "Doesn't change the way I feel about you, though." He sighed. "I miss you. I do." He coughed. "I miss the sound of your voice. I miss seeing your face at night and first thing in the morning. I miss the feeling that life's just better when you're around. At least mine is. Cause…I love you…I know I'm bad at telling you that, but I do, and I want to make it up to you. If I can. Because I want to do better. So, if you can – if you want to – I want to see you. I'll wait another three months or however long if that's what you want. If it's what you need. But I want to see you, if only to say…I'm sorry." He held the phone out in front of him, feeling a little wobblier than he realized. He stabbed his finger at the screen to hang up and slumped back, enveloped by the mossy odor of cold dirt. He nodded off, somewhere between sleep and oblivion.

His phone chimed. Rob sat up and searched for his cell phone. Not Emma. A text from Sareena:

Someone once told me he could understand wood. Me, I speak stone. Strong combo, don't you think? No "I" in team, right?

Below the message was a new sketch of the stone house, where a large section of granite blocks was replaced by a wall of glass that disappeared into the stone.

CHAPTER THIRTY-FIVE

Emma bumped against the heavy glass door of Haimon Young, Corporate Services. The receptionist behind the mahogany counter made a pulling motion with her arm. Emma pulled the door and it opened.

"Well, that was an impressive start," said Emma cheerily, trying to reverse her first impression. "Hope *that* wasn't the interview?" Emma laughed at her own joke in a pretense to be upbeat. Her heart was racing, her mouth was dry and she felt jittery.

The prim lady at reception smiled uneasily and looked at her screen. "You're Janeen?"

"No, I'm Emma. Connors."

"Right," said the receptionist, blushing slightly. "Sorry."

"That's okay."

"Just take a seat, they won't be long."

Emma smiled, sweat beads forming inside her navy suit, her good suit, her I-can-do-anything suit.

She took a seat in the waiting area, glancing at the magazines spread out on a large, glass coffee table: *Australian Company Director, CEO, The Financial Review.* How much could you read into a place from the magazines in the waiting room?

The big glass entrance door thumped, rattled, and Emma looked over. The receptionist made a pulling motion with her arm. The door opened slowly, effortfully, with enough difficulty for the receptionist to stand as if she was about to assist.

"It's okay, I got it," said a large, well-dressed woman of Emma's vintage, her voice hoarse and panting with exertion. "Sorry I'm late. I'm Janeen." She caught her breath, glanced at Emma and looked away.

"They're ready for you," said the receptionist. "I can show you through."

The receptionist ushered Janeen down a corridor. Janeen walked as if her shoes pinched, and she struggled to remove her old-style trench coat as she walked, half off the shoulder, belt trailing behind her down the corridor like a tail.

Poor Janeen.

Emma was glad she came early. She absently flipped through the pages of *Qualitative Finance*, pausing on the colorful graphs and charts. What was she doing here? This place was all wrong. Why did they even call her? Was she part of an affirmative action campaign? Her and Janeen. This didn't feel right.

Emma rubbed her temples, felty queasy. The comedown from that pill was messing with her. She felt anxious, distracted and fidgety, and her throat was dry, like she'd stuck a blow dryer in her mouth. Never again.

She pulled out her phone and slid the toggle on her phone and replayed Rob's voice message.

…if you want to – I want to see you. I'll wait another three months or however long, if that's what you want. If it's what you need. But I want to see you, if only to say…I'm sorry."

Emma dragged the cursor back on the progress bar to replay the message….*you want. If it's what you need. But I want to see you, if only to say…I'm sorry."*

Drag…to say…I'm sorry.

Drag. I'm sorry.

Drag. I'm sorry.

She was sorry too.

"Are you alright?" the prim receptionist looked concerned.

"I'm fine, why?"

The receptionist pointed at her own eyes.

Emma touched her face, damp with tears. "Fuck." She sniffed and retrieved a tissue from her bag. "Sorry." Why was she apologizing?

"There's a powder room just over there." The receptionist pointed toward an alcove with a large potted plant.

"I'm okay." Emma cleared her throat, dabbed at her nose with the tissue. The receptionist returned to her screen.

Emma fished in her bag for her pocket mirror, wiped flakes of mascara with the dry edge of her tissue.

"Emma," said a loud voice, startling her. "I'm Patrick." He clapped and rubbed his hands together. "We are ready for ya."

Emma stood and shook his hand, noticing his hairdo, short but for the faintest strip of tousled hair along the crown of his head, a micro-mohawk. "All good?" he asked. She gave him a thumbs up.

Patrick led her down a long wood-paneled hallway, with closed conference room doors on either side. Conference rooms 3, 4, 5. The downlights shone pools of mellow light on the warm wood; the effect was more high-end hotel than corporate office.

Emma looked down at Patrick's pointy shoes, the flash of bright Dr Seuss–striped socks peeking out from under his too-short trouser cuffs.

"We're in Conference Room 9," said Patrick, and gave the door a quick double knock before opening it.

Inside, an older, elegant woman in a collared shirt and pencil skirt stood to greet her. "Hi Emma," said the woman, her hair so bleached it was almost white, a shaved undercut made her face look extra pointy, like an elf. "I'm Deb," she said, "and you've already met Patrick."

Deb rattled off her job title and briefly explained what she did at Haimon Young, but Emma didn't catch most of it, just nodded. "Oh wow," said Emma at one point. "Yeah, great," which seemed to make Deb happy.

"Have a seat," said Deb, sitting down, lacing her thin fingers on the table.

"Hey, where did Janeen go?" said Emma.

Deb made a puzzled face and looked to Patrick, who grimaced.

Emma pumped her fist under the table, controlling a tremor in her hand. "The lady you interviewed before me," said Emma. "The lady with the trench coat."

Patrick steepled his fingers. "We've got a lot of interviews happening here today."

"Right," said Emma, sitting back in the swivel chair, its movement making her nauseous. She felt sad for Janeen. Hoped she was doing okay, wherever she was.

"So," said Deb, leaning forward. "Tell us a little about yourself, why you're interested in working for Haimon Young?"

"Well…" Emma took a breath. She felt dizzy. Her stomach churned. Sweat built on the sides of her nose. "It's a company," she said, "that uhm…" She stood up abruptly. "I think I'm going to throw up," she said.

Deb looked to Patrick.

"I'm definitely going to throw up." Emma looked around wide-eyed.

Patrick grabbed a small trash can and handed it to Emma,

who lowered her head into it, heaved and puked. A solid stream sloshed into the plastic bucket. She looked up, briefly. "I think it's just nerves," she said, and vomited again, hung her head in the can, heaving and spitting. She dry-retched at the smell, retracted her head and wiped her mouth with her hand. There she stood, holding the bucket under her arm. "Did you want to keep going or…"

Patrick looked shocked and disgusted.

"Are you okay?" Deb looked concerned.

"I'm fine," said Emma, sniffing and glassy-eyed. "I'll get going. I'm going to keep this, though." Emma motioned toward the trash can she had propped against her hip. "Sorry," she said, blinking, and walked out.

Emma found the toilets and cleaned up. She sat in the stall and breathed, her hand tremoring slightly, all joy drained from her body.

She took out her phone and called Rob. No answer.

CHAPTER THIRTY-SIX

Rob wedged a crowbar under the council notice on the door of the stone house. The plastic board came loose with a pleasing crack, then shattered, the sharp pieces falling at his feet.

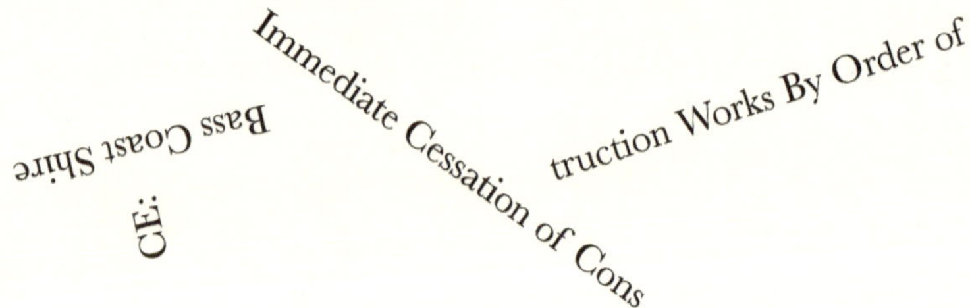

He kicked the plastic shards into the long grass and held the front door open for Sareena, who smiled as she entered, followed by the rest of her crew.

"Ooooh, this isn't the first time you been back here," said Sareena, hands on her hips, surveying the plastering, the exquisite carpentry of the curved staircase to the upper floor. She spied Rob's camp bed and portable cooker. "You been living here, dude?"

Rob blushed. "Well, idle hands."

Sareena nodded, hands clasped on the front of her tool belt as the rest of the crew filed into the house behind her, murmuring about the work completed in their absence, pointing at fixed joists, plaster and the bulkhead ready for kitchen cabinetry.

"Okay, listen up," announced Sareena. The crew almost settled down. Dani and Steph kept playfully elbowing each other and had a hard time keeping it together.

"Folks," said Sareena. "A minute of your time?"

"Sorry," said Steph, adjusting her hard hat.

Dani stuck her index finger in her mouth and put it in Steph's ear.

"Gross." Steph pulled her head away and shooed Dani's hand.

"Shut up!" Alex scowled. "Bit of respect, yeah."

Alex's new buzzcut with a tuft of hair sticking up at the front made Rob think of Tintin.

Sareena cleared her throat and resumed. "Okay, quick brief. First, it's good to be back here." The group murmured approval. "Council didn't want us building this house because the plans would've made the place too different from the original. You've got the new drawings. And you can see we're now honoring what was there. Making it more comfortable. Making the stone and glass work together, so the walls can flex, let more light in, and not have one material feel like it's dominating the other." She glanced at Rob, who stood motionless beside her, hands folded in front of him.

"Now," she continued. "The place already looks better than when we left it, but don't let Rob's guerrilla building fool you." She smiled at Rob. "There's a fuck-ton of stuff to do in here. And a few mistakes to fix."

"Oooh," they all said. Rob blushed and pretended to be offended, looking around with wide eyes like he didn't know what she was talking about.

Sareena smiled. "The first thing is getting that roof in order, so Jemma, what's it looking like up there?"

"It looks worse than it is. Reckon it's a week's work. I can patch and match most of it."

"Awesome."

"Kim, the roof tiles. What are you thinking?"

"I know you're worried about the moss."

"I was too, seeing dollar signs in my sleep, but the moss is only growing where the roof sags and messes with the water runoff, so Jem's work on the trusses should fix that. I do need a hand lugging shingles."

"I'll do that." Alex stuck out her chin and stuffed her hands deep into her pockets.

"Great," said Sareena. "Steph. Plumbing-wise, what are your priorities?"

"Aside from the roof, I want to finish putting in my PVC lines. We want to make sure there's not a scrap of galvanized pipe left in this place."

"Cool," Sareena said. "Rob, you got anything to add?"

"Ah," he cleared his throat and looked at them nervously. "I just wanted to say, I've worked with a lot of crews over the years, and you all…definitely have the nicest cars." The gag drew a half-hearted chuckle from the room.

"Better than your shitbox," someone called out, which got a hearty laugh.

"Yeah," said Alex. "A Mitsubishi? Seriously?"

"It's un-Australian," someone joked, and everyone laughed.

Rob smiled at the playful teasing. It felt familiar. "But seriously," he said, as the noise died down. Rob smiled and glanced at Sareena. "If I could do my time over again, I'd be proud to be part of this crew. You're one of the best I've seen."

"*The* best," someone called out. Someone else whooped and the others clapped.

"Okay, *the* best," Rob conceded, which got a loud cheer. "And your foreman..." He bowed to Sareena. "Best in the business." The group erupted.

Sareena curtsied as Rob clapped and the others whooped with abandon.

"Okay," she said, as the noise subsided. "Now let's finish this fucker."

The crew scattered and set about their tasks. The house soon filled with the banging and clanging of progress, the hum and screech of power tools.

Rob busied himself checking angles in the kitchen. Through a hole in the plaster, he could see Sareena in the other room. She was taking it all in, appreciating the organized chaos of a worksite, the patterns of activity. Alex walked up to Sareena and leaned in. "Can I talk to you for a second?"

"Sure, what's up?"

They pulled away from the others and tucked in closer to the wall.

Rob stayed still, crouched behind the wall where he could still glimpse them.

Alex looked flustered and nervous. She checked over Sareena's shoulder to see if anyone was watching them.

"Why are we back here?" she said. "I mean, really? I thought this guy was a dick?"

Sareena sighed. "You know," said Sareena, "You can't just discount people."

"Bullshit," said Alex. "You just couldn't say no."

Sareena gave Alex a hard look. "Excuse me?"

"Oh, come on." Alex scowled. "This place?" she opened her arms, palms up. "High-end property? Heritage. Prestige developer. The stone and glass and everything. Perfect for your career."

"So what? What's your point? What's good for me is good for you."

"No, it's cool. You're making your move, taking what's yours. I get it. I just kinda thought we were all about doing our own thing, not working with—"

"You done?"

Alex looked away.

Sareena put her hand on her hip. "What are you trying to say? That I'm selling out?"

"I didn't say that."

"Nah, but it's what you were thinking."

"I'm just saying, I think it'd be better if we could just build this thing alone, you know. Like, what's he really bringing to the table?"

"You serious?" snapped Sareena. "Look around. He's ready to build this place his fucken self. That's devotion. You don't see that? That's fire. Reminds me of someone else I know." Alex rolled her eyes. "Yeah, that's right," said Sareena. "Who took a chance on you? When you came to me not long out of juvie when you were all fire and no direction."

Sareena moved in close to Alex. "Hmm? Don't be too quick and sure to judge?" Sareena's eyes grew big. "You know that chip on your shoulder?" Alex looked away. "It's how you got into juvie in the first place."

Sareena paused, waiting for Alex to make eye contact, but she wouldn't. "Now," said Sareena, "I don't know what put it there. But you're the only one can take it down. And I suggest you figure out how."

Sareena walked away then turned around. "People can be more than one thing at a time, Al. I love ya, but you start picking fights on my site and you're gone. Simple as that."

Rob stood as still as he could. He stopped looking through the gap in the power point, then pretended to busy himself between the plasterboard and the floor. What had he ever done to Alex? It didn't feel fair to be so hated by someone he barely knew and to know there was nothing he could do or say to put it right. Some things were beyond his power to repair.

His phone buzzed and he scrambled to muffle it, quiet as possible. It was Emma.

CHAPTER THIRTY-SEVEN

Emma lay on the living room couch, texting from inside her cocoon of pillows and the quilt she'd pulled in from her bedroom. Kendry was in Byron and the house was empty. Too empty.

Emma needed to sort herself out. Get a job. Stop fucking around. She applied for jobs at random, including positions that were below and way above her experience. Applying for work now felt like online gambling.

She'd agreed to meet Erik. It felt important to see him again, if only to say goodbye.

She peeled herself out of her cocoon and headed to the shower.

She turned the corner onto Brunswick Street and there was Erik, already waiting. She immediately had second thoughts. He hadn't seen her yet. She could just turn around and leave, he'd never know.

"Em." He waved and walked over. "Hey," he said, leaning in for a hug.

Emma took a step back. "Seriously?"

Erik stopped short and pulled back. "Sorry."

They walked, side by side, not talking, pretending to be distracted by the buildings, the sky.

He stopped, suddenly, and turned toward her, oblivious to the two women in hijabs walking behind them on the sidewalk. "I just want to say I'm sorry," he said. "I was a dick." The women frowned as they passed around him. They gave Emma a sympathetic look. She chewed her lip. Erik didn't seem to notice the women at all.

Emma crossed her arms. "I guess we were never together," she said. "Not really."

He seemed puzzled by this at first and then his face softened.

"Still," said Emma, "a shitty thing to do, thinking with your dick."

He nodded, looked at the ground.

"Kind of glad it happened, though," she said. "Means I don't have to feel bad. I knew this would end, just thought it would end… better."

"I'm sorry."

Emma sighed. "You know you can keep saying that, but it doesn't actually change anything."

Erik stuffed his hands in his pockets, shoulders up by his ears. "What do you want me to say?"

"Don't say anything," Emma bit her lip. "Just be a better person."

He nodded silently. A truck passed and they walked in silence for a bit, feigning interest in opposite sides of the street.

"I *am* sorry," he said.

"I believe you."

A tram rumbled along its tracks.

"Hey, said Erik. "Can I show you this one thing?"

"What?"

"It's in there." He pointed at a yellow sign just down the sidewalk.

Pawn Shop

Cash — Jewelry — Loans

"I don't know." She shook her head. "I don't really want to go in there."

"Why not?" he said cheerily.

"I just don't."

"Aw come on, five minutes." He tilted his head to the side.

Emma took a deep breath and looked down the length of Brunswick Street. The fun shops were down there, the cool tailors, funky cafes and artisan jewelers. This part of Fitzroy was next to the public housing apartments where her dad's mate, Massimo, used to live.

The facade of small windows on the tower reminded Emma of the open window where she'd once taken refuge from the smell of cigarette smoke inside Massimo's flat. She must have been eight or nine then, and Emma recalled the thrill of seeing Melbourne from up there, sprawling and twinkling. It was higher than she'd ever been before and it both exhilarated and terrified her.

Though it had scared her, she stayed at the window while her dad and Massimo murmured on the couch behind. How adults could talk for hours was mystifying.

"No." She crossed her arms. "I don't want to."

He smirked. "Have you got some early-life pawn-shop trauma I should know about?"

"No." She rolled her eyes. "I just don't like them. The stuff in those places always makes me feel sad. Plus, I'm still pissed off at you."

"Okay. Well, do you want to meet up again or…?"

"Think I'll just go," she said.

"Okay." He looked around. "So, is that it then?"

"I don't know. I'm just not feeling fun right now."

"Fair enough. I'll just leave you alone then. Unless you want to call me some time."

She nodded vaguely.

He patted her shoulder and trotted up the steps to the pawn shop, the metal door scraping against the frame as he pulled the door open and disappeared inside.

She didn't feel safe loitering outside the pawn shop. Two skinny guys in stained track suit pants were sifting through garbage bags dumped outside the Brotherhood of St Laurence. Emma adjusted the shoulder strap of her bag, looping it over her head and crossing her arms over the strap.

She was annoyed now, felt trapped between leaving and going inside. Either option felt unacceptable, like defeat.

So what if she didn't like being around stuff other people had been forced to give up because it was their only way of paying the rent, or buying food, or settling a debt. Her own parents had shopped that way, through op shops and pawn shops, long before these places were cool.

The smell of mothballs and piles of old blankets would bring her right back there, putting on clothes that were several sizes too big so she could "grow into them," the feel of her toes finding the imprint of someone else's foot inside a running shoe. It's not that Emma was a snob, she just didn't feel comfortable so close to desperation. It felt precarious, reminding her that, whatever her hard work and good fortune had earned her, she was only ever a few mistakes away from being back there herself.

This was silly, wasn't it? Her not wanting to go in there. It was a preference, not a phobia. She *had* to go in there now, not for Erik, but to prove to herself this place held no power over her. She walked up the steps, tucking her hand inside her coat sleeve to pull open the sticky door.

It was warm inside, almost tropical. Guitars were strung up along the wall behind the counter, hanging by their necks. There were acoustic ones, their bulbous, hourglass frames. There were electric guitars too, painted in bright metallic colors that sparkled, even under these dim fluorescent lights. There was even one of those spiky, glam-rock guitars that looked more like street art than a musical instrument. Her eyes moved to a violin hanging up there, so small and delicate next to the other instruments, the runt of the litter. Emma would've thought someone who played the violin was someone who could afford to keep it.

Erik was down the back of the shop. The shop attendant, a round man with a walrus mustache, was handing him an acoustic guitar.

Erik propped his foot up on something and started to play, those long, creamy fingers sliding up and down the length of the instrument.

The skin on Emma's face prickled as the lyrics brought back a lost memory of her father. Her dad sang it differently, his voice smaller, frail, almost a whisper that whiskey alone drew from him. But this is what her father sang:

Tell me you'll stay
Oh, tell me you'll stay
Until the ghosts of our fathers they carry us away
Our lines are unbroken
Don't lead us astray
Be here in the morning and stay on all day
So, tell me you'll stay
Oh, tell me you'll stay
Until the ghosts of our fathers they carry us away.

It was an Irish protest song. Dad had sung it because his life was a protest looking for a cause. This had to be some kind of sign, even if Emma didn't believe in signs. Erik finished the song with closed eyes. He handed the guitar back to the man with the walrus mustache and they started chatting.

Her eyes moved down to the long glass cabinet underneath the instruments, filled with electronic gear: laptops, flip phones, old cameras and game consoles.

She could understand the odd person buying an item out of nostalgia. But Emma struggled to comprehend why young people liked this stuff. It wasn't the same as buying an antique lamp or something. These gadgets didn't do whatever they were made to do as well as new stuff could. Why would someone want a Discman, for god sake? She couldn't shake the suspicion that an entire generation was making fun of her, somehow, buying this stuff as an inside joke. "Look at this old crap. Lol."

"Hey, Em," came Erik's voice from the dimly lit back of the shop. "Check it out."

Emma averted her eyes as she passed the jewelry display cases. Those earrings, bracelets and rings used to belong to someone. How'd they get here? Stolen? Had someone died? Some of it would have been given up willingly when needs demanded, or after whatever had once compelled the owners of this jewelry to wear it faded.

She thought of her own wedding ring, sitting on the base of the reading lamp on her nightstand. She kept it there because she didn't like the way it jiggled on her finger, but it now seemed foolish to have left it there. What if someone broke in?

Flashing lights and electronic beeping interrupted her scheming the best place to hide her wedding ring.

"Oh, you fucker," said Erik, clapping at the side buttons of a full-sized AC/DC-themed pinball machine. He tilted his whole body as he smashed the buttons, the console ablaze with all the flickering lights of a rock-and-roll stage show. "Yes!" Erik beamed, having done something to set off the opening guitar riff of "Thunderstruck". "This thing is awesome," he said, without turning around.

Emma looked over his shoulder at the little metal ball zipping around a plastic chute. It disappeared and was then shot back into play through a tiny cannon.

"You know," she said, "that night at your festival…" She paused, waiting for him to respond, but he kept his attention on the game.

"Yeah," he finally said, still tapping the machine and his eye on the metal ball bouncing around inside.

"Well…" She looked him up and down, willing him to stop playing, but he only glanced at her. "We haven't really talked about it."

He licked his lips, concentrating on the ball rolling toward the flippers. "We talked about it outside?" He scrunched up his face as the machine made a disappointed noise.

She leaned toward him. "You have to be more careful with people's hearts."

He smiled without looking at her. "I know," he said, moving his head around to follow the ball. "I said I was sorry, remember, and you told me not to apologize anymore.

"I'm not just talking about other people, Erik. You need to be true to your own heart as well. It's not always clear what it wants."

He nodded.

"Hey!" She slapped her hand on the glass top of the pinball machine. "Can you *please* stop playing and look at me?"

"Okay." He raised his hands from the controls like he was being held at gunpoint and leaned back against the table, its lights flashing on the side of his face. "I thought we'd already talked about this, but okay, you have my undivided attention."

"Do I?"

His eyes narrowed. "What's with you? I thought we were cool."

"Yeah, no. I said I didn't want to come in here." Emma looked at him. "I don't like all this shit."

"But it's AC/DC pinball."

"Please. I just don't buy this, that you're so aloof, so cool and Zen about everything. And please don't say 'really,' or I'm literally going to freak out."

He took a breath. "What do you want from me, Emma?"

"I want to know that you felt something. That I was more than an afterthought, something you did on a dare."

"On a dare?"

"You know what I'm fucking talking about. Bag an older chick for the trophy case."

"You know what," he said, looking straight at her. "I think you *want* me to get pissed off. You want me to be the prick."

"You *are* a prick! You fucked that sour-faced Briley brat."

"Hey! What is with you? You have any idea how push-pull you are? Hold me close, fuck off, when am I going to see you again? You don't know what the fuck you want and now you want me to get mad at you so you can feel better. Then someone else is the problem, not you."

"That's the stupidest fucking thing I've ever heard." Emma turned as if to leave.

"Is it?" Erik called after her. "Let's look at *you* for a second. Bored housewife in midlife crisis seeks—"

"Fuck you!" she spat.

"Nice, Emma. Classy."

Emma looked away, tried to catch a glimpse of the world outside. Light. Open space. Fresh air. Everything in here felt dark and cluttered and hot and moldy and it all seemed to pile on the shame.

"Oi!" The walrus mustache man appeared behind the counter. "Youse are going to have to take this outside."

Emma craned her neck to look at the shopkeeper past the boxes of junk on the counter. "Are you serious?" she spat.

"Serious as a heart attack," he said, stone-faced.

"Right." Emma nodded. "Wouldn't want to degrade this place."

"Ma'am! I need you to leave."

"Sorry, mate," said Erik, and put his hand on Emma's arm. She pushed it off.

"Both of you." The shopkeeper fanned his hand, shooing them away. "Out."

Emma looked back at the man with the walrus mustache, who walked alongside them on his side of the counter, cell phone phone in his hand.

Emma stabbed her finger at him. "I don't need you to shepherd me out the fucking door."

"We're going," said Erik, raising both hands as he walked to the exit.

"Get her out, mate, or I'm calling the cops." He waved his phone.

"Pffft, the cops," she scoffed. "Fuck off, mate."

"Em, seriously."

"Oh, I'm leaving, don't worry." She swatted Erik's hand off her arm. "Who'd want to be in this place anyway? It's a shithole," she called over her shoulder. "At least I get to leave."

"Out!" He shooed them.

"Em, seriously. Let's go."

"You know what, fuck you and this dogshit place." She pushed over a stand of earrings sitting on the counter and flung a Hello Kitty statuette into the glass cabinetry.

The mustache ran for cover and tapped at his phone with sausage fingers.

Erik pushed Emma, still flailing, toward the door. She grabbed a stiletto heel and chucked it at the counter where it crashed into something glass.

Erik pushed open the door and moved her outside and down the steps. She stood on the sidewalk, panting, cars whooshing past.

"Was that fun for you?" said Erik.

"That guy was a dick."

"He was just a guy, Em."

She burst out crying and covered her face with her hands.

"Hey." Erik hesitated but put an arm on her shoulder. "Come on."

"I've blown up my whole life," she said.

"No, you haven't," he said quietly.

"I did." She struggled to find rhythm in her breathing, her mouth opening and closing silently. "I fucked everything up."

"You didn't." He patted her shoulder. "Well," he said, rubbing her back, "maybe just a tiny bit."

She snorted, and her nervous laughter turned into a cry. She wiped her nose with her sleeve. "What am I going to do?"

He put his arm around her and pulled her to him. "Well, what do you want to do?" She didn't answer. "Do you want to go home or back to my place?" he said.

Emma took a breath and slowly pulled away from Erik. She sniffed and dabbed at her eyes with the back of her hand.

"Well," said Erik, scanning the street, "whatever we do, we should get out of here before the cops come."

She laughed, wiping her eyes with the back of her hands, and the pair of them ran down the side street.

CHAPTER THIRTY-EIGHT

Rob sat on an upturned milk crate and stared out the big picture window of the stone house. The view gave directly onto Bass Strait where the gray water rippled from a passing breeze. It was bright outside, the light sharp enough for him to shield his eyes. Silhouetted figures walked past, flickering as they came between him and the light pouring in through the glass.

He could recognize them all from their shadows. There went Steph, with that unmistakable bounce in her step. There was Kim, a foot shorter than everyone else. And there went Alex, with her stiff march like she was trying to catch up to someone without breaking into a run. "Hey Alex," he called out. She stopped and turned to look over her shoulder. He waved her over. She took two steps toward him and stopped.

"All good?" said Rob.

She raised her eyebrows. "Yeah."

"Good." Rob flattened the hair at the back of his head. "I've been meaning to ask you what you want to do next?"

"About what?"

He smiled. "In the industry," he said, scratching his chin, "is there a trade you like more than the others?"

She looked up as if she was thinking about it, screwed up her face. "I don't know."

Rob laced his fingers together to stop them fidgeting. "You don't have to. Nothing wrong with general labor. It's usually a starting point, though. You could use it to move into something else."

"What, like carpentry?"

"Doesn't have to be." He watched her, waiting for her to speak. She was fiddling now, scratching at her palms.

"Probably gardening," she said at last.

"Oh yeah?"

She made a face like she was still thinking about it. "Yeah," she smiled. "Landscaping, I reckon. Be good to be outside most days."

He considered Alex. She suddenly looked younger, softer. He stuck his thumb out behind him. "What do you reckon we should do with the garden out by the shipping container?"

"Out there?" she jutted her chin toward the derelict yard, all chewed up with tire marks, the granite flowerbeds overgrown with weeds. "I'd go all natives," she said, self-assured. "Grevilleas, banksias. Stuff like that. Hardy. It'd get the birds in too. Parrots and that."

Rob tried to look her in the eye, but she wouldn't meet him. "What if…" he said, turning to look over his shoulder. "What if *you* did it?" He turned back to her. She was looking at him now, hands on her hips. She shrugged, a funny little one shoulder shrug, like she was pretending not to care. "Sure," she said. "I could do that."

"That'd be good," Rob said.

"You sure?"

"Yeah," he squinted, tilted his head to the side as if reconsidering. "Are you?"

Alex nodded, slowly. "Yeah," she said.

"Well, okay then." He pulled out his phone as if he had other things to do. "Make it look nice," he said.

"I will," said Alex and walked off. Rob cracked a smile as he checked his phone. No messages.

"Taking a break, Rob?" Sareena's shadow leaned to the side, the jet plume of her ponytail shooting out the back of her hard hat.

Rob looked up from his cell phone. "You heard from Aaron?"

Sareena raised her palms. "Said he was coming. He'll be here. Relax."

Rob glanced at his phone again.

Sareena took an audible breath. "Hey, I heard what you said to Alex." She tapped the milk crate with the toe of her work boot. "That was nice."

Rob nodded, barely looking up from his phone.

"She's pretty green," said Sareena. "You cool with that?" Rob nodded slowly, eyes still on his phone, looking for Aaron's number. "Yeah," he said. "She may not know everything, but she's got fire in her belly." He chewed his bottom lip and looked up at Sareena. "I have confidence in people who have something to prove."

She smiled. "Yeah, me too."

Rob craned his neck to get a better view out the window. "You know if Aaron's bringing Will?"

"How should I know?"

Rob frowned. "Said he would."

"Well, then," she chirped, "he will." She put her hands on her hips. "What's crawled up your ass this morning? Is this about whatever you've got going on in the shed?"

Rob looked at her sheepishly.

She smiled. "Yeah, I see you." She twirled her finger at him. "Don't forget, I know everything that goes on around here. I'm a wall of ears and eyeballs. Nothing gets past me." She turned to look out the window. "Oooh, it's them. Coming down the hill."

Rob eagerly got up from his milk crate and looked out the window. He frowned and turned to Sareena. "There's no one there."

Sareena laughed and clapped her hands. "Your face," she mimicked his wide eyes. "Priceless."

Rob rolled his eyes.

"Look at you," said Sareena, still smiling. "All worked up and impatient. Maybe you *better* sit down, Rob. Take a breather. You're going to hurt yourself getting all excited, a man your age. Don't worry, they'll get here, driving that little man van." Sareena laughed to herself and sauntered off, disappearing into the shadow of the hallway.

Rob put his phone in his pocket and looked around. The banging and sawing felt good, like all this effort was being poured into making the rest of the house look like this living room, solid and unpretentious, a beauty you could trust. He didn't even mind the low thump of doof-doof music they had playing upstairs. Work was happening. Full steam and full stride.

And there it was at last, Aaron's van bouncing on the uneven dirt road. He watched it come closer and park in the circular clearing. Will stepped out of the passenger seat and Rob felt a flutter of nerves, an electric current of affection tingling through his body.

No sooner had the boys got out of the van than Sareena was on them, tapping on her wrist, pointing at the house, giving them directions. Will made as if to follow Aaron but Sareena put a hand on his shoulder and redirected him toward the house.

Rob pulled out his carpenter's rule and a pencil. He crouched, randomly, near the entrance to the kitchen, pretending to measure the skirting board.

"Hey, Dad," said Will. "You want to see me?"

Rob took a moment, squinted at the meaningless measurement before looking up from his false labor. "Yep, great." He put an unnecessary pencil line on the plaster with a flourish and made a mental note to rub it out later. "Come on," he said, getting to his feet. "I want to show you something." He went out the back door, held it open for Will.

"What is it?"

"You'll see."

Rob pushed open the creaky door of the barn and invited Will inside. They made their way into the old place, the floorboards creaking under their boots. Will pointed at the pile of timbers and assorted hand tools laid out on a tarp. "What's all this?"

"It's mountain ash."

Will looked at him blankly.

"Found a stash of it under the house," Rob smiled. "Worth a small fortune."

Will put his hand on the grayed wood, caked with dust. "Looks kind of manky."

"It's not manky." Rob smiled. "It's old growth."

His son looked at him from under raised eyebrows. "And that's good because…?"

"You don't know?"

"Why would I?"

Rob cleared his throat. He came over and put his own hand on the silvery timbers. "Most of the timber you get these days is basically farmed. It comes from plantations. You get stuff like pine that grows fast so you can cut it down in a few years and use it right away. But this stuff…" He patted the timber, rubbed it with the palm of his hand. "This tree was king of the forest. It would've been growing in the one spot hundreds of years before someone cut it down."

Will frowned. "Wouldn't that make it shittier? Like, moldy, or whatever."

"Nooo." Rob scratched the stubble on his neck. "See here," he said, pointing at the lines of wood grain, so straight and tight they might have been raked with a comb. He rapped on the timber with his knuckles. "With all that time, the wood gets super dense. If you hit that with an ax, it'd probably just bounce off. This has had time to get strong, learn how to resist decay. New timber's weak. Unstable. This stuff here," he said, "hard as steel."

Will rapped his knuckle on the timber. "Kind of sad they cut it down then."

"Well, it wasn't us. And whoever did this is long gone." Rob ran his hand along the straight lines of wood grain. "Besides, you can still respect it. I reckon it depends on what you do with it." He turned to his son.

Will motioned toward the collection of unfamiliar hand tools laid out on the tarp. "Looks like you've got some idea."

"Yeah," said Rob. "What do you say we honor this piece of timber? Build something beautiful."

Will glanced over his shoulder at the barn door. "Shouldn't we be helping them?"

"Nah." Rob swatted away the suggestion. "She's got it under control."

Will sighed, looked nervously at the array of tools, the stack of timber, gray as old spiderwebs. "I don't know how."

Rob picked up an old hand plane and passed it to Will. "I'll show you."

CHAPTER THIRTY-NINE

Emma sat in a cafe on Sydney Road. One much like the others. This street used to be so grungy. Punk. It was casually trendy now. The cool people had become moms and dads pushing prams that looked like spaceships to cafes where they met spandexed friends for coffee and babycinos.

Emma sipped her latte, watching a new parents group bond, swapping stories, sharing advice, occasionally peeking into the nest of blankets where their little ones slept, cocooned from the world outside. For now. She remembered how long the days felt, and how quickly the years passed.

She picked up her phone and texted Kendry. *Can you talk?* and put the phone down, expecting an answer maybe today, maybe tomorrow, perhaps a week from now. Did they even allow phones at her "wellness" facility in Byron Bay? Emma's phone buzzed. That was quick.

Yes. Not in prison.

Ha ha.

What's up?

I ended things.

With Rob?

Erik.

Good.

Way to be supportive

…

I mean good for YOU.

Thanks

You ok?

Yes, ok. You?

…

Sick of people whinging

…

It's good you're there

Hmmm. No bar.

…

Kidding.

I know. It's good you get some r and r.

Rehab and relapse?

Emma typed *Be strong* and erased it; *I miss you* and erased it; *I love you* and erased it. *Love you*, she wrote and sent it.

I love you too.

The phone rang. It was Rob.

SUMMER

CHAPTER FORTY

Emma turned onto a dirt track, convinced she'd taken a wrong turn. The old wooden gate at the side of the road made her think she was trespassing in some farmer's field. The GPS showed no roads beyond this point. She drove on, fighting the steering wheel for control as the vehicle moved with the bumps and dips that wobbled her from side to side.

Rob so badly wanted to show her the house he'd been working on. The truth was Emma was curious to see it. That woman too, the tall one in the photos.

Twigs and gravel scraped under the car. There was no turning around on this narrow road. She could only go forward.

Rob had sounded nice on the phone. Familiar but different, more relaxed somehow. But Emma didn't know what she'd feel when she saw him. She half expected the rest of her life to reveal itself the moment she laid eyes on him. Then she'd know what to do.

The little car lurched up a steep hill, then crested it. This was like the peak of a roller coaster, just before the drop. From here, the path descended sharply into a wide green valley. Beyond the cliffs, the sea stretched to the horizon. The stone house appeared tiny, perched at the edge of the world.

Emma pumped the brakes as she descended toward the house, which grew larger as she approached and shapeshifted with the changing reflections in the vast window: trees, clouds, the ocean, her own car, the door, opening.

Rob came out the house. His hair was longer, and he'd lost some weight.

"You found it!" He beamed and walked down the steps to meet her.

It'd been eleven months since their last disastrous meeting in the Carlton cafe; it seemed both an instant and an eternity since she'd seen him face-to-face. This was Rob, even if he wasn't the man of her dreams, he was the man of her life, her memories. It was good to see him, and she smiled spontaneously.

"Looks amazing," she said, gazing up at the house.

"Thanks." He held his arms out for a hug.

Emma leaned into his embrace, comforted by the shape and weight of him, the strength and solidity of his body. They held onto each other, each aware of what the other might read into being the first to let go.

As Emma pulled away, he took her hand. *This was new.*

"I love all the native plants," she said, avoiding his gaze. "I bet it brings in the birds." The glossy leaves on the newly planted saplings fluttered in the breeze.

"How you been?" Rob said, his voice uncharacteristically quiet. "You look good."

"Thanks," she nodded. "Good. I mean…God this is awkward isn't it?" She gently let go his hand and nibbled the top of her thumbnail.

"It is a bit weird," he said. "But maybe weird's okay."

"Yeah." Emma looked away at the patches of freshly dug plants, poking out from their wind barriers.

"It's great to see you." He put his hands in his pockets.

She smiled and gently touched the round, springy leaves of a nasturtium. "You too."

He made shapes in the gravel with the toe of his boot. "Any luck getting a job?"

Emma turned away, shook her head slowly.

"Something'll come up," he said.

"Yeah." She forced a smile.

"You okay, Em?"

The wind blew in from the ocean and she slid her hands into the side pockets of her light jacket. "Yeah, it's just…" Emma sniffed, dabbed her nose with her sleeve and put her hand back in her pocket. "It's been a long time." She looked up at the facade of the stone house, her eyes following the huge V-shaped tear in the stone blocks filled in by a giant glass wall.

"This really looks great though." Her eyes wandered over the irregular-sized blocks of ancient granite. "You should be proud."

But he refused to change the subject. "What are you going to do, Em?"

She looked at him, turned away. "I don't know." She considered the house. "I'll be alright."

He nodded, slowly, as if weighing what she'd said.

"What about you, Rob? I know you've been building this place." She gestured toward the house. "It's amazing. Really."

"You want to see inside?"

"I do."

He opened the front door, and she stepped over the threshold. Inside, the place was a collage of her domestic fantasies, the way the rough stone met the sleek glass, the way the warm wood curved around the staircase and pulled her gaze upward, the way the ceiling beams drew her to the view of the ocean beyond the wall-sized picture window. It felt quiet and beautiful in here. Sacred. She took a deep breath, exhaling as waves swashed in the distance.

"What?" he said, quietly. "Don't you like it?"

"I do."

"I wasn't sure. You looked…unhappy."

She bit her lip. "I'm not." She followed the parallel lines of the wooden planks on the ceiling, the puzzle of stone blocks on the wall. "I was just thinking that I haven't seen you like this in a long time."

"Like what?"

She thought about it. "Excited," she said. "Happy."

Rob put his hands in his pockets and rocked back on his heels.

Emma nodded slowly. "It's nice."

He smiled and led her through the house and out a large sliding glass door that led to a side garden. "Wow," she said, stepping onto the swathe of native grasses, rippling in the sea breeze. "It's so beautiful." She took it all in, the house, the cliffs, the water, the sea air.

Rob hung back, giving her space. "You should see it on a sunny morning," he said. "You'd swear you can see Tasmania from here." He looked into the distance, pensive.

"What are you thinking?" she said.

He smiled a tight smile, looked down at his feet and sighed. "I was just…" He looked up at the horizon again, shook his head. "It's stupid."

"No, what?" She stepped toward him.

He half turned toward her. "It's weird that I have memories of this place and you don't."

She nodded. "Hmm," she said, softly. "I can see that. We've been doing our own things."

He flattened the hair at the back of his head with his palm.

They walked to the back yard, wrapped by the low stone wall that shielded the garden from the sea breeze. The sun broke through the clouds and their steps sent little bugs flying off the bright, dewy grass.

"You know," he said, walking beside her, "all that time we were apart…I didn't like it." He stopped and turned to face her. "It made me see what it'd be like if this all stopped. Us." He rubbed a knuckle across his bottom lip. "I asked myself what that'd be like and…I didn't like what I saw."

"What did you see?"

"It wasn't good," he said, quickly.

They looked at each other.

"I know it's hard," she said, before Rob averted his eyes again. "But can you tell me? Please. What does *not good* look like?"

He wiped his forehead with the back of his hand, the sun dimmed behind a passing cloud. "I saw nothing." Rob exhaled. "More like I felt it. Like the edge of that cliff." He pointed toward the end of the property, where the green field dropped away to the icy waters of Bass Strait. "I can just feel it there, even with my eyes closed. Even now. Feels like there's no bottom." He gritted his teeth. "That probably doesn't make any sense."

"No," she said, holding up her hand reassuringly, "I think I understand."

"Yeah?"

"Yeah." The wind blew a strand of hair loose and she held it back from flying in her face. "I'm sorry you felt that way."

He nodded, feeling helpless in the hold of her gaze.

"So, what does it feel like now?" she said.

"You mean right now?"

She nodded.

He ran his palm down the length of his face. "Well, it feels better." He smiled, his eyes bright.

"Yeah? How?"

His shoulders sagged. "Em, I know I disappoint you." She moved to contradict him, but Rob shook his head. "I know I do. Christ, *I* disappoint me. I'm fat and saggy. I'm not into travel or arty stuff the way you want me to be. I'm hopeless at conversations like this one. But I do love you. I know that, know it better than I know anything. This place…I built it thinking of you."

She looked behind him at the silhouette of the house, the way the stone picked up the colors of the cliffs that surrounded it, the glass that reflected the trees, the grass, and the water beyond them. "It's beautiful," she said. "Honestly. It's the most beautiful thing you've ever built."

"I had help."

"I heard. I saw."

"Oh?" His eyes widened.

"Instagram." She nodded slowly.

"Right." Rob scratched the back of his neck.

"You know," said Emma, avoiding Rob's gaze, her eyes moving over the freshly planted flowers in their new beds. "When I saw you in those photos, I was…jealous."

Rob tilted his head.

"I was," she said. "I saw how happy you looked. And it made me sad that I hadn't seen you like that. Not in a long time. At least not with me." She looked up at Rob. He blinked back tears.

"All this," he said. "I built it for you. For us. I want to buy this house, Em. And I want *us* to live in it."

"Rob—"

"I know it sounds crazy."

"Rob, it's beautiful. It is. And I love seeing you like this, all enthusiastic, but—"

"What's to decide? Look around."

Emma bit her lip, looked away. "I don't know if I can live here, Rob."

His eyes narrowed. "What are you saying? You don't know if you can live here or you can't live here with me?"

She sighed. "I need friends and family around me. I can't just live out here, away from everything. I'm not like you, I'm not…an island."

"We could work something out."

"Like what?"

He thought for a moment. "I don't know." He paused, looked out to sea. "I know it was bad before. I know I didn't see it."

"What didn't you see?"

He took a deep breath, turned back toward her. "That I gave up."

"Say more."

"Christ, I'm trying. I'm not good at this. You know that." He wrung his hands and glanced at the sky. "I let things go. I let myself go." He looked down at his belly. "I let the house go, said I'd fix it a million times, but I never did. And I let you down." He expelled a sharp breath. "I treated you like you were in my way, like what you needed didn't matter."

Emma nodded.

"It does though," he said, and smiled at her. "You do. And I'm sorry."

Emma held out her hand and Rob took it. He held her fingers to his mouth and kissed them. "I missed you," he said.

Emma moved closer and let Rob gather her in his arms. The shape of his body felt familiar, like coming home where memories live. And ghosts.

"What about *our* house?" She broke away from him. "We can't afford—"

"I knew you were going to ask about the money." He rubbed his chin. "Me and Sareena, we want to buy this place." Emma frowned. Rob's face softened. "As a business. You and me, we'd get the house. She gets the field, wants to build a trade school, sustainable building, a salvage yard, the whole shooting match. It's win-win. We could keep the old house, maybe Will can live in it, or we have a place in town, whatever."

She looked away. Her eyes caught the patina of an old wooden door on the barn.

"Will found that," said Rob catching the direction of her gaze. "The door. It's nice, isn't it? He's got a good eye."

Emma walked over and touched the scuffed and dinted wood with its marbled patches of ancient paints bleeding through each other.

"He's a good kid," said Rob. "A good man. Not afraid to go after what he wants. He's got courage. More than I ever will."

"I'm not happy with him quitting school."

"I know. But he can always go back if he wants. It's hard to pretend you like something you don't."

Emma paused and searched Rob's face. "Yeah," she whispered.

Rob put out his hand. She took it, his beefy, calloused fingers, warm and familiar. "I've got something I want to show you." He pushed the barn door open and led her inside.

In the middle of the room, lit by a shaft of light from the open door, was an exquisite wooden dining table. The tabletop was herringbone planks, their different grains and knots coming together in the middle, like a French braid.

Emma ran her hand over the varnished surface, smooth as glass. "This is beautiful."

"You like it?"

Her fingertips figure skated on the joints where the different colored woods came together. "I love it."

Rob moved to the far side of the table. "And look at this." He motioned Emma to come over. He pulled out one of the small drawers that lined the long edge of the table. "I put these in because I know you like your teas." She opened one of the small drawers. "Thought you could keep them in here," he said.

Emma misted up. "It's beautiful."

He looked at the table, not at her. "It's yours. I made it for you."

Emma's lip trembled and tears welled up. She wiped her eyes with the back of her hand, but the tears kept coming. "Thank you," she managed. It was perfect.

"Will helped."

"He did?" She smiled and wiped her nose with her sleeve.

"Yeah," Rob said, grinning. "He's actually pretty good on the tools." He handed Emma a paper towel from the work bench.

She dabbed her eyes and blew her nose. "Rob, I need to tell you something."

"Oh, what's that?"

She sniffed. "You're not going to like it."

His eyes narrowed. "Well, what is it?"

Emma's face got tense and contorted; she couldn't blink away the tears.

"Oh, Christ," said Rob. "Is it what I think it is?"

She looked at him, swallowed her bottom lip and nodded.

"Oh, fuck, Emma." He put his hand to his forehead as if he had a headache. "Why, Emma. Why would you *do* that?"

She shook her head slowly. "I don't know." She blew her nose. "No. That's not true." She balled up the paper towel and dabbed her nose with it. "I do know why." She cleared her throat. "I did it because I wanted to."

"Emma." He rubbed the back of his neck. "Who was it? Someone I know?"

"No."

"Well, who then?"

"It doesn't matter."

"It fucken does!"

"We were on a break. And why do you even care, Rob?"

"Because I care! What the fuck are you talking about?"

She swallowed. "We don't talk anymore, we don't do things together, we never have sex."

"Oh, please," he looked away.

"We don't."

"Well, what the fuck, Emma, do you have any idea—"

"How busy I am. Yes! I've heard that. You're very busy."

"Hey," Rob moved in close. "Don't try and turn this on me. You're the one who's been fucking around!"

"Fucked one person Rob, yes! And you know what, I'm *not* sorry. I'm sorry you're upset but I'm *not* sorry it happened. I'm grateful."

"Well, glad you're happy—"

"It was great. I'll be honest, Rob." He turned away again. "It was. I felt sexy and desired and alive."

"I don't want to hear this."

"You never *have* heard it." He glanced over his shoulder, annoyed. "Never," she repeated. "You never wanted to talk. About anything. Never wanted to do anything, go anywhere or try anything new. I got tired of waiting, Rob."

He turned away. "Waiting for what?"

"To live." She moved closer, his back still turned. "I'm not saying I want to be *with* that person. Build a life with them."

"Well, great. No issues, then."

"Rob."

"What?" He turned around, his face pouty.

"Are you really mad about this, or do you just think you *should* be?"

He looked at her, hard, then broke his gaze, his attention drawn to the table he'd built. Rob walked over to the table and put both hands on its surface. He leaned down, his head lowered between his shoulders.

"Rob," said Emma softly.

His shoulders trembled and he sniffed. "Fuck," he brought his fist down on the table and pulled it back instantly. "Ow." He turned, cradling his hand and rubbing his wrist. He winced and eased himself onto the floor.

Emma crouched and sat next to him. She put an arm around his shoulder. He leaned into her and rested his head on her shoulder. "I'm sorry," he said. "I'm sorry."

"It's okay."

He shook his head, wiped his eyes. "It's fucking embarrassing."

"What, crying?"

He nodded.

"You think this is the first time I've seen you cry?"

He took a deep breath, wiped his eyes with the palm of his hand. "When?"

"Christ, when not?" She squeezed his arm. "I know where you go. Out in your shed when you've had a few too many and you get all sentimental."

He dragged his sleeve under his nose.

"You only think you're hiding," she said.

He smiled, sniffed.

"Crying sober, though, that's progress."

He looked up at the pitched roof of the shed where cobwebs hung like tassels. "John Williamson." He clicked his tongue. "Gets me every time."

"True Blue." She leaned her head on his shoulder and hummed a few bars of the song.

Rob squeezed her arm.

Emma squeezed back. "I'm not trying to get rid of you, you old fart." She patted his hand. "I love you. You're family. Nothing's going to change that." She sat up, looked at him. "I want you to be a part of my life. I want to know that I can call you if I need to talk, or work something out. I want us to keep being parents, together. But I also know I don't want to go back to the way it was. I love you. I do. But I don't want to live together like we used to. I don't know what our day-to-day looks like yet but it's going to be different."

He sniffed, cleared his throat.

She touched his knee. "You act so gruff. What if everyone knew you were just a big softie."

He snorted and wiped his nose with his sleeve.

"It's going to be okay," she said. "We'll work it out. We're lucky, you know. We've got options. You see that, right?"

He nodded.

"It's going to be better, Rob. For both of us."

She hugged him and he held her, longer than he ever had.

They sat side-by-side next to the dining room table. Emma reached over and picked up the splintered handle of a hatchet, held it in front of her face. "My god," she said. "You gave that a good go." She smiled and glanced at the table over her head. "That's one hell of a table."

He smiled. "Fucken hell it is."

She laughed, put her arm around his shoulder. "I love it." She pulled him close and kissed him on the cheek.

CHAPTER FORTY-ONE

The listing party for the stone house was in full swing. The solid building stood vigil on acres of freshly cut lawn. Glimpses of Bass Strait played peekaboo through hedges and reflections of pink granite flashed off polished glass.

People milled about the grounds taking selfies as Erik played guitar on a small stage near the front of the house. Young people with no hope of buying real estate were there too. It all made for good photos, said the photographer from the *Home Design* magazine.

Will was at the mixing board while Aaron stood near the stage, dressed in a crisp white shirt and black cut-off shorts, his bear tattoo sniffing the sea air.

Erik finished his song. "Geez," said Rob, leaning toward Emma. "That fella's alright. He's no Tom Petty, but he's pretty good."

Emma smiled to herself and someone tapped her shoulder. "Mish! Oh my god, you made it." Mish came in for a hug. "This is my husband, Rob," said Emma, over Mish's shoulder.

"Nice to meet you." Mish shook Rob's hand.

"I'll let you two catch up," he said, spying Syed walking alone on the freshly mowed lawns.

"So, how you been?" said Mish.

"It's been weird."

"I bet. Are things okay between you guys?"

"I think so. Feels like we're moving into something new."

"You guys separating then?"

Emma made a face like she was thinking about it. "I don't know what we'd call it. I'm going to live in town, he's going to live here."

"Oh wow."

"Yeah, it's better that way."

"Well, that sounds good. Hey, tough break about the Haimon Young job."

Emma crinkled her nose. "That place wasn't for me."

Mish nodded. "Well, I'm kinda glad you said that, because I have a question."

"Oh?"

"I'm quitting Catch. That place is a shithole."

Emma chortled. "Well, you know what I think of it."

"Oh, it's a fucking mess. And the way they treated you was shitty. You deserved better."

"Thanks."

"I'll be honest. I want you to work with me."

"What?"

"I'm starting my own recruitment company. Specifically for migrant women. It's LinkedIn meets Fiver, for immigrants. Angie's coming too."

"Wow!" said Emma. "I had no idea."

"Well, you had other things going on," she said. "I want you to be my comms person." She touched Emma's arm. "Comms director, chief, whatever title you want."

"Oh, no," said Emma. "I'm flattered, but you want somebody… better."

"Don't be stupid. I want *you*. You're, and I mean this in the nicest way, you're old school."

"Thanks."

"What I mean is you're a purist, you take pride in your work. Plus, you're fun. I think you'll get along with the team I'm putting together."

Emma smiled then nibbled her lip. "Can I have some time to think about it? There's just been so much—"

"Of course." Mish put her hand on Emma's shoulder. "We're launching in six months. We haven't told Jarod yet. We're waiting until it hurts him the most."

Mish and Emma looked at each other and grinned. "Annual report time," they said together and laughed.

"What a dipstick," Mish sighed.

Emma laughed. "You know what? Fuck it! Yes! I don't have to think about it. I'm in."

"Really?"

Emma hugged Mish. "I'm so glad people like you exist."

"What do you mean?"

"People doing stuff. Trying to make things better."

"I only have a business plan and a website, let's not get too excited."

"You know what I mean." Emma pulled back. "You're shaping the world around you instead of the other way round. That's great. Gives me hope."

"Thanks." Mish blushed.

"Champagne?" Emma motioned to the trestle table on the lawn.

"Fuck yeah."

Rob reached Syed who was taking an unusual interest in the long, wide hedge near the cliff, crouching down, patting the ground with his palms. "You could put a pool here," said Syed, standing up, dusting off his hands. "Ground looks good. What do you think?" Syed pointed at the hearty shrubs that served as a windbreak. "Rip this out and put pool here?" Syed grinned.

"Anything's possible." Rob smiled.

"The band is nice." Syed scanned the crowd appreciatively. "Get buyers interested."

"About that."

"Hmm?" Syed squinted.

"The buyer," said Rob. "You're looking at him."

"Us," said Sareena, beaming as she joined them.

Syed looked incredulous. "You can't afford that. Can you?"

"Not separately," said Sareena. "But we can if we subdivide."

Syed shook his head. "Bad idea. Risky. The money's in the land."

"Nah, mate," said Sareena. "It's not just about making money. The value is in what we can do with the land."

"Ah," Syed mocked. "A master plan." He spread out his ringed fingers and wiggled them.

"Rob can have the house," said Sareena. "And then that part over there" – she turned and swept her finger across the level terrain of an adjacent field – "we turn that into an office and a trade school."

"She wants to change the building industry." Rob stuck his thumb out at Sareena. "Make it more sustainable."

"And you are the one who helps her do this?" said Syed, looking at Rob.

"Well," said Emma, walking toward them. Syed shielded his eyes to look at Emma's silhouette coming down the hill. "I figure," said Emma, "if you want to beat the competition in this trade, it's probably good to know what makes 'em tick." Rob smiled and held out his hand to help Emma down the grassy slope.

Syed looked at Emma. "You like this idea?"

Emma smiled. "I like it when everyone gets something."

"Hmmm." Syed moved his head from side to side as if considering the proposal. "I have other buyers." He looked at the ground and nodded slowly. "And I think maybe I keep it for myself."

"That's bullshit, Sy." Kendry's voice shot from the top of the hill.

Emma turned. "Ken, you came."

"Of course I came." She fluffed up her hair. "I'm not going to miss a kick-ass housewarming with all my favorite people." She turned to Sareena and stuck out her hand. "Hi, I'm Kendry."

"Sareena."

They shook hands.

"Geez," Kendry said, looking Sareena up and down. "You're a tall drink of water, aren't you?"

Sareena blushed. "You too."

"Now," said Kendry, turning to Syed. She hunched over theatrically and rubbed her hands together. "Where were we? Oh yes." She snapped her finger and pointed at Syed. "You were playing hard ball."

Syed furrowed his bushy eyebrows and looked up at the sky. "These are nice ideas, but…"

"Here it comes," said Kendry, smiling, all her teeth showing.

Syed put his hand on his chin. "Well, it's not what I had in mind."

Kendry cleared her throat. "Okay. So, you have a chance to make" – she pointed at everyone as she counted – "one, two, three, four, at least four people happy. Plus make off with what I assume is a shit-ton of money, all while kickstarting a new business and saving the building industry. Sounds like a good deal to me."

"Ken," said Rob, but Emma put her hand on his shoulder.

"Syed," said Kendry. "Look around." Everyone turned their heads and took in the scene. The rolling green hills, crawling with people, the rubberneckers and prospective buyers, the band, the lifestyle magazine, the photographer taking pictures. "You already got what you really wanted. Publicity. Legitimacy. Your name's out there. Congratulations, you're a player. It doesn't really matter who buys the house. Unless it's Hugh Jackman or Kylie Minogue. Are they here?" She pretended to look for them.

Syed squinted, the trace of a smile growing on his face.

"What if," said Sareena, turning to Syed. "What if, once we get the trade school up and running, we can work something out? Maybe we could send our best people your way and you give 'em a leg up. That'd be win-win, no? What do you think?"

"Yeah, Sy." Kendry rubbed her hands together. "Synergies. Does that sweeten the deal?"

He tilted his head from side to side. "What about you two?" he said, jutting his chin at Rob and Sareena.

"What about us?" said Sareena, with mock indignance. "You can't afford us," she smiled.

"I'm done with housing estates, mate," said Rob.

Syed nodded slowly.

"How about this…" Sareena steepled her fingers. "You come across a cool project, something heritage, and we promise to look at it. And if we take it on, we'll kick it back to you, but we get full control of the build and use our people."

"Oh zing," said Kendry."

Syed stood there, head bobbing, considering the proposal. "Market price?" He pointed at the stone house in the distance.

"Minus five percent," said Sareena. "Because I know you. You put a margin on everything."

Syed laughed and rubbed his chin. He looked at Rob. "You sure?"

Rob nodded.

Syed looked at Sareena, stuck out his hand and walked toward her. "Deal," he said, and shook her hand.

"Huzzah!" Kendry pumped her fists.

Emma looked at Rob. He seemed softer somehow, his gaze less penetrating. "I'm happy for you," she said, and his face reddened like a little boy.

"Thanks," he said, still blushing.

Emma smiled and gave Rob a hug, resting her head on the soft warmth of his chest. He squeezed her, rubbed her back, held her there, sinking into the moment. "You did an amazing job with this house," she said.

In the background, Erik breathed into the mic and they all turned toward the stage to listen.

Kendry and Emma's eyes met briefly. Kendry smiled warmly, just enough for Emma to notice.

"This is a new song," Erik wiped his forehead with the sleeve of his shirt. "So, I know you haven't heard it before. But that doesn't matter, you're still going to sing it with me."

He strolled to the edge of the stage. "Here's what we're going to do." He bent toward the small crowd gathered at the front of the stage and took out his cell phone.

"I'm going to record each side of the audience singing just one note. You people over here," he gestured. "You're going to sing first, okay?"

People whooped and clapped.

"All you people over there." He pointed at the other half of the audience. "You all just stay quiet for a second." Groans. "You're next," he said encouragingly.

"What's he doing?" Rob craned his neck to look.

Emma said nothing, just waited to see what happened next.

"Okay," said Erik, pushing buttons on his phone. "Now, all you people here I want you to sing one note. It's an F and it sounds like this." He struck the note on his keyboard a few times. People chimed in, held the note until it stabilized.

"Great!" said Erik, holding up his phone. "Hold that. Keep it going for as long as you can." He held his phone out and recorded them.

They sang and the single note hung in the air, the volume rising and falling as people lost and regained breath.

"Okay, great job." Erik beamed. "Now all you people over there, you're going to sing a G sharp." He demonstrated on the piano and the other half of the audience sang as he recorded.

He looked at his phone. "You want to hear what you sound like together?"

People clapped and cheered while Erik briefly fiddled with his phone and held it to the microphone. The two halves of the audience now sang together, with an eerie dissonance that kept going in an endless loop, longer than any natural human breath ever could.

Erik took a seat behind his piano. "Okay, this song is for someone special. It's called 'Lapse'."

Erik's piano wove in and out of the audience recording. Some people added their live voices to the chorus.

Rob moved closer to Emma and they watched their son moving dials on the mixing board.

"The world's a big place," said Rob. "How's he going to go out there?"

Emma watched her son. He was smiling. She saw in him the possibility of a life unscripted, with all the joy and sadness and wonder that lay before him. "I think he'll be all right." She took Rob's hand and squeezed it, finding comfort in the familiar shape of his fingers, the leathery feel of his skin.

Couples did things. They found workarounds, ways to enjoy the best of each other and avoid the inconveniences. They got bigger beds, or separate beds; they slept in separate rooms, or in separate houses. It was *their* marriage, after all, and they were free to make the rules.

The ocean sparkled in the sunlight and white caps fizzed briefly on the dimpled surface of the water. Way out, a tiny freighter ship steamed forward, leaving a frothy wake as it cut through the rolling waves.

ACKNOWLEDGMENTS

It's a persistent fiction that writers complete a book alone. There is always a team, whose expertise, labor, advice, patience and generosity contribute to the conception, creation and publication of a novel. I have a large cast to whom I owe a debt of gratitude.

I am most thankful to my wife, Suzie, for her precious insights, and for the years of open, honest and fearless conversation that have empowered us both to live our best lives together. You taught me to go after my dreams.

Thank you to my illustrious writer's group, Clare Strahan, Rachel Matthews, Sian Prior, Ilka Tampke and Suzy Zail. I'm blessed to have such talented writers review my work. Your feedback took me beyond the places I could travel alone and helped bring this story to life.

To my editors, Penny Johnson and Lorna Hendry, who quietly make me appear a better writer than I am on my own. I appreciate your skill and diplomacy and feel privileged to work with you.

To my cover designer, Bailey McGinn, you turned a mood board into a dramatic work of art.

I am also grateful for Tauseef Ahmed whose beautiful illustrations made the book feel real to me, even before I'd finished writing it.

Thank you to AJ Collins for doing such a wonderful job of the audiobook version of this novel. It's somehow comforting to know this book exists beyond the page.

To the people who shared their relationship stories with me in preparation for this book. Your courage and creativity demonstrate how relationships can change when people are willing to negotiate what togetherness looks like.

Finally, I want to thank my children, Charlotte and Alex, whose mature observations about life, relationships and what makes a good story found their way into this book. The future looks better for having you both in it.

With love and gratitude to everyone,

Yannick

ABOUT THE AUTHOR

Yannick Thoraval is an award-winning writer and teacher.

His work has appeared in national publications such as *The Conversation*, *The Financial Review*, *The Big Issue* and *The Australian*. Yannick was also managing editor of *Home Truths: An Anthology of Refugee and Migrant Writing*.

His debut novel, *The Current*, a climate fiction, was commended in the Victorian Premier's Literary Award for an Unpublished Manuscript. His second novel, *White Foam*, was shortlisted for Hachette Australia's Richell Prize. He has also won the International New Millennium Writings Award for Nonfiction.

Yannick holds a master's degree in history, a PhD in creative writing, and teaches fiction, creative nonfiction and communications at RMIT University in Melbourne, Australia.

www.yannickthoraval.com